DEATH RACE

The man gunned his motorcycle to full speed on the deserted rural road. The wolves poured after him, but he was pulling away when the machine hit the top of a ridge, bounded high, and came down with a crash.

The rider fought to regain momentum, but now the lead wolf had reached him. With an almost casual lunge, it closed its terrible canine teeth on his leg.

The trouser leg tore open like a wet paper bag and his calf was laid open in two great slices of white meat from knee to ankle. The wolf attacked again, locking its enormous jaws around his knee and literally somersaulting the machine into the air.

The overturned motorcycle roared on vainly for several minutes, its throttle jammed open, as the other wolves tore the faintly breathing man into raw, screeching strips. . . .

You will hear the sound in your nightmares!

Exciting Fiction from SIGNET

BLOOD SNARL

IVOR WATKINS

A SIGNET BOOK

NEW AMERICAN LIBRARY

TIMES MIRROR

Publisher's Note

This novel is a work of fiction. Names, characters, places, and
incidents are either the product of the author's imagination or
are used fictitiously, and any resemblance to actual persons,
living or dead, events, or locales is entirely coincidental.

SIGNET TRADEMARK REG. U.S. PAT. OFF. AND FOREIGN COUNTRIES
REGISTERED TRADEMARK—MARCA REGISTRADA
HECHO EN CHICAGO, U.S.A.

SIGNET, SIGNET CLASSICS, MENTOR, PLUME, MERIDIAN AND NAL BOOKS
are published by The New American Library, Inc.,
1633 Broadway, New York, New York 10019

First Signet Printing, January, 1982

1   2   3   4   5   6   7   8   9

PRINTED IN THE UNITED STATES OF AMERICA

PROLOGUE

That winter saw the first of the wolves move down from the Highlands. They were a straggling, undisciplined pack who foraged for thirty miles under the frozen moon and even crossed the English border, north of Carlisle. Next day, they were back on the high ground and no one was aware of their advance – except the petrified wildlife who had witnessed the casual savagery that marked their progress.

It was the raw winter of 1999 and a meagre number of Highlanders tried to shut out the pinching cold, by drawing mounds of bedclothes over their heads and dreaming of spring. They were the impoverished remains of Scotland's once bustling rural population. Their numbers had been cut with surgical speed during the years of their North Sea oil boom, when hundreds of families a month wedged suitcases into their cars and headed for the east coast towns, where they could double their incomes and reside in the uniform security offered to them by the oil company estates. The result was that many farms and smallholdings had been abandoned in the western Highlands, and the small villages in which dwindling communities still remained, were even more isolated than before.

The world, which paid very little attention to that remote and awesomely beautiful corner of Britain at the best of times, was at peace. A peace that ironically stemmed from the arms race. For years the Superpowers had been so heavily equipped that they resembled top-heavy knights of old and, unable to move without risking a holocaust, they became increasingly circumspect. However, the ponderous giants had their uses, and occasionally dealt out cuffs to belligerent minor nations. Thus it became unnecessary for Britain to keep a standing army stationed abroad, and the nation increasingly became preoccupied with lesser issues.

In Parliament, for example, members found themselves endlessly discussing Bills concerning amendments to the laws on prostitution, the provision of yet another television channel, the limiting of access to computerised credit information; in fact all the old perennials were dusted down and ventilated. The Press had a hard time. It was difficult day after day to be sufficiently ingenious to create stories out of such legislative mole-hills.

However, the time was ripe for pressure groups and ecologists made the most of it. Tighter laws were introduced to protect rare species of wildlife and, when it was reported that Britain's best guarded bird, the osprey, was breeding in Scotland after an absence of nearly a decade, thousands of tiptoeing visitors headed north. A misguided ornithologist who was unfortunate enough to be caught blowing one of the rare fish hawk's eggs, in order to carry off the shell for his collection, was jailed by a baleful magistrate who only regretted he could not order a flogging.

Red deer were another protected species and the vacation of ever more Highland mountain and pasture led to a steady build up of their herds. The quarter of a million deer of the early 1980s rapidly doubled, until some experts were advocating a severe gun cull. But no government would dream of taking up such a policy, with the weight of public opinion so firmly against interference with nature. Yet something had to be done. The landowners, a significant lobby in their own right, claimed that although the red deer feeds mainly on natural vegetation, it was causing a great deal of incidental damage. Tens of thousands of the graceful, high antlered animals roamed at will. They trotted, sniffed inquisitively – and trampled. Exuberant stags flattened fences, allowing cattle to stream out, and enormous damage was caused when a herd stampeded. They hopped into plantations, chewed the bark off saplings and disfigured trees by rubbing the velvet from their newly grown antlers.

People found them endearing at a distance. But it was not a problem that could be held at arm's length for ever.

One million red deer by the turn of the century? The Minister for the Environment looked up at his Parliamentary aide with a startled expression.

'Didn't realize it was that much out of hand. Better do something, hadn't we?'

His assistant who had the candour of youth, said, 'All that venison would be a boon if you'd agree to have them slaughtered.'

The Minister winced. 'Do you mind not using that word?'

'Venison?'

The Minister covered his eyes at the thought of losing the votes of conservationist and pet lovers throughout the country, and fluttered his fingers. 'No, the other one.'

However, the numbers had to be trimmed and it was decided, behind the practical glass façade of a government building in Edinburgh, that a small research team should evaluate the problem and recommend solutions.

There was no shortage of suggestions. They ranged from fencing off vast areas of the Highlands to the use of poison. The latter was thought to be quite a discrete solution by scientists at Porton, in Wiltshire, who produced with clinical efficiency a colourless liquid which could be poured into mountain streams and then relied upon to destroy any deer watering within the next ten hours. Thereafter the poison dissipated and was no longer a problem even if taken into town water supplies. But such cynical treatment of docile creatures moved even the Civil Service to say it was hardly cricket, and the idea was quickly dropped.

The eventual solution was discovered by EDNA (Ecological Data, Northern Area), a four-ton computer situated in the granite city of Edinburgh, which had never come face to face with any sort of sensitive creature, other than men in white coats and thick glasses who daily fed it with figures

7

clipped to millboards. Emotion, therefore, played no part in her reckoning.

The scientists had initially decided to concentrate their attention on a restricted area: the secluded island of Rhum in the Hebrides. The facts were fed in on a keyboard. Number of deer at large. Estimated annual increase. Area of land involved. Size of agricultural holdings and anticipated population growth. She thought about it for some ten or eleven seconds. Then started chattering. But her conclusions were so obvious that the men in white coats were embarrassed that nobody had thought of it before.

According to EDNA the most natural solution was to re-introduce a predator which last roamed the Highlands in 1743 – *Canis Lupus*.

Wolves? Weren't they ferocious? The ministry's team under Richard Unthank was pulled further into the project There were few wolf experts outside of zoos, and government scientists were paid to be adaptable.

It seemed sensible enough, and so some wolves were shipped in. Half a dozen pairs at first. Handsome, curiously shy creatures who seemed reluctant to leave the sanctuary of their cages. But after sniffing the sharp, clear air coming down from the distant mountains and peering across the spellbinding grandeur of the glens in autumn they moved cautiously off.

In the days that he had spent with the animals, checking their health and recording their behaviour prior to release, Unthank became attached to the pack and it was not long before he gave them names. Bent Ear . . . White Patch . . . Hollowbelly who was constantly hungry . . . the timid one known as Rabbit . . . and Darkmind. The latter was a menacing creature – at least half as large again as his companions – with an unnerving stare. He was the undisputed leader and most unpredictable wolf in the pack. Richard Unthank would have more than one disturbed dream about him before they finally met again.

Now as they spread out across the splendidly gaunt landscape, the comparison between the pack and their new domain was remarkable. At first they appeared to be in no hurry. But after fifty or sixty yards, and no sign of pursuit, it dawned on them that this was not a trick. They broke into a loping run, covering the springy heather with effortless bounds.

On a distant rise, the big male with a thick grey and black coat, and an upper lip that occasionally drew back to reveal fearsome-looking carnassial teeth, turned and looked towards the humans for the last time. To Unthank, who was anxiously staring after the pack, it appeared that Darkmind met and held his gaze. It was too late now for man to change his mind. The wolves were back where they belonged. Free and unchecked in an environment rich in ungulates and clear mountain water. Unthank pulled his eyes from the wolf and turned away.

For more than four years the pack flourished on Rhum. There were occasional accidents and illnesses, but healthy litters were born and the hunting was good. By the fifth year there were four dozen of the loose-limbed predators. The red deer problem on Rhum lapsed into inconsequence. No one saw a wolf unless he wanted to. If man chose to search them out, as he did on occasions for a television documentary or when researching a paper on wildlife, they were to be found. Otherwise, they were as elusive as the mist on the edge of the moor. No sooner did you move towards it than it slipped away.

It was an international forestry company – with a King Charles award for exports – which eventually sought help from London to control deer herds on the mainland itself. The company had acquired a lease on 300,000 acres of timber from a financially creaking National Trust. But no sooner was it neatly fenced off than the red deer trampled through. Almost as quickly as the horticulturists planted saplings, the ever-hungry deer stripped off the tender bark, leaving the naked plants to wither.

Couldn't a few of the Rhum wolves be shipped to Sutherland? They had proved themselves to be no trouble. They kept out of sight, as well as out of mind, yet their presence undeniably restrained the deer's vigorous mating habits. Unthank was uneasy about the idea. He accepted absolutely that wolves had a proper niche in the order of things. Nature was not a fool. But on the mainland? He rubbed his face anxiously, checked his figures and made twice as many trips into the hills as usual. But all seemed as before. Just as Nature intended.

And thus the wolves came to the Highlands. Not more than half a dozen at first but, even so, their usefulness was apparent to the company before a year had passed. The auditors reasoned delightedly that twice as many predators would double the effectiveness of their control over the never-ending deer.

By the turn of the century there were estimated to be two or three hundred grey wolves in the north of Scotland, but few people saw them or were bothered by their presence. Man and beast could live side by side in harmony, after all. Hadn't it been proved these past ten years?

Canis Lupus had returned to the northlands after an absence of two hundred and fifty years.

PART I: THE WINTER

ONE

Winter descended early that year, holding the whole of Britain in an icy embrace, numbing the population and paralyzing communications. It was particularly hard to take since it followed a series of unusually mild winters which inevitably lulled the population into shivering complacency. By mid-December the Thames froze over in central London. It had not happened since Victorian times when the river was a wider, more indolent creature, and the spirit of the old Frost Fairs quickly caught on. By Christmas Eve, boys were sliding beneath the lofty gaze of the Parliament building and under Westminster Bridge. Within an hour, a man with his arms folded expertly behind his back was skating gracefully down to Waterloo Bridge.

That same evening, the craze caught on and half of London seemed to be slithering and whooping their way across the creaking ice. It was already said to be three feet thick or more, and likely to get a lot thicker judging from a chilling long-range forecast. A hot-chestnut vendor wheeled his stall on, and then proceeded to defy the law of credibility by lighting a brazier on the frozen surface.

Within a week bonfires were started on the ice by other daring souls, including a spectacular affair at Greenwich, where merrymakers threw on bags full of salt and caused multi-coloured flames to shoot into the sky.

But it was not all fun. Not by a long chalk. The temperature sank so low that there were stories of birds freezing in mid-air and falling like stones to the ground. In the quarries of Dorset, the intense cold caused a petrification which split the rocks on its own.

Many people in isolated areas died when their cars broke down and froze before help arrived. Numerous others, shovelling a mountain of snow from their front paths in a frenzy of unaccustomed activity, died soon after of heart attacks.

The fact that, hundreds of miles to the north, tens of thousands of deer were already in trouble and beginning to die, was considered a small matter compared with the nation's growing discomfort at its own plight.

It was reported that a Northampton policeman, attempting to prise a tramp from a frost-laden bench in Wickstead Park, strained so mightily that a leg snapped off in his hands. The report, however, was never confirmed.

Certainly hundreds of people died who would normally have survived a benign winter. In a dimly-lit House of Commons, the Prime Minister, the Rt Hon James Beaconsfield, announced stringent power restrictions. No heating was to be permitted in homes and shops during the mid-mornings and afternoons.

'The grave news on the transport front,' he announced, peering over his spectacles at an unusually full House, 'is that one-half of all the ports in Britain are iced in, and some two hundred colliers stormbound in the estuaries. Furthermore . . . ' he rolled the words off his tongue with a Churchillian resonance that disguised his growing anxiety. 'Furthermore, our railways are experiencing the utmost difficulty in moving coal. Therefore, I earnestly appeal to every man, woman and child in this country to help conserve fuel by switching off unnecessary lights, and going to bed a little earlier than usual to avoid using heat.'

There were murmurs of discontent at his words, but the real outburst came two days later when he told members – by candlelight – that all television channels were to be closed down until further notice, to ease the load on the national grid. Aware that this would cut most of their constituents to the quick, several Opposition MPs were quickly on their feet.

'Resign, resign!' they chanted. 'Incompetence and a com-

12

plete lack of foresight!' someone roared. The Speaker tried in vain to call the House to order, and it is said that wild punches were exchanged in the gloom of the back benches.

Richard Unthank was in the Western Highlands helping with a head count of deer within a prescribed area. It was a random check and merely one of several methods of keeping an eye on the prolific animals. Some people likened them to rabbits. Introduce a hart to a hind at dusk and you could come back next morning and tend the herd, they said. This year there were as many of them as the staggeringly beautiful moorland and mountains could support. Yet the tall, rangy forty-year-old Unthank was a realist. He had a deep respect for the ways of Nature. She had an uncanny knack of balancing the fluctuations in all living things.

This year a rampant increase in red deer. Next, a winter of such ferocity that only the fittest would survive. In other words, a natural, ruthless culling that would decimate the exhausted herds, yet make them potentially strong and healthy again.

He grimaced at the wind that rounded Ben Dearig and scythed through the Scots pine and spruce on the braeside below him, like a giant's breath on the nape of a neck. God, it was cold. Yet the distant mountains had an awesome beauty that he was loath to turn away from.

He huddled up inside a heavy lambskin jacket and re-lit his battered cigar. He was as set in his ways as any bachelor. He loved the solitary life, researching among animals that never ceased to fascinate him. Perhaps he had achieved, without looking, what so many others spent a lifetime searching for – contentment.

A drizzle of sleet was being chased away into the distance by a spectrum of mauve, blue and yellow sunshine. His first glimpse of the sun for more than a month and probably the last for a long time to come. The air was clear and sharp up here; every breath as cold as a spear but, paradoxically, as invigorating as life itself. He shaded his grey eyes, the better

13

to see. On a faraway hillside, where royal thistles stood straight-backed in the snow, a solitary stag froze with natural caution.

There was no indication for miles in any direction of man's existence. It was as if time had stood still for ten thousand years.

On moments like these, he had a yearning for something more in his life. Someone with whom he could share such experiences. He chewed his cigar thoughtfully for a while, then jogged down towards the glen.

The old class-47 diesel engine, in faded blue and gold livery, gasped out a grubby mixture of black and petrol-blue exhaust fumes as it rounded a bend on the track north of Ullapool. It had seen prouder days as the name *Cyclops* on its flank indicated. Nowadays it leaked oil and its age showed as it began labouring up an incline.

Normally on a two-car train there was no need for the driver to peer anxiously ahead and wonder if they would make it. On any other afternoon they would cover the quarter-mile uphill section at fifty miles an hour with barely a snatched breath. But today the snow was lying in a soft mattress across the track. For as far ahead as he could see, all that was visible was a shallow white gully. No sign of the steep edges of the cutting that he knew lay below.

The wheels, already reduced to a cautious twenty miles an hour, spun as they fought to grip the steel rails. The two-foot thick snow was compressed in an instant to half an inch, but it cloyed and played havoc with the passenger train's momentum.

Slower and slower they progressed. Then, not more than a hundred yards from the crest, the driver gave up the struggle. People pressed the side of their faces to cold windows to see what the trouble was. The driver, who was a Sunday school superintendent at weekends, uttered a string of fluent, ungodly oaths and tried again. Several times he increased the power, only to cause an almighty scramble under the wheels. Jerking and gasping, the diesel progressed a few feet further. But now, with a fresh fall of great soft flakes blinding the day ahead, he shut down the engine. Stuart Abercrombie, the guard, jumped down and immediately vanished up to his waist. 'Hell's bells,' he groaned and waded to the front end.

The driver slid open the door to his narrow compartment and heaved the diminutive guard up. 'The old bugger needs a rest. He'll split his seams on this gradient if I push too hard. We'd best wait here for a break in the weather.'

Abercrombie took out his big silver pocket watch, fastened on a chain to his waistcoat, and shook his head. 'Station master's going to be annoyed if we're late again. Not to mention Doris. She's keeping a couple of mince pies hot for me.'

The driver glanced up at the brooding grey eiderdown of a sky, that threatened to smother them if it got any lower. 'They're the least of our worries.'

Cyclops settled down to wait and, before ten minutes had passed, was buried up to the bottom of its doors in gently heaped snow. The diesel looked like a great dejected sheepdog stretched out in a white wilderness. The driver kept the view ahead cleared by a single big windscreen wiper. *Cyclops* was appropriately named.

Unthank, too, was caught by the deceptively gentle fall of snow that refused to stop. He lengthened his stride but by now his leggings sank knee-deep into the whiteness.

He kept where possible to broken rocks, which were sufficiently exposed to be blown clear of snow. He was less than two miles from Ullapool but it was going to be a grind. Every step now was an effort. Instead of simply moving forward, he had consciously to raise his leg straight up out of the snow before moving it forward.

He did not see the train until he was almost on top of it. Even then, it was someone who let down a window and waved a frantic red scarf who drew his attention. He waited for them to barge open a frozen door and then swung himself up and into the muggy interior. A youth in a padded zip-up jacket pulled him farther inside and a woman with a beautifully angular face and attractive perfume poured him coffee from a vacuum flask. He lay back on the blue upholstery, spreadeagled his legs and nodded his thanks. The woman perched next to him, while the ten other passengers looked away, keeping their interest under control with typical British restraint.

'More coffee?' She was in her thirties and had a calm look about her which seemed perfect under the circumstances. She wouldn't get flustered in a hurry. 'Are you lost?'

He found his voice at last and looked out at the deceptive wilderness. 'Not really. I just wandered farther than was good for me. I'd have made it back to Ullapool all right, but it's nice to come across a big Saint Bernard like this.'

She smiled. 'We weren't exactly waiting for you. We were due in Ullapool ourselves half an hour ago. Then we got stuck. They are probably looking for us by now.'

Abercrombie, a short young man who seemed worried by the responsibility thrust upon him, set his Germanic, British Rail hat square on his head to keep up appearances and leaned across to Unthank. 'You all right, sir?'

Unthank nodded gratefully and stood up. He felt fine. The ache had disappeared from his legs and he drew a succession of deep breaths.

'Were you alone?'

'Yes.'

There was a stillness in the carriage. Most of the passengers were elderly and there were two small boys. They all listened, hoping to hear something that would allay their anxiety.

Abercrombie straightened up and cleared his throat. 'I want you all to sit down and hold tight. The driver is going to start the train with a bit of a jerk, to shake us out of this blanket. I don't want anyone falling over. Just brace yourselves and don't worry.'

There was a rapid bustling as all regained their seats. Teeth were clenched and older hands closed reassuringly over young ones. Unthank thought the woman looked rather white-faced, and smiled. For a moment he looked deeper into her eyes than he had done with any woman before. It gave him a physical shock of pleasure. But it was immediately overtaken by the great jolt of *Cyclops* heaving himself out of the surrounding snow and straining forward.

Ten yards were gained before the wheels spun again. They gripped, lost their hold and then slowly slid backwards. Only the sharp application of brakes prevented them losing more ground than they had advanced. Several bags and packages fell from the luggage racks. One hit Unthank on the forehead and made him wipe an involuntary tear from his eye. Nobody spoke for a while. The engine was shut off and they were again in absolute silence. Then one of the boys began to cry.

After a while the guard reappeared. 'It's all right. We'll soon be on our way.' He bent over the children and distributed some toffee that seemed reluctant to leave its paper bag. But when he caught Unthank's eye, Abercrombie shrugged hopelessly.

Unthank looked at his watch. It was well after three and the afternoon was drawing to an end. In an hour or more dusk would descend. If they didn't get out before dark they would be in real trouble. With the temperature at well below freezing, one or two of the frailer passengers might not survive the night.

He hefted on his heavy, wet coat.

Whoever she was, she knew. She didn't say anything. Simply, let down the window on a leather strap and put her head out. She gasped at the cold but withdrew her head smiling. 'I think it's almost stopped snowing.'

He shouldered his way through to the driving compartment from which the driver had still not emerged. The thickset Scot was sitting despondently over his controls. It was Abercrombie who was the most help.

'That's an awfully risky thing to do. Those drifts could be twenty feet deep and you won't know about it till you hit the bottom.' He came to a decision and gulped inside his uncomfortably-tight railway collar. 'I think it's my job to try for the station, not one of the passengers.'

Unthank patted his arm. 'Doesn't apply. I'm not a passenger.'

Abercrombie's face brightened slightly. 'That's true.'

'I'll make it in about an hour at the outside. You sit tight, and see you keep their spirits up.' He indicated the coach behind. 'With any luck they'll have a snowplough out here by six o'clock.'

As he went back for his gloves, Unthank was touched lightly on the arm by an old woman with a delicate smile who looked as frail as a brittle leaf. 'Take care, young man.' She beckoned him down and kissed his cheek with parchment lips.

He felt a bit of a phoney as he swung down into the snow. Faces lined the windows, grinning and waving. One of them was the woman with the cheekbones whose eyes he lingered on. Then he was trudging alongside and beyond the engine.

He walked on the sleepers. With upwards of three feet of snow to be traversed with each step he did not attempt any bigger stride. Once he glanced back at *Cyclops* but, by then, even the single clear patch on the windscreen was indistinct and he needed all his concentration for the way ahead.

The weather was as fickle as a jealous woman. No sooner had the rolling, grey snowclouds emptied, than the sun glinted between them. It made the going slightly easier. But he was panting as he forced himself on at a steady rhythmic pace. His laboured breath condensed in front of him and would probably have frozen if a light wind had not dissipated it.

A long downhill stretch gave way to flat track, which wound west and then north through cuttings lined with pine trees. It was after nearly forty minutes walking, when he stopped to hug himself and catch his breath, that he felt a new and uneasy sensation. An eerie prickling on the back of his hands and neck.

He was not alone.

Unthank swivelled around in the direction he had come

18

from to see if the diesel was miraculously labouring after him. But there was no sign.

He swung back, rooted to the spot. There was no movement on the ridges either side. Simply a glint reflected in the passing sunlight; perhaps a spur of granite. Yet someone was out there. Or something.

He held his breath the better to hear, while the silence grew more intense. Only his eyes moved, furtively behind narrowed lids. When a sleeve of snow rustled off a great branch fifty yards away he almost jumped out of his skin.

The silence returned. Powerful and hidden. The stunningly beautiful world encompassed by his vision echoed with it. Pine trees shrouded in white lined the embankment: a spectral congregation in a dazzling white cathedral.

He felt as if something unseen was moving ever closer to him. By now he was straining, listening for the faintest sound, until the veins stood out on his neck.

Unthank cupped both gloves to his mouth. 'Hello,' he called tentatively. 'Hello.' His words rolled up and over the crest, to be absorbed in the great nothingness beyond. There was no response.

Jesus, it was ridiculous. He broke his trance and moved quickly on. It was easier now: trees grew closer to the track and shielded it. Much of the snow lay trapped in their uppermost branches – a great veil linking spruce with spruce in an endless chain for several hundred yards. He lengthened his stride. Any undue vibration might bring tons of it crashing down on him.

When he reached the end of the trees, Unthank stopped again and looked back. He took off thick gloves and blew on his hands to restore the circulation.

Whatever it was his instinct had sensed was still there. He was quite sure of that. He squinted past the long angle of the sun, and into the light and dark of the trees. Nothing.

On he went, fighting a desire to run even though he was struggling for breath. His thick vest was clammy with perspiration, which trickled uncomfortably down the middle of his chest.

19

A few minutes later he saw smoke rising from a chimney on the edge of town. He began to run with great loping strides. It didn't matter now. Almost immediately he went sprawling into the soft, yielding snow and came up spluttering delightedly. There was a signal box up ahead, high as a pulpit. He had made it.

From quite a different direction, eyes watched and assessed the scientist. It was noticeable that he was both slow-moving and alone. He also had a lot of meat on his bones.

And yet man was an unknown quantity. The eyes blinked and turned away. For the moment they would leave it at that.

TWO

The red deer is one of the very few animals to have survived from the last Ice Age, and its continued existence is all the more amazing in the light of its ceaseless pursuit by predators throughout history.

Unthank thought about it as he stood in the bows of the Royal Mail boat, crunching her way through the milky ice that stretched across the Sound of Sleat.

The bearded skipper appeared momentarily from his bridge, jerking his head in disgust at the conditions. 'You don't need my help,' he called. 'You could walk back to Rhum from here.'

The scientist grinned and practised a boxer's footwork on the frosty deck to keep his circulation moving. The desolate view across the Sound to the sprawling grey-white land mass of Skye was breathtaking in its majesty.

Ahead of them, the deceptive ice stretched westward in an unbroken sheet as far as the eye could see. In a way, the ice was like the deer. It could not prevent itself being attacked and yet it always survived.

He tugged a thick Scandinavian ski hat further down over his ears and looked at their wake. Already the broken, bobbing ice seemed to be welding together.

No doubt the deer would survive until the next Ice Age. They were hunted by Stone Age man who scratched their fleeing outlines on the walls of caves and they were shot in their thousands by sporting gentlemen of the Victorian era who poured into Scotland by the train load. But none had wiped them out.

Unthank recalled reading of Prince Albert, Queen Victoria's consort, shooting a tame deer from the dining room window of his Highland lodge, no doubt to the excruciating discomfort of his retainers. And the Queen's doting habit when she recorded in her diary: *'Bertie's done it again. A particularly fine nine-point stag. What sport!'*

In the end it was the red deer who prevailed, and in the same way that it outlasted most other creatures throughout time. Despite its air of sad nobility, and though it gave hunters no more than a look of gentle reproach when mortally wounded, it suffered and survived its adversaries.

Now its most savage enemy had returned and was stalking the woods. One that this year was exceptionally strong and could surpass all others: could conquer the wolf and subdue man. *Winter.*

In the normal course of events, the animal builds up its strength during the summer and autumn and then ekes out its stamina over the grey months of winter. If by March the snow and ice still cling tenaciously to the land and refuse to be shaken off, countless of the oldest and weakest red deer simply huddle down and die.

This winter the whole species was endangered. Unthank knew they had sensed it. Hence, they were on the move. Winding their way down to the towns in an unprecedented way, to take their chance with man.

The scientist tapped his white teeth thoughtfully. He knew

21

that Nature always intended the fittest to survive. And yet he was uneasy.

Like the deer, he had a feeling of dread in his bones.

THREE

A pale sun crept up over the Cromalt Hills with the feeble strength of a bronchitis patient reaching the top of the stairs. There it rested on a bald headland and bathed the braeside in weak sunshine. Any warmth was welcome during the hardest winter in memory. The trees were badly frostbitten and hedges lay stiff as casualties under white bandages of snow.

Dunceford was not optimistic. He had been disillusioned too many times in his fifty years to be taken in by the first gleam in an eye. He regarded the sun in a way usually reserved for a visit from his mother-in-law, or for stepping into a tepid bath when what he really needed was bollock-roasting heat to take the everlasting chill out of his bones.

As he drove he listened to the rhythmic thud of his snow chains. He took several corners on the wrong side of the road, to save time. That might have seemed odd to anyone who noticed the lettering on the car door: *POLICE J B Dunceford (Sergeant)*. But in fact there was no danger of a collision on the little-used side road from Elphin.

He slowed to a crawl on bare hills where trees were almost as scarce as people. Yet this was the Drumrunie Forest. He reached the remains of an old hunting lodge and decided to call it a day. If he patrolled much farther, looking for vehicles in trouble, he might well get stuck himself and he was already miles from help.

He backed the Cortina carefully, pointed it along the line of his own tyre tracks and switched off the engine. A majestic stillness closed in around him, not broken until his stomach rumbled and he automatically reached for his sandwiches in greaseproof paper. They were delicious. Pork and pickle, washed down with hot coffee. He belched gently. Afterwards, when he got out briefly to clean the windscreen, he saw his first wolf.

It stepped out of the straggly bushes as quietly as a ghost, and stared at him. Dunceford was paralyzed and for an eternity nothing stirred.

He could feel his heart pounding while his hand fumbled desperately behind him for the door handle. The wolf took two more steps forward, less than twenty-five yards away. When he moved, it moved.

In a scrambling moment he heaved himself feverishly into the driving seat and slammed the door. It was all achieved in one great flailing movement, and the wolf did not try to take advantage of the situation.

It simply gazed at him with its cold green, slanting eyes, then turned and was gone. Later, when he told Constable Shaftoe about it back at Station House, he could barely recall any details other than its glinting eyes . . .

The next sighting occurred the same evening on a treacherously glazed main road near Kylestrome, in Sutherland. The nineteen-year-old son of a sheep farmer was half-driving, half-sliding his new girlfriend home after an evening at a pub.

She leaned her head on his shoulder as he motored carefully along; the windscreen wipers flicking clear the occasional flakes of snow. It was then that their long, probing headlights picked up two shapes moving across the slippery road ahead.

'Look out for those dogs,' she warned.

One crossed from the high to the low side of the road and was gone, but the greeny-yellow eyes of its companion were transfixed by the car lights. Then it, too, crossed out of sight. He stopped the car and got out, examined the verge and peered into the inky blackness.

23

The girl joined him, squeezing her hands under her armpits. 'Long way from their home, poor things.'

'Why, have you seen them before?'

'No. But you know there are no houses for miles.'

The young farmer glanced puzzledly up at the ice-hard high ground from whence the creatures came. And, when he restarted the car, he was silent for a while.

She snuggled up. 'What's the matter?'

'I'm not sure. But I'll tell you one thing. They are a hell of a size.'

She held his arm tightly, feeling the biceps. 'So are you.'

He was sufficiently diverted to forget his qualms. 'Occh! It's that Caledonian ale. It makes everything seem twice the size.'

It happened again two days later, on a Sunday. A father and his three small daughters were walking to kirk from their little stone home near Strathkanaird, in Ross-shire, when the youngest pointed ahead excitedly.

'Doggy, doggy!'

They ran on to investigate a shape sitting fifty yards off the track. It was sitting motionless on an outcrop of rock.

'Come back here,' called their father, who was short-sighted but refused to wear his spectacles in public. 'I said, come back. Right away!'

Instinct warned him and the anxious pitch of his voice halted the girls. They held their ground until he reached them. 'Hold hands,' he said quietly, trying to keep a rein on a growing feeling of alarm.

The wolf watched them intently, but made no move as they picked their way around it in a wide, careful detour. When after several minutes they reached the comparative safety of a road, the girl's father waved his stick.

'Off with you, you great brute!' he shouted. The wolf regarded him for a moment or two, then jumped lightly to the frozen heather and made its way farther down the glen.

The minister gave the family a lift home in his venerable, old Morris Minor car, but there was no sign of the animal. All three girls giggled on the back seat while their father told the clergyman. 'Sorry to put you to this trouble. But I think my bairns were a wee bit frightened. It looked awfully sinister, covered in spiky grey hair. Never seen one this low in the glen before. But it ran off soon enough, when I shouted.'

There were other sightings: at the Bridge of Grudie, far to the east at Maggieknockater and on the main coastal road near Banff. But, because of the remorseless, muffling snow and the numerous anxieties it brought in its wake, they were not put together. No one in Scotland was as yet aware of any widespread threat. Shadows moved at dusk and settled again, unseen.

There were no complaints when the Tuesday mail bus from Ullapool set out half an hour late. They were glad it was going at all. The thinly spread complement of passengers had no more than a quickly fading smile for one another before dusting the snow from overcoats or blowing closely on numbed fingers to bring them back from the dead. The driver sighed and squashed the remaining life out of his cigarette before preparing to move off. The engine shuddered into life and gave the slowly thawing passengers the sort of sustained shaking that could be matched only in a massage parlour.

The antiquated bus would be stopping at Elphin, among other places, before completing its circular route before nightfall and again parking by the jetty at Ullapool.

The town of small white houses was tucked away in the shelter of a sea loch on Scotland's north-west coast and flanked by broad, majestic mountains. It was purpose-built for herring fishing in the eighteenth century and its handful of symmetrical streets were a legacy of the slide rule precision of British Fishery Society architects. The same streets bore Gaelic name plates and, beyond them, the winter-harassed Highlands stretched out in a lonely splendour to the north.

The long gear-handle jolted into place; a final glance in the rear mirror at passengers hibernating under layers of clothing and occasional blankets, and off came the handbrake.

The woman with classic, angular looks, who had been marooned in the train, was now sitting on the long back seat of the bus. The fur coat bundled around her gave no hint of the graceful body inside. Behind the rear seat was a grill which separated the passengers from an area for mail bags and parcels. She was extremely tired after a journey from the Midlands which, so far, had taken three days. Normally it would be accomplished in a few hours. Yet she was as happy as she had ever been.

At the age of thirty-one, Emma Dancer controlled her own life, and did the things that she found the most satisfying. She was answerable to no one. Even so, the life she had chosen was arduous: invariably working in primitive conditions and often out in the open, on her hands and knees, in all weathers. At the moment her mind was dwelling on a listing she was about to start of fragmentary remains of prehistoric settlers, spread over two floors of the house she had rented on the outskirts of Elphin.

She was returning from a visit to the college of her former tutor: a professor in the Department of Archaeology and Antiquities at Birmingham University. It was with barely suppressed excitement that she had shown him the evidence of her excavations on a coarse, sheltered hillside near the sea. The hitherto untouched remains of an Iron Age settlement. She glanced up once again at the luggage rack with the natural concern that most women show for their offspring. But, in this instance, her attention was on a suitcase containing several carefully-wrapped fragments of crude pottery with traces of honey and grain embedded in the base, the rusted hilt and broken shaft of an unpretentious sword, and the time-eaten remains of a human skull. The skull she had examined and admired, even stroked, for hours. A light female cranium, preserved in peat, which had sent Professor Hector Fairfax into paroxysms of bright-eyed joy. He was not given to noisy outbursts at the age of seventy, but she had been able to measure his excitement from the little skips with which he traversed the room.

She turned and noticed that the other passengers were

26

staring at a frustrated farmer, digging up turnips from the frozen ground with a pneumatic drill. Ahead of them the road was no more than a track that a snowplough had cleared for traffic several hours before. It was the width of a single vehicle, leaving a sloping bank of downy snow hemming them in on either side. Any higher and it would become claustrophobic. She wondered how long it would be before they reached the village.

As she dozed, her thoughts drifted back to the train and the stranger with the frank gaze who had come and gone in a few minutes. He had drunk her coffee, exchanged a few words and then vanished along the tracks. Help had arrived soon enough, but he was not there to see the outcome. Curious . . . you could know some people for years and never be close to them. Others you met once – perhaps over the rim of a steaming vacuum flask – and you knew instinctively that you could share a lifetime with them . . . absolutely and irrevocably that you would be happy together. It was a ridiculously simple process. All stemming from a second or two when you looked deep into someone's eyes, and beyond. Except that sometimes, just as swiftly, when you looked again they were gone. Forever . . .

She settled into a warm stupor, hardly conscious of her breath condensing in the cold air, and recalled the past summer and all that had been achieved.

A dark-haired alert-eyed man joined her on the uncomfortably hard back seat. He was still breathing hard from the run he had made to get on board. But, once the snub-nosed bus was moving across the hard-packed snow, the driver was reluctant to stop for anybody. Kelso had scrambled aboard without help, despite his handicap, but received no welcoming smile from the driver. Merely a grunt as he proffered his fare. He fingered the heavy silver ring on the little finger of his left hand, twisting it unconsciously.

At twenty-nine, with his incisive style and abrasive manner, he had expected to be an editor by now. Or at least an executive sitting in a chauffeur-driven car. But, instead, he was shivering in a geriatric bus on its way across the arse-end of Scotland. He owed Fleet Street nothing after the abysmal way he had been treated. They had simply pushed him out of sight. As far away from the proprietor's sight as they could get him. Off to the land of the Caledonians where, as soon as you ventured out of doors, you were up to your balls in snow. Kelso grimaced. That must be making them laugh in El Vinos. He manoeuvred a small travelling flask from his pocket and glanced across at her.

'Excuse me, but you look extremely cold.'

She heard the voice only hazily between the fringe of her beaver skin collar and the brim of her hood.

He extended the flask. 'Would you care for a sip? It will help keep you going.'

'I beg your pardon?' As she struggled upright, her handbag fell to the floor. He retrieved it and, as he did so, she noticed there was something odd about his foot. Thicker and heavier around the sole than a normal boot.

But there was nothing slow about his expression. He had a quicksilver look; a lively and enquiring face that she somehow associated with the law. He would look well in a barrister's wig.

'I . . . I don't drink, thank you.'

'Oh, it's not a drink. More like anti-freeze. That is, it's ginger wine. Warms you up and makes you pant.'

'I'm really quite all right, thank you.' She smiled politely, ending the conversation.

Kelso nodded and looked away, out of the window. But after a moment or two he glanced back at her once again. Her eyes were closed and he narrowed his mind in concentration. Where had he seen her before?

She gave the impression of being taller than she was; fair hair curled slowly down to slim shoulders, a thoughtful face that was well worth a second glance, and tapering legs.

The movement of his body as he squeezed the flask into a back pocket, opened her eyes. She caught him looking at her.

'I'm sorry,' he said. 'I know you're trying to sleep. It's just

28

that I thought I recognized you. From London. But I'm not so sure now.'

This time she smiled tightly and with less grace. 'I don't often get to London.'

'Oh.' He pressed his fingertips together. It was unusual for him to feel ill at ease in a woman's company. 'Sorry.'

She realized how abrupt she sounded, and relented. 'You're not from up here, are you?'

'No. I don't even know where up here is.' He rubbed the dulled window clear of condensation. 'Not that there are many landmarks left to recognize.'

'We're getting quite close to Elphin.'

'Do you live there?'

'I've leased a cottage for a few months.'

'Really?' He chuckled at the thought. 'I hope you got the off-season rate.'

'It's not a holiday. I'm here to work.'

'In the winter? What do you do?'

He was not the type of man she particularly cared for. Too quick, too questioning, too forward. He was also younger than her – not that it would cramp his style. She imagined his ego would allow him to embrace women of all ages. The last real smoothie she had come across had been Maynard. And look where that had landed her. Maynard, the number one prize fart. Fart. Yes, that was about right to describe a confirmed bachelor who had wooed her ardently, until she fell, and only then revealed that he was already deeply in love *with himself*.

There was a familiar sour taste in her mouth. God, what a fool she had made of herself. But she smiled and said, 'I'm an archaeologist.'

'Aah. That accounts for it.'

Curiosity showed in her eyes. 'For what?'

'For thinking I recognized you. But it wasn't that at all. It's simply that you've got an interesting face. And that's the sign of an active mind.'

'Is it?' She was suddenly flattered.

'Certainly.' Kelso's attention was diverted by the bus momentarily losing its grip on the road and skating sideways before it found a more receptive stretch of surface. He pulled a face at the thought that they might get stuck out here within freezing distance of the bleak Atlantic coast of Scotland in mid-winter.

When next he glanced at the intriguing woman beside him, her eyes were closed. He envied her apparent calm. What on earth was he doing there anyway? He sank down into an uncomfortable huddle and thought back. Just two weeks earlier everything had been going so well. He was getting a front page by-line day after day. It seemed he could not put a foot wrong.

He got a job, using cooked-up credentials, as assistant registrar of an isolation hospital in St John's Wood, within coughing distance of Lord's cricket ground. Not that anyone was interested in the deserted pitch. In fact nobody who arrived at the hospital had the strength to lift a bat. Only the nurses were lively – or at least some of them, when they let down their hair and discarded their Lisle stockings and stringent blue uniforms.

His news editor received a story from a local stringer that several Bangladeshi immigrant families had been whisked to St Randolph's straight from Heathrow Airport. It was rumoured they had Dacca flu.

Every year during the 1980s seemed to bring a new and more virulent form of worldwide influenza. First Hong Kong flu, then the Siberian and Rangoon variations before it abated for ten years while winter took on a milder, more timid guise.

Now, as the Arctic again unleashed its pent-up fury across Europe, the killer flu virus that had swept the Indian subcontinent for several months seemed to be reaching out to grip Britain by the throat.

The Health Minister was infuriatingly complacent. *Absolutely not*, he assured journalists. *We are quite secure against such an outbreak and, even if it did somehow penetrate our protective measures, we have sufficient serum to vaccinate all likely victims. There is no cause for alarm.*

But, as the weeks passed, it became clear that the spread of the flu was beginning to reach epidemic proportions in the city, and strangely the distribution of vaccine seemed to make little difference. Using a great deal of journalistic skill, persistence and false charm, Kelso got to the heart of the matter. And then wished he hadn't.

By lavishing his attentions on one of the senior nurses who worked on the isolation wards, he discovered that the outbreak was indeed out of control. The first reports of the disease's arrival in this country were disbelieved and sat in a bureaucrat's in-tray until the overloaded hospitals demanded to know what action was being taken. By then it was too late.

However, there was a far more interesting aspect to the story which Kelso found out during a particularly hectic night in the arms of his 'reliable source'. He learnt that part of the extremely limited stock of vaccine was being secretly distributed to senior ministers; it was this particular gem that led to the picture that should have been the climax of his career. And almost ended it.

When a breathless Kelso burst into the night editor's office, with the photograph of an aghast Minister of Health in a discreet Harley Street surgery and a syringe of the precious vaccine in his arm, the print run was stopped. The front page was replated and the story of the year was ready to astound four-million readers. But, instead, within a short time a curious stillness fell on the newsroom. Word had come from the top and the presses were stopped once again.

His lordship was not only a press baron, but a close friend of the Minister of Health. The night editor picked up his phone and slowly his face became ashen. Yes, those responsible would disappear . . . immediately . . .

'Look, Kelso,' muttered the news editor, without moving his lips, and at the same time keeping an eye on the entrance to see if he could be observed in conversation with Judas Iscariot. 'Do me a favour. Just sod off somewhere. Anywhere. Up north, for instance. As far up as you can get. Scotland, if that's what they call that jagged bit at the top.'

'What for?'

'Whaddya mean, what for?'

'What I say. What on earth for?'

31

'Because I want a weather story. Yes, a good long one that goes on for days and days.'

Kelso rubbed his eyes in despair. 'You don't really mean that. You know damned well I could get just as vivid a story in fifteen minutes, sitting here. On the phone.'

The news editor's face set as hard and immovable as concrete. 'I've told you what we want. Now either do it, or resign. I'm not fussed. It's up to you.'

Kelso was stunned by the injustice of it all. 'But it was an honest story. I tell you, the man was using his position to jump the queue for vaccine. A Minister of the Crown.'

He got a flat look. 'So?'

'So why don't you believe me?'

The news editor considered the frayed end of his exhausted cigarette, as if contemplating its future. Then abruptly discarded it. 'It's not a question of believing you. It's much simpler than that. The owner of our newspaper has been jumped on from a great height, and he didn't like it. You have to understand that he's not a man of the world, like you and me. He's sensitive about being kicked up the arse by the Prime Minister's office. And because he's got the idea that you're responsible, he wants you to smart, too.'

'All right, all right. I accept it's his privilege to say what goes in the paper, and what doesn't. But there's no reason to send me to the other end of the earth.'

'But there is.' The lined face assumed a look of mock innocence. 'Because if he sees you walking about here smirking, in the next few weeks, he'll fire you. And me. And the editor.'

At that moment, two management executives appeared at the far end of the big newsroom and the news editor got swiftly to his feet, acting out his part to the end. At least, Kelso hoped he was acting.

'On your way. I mean it. ON YOUR WAY!'

'God almighty!' breathed the horrified driver, but hardly anyone on board heard his warning. He was fearful that anything louder might make the situation worse.

They were less than two miles from the village and had pulled over to avoid several red deer moving slowly along the wintry road towards them. He changed down to first and the bus reduced its headway, with a judder, to fifteen miles an hour.

The animals' heads drooped and most of them seemed too tired to care. Only a young hind was disturbed at being faced by the chugging single-decker. Her beautifully-rounded eyes widened with fright and she slithered as she backed away. A hart bucked aside and suddenly there were five or six bodies milling across the road.

Even at his reduced speed, the driver could barely avoid them. He wrenched the wheel hard and the radiator led the way into a dense drift at the side of the road.

Emma Dancer was jolted over the top of the seat in front. Martin Kelso, who was slumped in a doze, found the impact had the opposite effect on him. He was thrust down and under the two seats ahead. Belongings rained down from the rack. The driver rose out of his tilting seat but could not hold the bus. Its big back wheels lifted into the air as it settled into ten feet of snow, and the muffled engine throbbed erratically before dying away.

Kelso found himself sprawled out across the floor and, when he tried to move, discovered his club foot trapped awkwardly around a seat support. One or two of the passengers called out reassuringly to each other, and he was aware of somebody nearby gingerly feeling a bruised forehead and drawing in sharp breaths as they discovered how sensitive it was.

All that Kelso could think about was: *This is ridiculous. I shouldn't be here at all.*

They helped one another climb laboriously out and then stood in a pathetic group around the tilted end of the bus. Two passengers were cut and a woman thought she had a broken arm.

The driver set off for Elphin on foot with his hands deep in the pockets of his overcoat, which was nevertheless flapping

3

open at the front. He grumbled as he disappeared over the hill. 'Not my fault. Never seen so many deer so close to town. Not my fault. I don't know what they're bloody well up to.'

Kelso looked at the deer which had still not attempted to move on. They appeared to be exhausted.

An hour later, Jack Dunceford arrived with a couple of villagers.

It was dark before a tractor managed to pull the bus clear and, by that time, the sergeant's wife had met the last of the passengers who squeezed into the white Cortina. She wrapped a blanket around each of them and led them across to Station House where a great saucepan of beef soup was simmering.

Word quickly spread through the village and one of the people to look in was Sir Marcus Sheerwater.

The fact that he was Minister for Scottish Affairs made little difference to Sheerwater's attitude when more than two or three people collected in one place. To him they were potential votes, and he waded in with his reassuring smiles, words of encouragement and a firm handshake.

'Well done, Sergeant,' he said bumptiously when the two men could stand back and survey the scene. 'Think I'll just say a word or two before they start to disperse. Err, ladies and gentlemen. May I have your attention for a moment or two, please ... ?'

A hush fell on the assembly; Sir Marcus had a way with silences.

'I'd like to welcome you all here to Elphin and say how delighted I am that you are comparatively unscathed. I know some of you personally, of course, but to the others I say — come back and see us on a more agreeable day later in the year, although I'm sure you all realize that the warmth of our welcome is not dependent on the weather! My thanks, on your behalf, go out to Sergeant and Mrs Dunceford for their hospitality and ... '

Dunceford blushed. It was a rare sight. As the years passed, his resentment towards the force grew on a daily basis; he was now approaching retirement and had received no real recognition for his efforts. Thirty years' dedicated service and he would be handed, in return, a pittance of a pension and a silver police medal. But for the moment he basked in the MP's words. He tugged his jacket straight in readiness to respond, then put on a winning smile for the burst of applause.

Emma Dancer came across the room to shake his hand. He had seen her intriguing face around the village for the past month and knew she was poking into the history of the area. She appeared to be friendly with Sir Marcus Sheerwater and had, in fact, just introduced him to a pushy young man with a limp. That made her good enough for the sergeant.

He was just trying to think of something interesting to say to Emma, when Sir Marcus called across the room, 'Sergeant, I was just telling our journalist friend here that I'm giving a little party on Saturday. I wonder if you and Mrs Dunceford would care to join us for the evening?'

It was the first time that Dunceford had been invited to the MP's home on the hill, although he had been on duty outside several times when despatch boxes arrived from Whitehall. He swelled with pride and caught a glimpse of his wife sweating with excitement as she nodded vigorously in acceptance.

The room shuffled benevolently and everyone drew a little closer, hugging their mugs of steaming soup and making small talk. Outside, the wind from the hills drove the snow into the village in ever mounting drifts. Deep in the shifting shadows hunger reigned.

FOUR

The house on the ridge reverberated with unaccustomed noise. People danced, occasional bursts of laughter drowned the beat of the music, and the muted sounds carried far across the frozen hilltop.

It was midnight. The wind had died away and the glen lay stretched out in a coma, trying to recover from the paralysis of winter.

Martin Kelso had felt it worth booking in at the guesthouse for a week. Sir Marcus Sheerwater seemed to want to have a newspaperman around, hinting that the outcome of talks about a new North Sea oil initiative would be worth waiting for. Kelso would normally have declined any invitation that seemed like a sop to an MP's ego. But Sheerwater was also Secretary of State for Scotland and there could be something in it. Anyway, there was nothing better to do. So he stayed for the party and to see what transpired.

The trouble was that he was bored. Miss Dancer had not appeared with her gorgeous legs and so he simply sat and drank too many glasses of punch. Consequently, when he stepped out on to the terrace, he did not look where he was going. It was inky dark anyway. He put his weight down firmly in mid-air and was jarred by paving stones which were six inches lower than he had imagined.

Somewhere in front of him scampered his hostess's lapdog, which he had earlier been feeding with expensive little sausages on sticks.

He attempted to whistle to the dog several times, without finding the right pitch, and instead snapped his fingers into the shadowy darkness. 'Come back! Here, boy!'

Kelso swayed as he recalled the stern, meaningful look he

got a few minutes earlier when introduced to an off-duty police sergeant in an uncomfortably tight civilian suit. So he had drunk too much. Well, it was supposed to be a party, wasn't it? The newspaperman pulled a face. Didn't he have the right to forget himself once in a while? He glanced bitterly down at his surgical shoe. Things might get worse but, at the moment, it was difficult to imagine how.

The pug ran briskly up the garden, barking. Then stopped and gave a curious little whimper.

Kelso took several deep breaths in an attempt to clear his head and, as his eyes grew accustomed to the darkness, made out the muddled outlines of pine trees against the slightly lighter sky. The glen lay dark and satanic under clouds tinged with purple: the last reminder of a departed sun.

Cold as it was, he suddenly shivered with apprehension. For a moment, it was as if he was being chilled from the inside. Nearby, something was moving. He sensed it unmistakably. Something frightening that moved with great stealth like a nightmare on the edge of his consciousness.

'Here, boy.'

His tentative words were picked up by the petrified dog who hung on to them like a lifeline. It backed away from the mesmerizing shadows and began to scamper to safety. But something that Kelso could not see moved massively after the fleeting shadow and crushed it. There was a loud snap as if someone had broken a piece of wood in a single movement.

The newspaperman listened to the abrupt silence for a while, then took a few steps forward. He could not see a thing. Hesitantly he got down on his knees and reached out through the frozen bristles of grass ahead of him.

'Here, boy.'

His hand brushed against something damp, passed on and then quickly returned to it. It felt like fur, but it was wet and sticky. He drew back his hand and sniffed.

He had a dreadful feeling . . . but could not be sure. Slowly he put the damp, sour fingers to his mouth to taste them.

The door opened at the back of the house and a long thin

bar of light stretched out and saved him. It reached all the way to his feet.

'Mr Kelso,' called a genteel voice. 'You'll catch your death of cold out there.'

He unravelled himself and got up feeling rather foolish. Then stumbled back along the beam of light, wiping his hands on his trousers.

'What are you doing out there, Mr Kelso?' asked the feminine voice.

'Just getting some fresh air. I think I've cut myself.'

'Oh dear. Can I get you something?'

Kelso stepped indoors where it was warm and where there were other things to think about. 'Well, perhaps just a small brandy.'

Outside, the bar of light was squeezed tight and vanished. But, before it went out, it caught at its extremity a cold unblinking eye. A malevolent, almond-shaped eye.

FIVE

A Customs and Excise officer nudged his companion at Aberdeen Airport the moment that young Penny Bakersman swung into view. She had the sort of lithe walk that showed everything off in bold silhouette.

Eyes looked up from manifests, and remained fixed, as the lissom shape in calf-length boots came closer. To judge from her expression, her thoughts were miles away. Yet everything from her tilted nose to her jutting posterior seemed provocative. And men reacted accordingly. In this instance, a callow official who seemed fascinated by the approaching vision, moved across to intercept. He walked into an unnoticed case, and lost his peaked cap and millboard. But, scrambling up off his knees, he was still the first Customs man to offer her a card containing the printed words of warning.

'Anything to declare, miss? Madam?' He put his hat on, slightly askew.

'Nothing,' she said, eyes filled with concern. 'Except to ask if you hurt yourself.' She touched his hand solicitously and lingered there long enough to make him swallow hard.

He was aware of a uniformed colleague pulling a face full of exaggerated innuendo.

'I'm quite all right. Really. Very kind of you.'

She drew disturbingly close and he could smell a delicate perfume which flustered him even more. 'Positive now?'

He cleared his throat with a strangled sound. 'Have . . . have you anything to declare?'

'I don't think so. Say, what is your first name? You remind me of someone I met on the tennis courts last summer.'

It was too much for the gangling official. He flushed to the roots of his newly washed hair. 'We're not allowed,' he stammered. 'Not allowed to give our names.'

'Oh dear,' she sympathized. 'No dates, huh? Just like the Playboy Club. Well, I know just how you must feel. But rules are rules, I guess.'

She drew her travelling bag towards her, as if to leave, and he felt awkward about restraining her further.

'Would you mind opening your luggage?'

The oil tycoon's daughter, and sister of Franklin Delano Bakersman, had only a modest-sized grip. 'What, this?' She gave him a pleading look. 'I'd rather not.'

'Pardon?'

'It's embarrassing. Personal. You understand.'

He smiled disbelievingly. 'But you must. It's the law of the land.'

She gave a hopeless shrug and the Customs man dipped inside, to find himself looking at innumerable pairs of flimsy underpants. He picked one up, then hurriedly pressed it back.

She eyed him sympathetically. 'I told you so.' Then lowered her voice to share a confidence. 'I like to change my pants at least twice a day. I can't help it. I'm a very active girl and I get steamy under the crutch . . . Sorry! Is that an acceptable word in England? Anyway, they tell me it's normal and healthy.'

He stammered his thanks and chalked swiftly on the side of the grip. A half-salute and she was through.

She smiled back endearingly, as if she'd remember, and he was still blushing when she disappeared from view.

Franklin met her with an enormous hug on the other side of the barrier. 'Penny, you're looking terrific. Nice to see you again.' He sized her up behind his brotherly smile. If she got any sexier he'd be interested himself.

'Here, let me carry that.' He reached for the case.

'All right, but do be careful, Frank. I've got a sick friend in there.'

Franklin unfastened the case once they were in the limousine. Under the cotton pants and other underwear he found her white poodle, Cleopatra.

'Well, hello. You don't look as frisky as usual. Been sleeping?'

'I gave her a couple of tranquillizers.'

The thirty-year-old oil heir sighed. 'That was not a very bright thing to do. British magistrates have a habit of impos-ing enormous fines on people caught smuggling dogs into the country.'

'I know. But I'm not leaving her in quarantine for six months. She needs looking after, not locking up. She's very sensitive.'

He leaned back and closed his eyes. 'Sensitive? Aren't we all. But if you do things like that in this country you can get into a lot of trouble. You took an awful chance.'

She gave him a knowing look. 'No I didn't. I simply worked out what was possible. You show me a man, and I'll show you how to manipulate him.'

'How to what?'

She laughed delightedly. She had a beautifully square mouth and lots of even white teeth. Good teeth were a family characteristic. 'How to make him act foolishly.'

40

Franklin was now aware of her delicate perfume. 'I'm a man. Does that go for me too?'

She let her glance slide over him, as if the thought had not occurred to her before. 'I think so . . . I'll let you know.'

It was evening when Franklin Bakersman took the lift to the eighteenth floor of the Aberdeen Hilton, hummed as he walked along a muffled corridor and tapped on the door of Room 1807. He was short, handsome and full of himself.

'It's open. Come in.'

His sister was kneeling, open-legged, in the middle of the lounge in front of a dog basket, trying to entice Cleopatra to eat and drink from two bowls on the carpet.

He eased back the sleeve of his dinner jacket and glanced perplexedly at a rolled-gold watch. 'Aren't we supposed to be gliding downstairs, arm in arm, for dinner?'

'Oh, I forgot. Sorry. I've been so worried about Cleo. She won't touch her food.'

'That's all right. I know a brother ranks dismally low in any woman's list of priorities.'

She pushed back on to her heels. 'You try feeding her and I'll get ready. I'm starving. I'm going to gorge myself silly tonight.'

He helped her up and left his hands resting lightly on her hips. 'Good. That's what I wanted to hear. While you're in Scotland I want you to relax. Remember, that's all you're here for. Right?'

She shook her head slowly, teasing him. 'Wrong.'

Bakersman clenched his back teeth without allowing the smile to slip from his face. If she had arrived for some ulterior purpose, his father was behind it. J C Bakersman, the sceptical old sod who didn't trust his own son to run the overseas business for more than three months without checking up on him.

'Mother ask you to check how often I change my socks?'

She shook her head. 'Not mother.'

The stocky little oil heir was quick to anger and now he

41

took her by the shoulders, gripping a little too tightly for comfort. 'I think you ought to know, I like it here. I like being able to assert myself and make my own decisions. You can understand that.'

She levered his hands away. 'Let go. What's the matter with you?'

He walked around in a small circle, rubbing his forehead. 'I'm sorry. I really am. But the point is . . . ' He wagged a finger at her.

She waited expectantly, but there was only silence. 'Well?'

He sighed frustratedly. 'The point is that, at long last, I'm out of reach of that puritanical old sod. For once in my life I'm my own man, running the business smoothly and profit- ably. What more does he expect?'

She jerked her head. 'You know the way he is. He wants to know precisely what's going on all the time. He's suspi- cious.'

'Of what?' stormed her brother. 'Just name one thing that's gone wrong while I've been in charge here?'

'I don't have to.' She tickled him under the chin and he pulled away in irritation. 'I'm simply here to keep my eyes open.'

'What do you expect to find? Inefficiency, double dealing, what?'

'I don't know, and there's no need to shout. He trusts my judgement.'

'Your judgement?' he fumed. 'You've been engaged twice already and you're only eighteen!'

'Three times now, but don't let it upset you. It's just a hobby. I collect engagement rings.' As her tone hardened, he recognized the same cold depths in her eyes that he associ- ated with their tyrannical father. 'Look after the dog while I get changed.'

She unzipped her trousers and kicked them off as she went. She had a pair of endless legs and an extremely provocative behind.

He gazed after her and moistened his lips. 'Bitch,' he muttered, but not loud enough for her to hear. He knew how much reliance their father put on her judgement.

He bent down to examine the poodle and got a growl for his pains. He pulled a bellicose face. 'Don't give me any trouble, whitey, or you'll end up as a meat pie.'

His sister returned to the lounge snaking herself into a black velvet evening gown which hugged her contours down to the knees, before flaring out. Her shoulders and a vast expanse of bust were tanned and on public display. 'Zip me up, will you?'

He stood behind her and floated the tips of his fingers across her back.

'Stop it,' she said encouragingly. 'That tickles.'

'For somebody who's had three fiancés, you ought to be used to it.'

'I am,' she purred. 'But there's a time and a place for everything.'

She always was precocious. At the age of sixteen when their father caught her in a chauffeur's room over the garages she reacted not with embarrassment and shame, but with furious indignation at being interrupted. She told her brother later, perhaps out of bravado, that she didn't know what she enjoyed more: the struggle she had with the Afro driver of their pink Rolls-Royce, or the strap thrashing she got afterwards.

His thoughts were still far away when she interrupted his fingers. 'Let's go down and eat.'

The main restaurant was holding a dinner-dance for hotel guests, and she drew a good deal of attention as she moved gracefully through the tables with a half-smile for whoever was most interested.

A captain in the uniform of the Scots Guards rose to his feet, revealing muscular legs between his kilt and the white tablecloth. He had tousled hair and a jaw as square as an oak plank.

Long after they settled and Bakersman had mulled over the wine list, the big soldier was moving restlessly in his seat,

43

trying to engage her eyes. But now that he was interested, she made the task more difficult.

Eventually, when the band struck up, the officer plucked up his courage and walked across to their table. 'Hello, sir,' he said in the soft accent of the West Highlands. 'Remember me?'

Bakersman, whose thoughts at that moment were concentrated on the prospect of another two rigs coming into operation before the end of the year, withdrew the cigar from his mouth and looked faintly startled. 'Should I?'

'Captain Dougal Calder.'

The oil man could not recall ever having seen the giant officer before. 'I'm not sure precisely where it was we met, Captain err . . .'

'Calder. I'm a Campbell of Cawdor.'

Bakersman struggled to his feet and immediately regretted it. He was dwarfed. 'Are you indeed?'

The big, open face beamed. 'Indeed I am. We're a warrior clan.'

Penny smilingly indicated a spare chair at their table. 'Captain, why don't you sit down for a moment. My brother has never met a warrior face to face before.'

The guards officer laughed hugely and slapped his broad thigh. The word *brother* seemed to encourage him immensely.

'You may have forgotten, but we were introduced at your offices in . . . on the other side of . . . ' He cast a desperate smile at Penny, who was quick to help.

'Aberdeen?'

'Aberdeen. On the other side of Aberdeen.'

'You're interested in the oil business, Captain?'

'Absolutely!' He sat on the edge of the chair, absorbed in her amused eyes. Behind him, at the table he had just deserted, two other kilted officers smiled hopefully across.

'Are they friends of yours, Captain?'

'Ouch, no. They're MacDonalds. Pay no attention. They're a crude pair.' He finally tore his eyes away from her and turned to Bakersman. 'Would it offend you, sir, if I asked

44

your sister . . . It is your sister, isn't it? Aye, if I asked your sister to dance?'

The dance was a boisterous reel in which the Scot whirled Penny exuberantly around the tiny floor, within a cram of other dancers, whooping loudly.

They returned after five successive dances, laughing and gasping for breath.

Dougal Calder was glowing with pleasure when he confided in Bakersman, 'Your sister is a grand girl. She's got a lot of bottom.'

'I beg your pardon?'

'Bottom, grit, spunk. You know, a really grand girl.'

He returned for a moment to his fellow officers and held a whispered conversation. 'What did he say?' Penny asked from behind a cigarette, while attempting to appear disinterested. 'Something about me?'

Franklin rolled his cigar dryly across to a corner of his mouth, leaving just enough room for words to emerge. 'Said he likes your arse.'

She was faintly shocked. But the captain returned swiftly and said, 'I'm very much afraid I must go now. We have to be back in barracks by midnight and I'm officer of the guard.'

She reached out and covered his hand. 'How sad. You sound like Cinderella.'

Bakersman said cynically, 'Yes, if he doesn't get back by midnight they'll turn him into a civilian,' and coughed with laughter as he fanned the cigar smoke away from his face.

Dougal Calder bowed faintly to Bakersman. 'Nice to have renewed our acquaintance. Perhaps I can ask one last indulgence. Would you mind, sir, if I ask your sister to accompany me to the lobby? There's something important I want to say, as well as to thank her for an enjoyable evening.'

'Sure. Anything you like.'

She was gone for about fifteen minutes and when she returned she looked pale.

'You all right?'

'Yes.'

'He gone?'

45

She nodded and examined her slender fingers. 'Frank . . . '

'Yeah.'

'We're engaged.'

'What?' He leapt to his feet. 'Goddamit! What the hell are you playing at?' His serviette fell to the floor and some cigar ash broke off.

She glanced gently around as diners at other tables looked towards the disturbance. 'Take it easy, Frank. It was just a joke.'

He remained on his feet breathing hard for a while, then sank down. 'You sure?'

She nodded adamantly and he expelled his breath in a relieved sigh. 'Did he want to see you again?'

She raised her eyebrows, as if that was nothing to do with him. 'You're awfully inquisitive.'

'Well, somebody needs to look after you. You're only eighteen. And this guy's a Campbell. One of them Campbells are Coming. With big hairy legs and all. Well, I mean, somebody in the family's got to draw the line.'

This time it was Franklin's hand she patted, platonically. 'Don't worry. I told you I can handle men.' But she could see he was not convinced and added: 'Daddy knows it. Says I can see through them like panes of glass.'

Bakersman withdrew his hand icily. 'Is that why he sent you? To report back on my *inconsistencies*?'

'Frank,' she soothed. 'You're too sensitive by half. Just leave me to my own devices. You'll be all right.'

The Campbell of Cawdor inspected the guard at midnight: eight men, immaculately dressed and ramrod-backed. They spilled from the guardroom at the sergeant's shrill order. 'Turn out the guard! Come on, come on! Look lively. Stand still, stand still! Guard . . . Guard atten . . . shun!'

His apparently assessing eyes took in razor-sharp creases in khaki trousers and the restricted length of hair under their peaked hats; tapped one man's ankles with his cane to adjust

46

the symmetry of the back row. Then said quietly: 'Dismiss the guard, please, Sergeant.'

Off he walked, as the noise of screeched orders and crashing boots dissolved into the night. He quickened his step and ran the last few yards to the car park behind the officer's mess. Within twenty minutes he was braking sharply outside the Hilton.

At six o'clock in the morning the enormous Scotsman swung his legs out of the wide bed, tugged aside the curtain and stood looking down at the grey, sleeping city as he scratched his head.

Penny smiled lazily up at him. He was obviously still smitten. 'Thank you,' he said gently.

'Not at all. I always wanted to know what a Scotsman has under his kilt.'

Dougal Calder washed and then finished dressing in the lounge. He came across the white poodle while he was looking for his shoes. He knew enough about dogs to realize that she needed to be let out for a while.

'Come on, you scraggy wee bundle.' He picked the bitch up in one hand, tucked her gently but firmly under his arm, and left.

He set Cleopatra down in the lobby and pushed the big swing doors. She scampered through into the street and, within a minute or two, was far enough away to be completely lost.

SIX

It was common enough for stags to leap the sheep fences separating the high ground from the grazing areas. Four feet to the top of the wire and none too difficult with the advantage of the slope behind you.

But now, worn down by the attrition of the winter and

winds that sighed and moaned their way straight from the Arctic, not only the bolder deer chanced their luck. Tired hinds and their young launched themselves desperately at the barrier. Most succeeded. Some tangled their back legs in between two treacherous top strands, which trapped them like a metal tourniquet and resisted the harder they pulled.

The red deer left their share of bodies elsewhere, too: some emaciated in the snow, others drowned in peat hags blanketed by snow and in which they floundered in vain for a firm foothold.

Nature is without pity. Those of the black-nosed and exquisitely pale-eyed deer that could not evade it succumbed. Only man possessed the sentiment to save them, but this winter man was too involved with his own survival to care. The first few dozen deer to reach the towns seemed to find a haven. Local people regarded the inquisitive mild-mannered animals as a novelty and tossed out whatever scraps they could.

But the sympathy soon began to wear thin. As wearier deer appeared, there were some disturbing incidents. A cemetery was trampled and flowers eaten from pots on the gravestones. Then a huge stag knocked over a pram outside a grocery store in Inverness and the baby was dragged for fifty yards by blankets caught in a hoof.

As far south as Fort William, a heavy old hind got on to an escalator and, in trying to scramble off again, crashed over the side breaking a supermarket window and showering glass over shoppers.

A pair of hungry young stags clashed violently over the dust-bins behind a Chinese takeaway in Aviemore. They locked antlers and butted one another almost senseless, heaving and rearing through the restaurant and out into the street on the other side. Three cars collided in their anxiety to get clear.

But the final straw came at both Ullapool and Elphin, when dozens of deer abruptly stampeded through the streets at night. No one was certain what had caused it, but the clatter of hooves on paving stones and the thuds of jostling bodies scared the villagers.

Sergeant Dunceford met Temporary Constable Shaftoe

at the far end of Elphin the next day, atfer separately assessing the damage. The sergeant shook his head. 'If it happened in daylight a lot of women and children could have been injured,' he said.

Two hours later it did happen again. Several stags followed by a dozen hinds and calves galloped along the main road as if the dogs of hell were after them. Dunceford ran ponderously towards whatever it was that scared them, in a wood meandering down to a frozen burn. He was panting when he arrived and Shaftoe was close behind.

A strong movement through a thin screen of birch trees drew their attention and Dunceford signalled his 16-stone assistant to keep quite still. Whatever it was, they were unarmed and a long way from cover.

Dunceford picked up a piece of smooth stone and skimmed it between the tree trunks. Suddenly, there was a great commotion and a magnificent golden eagle flapped up from the fern-covered ground.

They could see fierce eyes, and an imperious curved beak, as it moved powerfully up and away. Shaftoe whistled in admiration. 'She must have a ten-foot wingspan. Never seen one that big before.'

They watched until it was a distant speck, then the temporary constable turned to go. But Dunceford was less certain. 'It would take more than that to frighten fully-grown stags.' He stared into the frozen ferns for a long time without venturing in.

It was his message to the divisional superintendent which, when woven in with other disturbing reports of deer movement in the glens, eventually spurred Edinburgh into action. But the options open to the civil servants were minimal. It was no good them even keeping London in the picture, since everybody in the capital who wasn't already confined to bed was dosing himself up with anti-flu tablets.

There was no doubt that Dacca flu had gained a grip on the south and that it would spread throughout the country before long. Vaccine was still in scandalously short supply and what there was could be moved only slower because of the iced-up railways and slithering roads.

The action they decided upon was a telegram requesting that Richard Unthank be given unlimited leave of absence from his duties on Rhum. He was to report to the mainland police and advise them on the problems being caused by the increasingly unpredictable behaviour of the deer herds.

Unthank was up in the hills when the message arrived. There is not much of Rhum; you can't go more than ten miles in any direction without walking into the sea, and trees are as scarce as a smile on your bank manager's face.

When he did get back, muffled against the frozen wind but tingling at the tips of his fingers and toes, he sat on top of an old-fashioned stove with a precarious funnel going up through the hut roof, and let the steam issue up around him as he thawed. With his big hands cupped around a mug of cocoa, drawing blissful warmth from it, he considered the summons.

One thing he had learned, cut off from the brisk pace that civilization sets itself, was to take his time and not rush into anything. If something was worth doing it would still be there tomorrow.

It was ten years now since he left London and buried himself in wildlife. Ten years since he had contemplated marriage. There was only one regret in his mind: perhaps by now he would have had a son. Or better still, a daughter to pull about gasping with laughter on a sledge, or to walk through the fields in springtime, a big hand in a small grasp.

But it didn't work out. He had spent six hectic months working at the Baltic Exchange in London, preparing to become something in shipping which would find favour with his highly critical, prospective father-in-law. And only succeeded in making himself miserable. It almost came as a relief when he discovered his slightly-superior fiancée in bed with her cousin who owned a string of racehorses. He accepted the escape hole and headed back to the Hebrides, where he had been posted briefly as a soldier years before, to bury himself in the solitude he loved.

But now if the deer needed help, and he could organize some assistance for them, he would leave again for the mainland. The bulk of the herds would soon be forced down from the hills towards the food and warmth of civilization. Tens of thousands of them moving inexorably closer to human contact.

And not only the deer were threatened by the severity of the winter. Squirrels, badgers, foxes. Those that could not hibernate and shut their eyes to the savagery of the weather, would probably not survive in great numbers. He had heard of more than one thermometer shattering; splitting right up the middle when the temperature dropped a sickening forty degrees in one night.

And what of the wolves? They too would be drawn down from the high ground once the big ungulates left. Without deermeat they could not last for more than a few weeks.

Unthank sighed and set down his mug. Perhaps, after all, there were some things that could not be put off until tomorrow. Within an hour, he had packed his bags and was heading for the mainland.

The Rt Hon James Beaconsfield sat upright in the back of the spacious black car and snapped, 'Am I surrounded by idiots?'

His aide, Marchant, did not know whether to nod or to shake his head vigorously. In this mood there was no placating the Prime Minister. The public's growing anger over the weather was being directed at Downing Street, and it would cost the party dear at the next election unless something positive was done.

'The match should never have been played in the first place,' he said tetchily. 'I don't care if it was an international, arranged six months ago.'

'No, sir,' said Marchant, scribbling something on a pad on his knee. 'The instructions banning the use of floodlights were explicit.'

'But once it had started, and seventy thousand people were inside Wembley Stadium, it should have been allowed to finish. Don't you see that? What idiot pulled the switch ten minutes from the end?'

'I understand that a power board official got to hear about the game and marched straight over there.'

Beaconsfield groaned. The lights had gone out at the very moment England were about to take a crucial penalty. There was uproar in the ground and at least thirty spectators were injured. His head ached and the last thing he wanted was to face a hostile Commons during Question Time. But it was too late; they were already turning into Parliament Square.

He could picture the scene: a Commons half-full but with every member in sight wearing an overcoat. Even the dignified Speaker had a hotwater bottle tucked between his seat and the small of his back.

'Would the Prime Minister tell the House why coal from the Midlands and now on its way to Europe cannot be diverted back to Britain? Surely it is the height of folly to take away from our own doorstep fuel so urgently needed to sustain British families?'

'Hear, hear . . .' Scores of feet drummed the floor. 'Hear, hear.'

He was on his own feet, apparently calm and sage, but with his hands clenched so tightly that the fingernails cut into his palms.

'I am sure the Honourable Member realizes that the eyes of the world are on Britain during this crisis and that they fully expect us to honour our obligations. We are contracted to supply our EEC colleagues with fuel, on which their industry depends. To cut off supplies now would be grossly unfair . . .'

He was interrupted by jeers and calls of 'Unfair to whom?'

' . . . I repeat, grossly unfair to our continental friends who are shivering just as much as we are.'

The Speaker was hard put to call the House to order and more than one Opposition member walked out in apparent disgust. But Beaconsfield saved the day to some extent by announcing that Britain was negotiating for the purchase of

United States coal, ' . . . with the same speed and urgency as a wartime operation.'

Back in the calm dignity of Number Ten, the Prime Minister picked up his briefing papers ready for another emergency Cabinet meeting that afternoon. 'Marchant, I want you to ask the American Ambassador to come over at three o'clock. Cancel any other engagements. Then I want to go over this television speech with Gerald. Anything I should know about?'

'Nothing that can't wait, Prime Minister.'

He did not bother the Premier with the information that Marcus Sheerwater had rung three times, long distance, asking for a personal meeting to alert him to what was happening to snowbound Scotland. Sheerwater had mentioned the plight of the deer. But that only made Marchant raise his eyebrows. Deer? He should try facing rows of angry MPs. They were like a pack of wolves.

He turned away, snapped up the small body of a mountain hare and loped down towards the trees. The others followed haphazardly and at irregular intervals.

Two, four, six dark shapes on the light night-grey snow.

They were hungry, but once again there were no deer to be found. Their eyes glinted. Nature was goading them. Every day they were obliged to work harder, move faster and at the end of it all to accept a less satisfying meal than before.

Yet their memories were still fresh of the time when they swept from the cover of the trees and raced up a white, seemingly empty hillside, only to see it erupt into movement as dozens of deer leapt to their feet, shook off sheets of snow and ran for their lives.

They had killed with abandon; raking, slashing, clamping their ferocious mouths until all was silent around them. A bloody, slippery, silent battlefield in which they settled to gorge. And then to sleep, distended and meat-drunk.

But the prey had thinned as winter increasingly became a menacing spectre on the horizon and now was almost impossible to find. They needed all their savage cunning simply to survive.

He smoothly accelerated and stretched out his graceful body, landing softly on his front feet. Effortlessly clearing streams and dark dips in the ground, as if floating. A huge branch snapped from its frozen tree trunk, unable to bear the harsh drop in temperature any longer, and the abrupt noise made them veer in another direction. His keen mind considered and discarded the cause of the disturbance. If anything, the agonizing cold made their sensations all the sharper.

When he stopped, they all stopped. He toyed with the winter-white hare protruding from either side of his mouth, clamped it under his paws and then tugged off its head and left the remains to be pulled apart by the others. But afterwards he was still hungry. The fur and fluff he swallowed made him sneeze and did little to assuage his hunger.

He ran, in a wide sweep, head bent to the ground, trying to pick up the scent of rabbit, fox or whatever might be breathing shallowly in a half-sleep. But winter had bitten deep into Nature's reserves and either the hibernators had yet to feel the first stirrings of a changing season, or the intense cold had got to them irrevocably and they would never emerge.

Before dawn he joined the others gnawing at the bark of pine trees. The wood was bitterly hard and rubbed their gums raw. For the second time that night he tasted blood, but this time it was his own and it filled him with a baleful anger.

Two of the pack harried one another, snarling defiantly and yelping in turn. They were all irritable and tired of casting around for food in vain. For too long they had kept to the high ground above the wire fences. But now they sprang at the wire and were immediately in new territory. One made it only at her third attempt and then took her spite out on a three-inch fence post, which she almost bit through.

He gazed down the glen where man ruled. It was unknown territory but here at least there was food. Here they would survive.

Were they not the greatest hunters in the northern hemisphere? Fierce, fast, cunning and with sharper sight and hearing than any other. They could not be stopped.

Darkmind led the way. The others hesitated and then streamed menacingly after him.

The snow was still falling and, Dunceford reflected as he peered through the station windows, in this kind of weather there was little to choose between night and day. He miserably nursed his third cup of lukewarm tea, and pretended that he had not noticed Constable Shaftoe, who was anxiously lurking on the threshold of his office. Eventually he deigned to look up.

'Well . . . ?'

'Two more dogs and a cat missing.'

The sergeant turned back to an empty view of the bleak hillside. 'How many does that make?'

'In all, five dogs and two cats in the past three days.'

'Mmm. Any sign of the carcasses?'

'What, in all this snow?'

'Well, start looking anyway.'

Shaftoe shifted awkwardly. 'Can I take the car?'

'You've got a bicycle, haven't you?'

'Oh, have a heart. What sort of an impact do I make, arriving to question somebody on a squeaky old bicycle?'

'You're not questioning anybody. You're looking for dead cats. Now stop bothering me. How can I think clearly with you muttering in the background?'

Shaftoe, who prized his position at the police house, realized he was beginning to irk his superior. He went away, only to return soon afterwards looking flustered.

He indicated the outer office agitatedly, unable to find words adequate to describe the latest arrival.

Dunceford sighed. 'Whoever it is, tell them to bugger off. Can't you see I'm busy?'

'Sir . . . Sir Mar . . . ' An irate figure pushed Shaftoe aside at the moment that he got out the complete name. 'Sir Marcus Sheerwater.'

Dunceford got up so quickly, he spilled the remains of the tea down his leg. 'Good morning, sir,' he said a little too heartily. 'How nice to see you again so soon.'

The sixty-year-old MP had a flushed and aristocratic face, as well as the air of a man accustomed to drinking port and being listened to. He tapped Shaftoe impatiently on the chest with a silver-topped cane. 'One of your men, Dunceford?'

'Yessir,' said the sergeant, chest out and arms rigidly at his sides.

'Well, tell him not to keep me hanging about outside, there's a good chap. I'm extremely busy at the moment, with a despatch case full of work from Whitehall. I'm sure you understand. Indeed, the very fact that I'm here, instead of calling you up to the house, is an indication of the urgency of the matter.'

'Absolutely, sir.' Dunceford pulled the best chair forward for the Scottish Secretary of State and frowned severely at Shaftoe before dismissing him with a wave of his hand.

Sir Marcus turned to Shaftoe. 'No, stay please. You may be able to help. The fact is, my Great Dane, Rupert, has disappeared.' He sat down, crossed one immaculately creased trouser leg over the other and fitted a cigarette into a holder while they watched respectfully. 'Must have wandered off yesterday. But I want him found immediately. Do you understand? I want a search. I realize it's not exactly your duty, Inspector . . . Oh, do excuse me. Is it Inspector yet?'

Dunceford blushed from ear to ear. 'Err, no sir. Still Sergeant. But please go on.'

'Well, Rupert has an impeccable pedigree. Been with me since he was a puppy, only so high.' He indicated a height level with the table. Shaftoe looked questioning at the sergeant. 'Always been high-spirited, as you know. Remember how he loved to romp about when you visited the High House?'

'Indeed I do, sir,' said Dunceford touching the back of his leg and wincing at the memory.

'I'm very worried. So's Lady Sheerwater. Needs his vitamins and a hot drink every day, you understand. We want him back as soon as you can organize it.'

Dunceford followed the brisk figure, who was as abrupt in leaving as he was in arriving. 'We'll do our best, sir. But I can't prom...'

The outer door slammed shut behind the front-bench MP and Dunceford was left looking at an empty space.

It was late afternoon when Martin Kelso clumped downstairs at the guest house and collected the wrapped sandwiches and thermos of coffee that he had booked an hour or two earlier. There was a snowplough heading south to Inverness that evening and he had talked the driver into taking him along. Somebody was playing a familiar lament on an old upright piano in the residents' lounge.

The hunched figure at the keyboard, with its back to the journalist, seemed familiar. Tall, tousled, wearing a sheep-skin jacket as if he half-expected the snow to follow him indoors, and peering intently at the sheet music in an attempt to avoid some of the wrong notes.

But the grey eyes and wide mouth that turned at his approach were not part of a face Kelso recognized. The man had a calm, outdoors look and was about ten years older than himself.

Kelso pulled his misshapen foot into line and paused by the piano stool. 'Playing that for me?'

'Why, are you going somewhere?'

'Ullapool, then Inverness.'

'In this weather? Hope you make it.'

Kelso stopped to fit the package of food into his overcoat pocket. Daylight was fading and he no longer had time to call, as intended, at the house of the singularly beautiful archaeologist. It was a nuisance having to rush off. But if he didn't take advantage of the lift, he would miss the story altogether.

'Which is the nearest big railway station?'

The lean fingers stopped in mid-span. 'Inverness.'

'Thought so. It is on the main line, isn't it?'

'Yes. Why?'

'Well I heard they're running two trains a day simply carrying snow.'

'Why would they do that?'

'Just what I want to know. Instead of carrying badly-needed coal or oil – and with half the rolling stock in Britain frozen up – they are shunting tons of snow about the country. Sounds crazy, doesn't it?'

'British Rail?'

'Yes.'

'I suppose they've got a reason. Why are you so interested?'

'I work for a newspaper.'

'Oh,' Unthank observed the sharp eyes, city shirt and carefully-tailored suit. Apart from the man's handicapped foot, it could have been himself ten years ago. How curious. It was his first reminder of the old hustle-bustle since arriving that afternoon and introducing himself to a despondent Sergeant Dunceford.

Kelso was well aware of the scrutiny. 'Something wrong?'

'No. You just reminded me of someone. Err . . . are you planning on coming back?'

'I doubt it.'

'In that case, as your room is next to mine, I'll probably sneak in tonight and pinch one or two of the blankets. It's going to be another nasty one.'

'Why not? Wish I'd thought of commandeering yours last night.'

They smiled and parted . . . and might never have seen one another again, but for the circumstances that were soon to touch both their lives . ; . as well as those of everyone in Elphin.

Kelso swung himself awkwardly up into the cab of the snowplough. His crooked leg stuck out momentarily and he glanced at it with a familiar resentment. As the engine throbbed into life and he huddled down into his coat for warmth, he heard the out-of-tune piano start up again.

Don't cry-ee. Don't sigh-ee. There's a silver lining in the

58

sky-ee. Bonsoir, old thing. Cheerio, chin-chin. Napooh, toodle-oo. Good-bye-ee!

It was a raw night. But the next day the weather showed how unpredictable it could really be.

The last of the winter snowclouds shifted towards Norway, losing height in the distance and leaving a clear sky. Soon afterwards, the first real sunshine of the year appeared over the western Highlands, like the prodigal returned.

It was a pale sun, emerging as if from a long illness. But it was enough to make the McDee girl skip down the path, happy as a fieldmouse and talking busily to an imaginary class. She was completely lost in her game. Her nimble feet directed themselves down the steep, stoney track, and only a small section of her mind remained alert.

Either side of the track was a dense stretch of snow-rimmed fern and, beyond it, pine trees stood with icy discipline in stiff rows.

There is always sound in a forest. Even the silences are full of movement. Creaks and shuffling, snaps and twittering. But a steady rustle and slither on one side made her stop. And listen.

The usual noises reassured her. But, when she walked on, a regular and massive brushing aside of ferns unlocked the fear in her mind.

She stood quite still again, dry-mouthed and trembling like a mole who is too shortsighted to see the fox standing over him, but instinctively aware of its presence.

In the acute focus of a moment she heard rasping breathing. But what she did not notice were great breaths of condensed air that arose not thirty feet away; her own anxious little puffs of breath obscured her vision.

When she stopped . . . whatever was following her stopped. But each time the dreadful unknown drew closer.

She set off again with her heart beating rapidly, willing her mother to appear around the next bend. Her foot slipped on the ice-skin of a stone and she fell, badly grazing her knees and bringing tears to her eyes. She ran on. Faster and blindly.

Whatever was following her broke into a loping run, scything powerfully through the damp undergrowth, its hoarse breath clearly audible now.

Even louder in her ears was the thudding of her own heart against her daisy-yellow anorak. Her matchstick legs would not move quickly enough. It was as if they were drugged. Terror dilated her eyes as she careered around the corner and ran full tilt into Albert Henry Tudor, a postman who was perspiring up the slope with a satchel full of letters.

'Wheeeeee.' He lifted her off the ground and swung her delightedly around in his long arms to absorb the impact.

She clutched him around the middle, sobbing with relief.

'What on earth's the matter, my little daffodil?'

Amy McDee peeped around the edge of his protective arms to see what had frightened her. But there was nothing.

His keener eyes travelled up and over the glistening hillside which the sun had edged with gold. He saw only fern and trees and countless more miles to trudge before he could finally ease off his tight boots for the day.

'A ghostie chased me,' she said fearfully.

'Did he indeed. And where is he now, pray?'

She noted the chiding tone and said reproachfully, 'I almost saw him.'

'Ah! Almost but not quite. Well, he's gone now. And, if it's your mother you're meeting, I passed her a little way back. You run and find her, and I'll have a sharp word or two with your ghostie.'

She waved several times on her gentle run down the hill. Turned and waved, and turned again. And whenever she looked, he was there. Tall, thin and reassuring.

But no one ever saw him alive again.

Lean, kitchen-weary Mrs Emeline McDee had given her youngest daughter a small bar of milk chocolate and left her dawdling twenty yards behind when she reached the spot where the postman had stood a short time before.

She swung the weight of her wicker-handled shopping basket into the other hand and stopped to regain her breath. Something glittered among the thick snow-topped ferns and took her attention.

She stepped into the damp undergrowth and prodded it hesitantly. It was part of a uniform jacket: torn and wet but strangely warm. On the collar was the brass crown of the Post Office. For no logical reason, she hurriedly dropped it and drew back. Then farther into the chest-high bracken she noticed a movement.

Amy's small hand reached into hers, from behind. 'Don't go in there, Mummy. I'm frightened.'

The very words gave Mrs McDee a courage born of example. 'There's nothing to be afeared of, darling,' she said with a calmness she did not feel.

Even so, she restricted her inquisitiveness to picking up a hand-sized stone and lobbing it into the greenery.

There was a violent disturbance and, with a great hiss, a golden eagle careered into the air, snapping and flattening the foliage on its way. Its regally curved beak and sideways stare pierced Mrs McDee's startled gaze as it laboured upwards with its talons gripping a soggy bundle.

A postman's peaked hat fell free and cartwheeled to earth, bouncing down the path.

SEVEN

It was Kelso who, without realizing it, killed Franklin Delano Bakersman.

He found his snow, packed in wagons and awaiting a journey south. But it was not the astounding story he had imagined. Great banks of snow had been pushed to either side of the main roads in Inverness and now the only way to dispose of it was to send it by train to the valleys and dump it there.

He phoned a couple of paragraphs over to his paper in London and then transferred to the news desk at their request.

'Martin! How are you getting on?'

'I'm bloody freezing. That's how I'm getting on. How much longer is this ridiculous exile supposed to last?'

'Just keep your head down for a month or two.'

'A month or two!'

'Let the fuss die down. Now, never mind about all that. You can do something for me. I've had a tip that there's an American, named Bakersman, up your way. Apparently he's planning to drill a third generation of oil wells in the North Sea. The idea is to bore straight down through the old, exhausted fields to the fresh oil-bearing strata which his company geologists now believe exists in vast quantities underneath.'

Kelso saw the possibilities right away. *Great News for Weary Britain.* Yes, he could do things with a story like that. *We're Sitting On Another North Sea Bonanza!* His interest quickened. *Billion-pound Quest Under Abandoned Wells.* It would be too big for Lord Danecliff to dismiss out of hand. And within a day or two, Martin Kelso would be back in London. Reinstated, with an all-is-forgiven, and on his way up again.

'Sounds possible,' he said with studied indifference. 'I'll look into it.'

'Hang on, Martin. It's not for you. We're sending Rooksby up to do the talking. Editor's orders. All you have to do is find out where Bakersman is, and we'll do the rest.'

'Nigel Rooksby? You must be joking,' he said indignantly. 'He's the bleeding ballet correspondent.'

'That was years ago. He's part of the newsroom now.'

'But he couldn't recognize a news story if it did the splits in front of him. I'm the man on the spot. For God's sake, leave it to me.'

The news editor said testily, 'You'll do what you're told.'

Kelso said something obscene.

'What was that?'

'Nothing.'

There was a long silence. 'The man's supposed to be staying at the Aberdeen Hilton. But he booked out yesterday with his eighteen-year-old sister and nobody seems to know where they've gone. Find out and ring me.'

The conversation ended abruptly and Kelso was left glowering at a silent receiver. Nothing would make him hand over a story like this to a fathead like Rooksby. It would be sacrilege. Not this story . . . not Martin Kelso's story. For that's what it had already become in his mind.

Death came a little closer for Bakersman when the reporter with the misshapen foot made a further phone call the next morning.

He squeezed into a phone booth on Inverness railway station and pressed some silver into the slot when a girl's voice answered.

'Aberdeen Hilton.'

'Miss Bakersman, please.'

'Room number?'

'I've no idea. She's been staying with her brother, Mr F D Bakersman, an American oil executive.'

'I see. One moment, please.'

There was a pause: long enough for her to take advice. 'Miss Bakersman is away at present, but should be back by the end of the week. Do you wish to leave a message?'

'Err, no. This is extremely urgent and personal. Is there a forwarding address?'

'One moment.'

There was another silence, then a man's voice came on. Older and more responsible. 'May I ask, sir, if you are calling about Miss Bakersman's dog?'

'Dog? Yes, as a matter of fact, I am. And I know she'd want me to ring her right away. I'm from the Kennel Breeders' Association. Major Wicksteed.'

'Ah. Yes, Major. Miss Bakersman can be contacted in Aviemore. The number there is 341.'

He went out on to the station concourse and asked a porter about train times.

'Where?' The railwayman cupped a hand around his ear.

'Aviemore.'

'Where?'

'AVIEMORE!'

'Oh, you mean Aviemore,' he said, putting a slightly different emphasis on the pronunciation. 'Platform Three in just a couple of minutes. It's two stops down the line. Going skiing?'

'No, I don't ski.'

'Pardon?' The hand went back to the ear.

'I don't ... Never mind. Thanks anyway.'

He returned to the booth, manoeuvred around the folding door and sorted out his small change. He rang the number which turned out to be an hotel. Were his dear friends the Bakersmans staying there? he asked in a voice soaked in charm and reliability. Yes? Good.

Next he made a reverse-charge call to London.

A familiar voice said, 'Newsdesk. Hang on.'

Kelso bent at the knees to observe Platform Three: a train was rolling in. 'Come on, come on,' he muttered. He tried shrill little whistles to attract attention over the phone.

'Yes?'

'Harry, can you hear me? It's Martin Kelso. I haven't got much time.'

'Just about. It's a bloody awful line. Sounds as if you're eating crisps.'

'You wanted the address of Bakersman, the American oil man in Scotland.'

'Oh, yes. Let me get a pencil.' Kelso puffed out his cheeks in exasperation and heard carriage doors slamming from across the platforms. ' ... Right.'

'He's staying in ... ' Kelso consulted a large holiday map of Scotland pasted to the wall in front of him, and ran his finger to the top right-hand corner. As far away as he could get. ' . . . Thurso. Castle Hotel, Thurso.'

'What's the phone number?'

'Harry, it won't help you. I've already rung and he's not using his own name. Tell Rooksby it's room seventeen he wants.'

'Got it. Anything else?'

'Yes. Tell him it's a man's country up here. He'd better slip something over his ballet tights.'

He rang off as the departure whistles were blown on Platform Three. In his anxiety to get the folding door of the phone booth open, he pushed instead of pulling, and struggled with its wooden folds before squeezing out through the gap.

'Jee . . . sus.' His run was slower and much more cumbersome than anybody else's. It consisted of putting one leg forward and dragging the other, solidly-built boot up to it. It never ceased to embarrass and enrage him and it scared a mother and child who heard the dragging run behind them.

A ticket collector was just shutting the barrier at the entrance to the platform. 'Sorry, it's going.'

Kelso burst through the half-gate. 'I know. I'm going too.'

Somebody opened a carriage door and he scrambled in as the train moved off. He fell back on a seat, gasping gratefully.

As the miles passed in metallic rhythm, he saw several groups of red deer moving southwards close to the embankment. But at the time it meant little to him. He was content to warm himself on the thought of Nigel Rooksby journeying eagerly north towards frostbitten Thurso.

Kelso's discomfort was forgotten when he arrived at the ski-centre hotel and found the Bakersmans in the dining room. The small, blond oil man did not seem to mind the intrusion. In fact, he insisted that the reporter sat at their table.

Kelso ignored the head waiter's disapproving attitude to his arrival – dishevelled and without any luggage. He could deal with waiters. After tucking hungrily into their rolls and butter, he thrust out the empty bread basket. 'Fill this, please!' The waiter accepted it with ill-grace and disappeared.

The reporter got on with his questions, although he found the man's younger sister a great distraction. She was wearing a snug cashmere sweater with nothing underneath. Every time he glanced in her direction, he saw the outline of her nipples. He tried hard not to look.

Bakersman realized that the newspaperman knew the essence of Parallel Oil's drilling plans and he decided there was no point in being secretive any longer. The company already had explicit drilling permission from the government and, once a national newspaper printed the facts and the Stock Exchange took account of the consequences, there would be nothing his father could do from across the Atlantic to pull him back.

The American talked through soup, Chicken Bangkok with butter, chutney and spices, through cheese and biscuits and coffee. He talked so long and in such enthusiastic detail that Kelso realized he had a second story, a natural follow-up on his hands too.

It seemed that most of the North Sea oil giants were beset by trouble. Technology had advanced so fast in the past thirty years that now it was beginning to trip over itself. Much of the automatic, self-correcting equipment that Britain's oil wealth paid for during the boom years of the 1980s was now often out of action. Bakersman said the equipment was so complex that even the technology required to repair it was prohibitively expensive. And, with much of the original oil flow drying up, companies were feeling the pinch.

Eventually, however, even Franklin Bakersman had said enough. He sat back and grinned. 'Look at my sister, Mr Kelso.'

The newspaper man did not want to. He knew his eyes would betray him, and he was right. She reached for a piece of cake and everything moved pendulously.

Kelso moistened his lips and turned back,

'Look at her. Look!'

The point of her brother's protestation was that Penny was

tucking into a great slice of chocolate gâteau, oozing with thick cream. Her wide, apparently innocent eyes devoured Kelso at the same time.

'The more she eats the slimmer she gets! It's incredible! Yet just look at her figure. There's nothing to it.'

Kelso swallowed on a dry throat. 'Oh, I wouldn't say that,' he croaked.

She put out a hand, touching his wrist and sending tingles up his arm. 'Frank, you're embarrassing the man.' She wriggled her shoulders and everything underneath shook from side to side.

'No . . . no . . . not at all,' he stammered. 'I can see you've got a lot of . . . a lot of . . . bounce.' Oh my god, he groaned inwardly. He was so confused now that he barely knew where he was.

But Franklin Bakersman saved the situation by abruptly changing the subject. He called the head waiter over and asked if the law allowed anyone to shoot deer locally. He was told no, only by permit and with the agreement of the Red Deer Commission.

He seemed disappointed and it was then that Kelso told him about the huge hen eagle that had been reported near Elphin, and which was said to have carried off more than one fully-grown dog.

'Can't the police do something?'

'Not much they can do. Time they pedal up, the thing's gone.'

'How big is she?'

'Ten or twelve feet from the tip of one wing to the other.'

'That right?' Bakerman's eyes narrowed with interest. 'Think they could use some help?'

'I wouldn't be surprised. It must be a lamb-killer too, and a lot of mothers will soon start getting worried about their children.'

'Well . . . ' Bakersman dabbed his mouth with a serviette. 'Perhaps later you'd show me, on a map, just where this place called Elphin is. Though I must say, it rings a bell in the back

67

of my head. I got it! Is there a Government Minister living there, name of err . . . '

'Sheerwater.'

Bakersman snapped his fingers in the air. 'That's the guy. He's asked me to meet him to talk about North Sea drilling. Maybe I should drop in on him after I've dispatched your eagle.'

A delicious smile spread across Kelso's face. Not so much at the thought of the American going shooting, but at the way the man's sister was gently brushing against his handicapped leg under the table. She'd noticed his limp earlier and now she leaned her leg against his, sympathetically.

He smiled wanly, like a grateful patient under treatment. But the more she persisted, the more sexually aroused he became.

How could he have known that he had just signed Franklin Bakersman's death warrant?

EIGHT

Alec McDee was a wiry Scot of indeterminate age, hewn from Highland granite, hardened by nine years' overseas service in the Black Watch and later embittered by unpredictable winters which extended beyond the sustenance provided by an autumn bank loan, and by summers that were often so waterlogged they rotted the feet of his cattle. He was a hill farmer and his greatest source of pride was his two daughters. But on this occasion he was showing the grim side of his nature.

'No bird tore the inside out of six ewes!' he exploded, crashing the butt of his shotgun down on the bare boards, inside Station House, making the dust dance in the rays of a watery sun. 'I tell you it must have been Sir bloody Marcus

Sheerwater's freak dog. He's big enough, he's savage enough, and you said yourself he's running wild.'

The sergeant ran a hand through his grey-streaked hair and deflected the double barrels away from his face.

'Now calm down, Alec, and stop pointing that thing at me. It won't help to blow my head off.'

The farmer swung away frustrated. 'Aah! I know I don't count for much against the Establishment. But I'll have the price of those ewes from him, and for any other sheep that are hurried into their graves. I'll have cash and an apology. And, on top of that, I'll have his dog's pedigree bollocks for breakfast.'

McDee, to whom ten sheep meant the difference between new dresses for his little girls or another penny-pinching vinegar-hard year, gripped the wooden stock until his knuckles showed white.

'If that creature shows its face on my land, I'll give it both barrels at close range. You won't even find the bits. Then, every day, I'll nail the rotting carcass of another ewe to his expensive front door until he admits liability.'

Dunceford, who was completely out of his depth against the far-reaching influence of a government minister, blocked the farmer's way out.

'Alec,' he said sharply. 'You keep away from Sir Marcus! There's a bloody great eagle in the area. There's your culprit. She's tasted carrion and she'll be looking for more. You know, as well as I do, this winter's frozen most of the wildlife to death. She's got nothing to eat. So, now she's looking for flesh. Old or new. It might even be a child she goes for next.'

McDee paused for a moment, aware of the logic of Dunceford's view, but allowed it to be swept aside in his tide of anger against the MP.

'I'll blow the head off every eagle I see. But it won't do much good, will it? Not if the high-and-mighty families hereabouts are shielded by the police, and their dogs allowed to get away with sheep killing with no more than a tut-tut and a finger-wagging.'

He shouldered past the policeman, lurching into the door

frame on his way out and almost jarring it off its foundations.

Shaftoe made a strategically delayed appearance from the inner room, in time to hear the farmer's parting shot. 'You can say goodbye to that dog,' said McDee savagely.

Dunceford squeezed his hands together indecisively, then finally made up his mind and swung to his assistant. 'First thing tomorrow, you and me – and anybody else we can drum up – are going out to nail that eagle. And we're not coming back till we get it. I don't give a damn if it takes a week and if you don't get a meal in between.'

The heavy-hipped Shaftoe frowned with dismay, and let his mind race over the possibility of eating a gargantuan meal – three or four times his normal size – that evening to bolster himself against hard times to come.

'I don't give a damn,' continued Dunceford, 'if you come back here looking like a walking skeleton. I want that bird.' He glanced over his shoulder to confirm that they really were alone. 'If I'm ever to get promotion, and if you want me to recommend you for a job as a permanent constable, then we have to do this right. Do I make myself clear?'

Shaftoe nodded intently.

'Good. Bring your father's old shotgun and a box of cartridges.'

'It's in our attic.'

'Get it down.'

'Now?'

'No, first you call at these farms: the MacClellands', Dewar's, Anderson's and the Tippermuir place. I'll do the others. Tell them we need a man from each for at least one day in the next three. Armed. Got it?'

'One from each.'

'Aye, that should give us a party of seven or eight guns a day.' Dunceford wiped a hand over his face and noticed it was trembling. He hoped it was fatigue, but he could not be sure. 'All right, let's get on with it.' At the back of his mind there was still a dark thought. An undigested fear.

PART II: THE PREDATORS

NINE

They came down out of the woods like a ragged army. Four, five, six wolves led by a huge grey male, loping ahead of the others at a steady twenty miles an hour. His was a species once regarded as the most dangerous predators in the northern hemisphere. *Canis Lupus*: the true wolf.

They had no equal, save one.

Their sharp vision, acute hearing and finely tuned sense of smell were supplementary to speed and strength. Fiercest and most cunning of all killers, save one.

The exception was man: perhaps because man had force of numbers. But here, with villages cut off from one another by snow, it was to be different.

The leader weighed nearly two hundredweight, yet moved with supple, effortless agility. Without altering his stride, he swivelled his head and snapped his traplike jaws at a startled grouse which heard the soft padded rush of his passing and jerked up – just in time to be severed at the neck. Blood darkened the snow.

The leader did a tight turn and swallowed a mouthful of soft meat, feathers and all. Then, as the first of his haphazard pack arrived with tails wagging to tear apart the plump warm body, he moved on towards the distant farm buildings.

They grouped in a loose arc on a lip of high ground, about a quarter of a mile from the farm. Sat there and watched the house, bathed in early-morning light. All except their leader, Darkmind. He worked quickly through the straggle of hedges and leapt cold drainage ditches until he was tight against the yard wall where he lay belly-flat, out of sight, and waited.

To an outsider, the attitude of the distant wolves might have seemed disinterested. But that was their way. The grey wolf in his wild environment often gained the confidence of the big ungulates by drawing casually alongside and looking in any direction, other than at the intended victim. Even playing with another member of the pack, tail-wagging and cuffing one another with front paws, before suddenly launching themselves sideways at the big moose, or wild horse, with snarling savagery. Going for a deep nose hold, to blind or cripplingly distract, while the rest of the pack came in from the back to tear at the exposed flanks.

Their snapping jaws could shear into the belly of a terrified victim six times their own size and disembowel it before it had time to realize what was happening. Often the victim died on its jellified legs, with its entrails hanging out, before crashing to the ground.

One of the distant wolves sniffed the clear air, tilted his head back and howled. It sounded mournful, but it signalled both his presence and his pleasure.

'That bloody dog!'

Alec McDee sat up in bed and tried to listen above his wife's heavy breathing. It would take a lusty set of bagpipes in her ear to awaken her before six o'clock. Her long grey days were crammed with arduous tasks and the alarm clock in her mind would tell her soon enough when it was time to set about the first twin requirements of the day: providing the house with warmth and its occupants with steaming porridge.

He walked carefully downstairs to avoid waking his small daughters, Amy and Lucy. In the hall, the girls' rough-haired terrier whimpered uneasily. McDee growled at it to be quiet and struggled into his heavy outdoor clothes. Then he broke open and loaded both barrels of his shotgun and slid a box of cartridges into the pocket of his duffle coat.

The door creaked, stiff with cold and signalling his intention across the quarter-mile to the Scots pines.

Outside he kneaded the warmth into his hands and stood

scouring the land for a sight of the loose-limbed, long-legged Great Dane. He whistled between two fingers, encouraging it although hardly expecting that it would trot forward unless tempted by the thought of breakfast. Even so, he rested the gun lightly in the crook of his arm in case it did.

A single barrel through the chest should be enough. He would rope the dog behind his tractor, drag it to the Sheerwaters' home and dump it in a bloodsoaked heap for them to discover. Then back for his own breakfast.

McDee whistled again, like an anxious owner seeking his pet, and set off across the fields.

The big wolf let him pass within twenty feet. He showed his fearsome carnassial teeth which could sever a man's leg, and his yellowed canine tusks which were ready to follow up by tearing the flesh into digestible shreds. But he made no sound. When a wolf has marked out its quarry, it will usually ignore any other distraction in order to concentrate on the kill.

And McDee was not the prey.

The hardbitten farmer, whose canny wife had more than once said he had something of primitive man about him, instinctively turned and looked carefully back. But in the glinting shadows, cast over the farmhouse by an unaccustomed and slow-ascending sun, he detected no movement.

It was some time before he found what he was looking for: a single set of canine tracks diagonally crossing a patch of frozen dew ahead. But before he could determine their direction – coming or going – he was made aware of the pack.

As if in response to some unseen signal, two or three of them stretched out their back legs along the cold ground, yawned and stood up. One extended his neck and sneezed. Another two ambled forward, going nowhere in particular.

Yet another grey-black head appeared blinking sleepily. Then a drab white wolf with only one ear.

The hair stood up on the back of McDee's neck and he spun around, eyes widening with the reality of the situation. The massive wolves settled in a loose circle, none closer than

73

thirty yards and not looking particularly belligerent. One even had its back to him. But he was effectively cut off from the farm.

In the tangled briar and dead rush stalks at the foot of the farm wall something moved. Too low a shape to make out. But big enough to bend a crab apple tree so that it finally gave up its winter-long struggle and cracked like a pistol shot.

In the distance McDee's head stretched clear of his fur collar, without otherwise daring to move. But he could see little in the face of the eastern sun. He prayed to God that somebody spotted his predicament and was on the way with guns. *Mother of Christ!* He had heard of the wolf experiments in a remote part of the Highlands but never expected to see any. He kept quite still.

The farmhouse door was on the latch. It was just after six in the morning and a kettle steamed on the hob. Upstairs Mrs McDee was hooking herself into an outrageously old-fashioned corset, and in the other room Amy and Lucy were sprawled asleep.

The wolf sniffed the doorknob, stood up on its hind legs and pressed its bulk against the door. There was a sharp click and it opened to let in a wedge of cold air.

Mrs McDee called drowsily down the bare stairs. 'Pour me a cup of tea, dear. The sweetener's behind the pot.'

The terrier, normally a tetchy and aggressive little animal, backed away with his tail laid low in submission. He died without protest. A long paw contemptuously swept the carcass aside, sending it crashing into the base of the dresser. The sound aroused Mrs McDee.

'I hope that's not mother's best crockery,' she called, in a voice edged with rancour.

The wolf went up the stairs in muffled bounds and into the wrong bedroom. The scent that Darkmind was looking for was here, but confused with the many other unfamiliar smells of man. There was a marrow-chilling scream, at which the big animal backed rapidly out and swung into the children's room.

Amy had her head under the pillow, and that saved her. At first she was faintly aware of the commotion and, when she heard a ferocious snarling and smelt fetid breath a few inches away, she lay rigid with fright.

The wolf, tangled in the bedsheets, snarled and cast about for his victim. But he was left with only eleven-year-old Lucy, standing frail and quivering in her limp vest and knickers.

Darkmind pounced, smashing her slight frame to the floor and wallowing in the smell of her fear. He snapped his jaws around her thigh with a sharp crack. And she died. Not because her leg was torn from her body, or because she was then taken by the throat on an awful thudding journey back downstairs. But of fright.

They hit the dresser on the way out, the killer and his victim. And, by now, the wolf was so confused by the noise and the blood which spurted up and over his muzzle, that he threshed about savagely, dragging crockery and tablecloth to the floor and tearing ruthlessly at the body. At last he had triumphed over the quarry whose scent lingered on the paths at the edge of the forest.

He was out of the door and loping back towards the high ground. The whole ghastly episode had taken less than two minutes. The girl's trunk slowed him down, but he would not let go until he reached the silence of the distant trees, where his pack could feed in peace.

Behind him, the quiet of the morning returned. And after a while Mrs McDee stumbled into the yard, aimlessly dragging a bloodstained sheet behind her. She seemed dazed and the air smelt sickly sweet.

From afar, McDee began to run. He knew in the pit of his stomach that he had been lured away from something horrific . . . *from god-knows-what*. He dropped his shotgun but it did not matter. The nearest wolf ambled out of his path, and the others watched him go as if they were now no more than bystanders.

A few minutes later the big wolf joined them. He tore off a forearm and settled with it under a tree, quickly gnawing to the bone. It was a sweet meat which titillated and pleased him. Some way off, the others whirled in a swirling circle over the warm remains. Even the tattered remnants of a thin, damp vest were gorged.

Darkmind stared back at the farm. Now that he acquired the taste he would strike again. Wherever he chose.

The wolves moved off at ill-spaced intervals and without haste. Each was a powerful self-sufficient predator. Yet they were intelligent enough to know that, together, they were invincible.

Their tracks vanished where the rocks began, and where edges of snow melted under the feeble vigour of the sun. But before long both the wolf and the snow would be back.

Richard Unthank sat in the tiny lounge of the boarding house at Elphin and played 'Rock of Ages' badly on an old upright piano. It was the best he could do from memory, and he wished he were home in his comfortably-uncomfortable bachelor flat on Rhum where he had piles of sheet music. He lifted the lid of the piano seat and found a mass of classical music in old folders, which did not interest him greatly; the more so since someone had spilled tea on it long ago, leaving the pages stained and undulating.

His fingers wandered over the keyboard. '*Greensleeves was my delight . . .*'

A feminine shape walked past and unclipped some letters from a wall board. She rested a tin of fruit and a jar of marmalade on top of the piano while she sorted the mail, and Unthank was immediately aware of them reverberating as he played.

He tried playing louder to compensate, but the containers shuddered the more.

Eventually, he cleared his throat loudly and jabbed a finger at the food. She said 'Sorry', without sounding particularly repentant.

'So you should be.'

'I didn't realize you were playing properly. It was all rather jumbled.'

'Oh, thanks very much,' he said with exaggerated gratitude. She continued towards the door and he glanced over his shoulder. 'Excuse me,' he said. 'Are you leaving?'

'I am,' she replied waspishly.

He indicated the tins on the piano. 'Well, perhaps you'd take your percussion with you.'

She swept them noisily into her bag, and it was only then that their eyes met. And locked. He was shocked at seeing the beautifully boney face of the woman in the train again. She was equally startled by his clear grey eyes and the Roman nose she had seen in her mind's eye more than once since their first encounter.

'Good God.'

She moistened her lips and shook her head faintly, without knowing what to say.

He repeated himself, 'Good God Almighty.'

She managed an embarrassed smile. 'Can't you think of anything more flattering than that?'

He was astounded. 'It you. From the train.'

She nodded breathlessly.

He suddenly found he was grinning. He indicated the piano and the tins. 'Sorry about all this. I'm not much of a pianist really.'

'I know. I heard you.'

The smile died on his face. But, as soon as he caught the gleam in her eye, they both laughed aloud. She even put out a hand to steady herself and he felt its touch through his sleeve.

'What brings you here?' she asked.

He shrugged, as if she wouldn't believe him anyway. 'I'm looking for wolves.'

'Really? I've just seen one.'

His smile quickly faded. 'Here in Elphin?'

'Five minutes ago. Over at the memorial hall.'

'Are you serious?'

'Absolutely. It's in the basement. Stuffed. A superb example. Must be worth a lot of money.'

He took a deep breath and then exhaled with obvious relief. 'I'm more interested in the live ones.'

She looked at him quizzically, wondering what had made him so anxious. 'Different to me then. I'm only interested when they're dead.'

They walked into the hall together, where the landlady was returning to the house laden with shopping bags.

'Hello, Emma. Nice to see you back. Got through the drifts all right, then?'

'Yes, thanks.' She looked gratefully at Unthank. 'I've picked up the letters.'

'Good. Oh, there was one telephone call. Your husband rang from London.'

Unthank twitched, and hoped the disappointment did not show. So, she was married. Probably had an influential, unbelievably rich husband and three gangling children. He might have guessed. She was too good to be true.

He edged around the two women. 'Well, I think I'll go up to my room and do a little work. Nice to meet you again,' he said formally. He suddenly felt very awkward and in the way.

TEN

Cecil Inkerman, who was overweight anyway, looked harassed. But who wouldn't after twenty miles of slithering driving behind a county council snowplough all the way to Elphin? And followed the entire journey by a juggernaut which kept much too close for comfort.

Next to him on the front seat, looking as relaxed as Inkerman was agitated, sat Franklin Delano Bakersman. At least, Inkerman assumed he was relaxed, judging from the way he puffed contentedly at an enormous cigar and answered any attempts at conversation with non-committal grunts. But it was difficult to be sure behind the American's dark glasses.

Inkerman had been Parallel Oil's senior public relations man in Britain for the past five years and, when the heir-apparent asked for the use of a caravan and a motorcycle, Inkerman scurried to provide them. He knew quite clearly who would be buttering his bread within a few years.

'Here we are, Mr Bakersman, sir.' He parked in a lay-by and leaned across his companion to open the door for him. The American nodded and tapped an inch of ash into the dashboard ashtray which was already crammed with cigar butts and cellophane. Most of it floated down on to the public relations man's trousers. Inkerman brushed it away with an apologetic smile, as if it was his own fault for getting his leg in the way.

'What's going on over there?' drawled the American.

Inkerman stared towards Station House, where there were a number of white-faced comings and goings. But later, when he went across to enquire, he was turned away.

When he reported back to the parked caravan, Bakersman patted him on the shoulder. 'Okay, I'll take it from here. You get yourself a room somewhere and I'll see you in the morning. I'm all tuckered out. Gimme a shout about seven-thirty.'

Inkerman noticed, beyond the American, that the portable colour TV was switched on and that there was a whisky bottle on top. It all looked very comfortable. He smiled waxenly, took his attaché case from the vehicle and made his way over to the boarding house.

At eight the next morning Bakersman sauntered into Station House, while his public relations man laboriously unloaded a new Japanese motorcycle from the top of their Range Rover.

There was nobody in the outer office and the American continued through to the sergeant's room, where Dunceford was sitting in his shirtsleeves with his head in his hands. Shaftoe was kneeling in front of the old-fashioned open fireplace, with an apron around his waist, laying paper and wood ready for a fire.

'Hi there.'

Dunceford surveyed the newcomer through the bars of his fingers. It was much too early for callers.

The American took off his dark glasses and smiled engagingly. 'Either of you fellas know where I can find the chief?'

The policemen looked at one another. 'What sort of chief had you in mind?'

'The police chief.'

'You mean the chief constable, sir?'

'Sure.'

'Ah, well he's in the city. The likes of him don't come here unless something really exceptional happens.'

'Well, where is he? Something exceptional just did happen. I got here.' The American laughed at his attempted joke, but the man behind the desk did not join in.

'I'm Sergeant Dunceford,' he frowned.

'Oh.' Bakersman extended a hand. 'I'm a visitor to your little town, and I just dropped in to say hello.'

Dunceford made no attempt to accept the hand. Instead he craned his neck slightly to see what the American was holding in his other hand. 'Is that a rifle you've got there?'

'This old thing? Oh, yeah. Point-two-two. I guess you'd just about call it a rifle.'

'Have you got a licence?'

'Sure.'

'Could I see it, please?'

'I guess so, just as soon as my gear is unloaded. Here's my card.'

Dunceford regarded the proffered rectangle of stiff white paper with suspicion, and made no attempt to take it. 'Mr . . .'

The American turned the card upside down. 'Bakersman. There, you see? Franklin D Bakersman. I'm in oil.'

'I see.' The dour Scot glanced severely at Shaftoe who had stopped polishing to take in the flamboyant newcomer. When his assistant reluctantly turned his attention back to the grate, the sergeant added: 'Well, what exactly can I do for you, sir?'

'I'm here for a little hunting. Thought you might be able to help.'

Dunceford raised a hand, as if he was stopping the traffic. 'That's a matter for the Red Deer Commission at Inverness.'

'I'm not interested in deer.' He lowered his voice as if to share a secret. 'I understand you could use some help in another direction.'

Dunceford got up and moved deliberately around the desk. His stare was particularly intimidating. 'I don't know what you've heard, sir. But whatever it is, take it from me, it's exaggerated. You've been misled. You'd best go about your business.'

Bakersman raised his hands lightly. 'Okay, okay. I was just trying to help. I heard you'd had some bother in the hills.'

'Bother?' Dunceford turned to Shaftoe, who was still on his hands and knees, for enlightenment. His assistant looked suitably blank. 'What sort of bother?'

The American grimaced. 'How about the sort that's been carrying off sheep and dogs for the past few days. What else would you call an eagle?'

Dunceford heaved a sigh of relief. He had just been through a nasty moment imagining that practically everybody in the locality, other than his divisional superintendent, knew about the McDee girl's death. But now he could breathe again. For the moment at least, he still had time to work out what to do.

He turned the short, handsome American back towards the door. 'It's not for me to say, sir, that you shouldn't shoot the odd wee bird. But I'd be extra careful if I were you. If you got lost, it's us who would have to poke about for you in the snow. And we get awfully peeved about that sort of thing.' He squeezed the man's arm a little too tightly for comfort.

Bakersman pulled himself free. 'I don't much like your attitude, Sergeant.'

'Oh dear.'

'I think I ought to mention that I'm a personal friend of .. ▪

of . . . ' He struggled to remember the MP's name. 'Sir Somebody-somebody. You know who I mean. It's on the tip of my tongue. It'll come to me in just a minute.'

Dunceford began to close the door between them. 'Be sure to let me know if it does.'

'Now look here, Sergeant. 'You hold your goddamned horses . . . ' But his voice petered out as the door clicked shut.

Outside, Inkerman unwrapped the protective plastic sheeting from around the Suzuki 250. 'Everything all right, Mr Bakersman?'

The American clenched his teeth. 'Fine. Just fine. Look, is it possible to hire British policemen for private purposes? I mean if I felt I wanted some help, say an escort or guard, while I'm in this part of the country, is that something you could arrange?'

'I doubt it. Our policemen aren't allowed to get involved in outside duties, unless of course there's a VIP in the vicinity: like a member of the Royal Family or a minister of the Crown. But the only person with that sort of pull around here is Sir Marcus Sheerwater.'

Bakersman snapped his fingers exasperatedly. 'Sheerwater, of course. I'll speak to him later. I particularly want that sergeant under me for a day or two. I've got one or two strenuous little security jobs I need doing . . . out in the snow. Pretty uncomfortable jobs really, but I've no doubt he's just the man.'

The oil heir tugged at his fingers and smiled grimly as they cracked at the joints. 'Okay. Let's have that bike and I'll make a start.'

By mid-morning Richard Unthank seemed to be getting somewhere, and nowhere. The *somewhere* was that he had learned about Mrs McDee and her shocked, surviving daughter, Amy. One was in a coma at the cottage hospital and the other in a state of shivering withdrawal.

The *nowhere* was his attempt to arrange transport out to the farm, where Alec McDee had returned the previous day and from whom nothing further had been heard.

In the end the scientist walked. He was used to legging it across the rugged winter hills of Rhum, where most of the time there was no alternative to your own two feet. Now he traversed the featureless white eiderdown of knee-deep snow guided only by the mountains.

He found the farm just as the wolves had earlier: nestling peacefully a quarter of a mile from the lip of high ground. He felt vaguely uncomfortable and glanced briskly around. But, with nothing in sight, he put it down to a mist that trailed under pregnant, low-slung clouds.

The farm door was half-open. He leaned inside and called, 'Mr McDee, are you there?' His voice echoed around the bumpy whitewashed walls and returned unmolested.

He tried around the back where undergrowth began close to the house, with frozen blackberry tangles and thick fern stretching across the clearing to pallbearing trees.

There was a damp and eerie silence in which a faint sound, when it came, was all the more distinct. He stepped awkwardly through the wet ferns towards it, stopping and listening every few yards. Then, through an indistinct screen of briars and hawthorn leaves he saw the source: a bedraggled lamb, apparently caught by the hind leg.

The lamb jerked its head in his direction and bleated, hoping for a mother figure to appear. Unthank had started to pull off his fur mittens when he was completely stunned by an enormous bang close to his face.

He smelt cordite as he reeled backwards, deafened and stung by a thousand pinpricks of heat. Then, just as suddenly, he was being roughly handled by a scowling, hollow-eyed Alec McDee.

'You stupid sod! What are you doing on my land?'

Unthank sank down on his haunches, covering his face and trying to stop his head gyrating. When he opened his eyes and cleared his vision, the first thing he saw was the lamb torn apart by shotgun pellets.

'God in heaven, what happened?'

'If you'd come any closer, you'd be dead. Lucky for you,

you were moving so slowly. Now clear off and don't come near my traps again.'

Unthank groaned and held his throbbing eardrums. He was propelled forcibly around the farm and back towards the high ground. McDee gave him a final shove on his way, but by now Unthank had recovered sufficiently to ask a question or two.

'What was that all about?'

'You walked in front of a set-gun. When you stumbled across the cord, it pulled the trigger on the cocked hammer wedged between two trees.'

'What did you expect to hit?'

McDee stared at him wild-eyed. 'One of those terrible things that killed my little daughter. There are lots of them, and they're all mine!'

Unthank shook the ringing from his ears. 'I'm a government employee, Mr McDee. I heard what happened and I came out to help. And I need your help if I'm going to do anything about it.'

The Scot did not seem to be listening. 'You tell them in town that I don't want anyone poking his nose in here. They're mine to do with as I choose.'

'You saw a wolf, didn't you?'

McDee raised his shotgun. 'If it wasn't for you, I'd have one by now.'

'A grey wolf? How many were there?'

'I won't tell you again.'

'I have to know how many, roughly what size, and which direction they took.'

The farmer levelled his gun dementedly. 'I'll kill you if you come back. Anybody and everybody who steps foot out here. They're mine now. I've got plans for every pox-ridden one of them.'

He fired one barrel without warning, dangerously close to the rangy scientist. Shot fizzed and scythed through the air, tearing on in search of a target that wasn't there.

McDee fired the second barrel in a mesmerized detached

manner. Fortunately for Unthank, the hammer clicked on an empty chamber.

Franklin Delano Bakersman took the Suzuki from Inkerman's awkward grasp and settled on the moulded saddle, gripping the beautiful bronze motorcycle between appreciative thighs. The public relations man wiped away a film of perspiration. All the time he held the machine he had been afraid that it would either run away or fall heavily on him.

'There you are, Mr Bakersman. Food and a storm tent in the panniers. It's hired for as long as you want it. When can we expect you back?'

The oil heir stood astride the bike and started the engine. He rolled the throttle and let power roar from the exhausts. Inkerman backed away, his face a mixture of distaste for the venom of the motorcycle and indulgence at the antics of his employer.

The American barely listened. Inkerman was one of innumerable faceless men who were always within finger-snapping distance, ready to agree with whatever he said. Outwardly he treated them with courtesy, but in all other respects he regarded them as wallpaper. Certainly not real people.

The vibrating power of the unharnessed engine was something to be enjoyed. It represented a freedom from the rigid constrictions of the business world.

'What?'

Inkerman cupped both hands around his mouth against the din. 'When will you be back, sir?'

Bakersman leaned his head to one side, to indicate that he still could not hear. He had been named after his father's idol of the thirties, Franklin Delano Roosevelt, whose New Deal between the wars had brought prosperity to a young and pushy J C Bakersman.

Inkerman made more of a megaphone of his hands. 'When . . . can we . . .'

Bakersman switched off the engine, so that the public

relations man was bellowing through a sudden silence.

'... expect ... you back ... sir?'

'No need to shout, Cecil.'

'No, sir.'

'Before dusk, I guess. If I get a shot at him today, maybe a little earlier.' He switched on, found first gear and moved slowly out on to the road.

Inkerman was relieved at seeing him disappear for a few hours. 'Good luck, sir,' he called. 'Mind the ice.'

Bakersman mischievously cupped a hand to his ear, then switched off momentarily. But the tubby man was not to be caught twice. He laughed merrily at almost being trapped and, as the younger man pulled away down the snow-covered road, his smile faded into a flat critical expression.

Bakersman was rich, influential and schooled in the fine art of polite indifference to the feelings of others. The world was at his feet. Yet he was dissatisfied.

At night, in the thinking time before sleep, he felt imprisoned by the inflexible confines of the empire he would inherit. In a way, he was more inhibited than the most humble ledger clerk. Competent as he was, he always had his father breathing over his shoulder.

He gritted his teeth, twisted the throttle and zoomed up the gentle incline that led towards the Glencanisp Forest, the lightweight rifle slung across his back.

This was freedom. He stood upright to savour the taste of it, and kept well to the left of the road which had been blown almost clear of snow by a curious wind that had then banked it up on the right-hand side, so that it sloped up to and completely over the hedge.

He pushed back the plastic visor of his helmet and let the cold wind stream into his face in an invigorating torrent. This was what life was all about.

He shouted exuberantly before dropping back into the saddle, happy at last, and luxuriating in the thought of Penny and her slim, neverending legs.

In his mind they were together at last. Alone in his apartment. She looked superbly provocative on the bed when he appeared ruddy and beaming from the shower, wearing only his bathrobe.

'Isn't it close in here?' he said, discarding the robe, just as he had rehearsed. 'Isn't it,' she agreed, reaching up to fondle and excite him.

She required a gradual and gentle build-up; whereas he needed ardour and almost immediate satisfaction. It was the eternal gap between what each knew to be ultimate fulfilment. But he was the initiator and his was the choice.

Wet and naked he swung on top of her, making her body jack-knife involuntarily, ignoring her muffled groans and animal noises and saturating himself in a slippery, sweaty threshing of love.

She was surprisingly receptive when aroused, and he liked that. But her face melted away into the road ahead. He dropped down a gear and leaned into the bend under the intermittent brilliance of distant sunlight winking between gaps in the heavy clouds, then took a dip and climbed on upwards.

He had never married. The drawbacks of his father's remarriage were too apparent for him not to be affected.

His father had brought home as his second wife a marble-faced actress, who had once played the lead in a black-and-white film opposite Ronald Colman and could never forget it. She was forever playing a part. And after only two years of J C Bakersman's profanities, including his insistence on hamburgers and ketchup as a main meal at least twice a week, she moved off to the comparative seclusion of New York.

There, she surrounded herself with statuesque dogs and faded actress friends. Her stepson was relieved for her. She never should have married his abrasive father. No longer did she have to feign tiredness, or announce with undisguised indifference: 'I'm plugged up, darling. Perhaps next week.'

Franklin was the only member of the family she ever got on with. Perhaps because each recognized the other's resentment of J C Bakersman's bulldozer mentality.

Four inches of virgin snow parted in a continuous bow wave for the Suzuki as the narrow road disintegrated into a rough track. He chugged slowly on, rising ever higher.

Eventually he came upon a barn, empty save for some rusty timber-sawing machinery, where he left the motorcycle.

He walked on up the bare slope. Ahead of him, some miles away, was the sea. He was on top of the frozen world where only mounds of inhospitable earth and occasional boulders would provide any protection from a wind that threatened to cut him in half.

But this was a place of eyries. He wrapped himself in a blanket and settled down in a cleft of rock to wait.

ELEVEN

For two hours after he returned from the McDee farm, Richard Unthank sat writing in the otherwise unoccupied lounge of his boarding house. The ringing in his ears made it hard going at first, but the vital importance of his report soon made him forget his own problems.

When he finished, he sealed one copy in an envelope and delivered it to the Station House, marked 'Sergeant Dunceford – Personal and Urgent'. The other he folded into his inside pocket and then went out, muffled to the eyebrows, to get a lift in the first vehicle that would take him to Ullapool.

It was no good him sitting by the phone, hoping it would be repaired. There was little prospect of downed lines being put right before a thaw. And already it was snowing again. Big ominous flakes which immediately settled in layer after silent layer.

Unthank was anxious to get his report to Edinburgh as swiftly as possible. So, he took it himself.

At about the time the tall man was bumping south out of the village in the cab of a friendly petrol tanker, Sergeant Dunceford got back to the station and shook the snow from his greatcoat.

Shaftoe was hovering with the letter. He knew how urgent it was; it had been impressed on him several times. He was also extremely curious to discover what it said.

Dunceford settled behind his desk, coughed importantly and slit open the flap. There were two pages of cramped handwriting, giving details of red deer movements and wild-life population in the area, and then a third page headed *Predators*.

It was on the last page that Dunceford concentrated. The first dates were several years old and indicated injections given to combat disorders ranging from malnutrition to distemper, and several words he could not understand.

Dunceford swore and scratched his head. Why couldn't people write plain English? It was not going to be easy to decipher. He crossed to the door. 'I don't want to be disturbed for a while. Understand?'

Shaftoe looked up inquisitively. 'Why?'

'Never mind why. You keep as quiet as a church mouse. I don't want to hear a squeak out of you.'

As he went carefully through the pages again, Dunceford became increasingly perplexed. Many of the words were in Latin. He pushed back his chair and thrust his head around the door.

'Where's Mr Unthank?'

'Who?'

'The scientist. The chap who left this document.'

'Oh, he's gone. Said he had to get in touch with his ministry as fast as he could. Got a lift to Ullapool. But he promised to be back by morning.'

Dunceford waved the sheets of paper in frustration. 'That's no bloody good. I can't make head nor tail of this.'

Shaftoe moved forward. 'Let me have a look, Sarge.'

Dunceford withdrew them. 'If I can't understand it, I'm damned sure you won't.'

The unkempt acting-constable looked hurt, and Dunceford sighed. 'All right. What are *pulex irritans*?'

'Who?'

'*Pulex irritans.*'

His lumbering assistant did not respond.

'Well?'

Shaftoe held his breath in intense concentration, but finally let it out like a Boxing Day balloon. 'I don't know. But whatever they are, they don't sound very appetizing.'

Dunceford paced up and down. Outside the snow was falling so thickly he could no longer see across the street. There was every chance that the main road would be blocked by nightfall and that Unthank would not get back for days. And he still hadn't made his mind up about what really caused the McDee girl's death.

'Nip down to Ardmore Cottage and see if you can find Miss Dancer. She's supposed to have all the brains around here. I'll write down this *pulex* thing. Ask her what it means. If she knows, ask her if she understands much Latin. If she says yes, then get her to step smartly over here. Got that?'

Emma appeared within five minutes. 'Hello, Sergeant.' She shook the snow into a wet patch on the floor and hung up her coat. She had a long slim figure, almost thin in places.

'Hello, miss . . . ' He dropped his eyes to the papers on his desk, uncertain whether or not to stand up. In the end he didn't. He had for some time fancied her from a distance and, at first, had mistaken her friendliness for a reciprocal interest. But not any longer.

'*Pulex irritans* are fleas.'

He turned to the third page without showing any detail. 'There are some entries here under *Canis familiaris*. What are they?'

'Dogs. Ordinary domestic dogs.'

He looked at her keenly, in order to impress on her the seriousness of the situation, but was embarrassed by the beautifully direct eyes that held his gaze.

He coughed formally. 'I've got some information here that

I'd like you to help translate. It contains quite a lot of Latin, and I didn't get that far at school.'

'I'll do my best. Let me see.'

He flattened the papers against his chest. 'You must understand. It's confidential.'

She nodded.

Dunceford glanced past her to make sure the door was firmly closed. 'It's police business, and that means nobody else must be told what you find out. Apart from me.'

She smiled uncertainly. 'I understand. May I see what you've got?'

'Yes . . . no! That is, I'd like you to study it here. Take my desk. Some of it is difficult to make out. It was written by Mr Unthank. Do you know him? He has pretty awful handwriting.'

'Sort of.'

'There, are you comfortable? I'll get you a cup of tea.'

He settled her in his chair and then roused Shaftoe. 'Two teas. Make it snappy.'

Dunceford closed the door gently and tiptoed to a corner seat, where he could watch her reading intently and making occasional notes.

'Anything yet?'

She glanced up politely. 'Such as what? You haven't told me what I'm looking for.'

He took a deep breath. 'All right. Some odd things have been happening that I can't account for. I've got a theory that a Great Dane has run amuck, but I need to know for certain.'

'Oh dear. Sir Marcus has a Great Dane.'

'Right,' Dunceford said grimly. 'And he's missing.'

She returned to the sheets and read with renewed intensity while Dunceford walked to the door on the outside edges of his soles, so as not to disturb her. 'Where's that tea?' he asked Shaftoe hoarsely.

'Coming, coming,' mouthed his untidy assistant with equal exaggeration.

'Sergeant!'

The urgency in her voice made him slam the door and jerk around. She looked ill; the blood was draining from her face even as he looked.

'What is it?'

'My God,' she whispered.

He had seen many cases of shock in his years on the force. Sometimes after horrific accidents, survivors who were at one moment chattering on about their escapes would jolt the next moment into trembling silence.

He covered her hand with a calm assurance he did not feel. 'All right, just relax. What have you spotted? Let me have a look.'

She was on the last page and her finger extended limply to two words which were underlined: *Canis Lupus*. After them, the scientist had written 'possibly half a dozen'.

He read the words hesitantly. '*Canis Lupus*. What's that?'

'Wolves.'

His mouth was dry, incredibly dry. He could hear his wrist watch ticking. It was Shaftoe who broke the silence by quietly opening the door and bottoming in backwards through the gap, with two cups of tea.

'Get out!' Dunceford said quietly.

'What?'

Emma was biting the side of her hand and staring out at the thickening snow. 'There are a lot of isolated people living out there, Sergeant. You've got to warn them.'

'Outside!'

Shaftoe was propelled backwards. He stood mystified, looking first at the tea and then at the door which closed just a few inches from his face.

Eventually the door jerked open again. 'Where's that tea?'

All Shaftoe could do was thrust it through the gap.

Dunceford looked as if he'd had a death in the family. 'Bring the car around the front,' he said tersely. 'Lock the front door behind you, and don't let anybody in until I say so. No exceptions. Then get two shotguns and load them. Have you got that?'

'Got it.'

The door shut in his face.

TWELVE

Bakersman lay on a groundsheet, staring at a scattering of
rocks and aware of how numb he had become stretched out on
the cold inhospitable earth. It began to snow again, but the
ache in his bones seemed to make him insensitive to any
further drop in temperature.

He had not seen any movement for three hours. Even a
short-sighted mole would have been welcome, but there was
nothing. Certainly no sign of an eagle. The winter had been
much harder than he had ever imagined back in his double-
glazed paradise in Aberdeen. He vowed never again to be
pernickety about draughts.

The snow blurred his glasses and he was lying on his back
polishing them when the first wolf appeared. At first Bakersman did not see it. But when the female began scratching
herself and snuffling, he rolled over on to his chest and
peered through out-of-focus eyes.

Jeeesus. He tried to fumble his glasses back on, but only
partially succeeded and missed one ear completely with the
spectacle arm. His other hand swam for the rifle.

A third, fourth and fifth wolf emerged from the rocks not
thirty yards from him, nuzzling and then stretching their
great lean bodies beside a frozen pool.

He did not know what to do. First he wriggled back into
the protective cleft of rock, then edged forward again. Heart
pumping wildly, he was both alarmed and elated at the same
time. It was impossible. God, there were no wolves in this
part of the country, not roaming free.

93

Yet here they were. Unmistakably. With slanting Byzantine eyes and mouths as long as jagged saws. Like man, they were creatures that had to kill to survive.

Bakersman was trembling. He raised his rifle, sighted the wavering barrel, then lifted his glasses and wiped away the stinging perspiration.

What happened next made him abandon his idea of opening fire.

There was a lot of affectionate head rubbing among the wolves and one big spiky-haired black and grey male enthusiastically licked the genitals of a she-wolf. He tried to mount her sideways, but she moved around in a circle thwarting him, and finally she tucked her tail between her legs and sat on it.

A shabby white wolf with a torn ear tried next and was much more successful. The she-wolf needed little courtship from him. She swept her tail aside, exposing her vulva. The white wolf mounted precariously and clutched his front paws around her stomach. He thrust into her with a remote look on his face, rocked and adjusted the weight on his hind legs.

The wolf's heavy penis expanded as it pushed into the female vagina and locked inside her as it swelled. Semen spurted.

By now the two big animals were fixed together inextricably and so they would remain for some twenty minutes. After the first coming, the male lifted his hind leg over the she-wolf's back and turned his back to her, still welded together.

Bakersman stared incredulously at the partners, lying tail to tail and locked by their genitals. By now a thicker sperm had passed into the female, and only a psychological bond remained.

The oil-man felt vaguely confused. He was aware that he could be in danger, but was totally engrossed in the scene before him. If only Penny was here.

The other wolves seemed scarcely interested. Even the frustrated grey and black wandered off, leaving the mating pair to their curious honeymoon.

Abruptly Bakersman decided to act. There seemed no time

94

to consider the consequences. He cocked the rifle, remembered to breathe out most of the air from his lungs to avoid any shake; he'd try for the bitch first. He squeezed the trigger gently. His first shot hit the female in the flank, making her yelp forward in pain. The torn-eared male was dragged with her, indivisibly secured by the genitals.

The rifle fired again and again, it seemed to have a life of its own. The sound cracked across the hilltop and sent the other wolves bolting in all directions, unaware of who or what was attacking them.

The second shot missed and the third caught her in the neck, causing her body to shudder and twitch uncontrollably. The big male whimpered and tried to drag his partner across the frozen ground to cover. But she was too heavy and he succeeded only in scrabbling around in a desperately painful circle.

Bakersman scrambled up on to his feet, losing his glasses completely and reloading with clumsy fingers. He was certain only of one thing: the blurred double outline of two wolves with wine-dark stains widening across their coats.

He had his rifle up for another shot when an express train hit him. Or, if it wasn't a train, it was travelling at much the same speed.

As he was hurled off his feet in a confusion of upturned sky and crunching pain, he glimpsed an enormous wolf. The impact dislocated his arm and the rifle vanished.

But the wolf had come at him so violently, and with such irrational fury, that it stunned itself as they both thudded back into the granite. The impartial rockface saved Bakersman's life.

Sick with pain from his neck, he got up and staggered back across the uneven hilltop. Several times he missed his footing. And the only way he knew he had reached the trees was when his forehead cracked into a branch, and searing pain and lights confused him even more. How many times he went down on his knees, he could not tell. But somehow he reached the open ground leading down to the barn.

Somewhere behind him, the wolves had collected their

scattered wits and began to howl excitedly. It was the beginning of the chase. Yet the eerie sound barely penetrated his consciousness; he was only aware of the nausea which threatened to gag him, and one arm swung uselessly at his side.

The wolves, as is their habit with prey, pursued him in a long straggling line. On this occasion the ragged-eared male was leading, and Bakersman was aware of him coming up fast as he stumbled into the barn.

In a rising panic, he thought he would not make it. He could almost feel great claws raking down his back. But something – perhaps faded human scents and suddenly unfamiliar surroundings – put the leading wolf off long enough for Bakersman to slam the door with his remaining arm.

The heavy wood hit the predator in the side of the mouth as it bounded forward, catching its long muzzle and squeezing it against the jamb. The wolf gave a strangled snarl and thrust half of its face inside. But the American had just enough time to heave his shuddering back against the door.

The pressure on the animal's mouth must have been enormous. Its three-inch fangs snapped at the empty air. Then it whined, like a chastised house dog suddenly aware of its plight, and dragged itself backwards and free. The lopsided door banged shut, and Bakersman swung over the locking crossbar before slumping down in a sobbing heap.

Five minutes later – or perhaps fifteen, he could not tell – he came out of an exhausted coma: alerted by a slithering and scratching coming from the high roof.

He wiped his eyes, trying to clear the blurred focus, and glimpsed enough to recognize *Canis Lupus*, a savage wolf face peering down through the square of corrugated plastic which acted as a roof window.

The mouth opened in a snarl and there was a frantic scrabbling as the animal lost its tilted balance and slid away out of sight to drop with a thud outside.

Bakersman let his tear-stained face loll back against the wall. 'Oh mother. Oh Jesus. Help, please help me.' For someone who just a few hours ago had everything, it had been an awfully short step to having nothing.

He had a feeling that he was going to die.

He jarred his dislocated shoulder trying to sit up. 'Jesus Christ,' he moaned. 'Where are you when I need you?'

The sagging figure of Jesus, frozen in time on the Cross, stood out clearly over the church of St Andrew the Martyr.

Stepping out of the church porch, Sir Marcus Sheerwater looked remarkably healthy in comparison. He patted his chest and breathed in the clear, sharp air.

Sergeant Dunceford was waiting anxiously to talk, but the MP held up a restraining hand.

'Not now, Sergeant. I'm expecting an important phone call from the Prime Minister's office in about half an hour. Of course, it's not for me to say, but it could be good news.'

The sergeant was still panting from his run. 'Sir . . . '

Sheerwater's eyes narrowed with pleasure and he glanced around. They were alone, and the delicately falling snow settled on their shoulders. 'It could be a reshuffle.'

Dunceford continued to fight for breath, as the MP lowered his voice with unnecessary caution. 'A reshuffle, man. A Cabinet change-round. Do you understand what that means?'

The thickset policeman shook his head, not because he was incapable of understanding but because his mind was full of something more urgent.

Sheerwater looked smug. 'Well, wouldn't you say that an appointment as Britain's Oil Minister was a significant improvement on the Scottish Office? Granted, it's speculation on my part at the moment, but the PM doesn't put you on stand-by for an urgent call every day of the week.'

The words finally penetrated and Dunceford said laboriously: 'Are err . . . are congratulations in order, sir?'

A pair of fur mittens were lifted to curb any premature enthusiasm. 'No, no, no, Sergeant. I could be quite wrong. But, I do have a feeling he isn't simply ringing to tell me that we've been cut off by the snow.'

Dunceford hurried after the parliamentarian as he stepped briskly towards his imposing home. 'Sorry to chase you up at church, sir. But there's some trouble.'

'That's all right. I don't normally mind being bothered wherever I am. On this occasion, I was on my knees thanking God for seeing fit to bless my career. But, if you would just give me an hour to talk to Downing Street first, I'd be obliged.'

Dunceford caught hold of the statesman's arm and stopped him in his tracks. 'I think you'll find this is more important, sir.'

Sheerwater glanced at him sharply. 'That's a matter of opinion, Sergeant. We'll talk about it in an hour.' He walked resolutely on.

The policeman was left in an agony of indecision. He twisted the fist of one hand against the palm of the other. 'I'm sorry,' he called sarcastically. 'Sorry to have bothered you.' There was an edge to his voice which made it clear that to wait was not good enough.

The older man turned in astonishment. 'What?'

'I don't mean to be offensive,' stammered the sergeant. He was, however, determined to share his secret with somebody in authority and to lift the responsibility from himself.

'All right, let's not argue, man. What is it?'

'Those wolves that were settled a few years ago at Creag Riabhach and Cape Wrath way . . . do you remember?'

'Yes, yes.'

'They're on the move.'

'What?'

'I've reason to believe a pack of them has arrived here.'

'Here. You mean in this part of Scotland?'

'No, I mean here in Elphin.'

The expression on the Minister of State's face surprised Dunceford. He did not look alarmed. Quite the opposite – he smiled indulgently. 'I see. Well, quite frankly, Sergeant, I doubt it. But what makes you think so?'

'First, the McDee girl disappeared. Her father claims she was carried off by an animal, probably a wolf.'

'But you told me yourself, he was hysterical. And didn't he talk of one animal? How many of these creatures are there supposed to be now?'

'Several. I've a report here from a wild life expert, sent up from Edinburgh. He thinks there could be six in the vicinity.'

'Well, where is he?' The MP looked at his watch. 'I'd like to talk to this . . . expert.'

Dunceford's hands flapped at his side. 'He left. But he should be back in a day or two.'

Sheerwater shook his head in disbelief. 'Left? He can't be very worried about us then. Tell me, Sergeant, how many of these . . . things have you seen? Precisely how many?'

Dunceford shifted uncomfortably, dislodging some of the loose snow from his head and shoulders. 'Well, none actually.'

'Umm. So, there may be only one of these animals that nobody has seen. Or there could be half a dozen. And the only person who claims to know anything about them has gone off to enjoy himself for a few days.'

Dunceford clenched and unclenched his hands. He was beginning to wish he had never raised the subject, and in his mind he blamed Richard Unthank for his predicament. He was being made to look a fool in front of the only man in the area who had any real influence: Sir Marcus Sheerwater, the only man who could recommend his promotion to inspector with any likelihood of it getting the chief constable's attention.

The MP did not comment further, but took the big sergeant by the elbow and steered him to his elegant high-fronted house. 'Come in for a moment or two, old chap.'

The invitation did not extend farther than the spacious, sparsely furnished hall, with its white walls and polished pine floor, but it was enough for Dunceford. The policeman stood awkwardly, trying to make as little mess as possible while he thawed out.

Sheerwater returned from an inner room with a glass and decanter. 'Drink?'

'Err . . . I don't think I should on duty, sir,' said Dunceford, but he was ready to be convinced otherwise.

Sir Marcus shrugged, took out the thick glass stopper and poured himself a generous measure of whisky. He sipped it appreciatively. 'Umm. Now let's look at the situation sensibly. You know how truculent McDee is. At times I'd say he is almost unstable. I mean, what about that ridiculous idea of his that my dog was systematically killing his sheep. Now, tell me frankly, Sergeant, how much reliance do you put on his word?'

Dunceford shook his head.

'And the man from Edinburgh. He has actually seen any wolves in the vicinity?'

Again Dunceford shook his head helplessly. 'No, but he's going by the signs.'

'What signs? Signs in the snow? I'd be very surprised in this weather if he could make out his own feet, let alone the tracks of unidentified animals.'

The sergeant could only bite his lip and nod.

'Look, Sergeant, I must be ready to take the call from London. So, perhaps you'll excuse me. Meanwhile, you look into these claims and let me know if there's any substance to them. If it's a matter of public safety, come back by all means. But I strongly recommend that nothing is said that alarms families. Not on the strength of the views of an outsider with a lively imagination who's only been here about ten minutes. Now, wrap up well against the snow. We don't want you going down with flu. You're much too valuable to Elphin.'

Dunceford smiled gratefully as he stepped out into the deep drifting snow.

He looked back from the road and caught a rare glimpse of Lady Sheerwater peeping out through lace curtains. She smiled as if they were close friends and fluttered arthritic fingers at him.

Dunceford pretended not to see her. He was feeling too ashamed of himself.

But when he got back to Station House, Shaftoe was all agog. 'What did you decide, Sarge?'

Dunceford stripped off his heavy coat and flung his hat at

the floor. 'About what?' he snapped.

'About the . . . the wolves.'

'What are you on about? Use your commonsense, man! There aren't any wolves in this part of the country!'

A red double-decker bus left Regent Street and was turning cautiously into Piccadilly Circus when it came across a patch of sheet ice. Out of control, it slid across the junction and into the statue of Eros. Its front wheels mounted the circular steps and knocked the young god's bow from his grasp.

The Prime Minister's Press Secretary learnt the information within five minutes from a Press Association machine, which disgorged a continuous sheet of news day and night in his cluttered office.

He soft-footed his way into the Premier's study and whispered in Mr Beaconsfield's ear. The bushy eyebrows rose fractionally behind their spectacles, a hand smoothed the flat grey hair and then the great mind moved on to matters of more importance.

There were three other people in the study: the portly, affable Home Secretary, a formidable woman Director of the Nightingale Institute of Medical Research, and the Minister of Health who had arrived late.

James Beaconsfield addressed himself to the suave, debauched looking face of the Health Minister. 'Eric, we've just been running through the medical situation facing us. I've got your report on Dacca flu for England and Wales and I spoke a few minutes ago to Marcus Sheerwater in Scotland. It's really a question of what we do next.'

The Health Minister took off his glasses and tapped the stem against his teeth, nodding intently. 'What did Marcus have to say?'

A perplexed line creased the Prime Minister's forehead. 'He sounded brisk enough at first, but then got rather depressed. Perhaps the poor chap has caught it himself. Anyway, at least he confirmed that Scotland is as badly affected as the south. They need as much vaccine as they can get.'

101

The Health Minister spread his hands. 'I sympathize with him, marooned up there in the Highlands, but we just do not have enough to go round. Did he give you any figures?'

'No, he went strangely quiet. Seemed almost to be waiting for me to tell him. He's an odd chap in some ways.'

The woman virologist, who at thirty-eight had become Britain's youngest Dame in the last Birthday Honours, largely for her research into viruses, gave the Cabinet ministers a discourse on the Dacca Influenza-A pandemic.

Her deep, composed voice was in keeping with the fact that she had almost totally subdued her femininity in order to compete at the highest level in a man's world.

When she finished, the Prime Minister invited further opinions. 'Eric?'

The Health Minister pulled a disparaging face. 'The situation is already out of hand. In normal circumstances, Prime Minister, there might be a chance of blanketing all points of known contact and limiting the spread. But, frankly, with most of our medical energy being directed at coping with extra road accidents, hypothermia, frost-bite and a thousand and one other emergencies, there is little chance that we could mount such an exercise.'

The Prime Minister turned away to talk to the Home Secretary in a quieter voice while Dame Pamela had time to notice the Health Minister's eyes on her legs. She gave him a splintered smile and tugged her knee-length dress a little lower.

Beaconsfield closed a folder on his desk, signalling the end of the meeting. 'Thank you for coming. It must be apparent to us all that we need outside help to cope with the epidemic. I will see what can be done.'

Within twenty minutes senior civil servants were working on a draft message to the World Health Organization, seeking preference for Britain over the supply of vaccine.

The PM's personal assistant was waiting anxiously for the final version to be cleanly typed when he was handed the gist of a message relayed by the Department of the Environment from their Edinburgh office.

It concerned the movement of red deer, Arctic birds and an unspecified number of wolves in the north-west Highlands. He looked at the statistics without properly comprehending them.

'What on earth have they sent this to us for?'

'Thought you might want to know, I suppose.'

'For Christ's sake, man. We've got an epidemic on our hands. Spare me this sort of stuff.'

He crumpled the note and tossed it into a waste basket. Later that day it was collected and shredded in the usual way. No one in a position of authority in London had paid any attention to it.

THIRTEEN

Franklin Delano Bakersman forced himself to walk slowly around the barn, hunched as he was. His dislocated shoulder had resolved itself into a dreadful ache which only became unbearable if he moved his head.

He had heard nothing from the wolves for over an hour. Perhaps they were gone. He felt ill and nauseous. He could not last much longer without medical help: he had to take a chance.

Gingerly he opened the big door and peered out. The woods were silent and there were no animals in sight. Nothing stirred save distant ferns exposed to a breeze.

He wheeled the Suzuki close to the door and propped it up ready to use. Then with infinite care he opened the creaking door wide. It was now or never.

He pressed the starter button and, as the engine roared into life, let out the clutch with a great jolt and careered through the opening.

Wolves streaked out of the trees on either side of him with nightmarish speed. He wobbled wildly and yet the Suzuki seemed to be moving in slow motion.

He saw a set of fearsome carnassial teeth widening to reveal massive bone-crunching molars beyond. Then, at last, the engine responded and he surged out of reach.

He built up speed so rapidly that, for a moment, he could barely control the motorcycle with what amounted to one hand. The front wheel wavered, righted itself and he zoomed up the other side of the dip.

Wolves poured after him but none could exceed thirty miles an hour, and he was touching fifty as he cleared the top of the ridge. The thump of the machine landing wrenched his neck agonizingly and he lost his concentration in a stinging haze of pain and tears. 'Oh, my Christ,' he sobbed into the wind. 'Oh Christ, my neck!'

Snow lay frozen on a threadbare carpet of rotted leaves, leaving them slippery and treacherous. The back wheel slid away and the front spun frantically, fighting for a grip. He took the weight of the bike on his foot as it slewed around and came almost to a complete stop, with the engine still racing.

In a moment or two the first of the wolves cleared the ridge and bounded down towards him. The back wheel took hold and he pulled away again. But now his shoulder was on fire with pain and he could no longer twist the throttle to increase speed.

A wolf closed on one side and ran abreast of the bumping machine. Then with a casual lunge it closed its terrible canine teeth over his leg.

The trouser leg tore like a wet paper bag and his calf was laid open in two great slices of white meat from knee to ankle. The leather boot held it together and, although he was aware of a great force being exerted against his foot, he was barely conscious of the wound until blood welled out several seconds later.

Even then it was his foot slipping on the suddenly greasy foot-rest that made him look down. He had little time to take it in. The wolf attacked again, locking its enormous jaws around his knee and literally somersaulting the machine into the air.

The Suzuki went over its handlebars, then over and over again. Bakersman was caught in an horrific cartwheel with the wolf jaw-locked on to him. His scream choked off at the second bounce when the half-hundredweight Japanese motorcycle landed on his chest and crushed most of the remaining life out of him. The wolf was flung clear, but when it tried to run it collapsed on to its chest with both forelegs broken.

The engine roared on vainly for several minutes, its throttle jammed open. And only when it spluttered and sank into silence did the other wolves venture close, with tails wagging, and tear the faintly-breathing Bakersman into raw, screeching strips.

Kelso was having the time of his life. After phoning his North Sea oil story to the paper he settled down for a day or two with Penny Bakersman. She was a lot younger than him, but for a reason he could not fathom, she responded ardently.

Perhaps it was the disrespectful way he treated her. She was so accustomed to servility that his take-it-or-leave-it attitude seemed refreshing.

He did things he had not done for years. Bought her chocolates and flowers, had his new suit sent up from London – even though it did not arrive until the following spring when rail services eventually untangled themselves – and danced.

Dancing was something he had never tried in public. It was so different to the privacy of his room, where a clubfoot could be overlooked if you avoided the mirror. She forced him into it, one evening when he was two parts gone on white wine and an enormous helping of sherry trifle. He half-glided, half-clumped after her seductive movements, but since the band was painfully loud and everybody seemed intent on jostling everybody else, he forgot his disability and ended up laughing and clapping for more.

They never actually got to bed together. Not because of any shyness. It was more a mutual deference . . . a drawing back from anything that might edge their affair into an inevitable decline.

He found her breathtaking and it got worse for him every day.

Maybe, he thought one night when he lay on his bed smoking and staring at the blank ceiling, some day he might even ask her to marry him. But the accompanying fear of a scornful whatever-put-that-idea-into-your-head made his courage shrivel.

The following morning at breakfast, when he was scrunching into his fourth slice of wafer-thin toast and chunky marmalade, a receptionist interrupted them. Kelso's newsdesk had left an overnight message congratulating him on the story, and somebody called Rooksby had phoned twice from Thurso.

'Nigel Rooksby?' he asked innocently.

The hotel man nodded. 'He seemed most agitated. Wants you to call him back.'

Kelso shook his head. 'No. I've never heard of him.'

Penny smiled anxiously. 'Any messages for me?'

'Sorry, madam. Nothing.'

Kelso caught her eye. 'Your brother?'

'Umm. It's not like him to leave me stranded. I hope he's all right.'

Kelso noticed she wasn't wearing a bra again. It was a disturbing habit. He stretched for the marmalade and brushed against her. 'Of course he is. And you're not stranded. Come upstairs and I'll resuscitate you.'

She rapped him on the nose with a finger. 'You could be arrested back home for making a suggestion like that. I'm only a girl, you know.'

It was meant as a joke, but it was too close to the truth to amuse him. He was quite a few years older than her and shopsoiled. Maybe that was why his feelings were bruised.

Kelso glanced sourly at his misshapen foot. 'I'm going up anyway. This bloody thing's playing me up again.'

FOURTEEN

The temperature dropped another few degrees and winter seemed to stretch endlessly towards the horizon. For centuries Britain had been colder than Europe before the Ice Age, and further such winters would inevitably one day bring Scotland back into its frozen arms.

The tracks of the glaciers were everywhere for the keen eye to detect in detail. Even the staggeringly beautiful valleys and the mysterious lochs owed their birth to a restless, slow-moving continent of ice.

But the fact that Scotland's mountains and forests and summer grandeur were no more permanent than a blink of the eye, meant little to Darkmind. He knew nothing of the reality: of the limitless, paralyzed periods of history that had gone before, when the land was covered in ice hundreds of feet thick, and which would one day return.

He was too engrossed to think. He concentrated on rapidly eating the long, jointed portion of meat wrenched from the man's trunk. It was sheathed at one end in a tough leather boot and he gnawed open the indigestible covering in order to get at the sweeter meat inside.

He ate well away from the others, clamping the joint under his front paws as he snuffled and chewed appreciatively. But a fully-grown wolf can eat ten pounds of meat at a time – fifteen or more when ravenous. And there were others in the pack. He was aware of them snarling and bickering over the remains, and bolting down whatever they managed to snatch.

The winter had been bitterly hard. Sometimes the murderous frost snapped great branches from trees helplessly pregnant with snow. And, although at first the wolves fed regularly on deer meat, the hunting became increasingly

107

arduous. Until the time came when there were no longer any deer on the mountains.

There were numerous wolf packs in the Highlands and, for a while, they were the better off for having to properly hunt for prey. They ranged far and low through the open forests. There were many of them now, and they could hear one another howling at night across the frozen countryside. It was like days gone by: a time that none of them could remember yet all could instinctively sense.

They knew full well where the deer had gone. But to follow would be to risk facing man, whom they saw simply as a larger predator than themselves. A predator with more food than he needed.

Darkmind's pack grew increasingly haggard and snappy. The day eventually came when their smouldering mal-evolence erupted into internecine hostility, and they killed and ate the weakest in the pack.

They found an isolated stone cottage where the sole occu-pant, a recluse, had died a week earlier. Darkmind led them to feast on the corpse, and then their gaunt half-starved shapes ran through the shadows ransacking each room. Before long they were menacing the surrounding countryside in an ever-widening circle.

Everything that moved died in the first two days of their new-found gluttony. Scraggy chickens and a terrified, pauper-thin terrier hiding in an abandoned barn . . . then a great pig that had itself only survived up to then by truffling through the edible evil-smelling mess of its sty.

But when the last of the pork was gone and the wolves' distended stomachs, for which they paid with agonies of cramp, shrank back to normal, they realized the outlook was bleak.

Desperately they grubbed for moles, tubers and shrivelled fruit – until even that became impossible in the petrified earth. They clawed at trees to dislodge forgotten birds' nests and gnawed the iron-hard bark in search of insects.

Snarling and more aggressive than ever towards his humili-ated pack, Darkmind had been the first to attack a human.

On more than one occasion he was ready to pounce, but withdrew at the last moment and filtered back into the trees, unseen. But once the pack finally drew blood, it followed up with growing confidence. A pattern was quickly established. Their belly-slithering stealth would be followed by great bounds of savage exuberance.

No longer would they avoid the noise and the confusing scents of the lowlands.

. The pack was ready – the first of several to venture down the mountainsides – to tunnel through the whispering sea of frozen ferns to where the roads began and smoke curled from narrow chimneys.

Only Darkmind hesitated. He was pulled in two directions. First, there was the predatory instinct that urged him boldly forward. But equally pressing was the need to find a den where Whitepatch could give birth to their cubs.

The other wolves moved in an anxious, erratic circle while Whitepatch nuzzled his face and licked the sensitive area under his back legs. He stretched his neck, blinking contentedly at the sky, before loping away.

Whitepatch gave a strangulated howl which degenerated into a whine. Longrunner and Hollowbelly looked up from the polished bones they had been scrunching, silencing her with flat stares.

One by one they followed Darkmind. All, that is, but Whitepatch. She had motherhood on her mind as she took a different route down through the clearing.

Cecil Inkerman was justifiably agitated. Next morning, after breakfasting fitfully on two eggs, sausages, fried bread and a generous helping of baked beans, he was too edgy to finish it off with more than a single slice of toast.

If anything happened to Franklin Bakersman, the old man would almost certainly blame him for abetting his son's hunting trip in mid-winter on unaccustomed mountains. And alone.

Some fathers never see their sons as they really are. To

them they will always be vulnerable, slightly irresponsible youths. Certainly not calculating, self-sufficient men.

Inkerman raised a large pair of German binoculars and again stared out through the oblong window at the back of the caravan. But the more intently he scanned the desolate braeside, the more queasy he became.

Somebody had to do something quick. He could hear J C Bakersman's high-pitched voice barking out questions to which he had no convincing answers. *What? Why didn't you go with him, you great bag of lard?*

If the thirty-year-old managing director of Parallel Oil was sprawled out on a frozen hillside, perhaps with a broken leg, he could die of exposure within a few hours.

Inkerman paced up and down. *Of course, it could all be a mistake. But why wasn't he back by now? He had a new Japanese motorcycle . . . the best on the road.* Inkerman crashed a fist into his palm. *Bloody Japanese . . . always breaking down. He could strangle the lot of them! How could they do this to him?*

He struggled into his overcoat, stuffed a half-slice of toast into his mouth and hurried over to Station House.

Acting Constable Shaftoe was massaging his right ear with the help of his lightly inserted finger when Inkerman burst in and made for the inner door, marked *Sergeant-in-Charge. Private.*

Shaftoe, who was reputed to be a slow mover, broke all records. He jerked up out of his chair and blocked the doorway with a meaty arm. Their faces came to a halt only inches apart: one distraught, the other stolidly immovable.

'Yes, sir?'

'I want to see the officer in charge, immediately.'

'Oh? What about?'

Inkerman tried to get under the arm, but it moved down, squeezing against his head.

'Careful!'

'Oh, sorry sir. Now what is it that's so urgent?'

'You're not the Sergeant!'

'True,' said Shaftoe, meeting him eyeball to eyeball and

110

not giving an inch. 'Sergeant Dunceford is out. But I'm his deputy.'

Inkerman glanced doubtfully at the unkempt figure. 'When will he be back?'

'Who?'

'Who the bloody hell do you think? Bunceford, or whatever his name is.'

'I couldn't rightly say. Might be some time yet.' Shaftoe studied his chewed nails diligently.

'All right. I want to report a missing person. My colleague ... that is, my managing director went off into the hills yesterday to do some game hunting and hasn't come back. I'm afraid something untoward may have happened.'

He spoke so rapidly, Shaftoe had difficulty in understanding him. 'Unto what?'

'Untoward. Something unexpected.'

'Oh.' Shaftoe worked his braces out like chest expanders. 'I'd better take a note. What do you think's happened to him?'

'I don't know. He might have broken a leg ... or got hopelessly lost in all your bloody snow. Perhaps he's lying doubled up in pain somewhere, while you're standing there humming and hawing.'

'All right,' Shaftoe admitted reluctantly. 'Sergeant should be back in twenty minutes. He'll see to it then.'

Inkerman ran tense fingers through his hair. 'Can't you do something right away? Make a few phone calls, or start organizing a search party?'

Shaftoe sat down at his own shabby desk, on which one leg was slightly shorter than the others. 'I'm not authorized to use the phone.'

'Why on earth not?'

'Well, according to the last bill we had in, somebody was making a lot of personal calls. Not me, but the Sergeant got very upset.'

Inkerman groaned at the ceiling. 'Jesus.'

The untidy policeman pulled out a blunt pencil and licked the end. 'Never mind, I'll take the particulars. Name?'

'Inkerman. Cecil Inkerman.'

111

Shaftoe looked up, puzzled. 'Surname?'

'Inkerman. As in ink that you write with. INKERMAN.'

The burly assistant wrote laboriously and shielded it from view with his other arm. 'Err. Address?'

'We have a caravan about fifty or sixty yards down the road there. JVR 272.'

'No, no. Where's your home?

'For pity's sake, what do you want that for? You can get all that bollocks later. I'm telling you that the leading executive of Parallel Oil Incorporated is probably lying injured in the snow, and certainly in need of urgent help. Now for heaven's sake start the wheels turning to find him. I'll be back in ten minutes. You find Bumford. I'm going to alert Sir Marcus Sheerwater.'

Shaftoe was roused to his feet once again. 'Oh, I wouldn't do that if I were you.'

'What?'

'He doesn't like being woken up too early.'

Inkerman could scarcely believe his ears. 'Look,' he said hoarsely, 'the man who is missing is Franklin Delano Bakersman. Perhaps you've heard of him.'

Shaftoe shook his head.

'Well you take it from me: he's probably the most influential American ever to set eyes on this . . . on this village. And when Sheerwater hears he's missing, he's going to have a fit.'

Shaftoe shrugged helplessly. 'Well, I wouldn't know anything about that.'

Inkerman closed his eyes and left. He missed his footing on the steps as a result, but was past caring. He talked anxiously to himself as he climbed the slope towards the MP's high-fronted residence in the distance. If anything happened to Franklin Delano Bakersman, the man's father would have his guts for garters.

Emma Dancer's long tapering legs were a disadvantage on a Shetland pony. Either she had to bend them right up and grip

112

the barrel-shaped animal with her knees at the base of its neck, or they dangled incongruously and trailed in the snow.

She had meant to spend the day working in the remains of a buried settlement, but the snow drifted too deep for it to be worth while. The fact that she had made a wasted journey became obvious as soon as she reached the centuries-old site but, after nearly four months of indoor work, she could hardly wait for a thaw.

In the distance, beyond the great snorts of condensation emitted by her sturdy pony, she could see the solitary peak of Stac Polly watching her wrathfully under a heavy grey sky.

The pony was eager enough to retrace its steps but, when she saw a scattering of ravens hopping and fluttering behind a thin screen of trees, she reined in.

There was something curious going on. Nothing else moved and, cautiously, she investigated. She came across the beautiful motorcycle lying almost unscratched under a spruce tree: its violent crash having been cushioned by snow. She sank to her knees, puzzled. Then discovered a gauntlet with something solid still inside, and instinctively drew back.

There were several other scattered remnants which she could not individually identify but, when considered together, they led her to an increasingly horrifying and grotesque conclusion.

Emma was not normally given to panic. Quite the opposite. Usually, the more fraught a situation became the more determined she was to overcome it. But this was different. She sensed an overpowering and unseen presence and glanced around wildly.

The ravens flapped heavily into the distance as she stumbled back to the pony. Somehow she got on and, with a feeling of growing terror, urged it down the slope.

FIFTEEN

The purpose of a gin trap is to hold and maim its victim. So that, even if the prey eventually escapes, it will never be the same again.

The design is brutally simple. There are two iron jaws each containing a row of spikes, which snap together with blind force when something exerts weight on a central pad and releases a spring. The something is usually a foot: an animal's leg which, under the fur, is thin and consists of delicate bone.

The bull-spring which clamps the jaws together cannot be forced open by the victim, and the whole apparatus is chained to an iron stake embedded some distance away. Gin traps are illegal in the British Isles.

McDee's was a big one: more of a bear trap. The jaws were nearly two feet across and rusty from lack of use. But he ignored the rust and concentrated on filing the teeth into a series of raw edges. His long straight hair was constantly falling in his eyes and he flicked it clear with an occasional jerk of his head as he worked with wild-eyed concentration.

Next he buried the trap and a pair of working gloves, with loving care, deep in a pile of rotting manure. After two days, when he felt that all traces of human contact had been subjugated by animal scent, he excavated them. Then he pulled on the smelly gloves and set to work.

He had hardly eaten since his eldest daughter had been carried off, leaving only a smudged dribble of blood on the stairs to mark the passage of a clutching hand. During violent headaches and moods of bruised despair, he had kicked down nearly every door on the farm, imagining himself to be face to face with the killer. Now, at last, he was glad to have a real purpose.

He picked a sandy spot not too far from the farm where two tracks converged, squeezed together by a stream on one side and a confusion of brambles on the other. McDee got on his knees and scraped out a shallow pit about two feet square, levelled the bottom and then carefully bedded the trap. He ran out eight feet of chain and anchored it to a metal stake. Next he carefully buried the trap, laid a pad on top to await an unsuspecting foot, and spread his remaining soil across it all.

He backed away, pulling his kneeling sack with him and giving the ground gentle sweeps as he did so. He examined it meticulously, made one or two delicate adjustments to the surface, and finally seemed satisfied.

McDee had only one trap and he knew he was not likely to get another. So he went back to the farm to prepare a quite different ambush, which was just as well. Since, when the wolf came, its natural suspicion allied with keen eyesight and acute sense of smell warned it away from the junction of the paths.

McDee took his worn but ferociously sharp butcher's knife and picked out a plump ewe from a huddle of sheep in his barn. He dragged it outside, clamping its writhing body between his legs and stabbed it through the side of the neck.

Blood spurted over his hand, warm and sticky. The sheep jerked violently, then lay still and eyed him with a degree of trust which was not reciprocated. When it sagged lifelessly, McDee cut into its breast with relish and sliced open the flesh between the rib cage. He stuck his arm into the cavern and drew out a tangle of shuddering tubing and intestines. It smelt foul but that did not wipe the crazed smile from his face.

He dumped the jellied mass on to one of Lucy's already-stained sheets. It seemed appropriate that the sheet should help avenge her death.

McDee bundled it up and took it, together with a selection of items he had prepared the previous evening, to an oak tree by a sheltered spring where deer sometimes watered in the summer; an awkward secret place rarely visited by humans.

115

There he unrolled a waterproof wrapping and lovingly took out a six-inch steel shark hook, attached to a stainless steel trace, and ten feet of heavy-duty nylon fishing line.

He rested a ladder against the well-worn tree in which his daughters had so often played out their fairy-tales, and knotted the cord firmly around a branch. That left the hook dangling nearly five feet from the ground.

He dug the hook into a chunk of slippery, spurting liver, draped some more intestines around it, and let the dripping bait swing in the breeze.

McDee scattered some smaller pieces of offal around the base of the oak and, again, stepped back to scrutinize his work. He squeezed his hands in feverish anticipation, reluctant to give up the picture of a trapped wolf that filled his mind. But the sooner he removed his presence, the quicker the bait could work.

Even McDee was surprised with the speed at which one of his traps was sprung.

When he crept back through the undergrowth two hours later, unable to contain himself any longer, he had snared a she-wolf.

Whitepatch came down the trail alert and without fear. She was a predator and herself to be feared. Only man disturbed her. As a cub on Rhum she had thought of him as the main enemy but then, after being netted and shipped to the mainland, came to accept him as a superior. Just as she accepted Darkmind as the dominant figure in the pack.

She detected McDee's scent a mile from the farm and, where the trail dissolved into a wider path, his odour was strong and recent.

She sniffed at the barely disturbed earth over the trap and backed warily away, before going into a crouching detour and on towards the farm where there were chickens and the exciting smell of sheep. After devouring a kill, there would still be plenty of daylight in which to find herself a den.

She gave a short gruff bark, urinating in her eagerness to

116

close with the prey. Her steady economical lope soon brought her within sight of the dripping intestines hanging from the tree.

At sixty yards, Whitepatch came to a halt, wrinkling her nose and taking in the full flavour of the reeking meat. She stood sideways on, appearing almost disinterested for a while, but testing for any indication of an enemy.

Eventually she approached. Closer and closer until she was directly underneath, and the blood dripped tantalizingly on her upturned face. A coarse tongue flicked out appreciatively and her handsome eyes never left the swaying offal, suspended just out of reach.

She growled and struck upwards with her paw, scything the air and missing by some eighteen inches. Finally she bottomed away, and leapt upwards.

A light wind caught the bait and moved it, so that she fractionally missed the steel barb and grabbed only some superfluous meat between her teeth. It was quickly bolted and she turned back for more.

This time her snapping jaws took the whole bait and the weight of her leap helped the shark hook bite into the recess of her upper jaw.

The jolt when the line came up short almost broke her neck and she was flung backwards: all her ninety-eight pounds suspended by the mouth. She was in agonizing pain, but the choking pressure on her neck prevented her making any sound other than a subdued gargle, rather like a sink emptying.

She recovered sufficiently, through a haze of blood, offal and saliva, to squirm her rear quarters. But a renewed dagger of pain in the mouth made her stiffen into immobility, other than gingerly to touch her back legs on the ground.

That left her standing painfully on tiptoes, her disfigured mouth trapped as surely as if it was nailed. It was all she could do to find enough room in her windpipe to pant excruciatingly.

McDee found her an hour later, crucified by the mouth. He could hardly believe his good fortune. He ventured around

117

the semi-conscious wolf grinning like a small boy on Christmas morning.

Only when he saw the point of the hook protruding from her muzzle, with blood drying darkly down her chest, was he satisfied. Caught on her tottering back legs in a slow but perpetual dance, the wolf could bring none of her strength to bear.

McDee clapped his leathery hands gleefully and went into a shuffle. 'Who's afraid of the big, bad wolf?' he sang off-key. 'Big bad wolf. Big bad wolf. Who's afraid of the big, bad wolf? Certainly not McDee.'

Later he drove the tractor over to his dilapidated and rarely-visited neighbour, Morgan Grenfell. He drove recklessly without heed either for the vehicle or his own safety, and on the way he cackled with anticipation of what was to come.

Grenfell was a bachelor and the sole survivor of three farming brothers. He lived alone in piglike conditions, raising giant porkers and talking to them for hours on end, in the foulest language, about the things he could never discuss with people.

What now drew McDee to him was his dogs: two ugly bull terriers. Short, heavy-shouldered dogs with nasty pink eyes and vicious teeth which they bared at anything that moved.

McDee dragged a bottle of Scotch from the lining of his coat pocket and filled a mugful for the startled Grenfell before they fell to talking. Their conversation ended with McDee pushing forty pounds worth of crumpled long-hoarded fivers across the uneven table and taking the dogs by their leashes.

The other farmer sympathized clumsily over Lucy's death and already knew about the wolves. He had heard them howling for the past three nights and was now even sleeping with his pigs. The stench from his caked trousers confirmed the fact, although it went unnoticed by McDee whose mind had already darted back to the wolf, suspended in pain. But that was his secret.

Within half an hour he was back with Whitepatch, who was

118

in a dazed swirl of semi-consciousness. The bull terriers snarled and yelped in their eagerness to get at her, but McDee tied them to the tractor.

With almost sensuous pleasure he took out his knife, wiped the wickedly-sharp blade and positioned himself behind the wolf. Whitepatch wagged her tail in weak submission.

McDee stretched out one of the wolf's hind legs and stroked the blade across the main tendon just above the joint. Then repeated the exercise with the other hind leg. A meagre trickle of blood ran down to the paws, but nothing more.

Next he released the nylon cord so that the wolf collapsed to the ground, and then went back to the dogs – to watch.

Whitepatch tried to lick away the blood around the hideously protruding hook, and got up weakly. She was only half successful. Her forelegs responded, but the hamstrung hind legs would not.

McDee hugged himself, leaned back and laughed. Laughed until he cried. Then he released the dogs.

They went for the wolf like bullets, almost colliding in their haste. The big she-wolf managed to snarl and half-snap, giving herself just enough time to swivel on her bottom and scuff along on her forelegs.

The sight of the wolf desperately dragging herself along while the dogs snapped at her neck was almost too much for McDee. He jumped about delightedly, urging them on until he was hysterical.

The bull terriers had the time of their lives. One dug its serried teeth into the lean grey flank and hung on grimly. The other bit deeply into the neck of *Canis Lupus* and was dragged along the bumping, yelping fur-strewn path.

Whitepatch kept rowing with her front legs, but the power gradually ebbed until she gave up and lay on her side, panting and exhausted, while the uncompromising dogs bit through unprotected flesh and literally worried her to death.

McDee joined in, kicking the carcass until his toes were sore inside his heavy boots. He pulled off the dogs, their pointed white muzzles stained with gore, and tied the nylon cord to his tractor. Then he towed the she-wolf back to his farm.

He knew that, sooner or later, her mate would come looking for her. And he wanted to be ready.

He wiped an arm across his eyes and sighed contentedly. It was the most enjoyable day he had had for years, although one might not have realized it to see him sob as he drove home.

SIXTEEN

Richard Unthank had a nightmarish journey back to Elphin on the snowplough, which itself was twice buried up to its nose in snow which slid treacherously back down from the masses piled steeply on either side of the vehicle.

He fell into bed after discarding only his boots, woollen hat and coat in an uneven trail leading to his double mattress, and dreamed wearily about digging himself out of an endless snowdrift. Nevertheless he slept and next morning, after a roasting bath, he was the first guest into the breakfast room.

Inkerman appeared half an hour later, moving slowly and wincing as if he was in a delicate condition.

Unthank glanced up from his scrambled egg. 'Morning.'

'Morning.'

'Any news?'

'About what? You've heard something?' The public relations man was suddenly alert to the possibility that his missing employer might have returned during the night.

Unthank shook his tousled head and looked blank. 'No, I've been in Edinburgh for the past few days.'

'Oh.' Inkerman stared from a window at the incredibly beautiful white-shrouded landscape. The sky was an undecided mixture of metallic greys and blues, but more promising than he had seen it for weeks. 'You should have stayed there. Nothing would have dragged me back here.'

'It's my job.'

'Uh-huh.' Inkerman served himself from silver dishes on a sideboard and poured tea for them both. There were few guests at this time of year, and the staff were hard to find before midday. 'What do you do?'

'I'm an environmental scientist of sorts.'

'Sounds like a nice secure job. Get a pension at the end of it, too?'

Unthank noticed the forlorn note in the voice of the man with a big waist and pineapple hips, and merely nodded.

'You're lucky. You don't know how lucky,' said Inkerman. 'It's not easy to get new jobs at our age.'

Unthank raised an eyebrow. The other man was about fifty years old and out of shape. He estimated that he himself was ten years younger and had a lot more puff, but he let it pass.

'Why, are you about to lose yours?'

But Inkerman did not answer; he was no longer listening. He cocked his head to one side, crossed to the window and looked obliquely up the road.

In the distance, a police car was approaching at speed, with its siren blaring frantically.

'What is it? What's happened?' Inkerman could see the Suzuki in the back of the estate car, and he hurried across the road plying Dunceford with questions before the ashen-faced police sergeant could get out of the driving seat.

'There's been an accident.'

'Jesus. What sort of accident?'

Unthank joined them, tugging a napkin from his shirt front. 'Anything I can do?'

The policeman signalled Shaftoe to help him at the back of the car, then turned angrily on Unthank. 'Where the devil have you been?'

'Having my breakfast.'

'No, I mean for the last couple of days.'

'Edinburgh. I left you a note specifically.'

Inkerman could wait no longer. He shouldered between them. 'For God's sake, Sergeant. I want to know what's happened.'

'There's been an accident, that's all.'

'That's all?' echoed the shorter man unbelievingly. 'That's all? Wasn't anybody hurt?'

The two policemen ignored him as they strained to lift the gleaming Japanese motorcycle down on to the road. Only the front lamp was smashed. Otherwise it looked in the same mint condition as when it had left.

Inkerman bent anxiously past them and ducked into the rear of the Cortina. A grey blanket covered a long, narrow hump. He gulped and withdrew the top flap: underneath was a three-foot long tool box. The sergeant moved him out of the way and the two men carried the box into Station House.

Inkerman had time to resume his search of the car, but now it was empty.

He hurried into the police house, stumbling over a pair of boots, so agitated he was almost unintelligible. 'Where's Mr Bakersman? That's his bike out there. I tell you that's his bike.'

The sergeant disappeared into the inner room and muttered to Shaftoe. 'Get rid of him.'

The bulky, untidy constable was not unsympathetic, but he too had a lot to do and not much time to do it in. He ushered the public relations man back to the porch. 'There was an accident.'

'Oh, my God. Was he badly hurt? Is he in pain?'

Shaftoe could not bring himself to speak now that the moment of truth was upon him.

'Well?' demanded Inkerman.

'Yes, he was hurt.'

'Can I see him?'

'No.' Shaftoe bit his lip and raised his head. 'He's up there.'

Both Inkerman and the loose-limbed scientist gazed up at the first floor, assuming that was what the policeman was

122

talking about. Inkerman even stepped out into the road and stared at the bedroom window. 'Where?'

'He's dead.'

Inkerman's mouth sagged open. 'What?'

Unthank helped the public relations man back to the guest house, and gave him a scalding cup of tea to counteract the shock. But Inkerman's hand shook so much he spilled most of it into the saucer.

'I saw him only yesterday. He can't possibly be dead . . . ' His fingers dug painfully into Unthank's arm. 'And who's going to tell his father? Not me.'

Unthank rubbed his forehead and tried to think coherently. 'That's not the real problem.'

Inkerman came out of his daze a little, curious to know what the taller man meant. 'What is it then?'

'It's fairly obvious if you think about it . . . Where's the body?'

'Still there. Where the accident happened, I suppose.'

'No, I don't think so. The police wouldn't leave him there. How tall was he?'

'I don't know. Quite short really. About five feet two.'

Unthank made a funnel of his fingers and expelled his breath thoughtfully. The fears in the back of his mind re-emerged.

'That tool box they took in. Could he have been inside?'

Bewilderment creased Inkerman's face. 'A five foot man . . . in a three foot box?'

Everybody was in a panic by midday. Everybody that is but Sir Marcus Sheerwater. While Sergeant Dunceford dithered, wondering how on earth he could keep the lid on a second mysterious death in a few days, the MP sorted out the problem in a matter of seconds.

'You can't hush-up a thing like this.'

Dunceford and Shaftoe regarded him wide-eyed. 'No, sir?'

'Of course not. I want a full inquiry. So will the procurator fiscal.'

'Right away, sir.'

Cecil Inkerman was a bag of nerves when it came to informing his head office. It took the best part of an hour to contact someone in authority and make them understand what he was stammering about. Minutes later he received a crisp, urgent message asking him to repeat his garbled report. Inkerman phoned through a shaky confirmation.

But it was Sheerwater, at his autocratic best, who really made it sink home. He drafted a telegram to J C Bakersman in Texas. The MP had spent several years as a British Army officer in the colonies and was accustomed to sending dispassionate messages to bereaved relatives.

REGRET TO INFORM. YOUR SON FRANKLIN KILLED IN ACCIDENT. ESSENTIAL YOU MAKE CONTACT. MARCUS SHEERWATER.

The one sound act that Inkerman did accomplish was to get a message to Penny Bakersman at Aviemore. A pageboy scoured the hotel trying to locate her and the handicapped newspaperman.

He did not imagine they would be in their bedroom in the middle of the afternoon, but he was wrong. Martin Kelso was lounging back against a propped-up pillow, in his vest and trousers, reading a newspaper and basking in the tropical warmth of the central heating.

Penny was huddled next to him with her head under his armpit and one hand nestling in the warmth of his crotch. But it was not a blissful moment. She had been sulking and, as a result, he was studiously ignoring her.

'I thought that staying with you was going to be exciting,' she complained.

He grunted and turned over a broadsheet page.

'Nothing's happened for days. We haven't done anything, or gone anywhere. Hell, you must be as bored as I am.'

He regarded her remarkable shape from around the edge of his page and shook his head. She was partially dressed, but few buttons were done up and he slid his hand unhampered across the firm contours of her buttocks. They were superb marble bastions. Then he let go, and returned to his absorbing account of a football match played in a blizzard.

There was a knock on the door. 'Telegram for Miss Bakersman.'

She got up hurriedly and pulled herself together. 'Push it under the door, please.'

Telegrams were nothing unusual in her life. Her mother used to send one a week, reminding her about changing into warm underwear or urging her to visit one or other of her numerous aunts and god-parents scattered around the world. And her father seemed to conduct his business, as well as intimate family relationships, by cable.

She slit open the pale orange envelope and let the message dangle while she finished with Kelso. 'There's a lot more to life than arsing about in bed.'

'Umm?' He started on the financial pages.

'I'm fed up. Do you know what I want?'

'Yes, I know what you want,' he muttered thickly, without taking his eyes off the paper.

'What was that?'

'Nothing.'

She sighed exasperatedly and read the telegram. She skipped through it once, then read it again more carefully. Then a third time, puzzled. The words did not sink in, because she refused to let them.

Eventually she let out a little whimper and swayed on her feet. Kelso saw the colour of her face change to a porridgey grey. He swung his feet off the bed and grabbed her just before she fell.

'What is it?'

She gripped his bare arms, digging her nails in to screaming depth without even realizing it. Kelso, frightened by the change in her, shook her like a child. 'What the hell is it?'

'He's dead . . . Frank's dead.' Her eyes swam, and her head wobbled as if it was no longer firmly fixed to her body.

'Who's Frank?'

'He's dead,' she moaned. 'It says so, there . . .'

125

Kelso prised her loose and picked up the flimsy slip of paper. 'Your brother? Good God!' He sat her on the bed and then quickly began to dress. Franklin Delano Bakersman alive would rate a couple of paragraphs in the paper, but the same man dead was worth a double-column top and a picture any day. He combed his hair with rapid thrusts of his fingers, but no comb, and struggled into a jacket.

'You stay here. I'll get you a headache pill, or a tranquillizer or something . . . I've got to make a phone call. You sit there, and you'll feel better in a minute. I'll be right back.'

SEVENTEEN

Inkerman had a gleam in his eye by next morning. There was hope for him yet. The company president was flying in to Britain from Dallas, and a helicopter was waiting to whisk him north. A message, sent ahead, instructed Inkerman to gather together all of Franklin Delano Bakersman's personal possessions.

The trouble was: there weren't any, apart from a completely undamaged watch, which the police were holding on to for the inquest. But they had found nothing else: not even a bunch of keys or pencil.

'I must get out to the spot where he crashed,' the public relations man explained to Unthank. 'For some obscure reason, the police say it's dangerous. But if I leave it any longer, the snow will bury whatever's left.'

The tall scientist shrugged. 'What can *I* do?'

'You seem to have some pull with the police. At least they're letting you roam about.'

'Yes, but that's only because of the research I'm doing.'

'Okay. Let me come with you. I won't interfere with anything you're doing. But, if I'm going to keep my job, I just have to carry out the old man's orders.'

'Look, the police are right. It could be risky. Somebody should have told you. There are wolves in the vicinity.'

'Wolves? They're the least of my problems. It's J C Bakersman who'll tear me to bits. Anyway, I thought that your Highland wolves and wild dogs were supposed to be up along the north coast, a long way from here.'

'Take it from me, they've moved. And they're nothing like dogs. They're savage and they hunt voraciously.'

Inkerman nodded impatiently, determined not to be side-tracked. 'Just take me along, somewhere near the spot. And then go on with your own observations. I won't get in the way.'

Unthank turned away. 'I can't possibly.'

Inkerman restrained him with tears in his eyes. He made a sad, plump figure. 'Listen, if you don't help, I'll go on my own. I've got nothing to lose.'

'You've got everything to lose.'

'Let me be the judge of that.'

The younger man regarded Inkerman for a while, then pulled a wry face. 'All right. I'm leaving in twenty minutes. You'll need climbing boots, a tough anorak, a haversack with a vacuum flask, some chocolate and a compass. If you're not by the front door when I'm ready, I'll go without you.'

Inkerman beamed as he wiped his eyes with the sleeve of his jacket. 'You won't regret this.'

Unthank regretted it within an hour. The two men set off resolutely enough and covered three miles in remarkably good time, but then the snow began to harry them and they turned into plodding snowmen.

Inkerman was sweating profusely under his double lining of clothes, but insisted on showing how vigorous he still was by forging ahead. The problem was, it was asking for trouble with so many snowdrifts about: blundering forward in a straight line.

He sank up to his chest on one occasion. Somehow he managed to keep upright and Unthank heaved him out by the collar, but only at the expense of a lot of stamina. They trudged on and up towards the bleak heights of Cul Mor and Cul Beag. And, for a while, a light wind from behind whisked them along like corks on a sloping white sea.

Inkerman got his second wind and was beginning almost to enjoy himself, when his companion suddenly brought him crashing down from behind with a cumbersome rugby tackle.

He spluttered up out of the wet snow like a great, indignant walrus, but Unthank's gloved hand clamped across his mouth. The other glove was jabbed forcefully to the west.

Moving down from the barren windswept slopes were three, four, five animals. Large, mainly grey and black, and moving with a casual grace.

Inkerman looked at the younger man for enlightenment. 'Wolves.'

It immediately crossed Inkerman's mind that the very idea of predators might make Unthank want to turn back, even though the men were almost at their destination. 'They look harmless enough to me.'

The scientist knelt up and adjusted his binoculars. 'Do they?' He focused on the leader, and noted the big male's dark and light grey colour variations.

The line of wolves halted behind Darkmind and blinked across the quarter mile of hillside at the two men. Inkerman also knelt up. 'They've seen us!'

'I know.' Unthank felt a surge of pleasure at recognizing the big wolf from Rhum and yet he also knew that, from this moment, the pack would be marked for death.

Darkmind exchanged no more than a steady glance with him as the wind ruffled his thick coat, and he moved on in his own time. Unthank knew that the clear, sharp eyes would have picked him out and unlocked a memory.

Inkerman stood up, bolder now that the animals were loping on into the distance. 'They know who's boss.'

'They certainly do. And it's not us.'

Inkerman took off his fur hat and ran fingers through his

hair. 'Pheew. I've never seen a wolf like that before. Handsome. I'd like a really close look one day.'

Unthank grimaced. 'I'm going to see what they're up to. Do you think you can look after yourself now? The place you want, according to the police, is up there just over that ridge. You probably won't see much in all this snow, but don't stay more than ten minutes. Then strike straight back down here, use your compass and head for home. Ten minutes. No more.'

'Fine. You look out for yourself, too. You could be in trouble if you catch up with them unexpectedly.'

'That's not likely. They move faster than you imagine. It's deceptive. All I want to do is get some idea of their runway: their hunting route. Wolves usually follow a pattern. Anyway, I'll see you back at the guest house before dark.'

They waved one another goodbye. Not for the last time. But, by the time they next met, one would be quite unable to recognize the other.

Not all wolves run in packs. There are some who hunt alone because of their individual peculiarities. One or two are unusually skilful and others perversely greedy. But, more often than not, lone wolves have been driven from the pack because of their social attitude, sickness or derangement.

The latter can be viciously unstable as Darkmind's pack discovered. They drove out one of their number after an irrational and murderous fit left him foaming at the mouth.

Now he followed the others at a malevolent distance: slavering in their tracks, bolting down any food they overlooked or discarded, and fighting a continual battle with his own tail, snapping and snarling in dizzy circles. A highly dangerous and unpredictable predator.

Cecil Inkerman ate too much. He knew it, his wife and tubby academic son knew it, but he enjoyed his double helpings of everything so much that no one did anything more than tease him about his paunch.

He had a shotgun hanging upside down on a webbing strap over his back. He had not fired any sort of weapon for more than twenty years but, with a pocketful of cartridges and only J C Bakersman on his mind, felt no cause for alarm.

He discovered marks of a motorcycle impact on two trees and even a thin scattering of headlamp glass. He felt around on his hands and knees for a long time, shoving back the snow and sifting it through his gloved hands.

All he found was a pair of spectacles with the right lens shattered into a cobweb of fragile glass. Carefully, he put them away and stood up. He had been there fifteen minutes already.

The last of the wolves had been watching him for some time, its upper lip snickering back and its tail swishing restlessly. But Slack-Jaw was undecided. The disease that attacked his nervous system was quiet for the moment and he was content to crouch and watch the curious movements of the human, while his saliva dribbled on·to the snow.

It was the man himself who prompted the attack. He straightened up, as if he had sensed something, cocked his head and listened intently to the distant stirring of the wind in occasional trees. Then turned, dreadfully slowly, to find out what was behind him.

Slack-Jaw wriggled forward to within thirty yards and halted, ears pricked forward. Only his tail moved now, in strong regular sweeps.

Inkerman tried to force his paralyzed mouth into a smile. 'Good boy,' he croaked, with the desperate thought that he might win the creature over. But the idea vanished abruptly as the black, spiky-haired wolf started forward.

'Aaaaah!' Inkerman, with only a second or two left to do something, struggled to pull the shotgun off his back and over his head, but the thick strap caught under his chin. He was also aware of an excruciating pain in his knee as a result of the sudden tightening of muscles.

Slack-Jaw was not the fastest wolf in the pack but he was one of the most deadly. He plunged through the belly-deep

130

snow and launched himself at the human who was still flailing his arms.

Inkerman went over backwards, actually hugging the demonic animal that he was trying to escape from. Yellow teeth scissored past his face and tore off half of his ear, but he barely felt it. He was desperate only to get away. A gush of warmth down his jaw and neck made him realize he was bleeding.

'Oh God . . . Ooooh my . . . ooooh.' He staggered back to his feet and miraculously found that the shotgun was now in his hands, but the wrong way up.

Slack-Jaw had backed off, giving himself space for another leap and now closed in fast. The unwieldly public relations man closed his terrified eyes and gripped the gun by its barrels.

It was a do-or-die haymaker of a swing which caught the wolf on the neck, with a thud that could be heard halfway back to Elphin. The stunned predator fell into the snow with a strangled whine that sounded like the movement of a badly rusted door. Inkerman did not wait to see the outcome.

He ran blindly down the slope, toppling heavily into the snow and losing the shotgun. His hat and gloves soon followed. His chest heaved and blood, which continued to wash down his neck, froze in a rosy circle on the shoulder of his padded jacket.

He babbled to himself as he ran. There was no thought in his mind of using the compass. He just kept staggering on, getting up almost as many times as he fell down.

On the last occasion, he reached the reassuring solidarity of the A.835 road, and it was there that a farmer on a tractor found him spreadeagled nearly an hour later.

His fingers became so cold and stiff, clutching the icy surface of the road, that they looked almost black when he arrived at the infirmary.

EIGHTEEN

Penny Bakersman and her limping journalist arrived in the village about an hour after J C Bakersman and his entourage. They booked the grandest double room at the guest house and Penny went straight upstairs to fling herself sobbing on to the bed. The journalist left her dabbing her eyes and hiccuping and went across to Station House to find out what was going on.

Acting Constable Shaftoe had his sizeable foot on a chair, trying to get a shine on his dull toecaps. He was also for once wearing the dark regulation tie, although his blue police shirt would not button around his muscular neck and had given up the struggle, leaving an even untidier impression than before.

'Good afternoon.'

'Afternoon, sir.' The station assistant straightened quickly, concealing the shoe cloth behind him. 'Are you here for the meeting?'

'No. What meeting?'

'Oh.' Shaftoe stopped holding out his chest and exhaled. 'It's official police business.'

'Well, perhaps you remember me? I was here a few days ago. My name's Kelso. I'm a journalist.'

'Oh dear.' Shaftoe glanced uncertainly towards the sergeant's door.

'I'd like to get some details from you about the death of Mr Franklin Bakersman.'

'Oh?'

'You know . . . the accident that was reported yesterday. He was an American oil executive. A friend of mine, as it happens.'

'Sorry.' Shaftoe shook his head vigorously and put up both hands to quell any argument. 'I'm afraid we're closed.'

'What do you mean, closed? This is a police station, isn't it? Police stations don't shut down for the weekend.'

'This one does . . . So, you'd best come back the day after tomorrow.'

'That's ridiculous! On whose authority?'

'The Sergeant's.' The big assistant shrugged hopelessly. 'What he says goes.'

Kelso was about to dispute the point when the inner door opened and several men streamed out, talking in low voices. They showed deference to a small, slightly-built man with a parchment face and an expensive coat slung around his shoulders like a cape. He looked ill to Kelso, but also vaguely familiar.

The journalist stepped forward. 'Mr Bakersman?'

A pair of ferrety eyes fastened on him.

'Mr Bakersman, I knew your son. I'm most terribly sorry.'

The eyes continued to assess him, then fell away. At his side a brisk, bespectacled aide turned to Sir Marcus Sheerwater. 'Who's he?'

The MP coughed discreetly into his hand and leaned across to the oil man's wrinkled ear. 'A reporter from a London newspaper. I don't think we want any unnecessary publicity, do you . . . ?'

The aide didn't need any instructions from J C Bakersman. 'Get him outta here,' he said in a high-pitched Southern accent. Nobody acted on his words until Sir Marcus nodded his assent, then both Dunceford and Shaftoe stepped forward at the same moment, bumping into each other, before crowding Kelso towards the main door.

'Hey, what are you doing? Let go of my coat! This is a police station not the bloody American embassy. Watch it, this coat cost me a month's salary.'

Kelso was outside almost before he knew it and the door closed irrevocably on him. He stood swearing in the ankle-deep snow, then limped grumpily back to the guest house.

He clumped upstairs. 'Penny,' he said urgently, stripping

133

off his coat. 'I want you to do something for me.'

She sat up red-eyed and sniffing miserably. 'I'm not going outside. I look a mess. I don't care what it is. I'm not facing anybody looking like this . . .'

'You've got to. It's your brother.'

'Frank?' She turned eagerly. 'Have you found out something I should know?'

'No. And that's the whole point. The police are not saying anything. Not a dickie bird. And that's very odd. But they'll talk to you, his sister. So, for my sake, tog yourself up and find out from them what happened. Okay?'

'I'm not doing your prying for you.'

'Who's prying? You're his sister. You've a right to know. And you want to know for your own peace of mind, don't you?'

'I guess so,' she sniffed despondently. She stripped off a jersey, ready to wash her tear-stained face. 'I'll find out what I can.'

He plonked himself down on the end of the bed and searched his pockets for a cigarette. He did not smoke for enjoyment any more; it had become simply a way of easing the frustration. She was a stunning girl, but she had an unfortunate knack of getting right up his nose. He discovered a stray cigarette in the lining of a pocket, considered it morosely and then broke it in two and discarded both halves.

Her sing-song American voice reached him from the bathroom. 'Honey. Honey . . . you there?'

'Ummm.'

'Sorry I've been so miserable. I'll make up for it tonight. I promise.'

'Fine.' Kelso looked out through the lace curtains at the snow, which was again falling with heavy stealth. He seemed to have reached the point in his life that he had once dreamed about: living with a beautiful girl who couldn't get enough of him and, at the same time, being paid by a newspaper for doing what he liked best. Yet still he was oddly dissatisfied.

Half an hour later they walked together to Station House, where Kelso made her go in alone. He stood in a doorway

134

farther along the road, hopping from one foot to the other, until she reappeared. It didn't take long.

'Martin!' She ran to him excitedly. 'Father's here . . . in town. They said he's staying with a parliamentar . . . parliamen . . . somebody from the House of Commons.'

'I know, I saw him earlier.'

'You saw him? Why didn't you say?'

'I wanted it to be a surprise,' he lied.

She pulled away, looking more relieved than she had for the past two days. 'I must go and see him. He needs me. He must be beside himself with grief.'

Kelso restrained her. 'I need you, too. Now hang on a second. What did the police say about Frank?'

'Not much. Just that he was in a motorcycle accident and that the funeral arrangements are in hand.'

'Did you see the body?'

'No, they wouldn't let me. They said it was to do with your inquest laws over here.'

Kelso's eyes narrowed. 'Did they indeed?'

'Martin, I'll see you later.' She kissed him on the nose and then was gone, hurrying up the road towards the solemn, narrow-windowed High House.

Richard Unthank squeezed the bridge of his nose and shut his eyes. It was getting dark and there was no way he could get to the infirmary now that the snow was falling heavily.

He sat by a big open fire in the shadowy lounge and sipped the hot meat-extract drink. Once again he went through the day's events, to see if he'd overlooked anything that might have helped Inkerman get safely back to the village. But there was no way round it. He had been obliged to follow the trail left by Darkmind and, although it had petered out on frozen boulders of the slopes overlooking Loch Lurgain, the hour he had spent tracking the wolves was invaluable.

There were five of them, all right. Three males and two she-wolves and, judging from their droppings and the speed at which they travelled, they were in reasonably good shape.

135

He got one good look at them padding along a faraway ridge, outlined momentarily against the leaden sky, and, if the snow eased up tomorrow, he would pick a spot overlooking their runway and obtain more information. It was still too early to alert the police to his discovery; they would probably insist on seeing for themselves and frighten the pack away.

A firm hand gripped his shoulder, bringing him back to reality, and he looked up to find the limping journalist smiling at him. 'Hello. You couldn't stay away from the old place then?'

'That's right. Mind if I sit with you?'

'Not at all.'

They perched either side of the big stone fireplace and watched flames dance up the sooty chimney. After a while Kelso said, 'I was with Bakersman's sister when she heard he'd been killed. We came right back.'

Unthank nodded into the mesmerizing flames.

'Do you know the circumstances?' asked the reporter.

'No. Only that there was a crash of some sort, and I suppose he broke his neck.'

'Umm. What caused it?'

Unthank glanced briefly into the reporter's astute eyes, but the man was rubbing his disabled leg as if the question didn't really matter. Did the newspaperman suspect? God, he didn't even know for certain himself. And the police were not giving anything away.

'No. I offered to look at the remains, but the police said they didn't need any help.'

'How could you have helped?'

'I studied pathology as part of a science degree.'

Kelso sipped his drink noisily after blowing on the steaming surface. 'Curious that,' he said casually. 'They wouldn't let his sister see the body either.'

When the housekeeper next bustled through from the hall, the scientist called her over. 'Mrs Galbraith, where do the police keep bodies here before burial? We were thinking about that poor chap in the motorbike crash. Is there a mortuary?'

'I really don't know, sir. Hang on a minute, I'll ask.'

She rustled off in her full-length dress, which would not have been out of place in Victorian Scotland, and they heard her call to somebody down the cellar steps. She returned, patting the bun at the back of her head. 'He says they use the mortician's like everybody else. That's MacDonald's Undertakers, by the church.'

'Thank you.' Unthank drained his cup and stood up. 'Well, I think I'll say goodnight.'

Kelso watched him curiously. 'You're going to bed? A little early, isn't it?'

'I'm an early riser. Anyway, I usually take a stroll before I turn in.'

'In the snow? It's coming down by the hundredweight.'

'A little snow never hurt anybody.'

Kelso stood up, too. 'I think I'll join you.'

'No thanks. I prefer to be alone when I . . . ' He broke off before he could say too much. But the newspaperman finished the sentence off for him.

' . . . when you break the law? Look, if you are going to creep about an undertaker's in the middle of the night you'd best not do it alone. It would only take one lid to open unexpectedly and you'd die of fright.'

'I never said I was going to visit the undertaker's.'

'You didn't have to. I could see the curiosity coming out of your ears.'

'All right, so you've guessed. But why do you want to come?'

'I'm a newspaperman. It's my job. I knew something was wrong as soon as I arrived here. It's in the atmosphere.' He sniffed inquisitively. 'Can't you smell it?'

'No, I can't. My reasons are all logical. I don't go by instinct. But we both need an answer, so let's take a look.'

The housekeeper called after them on the landing. 'Mr Unthank, you're wanted. There's somebody here to see you.'

He let Kelso pass him. 'Meet you in the hall in ten minutes.'

'Right.'

137

The attractive woman with the high cheekbones was standing at the foot of the stairs. The sight gave him a jolt of pleasure. Even though he barely knew her, she had been on his mind for days.

'Hello, Mr Unthank.' There was a flush in her cheeks which might not have been entirely due to the sharp weather. 'I heard you were back. Can I talk to you for a few minutes, please?'

'Of course. I'm really delighted to see you.' He led the way back into the lounge where the shadows of the fire flickered along the walls. 'Let me take your coat. Have you come far?'

'I've got a cottage just a few hundred yards along the road. Kyle Lodge. The one with the whitewashed walls and a fox on the weather vane.'

He shook his head, as if he still could not believe his luck. 'If I'd known you were there, I'd have dropped in before now.'

She caught his gaze and held it. There was an instant chemistry between them; he had known on seeing her in the train. It only takes a glance. Now, here it was again.

She sat down and stared at her interlocked fingers to avoid being distracted. '*Canis Lupus*,' she said quietly.

He was surprised. So surprised he could not think of a thing to say. He quickly closed the door, so that they were completely alone. 'Say that again.'

'No need to. I can see the effect it has on you. The police asked me to interpret some of the Latin in the notes you left. So, I know what you think.'

He laughed cynically. 'It's nice to know somebody understands. The police told me, when I got back, that it was an interesting but basically unrealistic theory.'

His voice slowed as his attention was drawn to the beautiful symmetry of her face. She had a calm, aristocratic look. Good bones and a wide mouth, and her eyes seemed to be a peculiar shade of yellowy green in the half-light. A trick of the fire, but he was reminded of wolves.

'What's the matter?'

138

'Just for a moment there . . . you reminded me of somebody.'

'Anybody I know?'

'No.'

She brought him back to earth. 'I'm frightened. I think you had good reason for reaching the conclusion you did. But I know that Marcus Sheerwater has talked it over with the police, and they're going to ignore it. Now, if you're right, somebody could get badly hurt soon. But nobody outside has been warned of the danger.'

Unthank's heart went out to her. At last, someone with the commonsense to take heed.

'It's more than just an idea. I saw the pack today, on two separate occasions, just a few miles from here. I recognized them too. Their leader was brought over from Rhum a couple of years ago. They're dangerous all right. Normally, of course, it doesn't matter. They kill red deer and that's enough. The trouble is that now the deer have moved much farther south towards the industrial areas where wolves won't venture, they are naturally casting about for a replacement.'

'Did you hear about the man on the motorcycle?'

Unthank lifted his head in interest. 'Yes. What do you know about it?'

'Not much. Other than it's got the police worried stiff. When I asked Sergeant Dunceford about it he almost snapped my head off. And that's very unusual. He's got a soft spot for me.'

'What do *you* think happened?'

'I don't know, but I've a sense of foreboding. I've had it before when something evil has happened.'

Unthank looked at her in silence, and made his mind up. 'I want you to meet someone. Upstairs. Err, I don't even know your name . . .'

'Emma Dancer.'

'Upstairs, Mrs Dancer, I'd like you to meet somebody.'

She got up gladly: relieved that someone else was getting involved in what up to now had been irresponsible thoughts in her mind. She was not married, but to correct the laconic

139

man with the steady grey eyes seemed faintly ridiculous.

She was as surprised as Martin Kelso when he opened a bedroom door to Unthank's knock. He quickly finished tucking a thick shirt into his trousers and zipped up the front with reckless speed. They were both taken aback.

'Hello again! Emma, isn't it?'

'Hello.' Suddenly she was in the company of two quite different, physically attractive men. After months of comparative isolation, she was stimulated to sense them competing for her attention.

Unthank invited her to sit on the edge of the bed, then explained what he and the journalist were about to do and why. Emma listened intently and made her mind up both immediately and firmly. She wanted to go with them.

They both shook their heads adamantly, but she was a determined woman. 'You need a lookout. You also need somebody who knows their way about.' She got up and gulped. 'Come on, let's get on with it. I don't know what we'll find but, if we don't, I'll never sleep soundly again.'

Getting into the undertaker's was comparatively easy. They tiptoed around the back where there was a lean-to. Emma led the way inside and reached her hand up into a vase on a shelf. She took out a key and handed it to Unthank.

'I told you, you needed me,' she whispered.

'How the hell did you know where to look?' asked the journalist hoarsely.

'This is a stone mason's as well as the funeral parlour. They sharpen my cold chisel and scrapers for digging.'

Unthank creaked open the back door. 'Shuuush.'

No one lived in the building, but they could not afford to switch on any obvious lights. Martin Kelso had their only torch and, in a workshop full of benches, coffins and wood shavings, he shone it eerily under his chin and tapped Emma on the shoulder.

She gasped and laughed, but it only seemed to irritate Unthank.

'Where do we start?' asked the journalist.

Emma kept her voice down. 'There's the ground floor and a cellar. Perhaps we'd better split up to save time.'

'Right,' said the scientist. 'Martin, you stooge around up here with the torch, and I'll take Mrs Dancer down to the cellar. At least we can put the lights on down there.'

'Hmmm,' said Kelso unenthusiastically. 'Emma, wouldn't you rather stay up here with me, among the coffins and marble headstones? I mean, going down there with him, you never know what might lurch out of a dark corner. And what if you saw a faceless . . .'

Unthank interrupted in an urgent whisper. 'Why don't we just get on with it? Come on, Mrs Dancer.' He towed her towards the squeaky stairs.

On the way down, past cold walls of flaking plaster, she was glad of his hand and squeezed it tightly for reassurance.

Alone upstairs, Kelso began his own search. He swept the torch ahead of him in an arc and was startled to see a shape facing him, until he realized it was his reflection in the shop window. He grimaced and moved on. A moment later he crashed into a tall, inanimate figure which toppled heavily away from him. With a great groan of exertion, he engulfed it in his arms and strained to prevent it crashing to the floor. It landed with a muffled thud, with him sprawled on top.

Richard Unthank scrambled back upstairs to find out what the commotion was about. He picked up the rolling torch to reveal the journalist with his arms still wrapped around a life-sized stone angel.

'What the hell are you up to?'

Kelso regarded him sheepishly from the floor. 'I don't often get the opportunity to be this close to a woman. It's all a matter of grabbing your chance.'

'Here, take my hand.' Unthank hauled him back to his feet and resurrected the monument. Then he returned to the cellar where a single, bare bulb threw a shadowy but thankful light down a long arched room.

Emma moistened her lips and began to regret ever coming. There was a line of five coffins: two lidless and empty, and

141

the others with their pine tops set firmly in place.

'I suppose we have to look inside,' she said without enthusiasm.

Unthank moved along the row, examining the top of each casket. 'No need. These two have names on: Fraser and MacDowell. This is the only one that's not marked.' He took a deep breath and put his hands on the lip of the last coffin lid. 'Here goes.'

He was surprised by the expression that met his. The occupant's face in repose had an almost disappointed look about it. The skin was the pallor of pale green marble, and belonged to a woman. The body smelled faintly. He could not quite place the aroma and did not dwell on the thought too long. He let the lid drop back into place. 'Not there either.'

Emma glanced at his weathered, clean-cut face. 'What do we do now?' She had not realized until that moment just how much taller he was than her: head and shoulders. That would make him about six foot four, although he did not give the impression of being all that tall from a distance. His outdoor shoulders, wide hands and feet gave him a spread-out look.

While she was looking at him, the light went out. Without warning.

'That you, Martin?' Unthank's question echoed along the brick-domed ceiling. But there was no response.

Her hand crept back into his and they edged between the coffins to the comparative security of the wall. From the direction of the stairs something moved slowly and deliberately towards them. Her grip tightened until it became almost a tourniquet around his fingers.

It was as if someone was approaching inexorably with one foot dragging behind the other up to it.

The torch flicked on under Kelso's chin. His mad smile made them both grimace with exasperation.

Unthank loosened her hand reluctantly and felt his way back to the foot of the stairs, flooding the cellar with dull light again. 'Come on, let's get on with it. Find anything upstairs?'

'Not a thing.'

Emma called from the far end of the underground repository. 'There's something here. A freezer I think.'

They joined her beside the big white enamel chest, which was plugged in to an electric socket in the wall. When she lifted the lid, freezing vapour drifted out.

'Not much here. Just a few bottles and a . . . box of some sort.'

Unthank bent over the edge. 'That's it. That's the one the police brought back from the Bakersman crash. Give me a hand.'

The two men strained to lift it out of the freezer and on to the concrete floor. Unthank drew a deep breath and opened it. For a moment they found it difficult to focus in the half-light.

There were a pair of goggles, a rifle, a torn leather boot and some tattered clothing. There was the shoulder and sleeve of a jacket which was caked stiff, although none of them could identify the stain in the gloom. But nowhere was there any sign of Bakersman or his remains.

Kelso returned to the freezer, rummaging inside. 'There's something else here,' he called.

It was a large plastic bag and he swung his feet off the ground in order to get his head sufficiently far down inside to read the label. *F D Bakersman*.

He regained his balance and got a firm grip on the bulky bag without considering what might be inside. It was about the size of two or three large turkeys.

The plastic was heavy with ice and bumped crustily against the side of the freezer. He needed both hands to heave it out to Unthank, who brushed away some hoarfrost and loosened the neck in order to examine the contents. Whatever it was, it was not a body.

She nudged his elbow. 'What is it?'

'I can't see. Bring that torch over here.'

Kelso chewed his lip pensively and Emma Dancer swallowed hard. But it was Unthank who had to work up the courage to open it.

He slid his hand gingerly inside, but felt only frozen chunks of meat. In vain, he tried to pull one out: the contents were rigid and unyielding. Eventually he dumped the entire bag upside down on the concrete and dropped it several times to loosen its grip.

He delved inside again and this time pulled out a long joint almost devoid of flesh, apart from some remnants of rubbery gristle at one end.

He dipped in a second time and retrieved something white and, at first, barely recognizable. A human hand. Unthank stared at it in horror, but could not manage to let go until her scream made him drop it.

'Oh my Christ!'

He jerked back, rubbing his tainted palms frantically up and down the seams of his trousers. He gave a moan of anguish and Emma instinctively put an arm around him. They were both trembling.

Kelso drew them away. 'Come on, let's get out of here. Enough's enough.'

The reporter helped them to the stairs and was then himself obliged to return to the scene to pick up both the frozen hand and forearm joint from the floor. Steeling himself, until he was shuddering with determination, he snatched them up and thrust them back into the plastic bag. Then he heaved it all into the cabinet and slammed the white lid down.

He knocked over a trestle table in his haste to get out, but did not stop to pick it up. All any of them wanted to do now was to get away; to put as much distance as possible between them and the macabre remains.

Emma was crying quietly when they reached the guest house. Unthank had a quiet word with the journalist, and they agreed that he would take her home and that the two men should talk in the morning.

He found her white-walled cottage by the light of an occasional moon, which skipped capriciously in and out of lumbering clouds. On the roof, he noticed the weather vane fox at full stretch.

He sat her down, shivering, on a sofa and then made two

cups of steaming cocoa in the tiny kitchen. It was while they were huddling close together, sipping it, that they heard the wolves for the first time: howling in the distance.

At first Unthank thought it was his imagination but, when she jerked her startled eyes towards him, he knew it was a fact.

They were a mile away. No distance at all across land that favoured them.

The pack nuzzled Darkmind affectionately. In turn they licked his face and rolled on their backs, showing submission and deference to their leader. They would soon be ready to hunt again.

Darkmind's almond eyes blinked as he stared at the small community in the distance. He was in two minds again. Emotion moved him to find his mate, Whitepatch. But instinct urged him, first, to kill and eat.

For the moment they cancelled each other out. But during the night his nagging hunger would grow and, by daytime, the need to run down fresh prey would be decisive. His nose wrinkled as he remembered that the smallest of his human victims had been the tastiest. He would seek more of that size. Several more.

NINETEEN

Dawn provided the wolves with a natural meal. Gusts of wind swept layers of fine snow over more than a hundred wild duck sheltering up against an earth bank. By first light, when the winds died away, the birds were covered by a deep drift.

Darkmind and his pack detected movements and burrowed, snuffling and excited, under the snow. They tunnelled briskly for more than thirty yards before coming upon the first of the plump ducks.

After the first half-dozen died in a squawking flurry of blood and feathers, the others huddled mutely together, resigned to the inevitable.

None of the big wolves went hungry, and none left the scene of the slaughter without staggering from the distended weight of his stomach. They were meat-drunk. That day, therefore, Elphin had a respite.

Kelso was up exceptionally early. There was no sign of Penny and he assumed she had spent the night with her father in the aloof atmosphere of Sir Marcus Sheerwater's house on the hill.

The reporter glanced at the tight covers and undisturbed pillow on her side of the wide bed, scratched the sleep out of his head and began to tug on his socks. He would soon be much too busy to bother about her. He shivered. It was six a.m. and another ruthless morning, but he had a lot to do before most other people stirred.

He spun the hot tap in his washbasin and let the water gush out for a while. When he tested it, the icy chill made his eyes cross. He walked around the room dressing in a desultory fashion; a vest here, one leg in his crumpled trousers there. Then back to test the water. God in heaven, it was still freezing. He bent to read a handwritten note fastened to the splash-back above the basin. *NO hot water before seven a.m. and after ten p.m. GUESTS are asked to inform the house-keeper when they wish to run a bath.*

'*Now* you tell me,' he yawned. He cleaned his teeth and abandoned washing in favour of a quick splash of cold water to the face and a furious rub with a towel to restore his circulation.

Bakersman's fate occupied his mind. Whatever it was that had got the man, it had been gruesomely effective. And there was little doubt that Unthank knew more than he was saying. After all, Edinburgh would not send an environmental scientist to the back of nowhere just for the fun of it.

Kelso squeezed his misshapen foot into the built-up shoe, stood up and tested his weight. Right. He drew the bedroom curtains and was surprised to see how much higher the level of the snow had risen during the night. A car parked in the street was now no more than an undulation in a wide white expanse.

He shook his head. If it wasn't for the Bakersman mystery, he could easily have started work on a Highland-villages-marooned-by-the-snow story.

Kelso limped along the corridor to Unthank's room and knocked. There was no response, and so he opened the door and leaned apologetically inside. 'Hey, are you awake? Sorry to disturb you so early . . . '

He switched on a wall light to discover that the long, lean scientist had not slept there overnight either. The bed covers were smooth and untouched. 'Dirty beast,' he said absently, glancing about for luggage.

Kelso found a suitcase tucked away in the wardrobe, and swung it out on to the bed. Then, he shut the door to make sure nobody saw what he was up to. Inside, under spare shirts and socks, was a folder containing sheets of notes, a copy of the Red Deer Commission's annual report and half a dozen photographs, which he glanced through.

One picture was of two stags roaring at one another in the rut; another showed more than a hundred deer on the move down a hillside; and there was one of Unthank, weighing a long-legged calf with the help of handscales and a harness under its belly. But it was the final two pictures that riveted his attention.

One was of a grey wolf, crouching on the ground with its head back and its mouth open in full cry. The other showed three animals photographed from the air: they were close together and moving at full stretch across open countryside, but in the distance were rows of houses and the ugly shape of a power station. Scrawled in ink across the back was the previous month's date and the caption: *The farthest south that wolves have yet been spotted. Lennox Hills, north of Glasgow.*

Kelso gave a little whistle and set the picture aside. Then he settled down to read what he could of the notes in Unthank's cramped handwriting.

After less than ten minutes he was back in his own room, where he pulled his portable typewriter on to his knees and hammered out a first draft. Jesus, he breathed as he paused to read what he had typed. The words tumbled out, taking care of themselves. The only problem was his fingers which, in their excitement, got in each other's way.

He wrote: *Savage wolves, forced down from the remote north-west Highlands by the severe winter, are believed to have killed American oil heir Franklin Bakersman. His mutilated body was found yesterday close to where his motor-cycle had crashed on a hunting trip. Police are keeping details of the death secret, but fears are growing in Scotland that man-eating wolf packs could soon terrorize much of the countryside . . .*

He wrote all that he had gleaned from Unthank's notes, as well as a fair amount of speculation. But it was still a powerful story, and he could hardly wait to phone it over to London. My God, he thought, this will make the back bench sit up and take notice.

Kelso hurried downstairs, clutching his copy, and almost colliding with Mrs Galbraith in her curlers who was carrying a pot of tea, a cup and saucer up to her room.

'Ooh-eer!' She gave a wavering cry as he squashed past and clumped down the stairs, three at a time. He was so excited at the thought of what the story would mean – his eventual return to Fleet Street with an enhanced reputation for landing on his feet – that he could have pinched her frugal bottom for the sheer joy of it.

'Can't stop,' he called. 'Got to make a phone call.'

'Oh, Mr Kelso. Could I have a word with you?'

'Later, darling. Later.'

He settled himself on a high stool by the reception counter

in the hall, smoothed out his half-sheets of copy and caught his breath. Ready? Right.

Kelso picked up the telephone and dialled 0 for the exchange operator to make the connection with London. It was silent. *Odd*. He pressed down the receiver cradle and started again, but with the same result. Total silence. No dialling tone, no engaged tone, nothing.

He swore and went through the ritual once again.

Mrs Galbraith plucked at his sleeve. 'Excuse me, Mr Kelso,' she said politely. He gave her a barely-considered glance and shook the hand-set violently to make it come to its senses.

But her voice wore through his consciousness. 'The line's down, Mr Kelso.'

'What?'

'The telephone line's been brought down by the snow. We've had the biggest fall I can remember since I was a girl. I wouldn't be surprised if it's snapped in half a dozen places between here and Inverness.'

'What?' he groaned.

'Aye, it's happened before and likely it will happen again.'

He wrapped his hand across his forehead and closed his eyes in despair.

'Don't worry, Mr Kelso. They'll have it working again before you know it. In a week or two.'

Kelso stared at her honest face for a while and finally managed a weak smile.

'So soon?'

Mrs Galbraith did not understand why he urgently needed to contact London, but then she was accustomed to the idio-syncrasies of people who bustled in from the towns and who, at first, were always looking at their watches and measuring their time in seconds.

He seemed to have a headache and so she tried to be helpful. If it was a reliable method of communication he wanted, why didn't he try Mr McIver?

149

Kelso was ready to grasp at any straw. He waded out through waist-deep snow to a row of weatherbeaten cottages where McIver lived.

He raised his fur hat to a bedraggled woman who answered his knock, wiping her kitchen-wet hands on a stained pinafore.

'Is Mr McIver home?'

'Andrew?'

'Err, yes.'

The woman was intrigued by his London accent and shouted, without turning her head away or taking her eyes from his face: 'Andy. Some gentleman wants you!'

McIver had a curious, weasely face and a gap in his teeth, but he seemed anxious enough to accommodate Kelso. 'How can I help you, sir?'

'I understand you breed homing pigeons.'

'Indeed I do.'

'Are they reliable?'

'How do you mean?'

'Don't get me wrong. I'm sure they're thoroughbred. But can they fly long distances in this sort of weather? I mean, are they up to it?'

'Aye.' There was more than a hint of curiosity in the little man's voice, as he wondered who it was questioning the stamina and quality of his birds.

'Good, then perhaps we can talk. I have a proposition I'd like to put to you.'

McIver seemed pleased to show the reporter his loft and aviary, which were considerably brighter and better venti-lated than the rest of his home.

Kelso admired dozens of sleek birds in subtle varieties of grey, white, black and incandescent mauve; some fat and sleepy, others ruffling their feathers and pecking their plump chests for unseen delicacies, and the rest perched in rows and staring back at him, unblinking.

'They fly between here and Edinburgh?'

'Aye.'

'How long does it take?'

150

'Three or four hours. Depends on the bird, but they usually fly at about forty miles an hour.'

'Can they take a message?' he asked anxiously.

'Of course.' There was a momentary twinkle in the Scotsman's eye. 'But they're not like budgerigars, you know. They can remember only a few words at a time.'

Kelso pressed on. 'What I really want to know is, can they carry a reasonably long message on their flights?'

'Well, that depends on how heavy it is. I can put a capsule on this one's leg.' He reached into the wire enclosure which partitioned off one end of the loft. 'You could get a small sheet of paper in here. It depends how small you can write.'

Kelso felt a wave of relief. At last he had a way of contacting his newsdesk, via their Edinburgh office. The photographs he had appropriated would have to wait. The guts of the *Wolves threaten homes after killing oil heir* was enough to get the paper in a tizzy. The day news editor would organize a helicopter and he'd be out of it and writing an I-was-there piece for the paper by tomorrow.

He pulled out his wallet. 'Right. I want to hire a bird. No, make it two birds, just to be sure. You know, belt and braces.' He stuffed three five-pound notes into McIver's doubtful hand. 'That enough?' He added a fourth. 'Okay?'

'Okay for what?'

Kelso sighed and took the fancier lightly by the shoulders, to make sure they were eye to eye and that the man was concentrating on his words. Perhaps he had not made himself clear.

'Look, please. I want to hire two of your best pigeons to fly down to Edinburgh, each with an identical message on its leg. That's all. When either of them arrives, the job is done . . . and they're yours again. It's as simple as that.'

Understanding dawned across McIver's face and he handed back the banknotes regretfully. 'No traffic will be able to cross the Dirrie More in this weather. It will be blocked solid by all the snow we had last night.'

Kelso had travelled the Dirrie More in much milder conditions and knew that the mountainous road route between

Ullapool and Inverness, whose Gaelic name meant the Great Ascent, was formidable at the best of times. But he could not understand what bearing that could possibly have on racing pigeons.

'What's that got to do with it?'

'It's the only way of getting the birds south.'

'What are you talking about? I don't want them to take a bus. Why can't they fly?'

McIver revealed the gap beween his front teeth in a sad smile. 'You don't seem to understand, sir. Pigeons fly only the one way. That's home. In other words, you can take these birds to Dundee, Aberdeen, even London if you like. But they'll still only fly in one direction: straight back here.'

At last Kelso understood. He shook his head and left a single pound note for his trouble. He'd just have to find another way. There must be an alternative.

A journalist without a newspaper. What a farce. It was like trying to tap dance in your socks. He was willing but helpless.

TWENTY

They awoke with deceptively bright sunshine streaming in through the bedroom window. Unthank was the first to emerge from under a dishevelled mountain of sheets, eiderdowns and greatcoats. He was still dressed, but his clothes were grotesquely crumpled. Also, his mouth tasted as if it had been open all night.

Only later, when prodded by his foot and offered coffee, did Emma Dancer stir.

She struggled slowly up on to her bottom, grimacing at the world, and practised opening and closing her sticky mouth. 'What are you doing in my bedroom?' she asked drowsily.

'I just got out of your bed.'

'Oh.' She looked forlorn as she remembered the previous night's events. 'Was it worth it?'

He sank down on the end of his bed, sipping his coffee. 'I wouldn't call it particularly memorable. You had your boots on, two pairs of trousers, innumerable woollies and my hat. It was like sleeping with a giant teacosy.'

'I'm sorry.'

'Don't be. I consoled myself with the thought that it would probably be much better next time.'

She finished her coffee and stared out at the deceptive sun. It did nothing to dispel the invisible, vinegary cold. She forced a smile. 'Been up long?'

'An hour or so. I've been sitting in your kitchen, mulling a few things over.'

'Such as?'

'Oooh . . . If you must know, I was thinking about your husband.' He did not want to say it, but the thought had been on his mind for a long time.

'What husband?'

He looked into his lap, embarrassed that she should deny what he believed to be true. 'I heard Mrs Galbraith mention him the other day.'

'Did you now?' She drew her feet up and swung them out on to the floor. If he thought she owed him an explanation, he was wrong. The fact that she was unmarried suited her well enough most of the time, and yet . . . when other women proudly paraded their husbands and children, she usually felt hurt. A sense of unfulfilment perhaps. Unthank pressed his hands together awkwardly. He had thought two or three times during the last few days that, in Emma, he had finally found the woman he was looking for. But she had been such a long time arriving that, over the years, he had grown accustomed to loneliness, and there were aspects of it he loved. Only the week before he had stood on Suilven, the towering chieftain of a mountain, weathered out of soft sandstone, and realized that the whole magnificently desolate vista belonged to him alone. At that precise moment, he was the only person who mattered in the world. Unthank's mother had run away from home before he formed a clear memory of her. She was a deeply religious woman who spent innumerable winter evenings being individually schooled in church teachings by a haunted-looking rector, who was himself the victim of a loveless marriage.

Unthank's father never again mentioned either of them, after they ran off to Eire and started a preparatory school. The rector was unfrocked and died within a year or two, but his mother never reappeared, and the boy was raised by his solitary father. For years his only contact with women was when he was taken for Sunday afternoon 'treats' to have tea with remote aunts.

The real loves of his life were dogs. He had his first lolloping bulldog when he was thirteen and, although he called it Satan and pretended it would hurl itself at anybody who made a threatening move towards him, it remained basically a great soft, cuddly animal until it died.

Since then he had cherished, in turn, four different dogs. But the last, a clear-minded Welsh collie, caused him so much grief on dying that he resolved not to have another for a year or two. He still missed the black and white shape huddling against his legs by the fire in the evening and, sometimes, without thinking, reached down to ruffle the thick hair on the back of her neck only to realize she was just a memory.

His father too was dead now. Unthank crossed to the piano and let his fingers wander across the white notes. *Abide With Me.* Simple, moving chords.

Emma returned while he was playing and touched his arm briefly, and he felt closer to her in that moment than he had to anybody for years.

'That's really beautiful.'

He glanced at her and then away again. 'There are a lot of beautiful things around here. Have you seen Loch Maree in Wester Ross? They say it's the most enchanting of all the Highland lochs. And there's a small, grey stone cottage I know near Kinlochewe that stands at the foot of a great mountain with snow-covered slopes that were veiled in mist

154

and escorted on either side by silver birch trees. It's so staggeringly beautiful that, whenever I see it, it takes my breath away.'

She smiled softly and slipped her hand through his arm. 'You love Scotland, don't you?'

He nodded, and she went on, 'And you love to be alone, don't you?'

Unthank leaned his head into the crook of her arm and gently nuzzled the soft, side of her breast. 'I've never had an alternative, until now,' he said barely audibly. She gazed into the distance, part mother and part lover, and squeezed his head closer.

Kelso clutched the large brown envelope containing both the stolen photographs and his dramatic news story as he clambered up through the snow to the MP's pulpit-like house.

A butler kept him waiting in the porch and then solemnly informed him that Miss Bakersman was indisposed. But Kelso was not in the mood to be put off. 'Is that what she said?' he demanded. 'Or what somebody told you to say?'

At that moment the reporter glimpsed J C Bakersman, an aide and a woman crossing the far end of the hallway, and called round the affronted butler: 'Mr Bakersman. Mr Bakersman, sir! Can I have a minute?'

The group paused and Kelso heard the murmur of their voices. Then the aide appeared at the door. 'Oh, it's you,' he said in a disinterested voice. 'Sorry. Mr Bakersman is terribly busy.'

The door began to swing shut, but Kelso jammed his stone shoe in the gap and prevented it closing farther. 'Tell him I'd just like a word. It's important to me.'

'He doesn't want to talk to you.'

'How do you know?'

The aide appeared exasperated. 'Look, what's it about?'

'I'm told he's got a company helicopter flying in today. Can I get a ride in it, out of here? It's urgent that I return to London.'

'Sorry, friend, it's fully booked.'

The door began to close again, only to swing back when it contacted his extra-thick sole. 'Then will you at least put this letter on board?'

'Sorry. Company regulations.' Cold eyes looked pointedly down at his obstreperous foot until Kelso withdrew it. Then the door clicked shut.

But it was not a wasted visit. As Kelso stood balefully outside, Penny appeared from inside the house with a cardigan draped around her shoulders. She hopped and skipped through the snow to kiss him.

'Miss me, dahlin?'

'Yes, when are you coming back?'

'Not for a little while. You keep out of the way for a teensy-weensy bit longer, then I'll be back draining you of all your strength.' She made an encouraging animal noise at the back of her throat as she slipped seductive hands under his coat and massaged his back.

'What the hell's going on? Everybody's shunning me. If it's body odour, for God's sake tell me and I'll have a bath.'

'Dahlin, calm yourself down. It's simply that Daddy doesn't like newspapermen. He thinks there's something mighty odd about a man who earns his living by telling lies about the people who matter.'

'Lies?'

'Lies, exaggeration . . . what does it matter?' she soothed. 'Just keep out of his way until after the funeral and all.'

He gritted his teeth and remembered the most important matter on his mind: the story. 'All right. But you've got to do something for me, too.'

'What sort of thing?' she asked suspiciously.

He pulled out the envelope. 'I want you to give this to somebody on board the company helicopter. The pilot will do. Tell him you want him to post it Express Delivery in the first city he gets to.'

'Sure,' she said doubtfully. 'What is it?'

'A snow story. Last night was the biggest fall they've had in the Highlands since the kilt was invented. Look, I'm a

156

newspaperman, whatever your father's opinion of me. And that means I have to produce stories in order to keep my job. All right?'

'All right, dahlin.' She stood on tiptoes and kissed him. 'I'll see to it.'

'You will? I love you.'

She was the fifth, or possibly the sixth, girl he had told that he loved that year. Not that he felt any commitment. With his main story on its way, he was ready to pack his case and head back to London just as soon as they sent for him.

TWENTY-ONE

Darkmind left the others on the high ground and cast about for the scent of his mate with increasing desperation. He swept back and forth in a great shelving search, gradually descending the slope on which he last saw her.

Eventually he sniffed the earth and whined eagerly. It was night, but there were traces where she had raked the surface and urinated as a scent-mark. They were comparatively recent.

He raised his thick fur-rich neck and howled. It was a questioning call of exuberance. Higher up the slope, the other wolves stood and turned their heads to listen. But there was no answering call, and they did not interfere.

Darkmind lowered his bulky head, dropped his tail and bounded down the hill. A red squirrel, not fully awake after a winter's hibernation, scrambled for the nearest tree to escape the dark irresistible force that swished past. But he need not have bothered. Darkmind was too intent on his destination to deviate from his course in order to crunch the life out of such easy prey.

The great wolf slowed as he approached the junction of the

two paths, and then sank into the verge while he tried to analyze the muddled odours ahead, in which Whitepatch and man were intermingled.

He peered intently through the darkness, his night eyes watching for any unnatural movement and his delicate ears pricked forward. But, for the moment, he relied mainly on his nose, which made it possible for him to detect a scent in a manner a hundred times more sensitive than man's.

From here on he would stalk – enjoying the primitive pleasure that it gave him as he bellied forward and sniffed the scarred tree. He licked the discoloured snow where blood had dribbled from his mate's incessantly dancing legs. And he whined, understanding at last. It was a tragic and fearful noise.

Later he moved menacingly on towards the farm.

In the kitchen of the silent farmhouse, McDee was aching to go to the lavatory and fervently wished that he had relieved himself earlier. But now he could not afford a moment; he was all set.

The farmer was sitting at the end of a long, bare table facing the door which he had opened to the yard and the night. His shotgun rested in front of him, propped on top of a pile of encyclopaedias, which he had bought by mail-order when Lucy was born, so that she would grow up to be more clever than him. They had hardly ever been opened.

He was drowsy now. He dreamed a curiously happy version of what was to come. He was particularly content that he had a clear view of a post embedded in the middle of the yard with the she-wolf's head impaled upon it.

The head wore a sleepy, enforced grin where the tip of the post skewered through the lower jaw and roof of her mouth.

The yard itself was illuminated by a single electric light bulb which normally lit the porch, but which McDee had now bent on its bracket to shine outwards. He himself was well back in the gloom, his finger curling and uncurling from around the trigger, a heaped box of cartridges at his elbow.

Darkmind stood winter-still in the frost encrusted night, staring into the compound from two hundred yards away. He

158

saw Whitepatch's head, the dried blood around the corners of her mouth, and the hacked fur which came to an abrupt end at the nape.

He detected McDee's heavy sweaty odour too, but it did not stop him coming in at a rush. So swiftly in fact that the farmer was still occupied by his private dreams, unprepared for the moment.

The wolf, who was longer than any man in the Highlands, soared over the four foot yard wall and was leaping forward with incredible ferocity when the first cartridge went off. McDee had come back to reality with a jerk and fired almost instinctively.

Most of the shot bit into the side of the kitchen door, sending up a hissing cloud of plaster dust. But some metal pellets escaped into the open and blasted the she-wolf's decapitated head off its stake, so that it rolled about the ground like an awkward rugby ball.

Darkmind swerved away at the explosion and took a few pellets in the foreleg. For a moment the leg felt as if it had been touched with a hot poker. Then, just as suddenly, the pain was gone and so was he.

McDee got up hurriedly, upsetting the box of cartridges, swearing and bruising himself as he groped blindly for the scattered ammunition without taking his eyes off the kitchen door. At any moment he expected a crazed wolf to crash through at him.

But nothing happened. He built up a desperate little pile of cartridges again, and even had time to swiftly wipe the sticky perspiration from his face with his arm.

A soft thud made him duck and swing the double barrels up at the exposed rafter-and-slate roof. A scrabbling, sliding rush put the matter beyond doubt. The bugger was up above him! He squeezed both triggers, recoiled from the double shot and was engulfed in cordite fumes, as well as a shower of grit and slate chippings.

He broke open the gun and rammed in another cartridge. The second one snagged and he threw it frantically aside, snatching up another.

159

There was a rending crash overhead as the wolf slid down the outside incline, hitting the lamp bracket and shearing it off, leaving the entire farm in darkness. Something heavy thudded to the ground but, in the confusion, McDee could not be sure what.

He crouched there, barely breathing, for a painfully long time. Then inched forward to the doorway which he could only identify by its grey outline. A dim-edged moon gave some light, but the advantage was now almost completely with the wolf, if it was still alive.

McDee grew more courageous with each moment. They had been two good shots and no normal animal would remain immobile through such a din, as well as through the traumatic silence which followed. He reached the opening and peered cautiously through.

The wolf snarled and leapt, his breath sickening McDee with its stench of death and offal. Its carnassial teeth snapped past his ear, tearing the lobe, and clamped into the door post. They jammed deep into the wood, giving the panic-stricken farmer just enough time to slam the door shut.

In the darkness of the room he backed wildly away, crashed over the table, and got up only to lose his balance on the treacherous cylindrical cartridges which still littered the floor. But, laying sobbing on the rush matting, he was at least able to reload and cock.

Inexplicable tears blinded his eyes and his breath came in a stutter. But somehow he fumbled his way back to the chair and managed to realign his shotgun on the jumble of books on the table, which at least gave him height and direction.

He was sure the wolf would not wait long, and he was right. The only error he made was over the direction of attack.

McDee was rigidly intent on the door when the wolf came through the window. The animal hit the glass and wooden dividers at full stretch, taking the impact on his thick skull.

Nearly two hundredweight of prime fighting predator came in with a welter of glass, splinters and displaced putty. McDee was crushed to the far wall, his face distorted. His shoulder broke with a distinct snap and the impact of his head on the plaster was such that it left a two-inch dent in the wall.

Darkmind lunged at the man's neck, shearing through soft flesh with the last premolar and first molar on each side of his mouth. McDee's head fell back under its own weight, leaving it gurgling open at the throat. His knees jerked up in a great spasm and his fingernails clawed desperately at the flagstones. Even after death, he still twitched and tried to get away,

TWENTY-TWO

Kelso was told to be at the school playground by nine o'clock the following morning if he wanted to meet the helicopter. He found the snow had been swept back and strips of orange canvas laid out in a T-shape across the frozen tarmacadam.

There were several people waiting, mostly from J C Bakersman's party, and they kept well clear of the reporter, confining their interest to an occasional glance in his direction.

Kelso walked up and down, shaking his heavy-footed leg which had been tingling and playing him up for some days. He was glad when, at last, a familiar figure arrived and he smiled hugely.

But Unthank had a hostile look on his face. 'You stole my photographs, didn't you?' It was more a statement than a question.

'No, I didn't.'

'You opened my suitcase, rummaged about among my private belongings, and then deliberately took them away.'

'No, I didn't.' Kelso put out his hands to show his sincerity, but they were knocked aside.

'You're a bloody awful liar!'

'I'll tell you what happened, if you'll give me a chance. I

went to your room to speak to you about what we'd seen. You weren't there. I'm a newspaperman . . . remember? I couldn't possibly hold on to a story like that. It's too hot. It was raising blisters on my hands. You understand that, don't you? So, I looked for confirmation. And you, an environmental scientist, were the most likely person to have it. I found it, didn't I?'

'You should have asked me.'

'How? You were with a woman . . . all night, for all I knew. I had to take the law into my own hands.'

'That's no excuse.'

Kelso turned away in disgust. 'For Christ's sake, man. We're talking about public safety and people's lives. You can't play George Washington with this sort of information. Don't you think that families with children have a right to know and protect themselves?'

'That's a matter for the police. Not you. It's a matter of judgement. But that's not the question. The question is, where are my photographs? Because I want them back. Right now.'

Kelso spread his hands. 'Can't help you. By now they'll be in Fleet Street, and probably on the front page next to a story by Martin Kelso. Hang on a few minutes and you'll see for yourself when the helicopter brings some papers in.'

Unthank's grey eyes hardened. 'You don't give a damn for people. You're only interested in your own self-aggrandizement.' He even drew back his fist, but Kelso's quizzical face made it impossible for him to deliver a punch.

'You wouldn't strike a cripple . . . not a big strapping fellow like you.'

'Wouldn't I just.'

But any altercation they might have had was halted by the fluttering beat of a helicopter engine approaching from the south-east. It hung briefly over them, as if impatient to come down out of the frozen blue sky, and then set down in a flurry of agitated snow.

J C Bakersman ducked out under the blurred rotating blades, and spoke briefly to an aide who pointed Kelso out to him. Penny was also helped down from the helicopter. She had been crying again, and the reporter wondered why. But

162

not for long; he was soon fully occupied with a problem of his own.

The short-tempered oil tycoon walked purposefully across and fixed him with an unblinking stare. 'Your name Kelso?'

The engine died away and there was an audible silence.

'That's right.'

Before Kelso had time to react he was lashed painfully across the face with a leather glove. It cut his unprotected mouth and brought stinging tears to his eyes.

Veins pulsed in the American's scrawny neck which was the colour of boiled ham. 'You two-faced son of a bitch,' he hissed, so that nobody else could hear. 'They tell me that, while my son was dying, you were screwing my daughter. Huh? That amused you, did it?'

Kelso shook his head vehemently, and felt the glove lash his face from the other side. He wrenched it from Bakersman's debilitated grasp and flung it far away. Then Kelso clenched his own fist. But the oil man danced in front of him, inviting trouble.

'Hit me. Go on, I'd love you to. Hit me and I'll sue you into the ground. I'll squeeze you like a lemon for every cent you ever made, and then every penny you earn from now until the day you die.'

It was the venom in his voice, not the threat, that stopped Kelso.

The old man, breathing hard, stumped back to a group which now included Sir Marcus Sheerwater, hovering on the fringe. He paused on the downslope to Elphin and called, 'There's something else! Your newspaper said to be sure and tell you: you're fired. Sacked. Out. They've got no place for mendacity. All those lies you wrote about my son . . .'

Kelso turned to Penny for enlightenment and she approached slowly. 'What's he done?' he asked bewilderedly. 'What's the old sod done in Edinburgh?'

She shook her head helplessly and handed him the morning's newspaper. Kelso snatched it eagerly and scanned the front page without finding a mention of the wolves. Then page two, and three. Soon he was ripping over page after page until he was at the back. Nothing!

'I don't get it,' he said hollowly.

'He found out about us. I don't know how. Somebody told him you were screwing the arse off me. Off me . . . his little girl. And on top of Frank's death and all. He had to take it out on somebody, otherwise he'd go off his head.'

'But he said I was sacked.'

'I know, and I'm sorry.'

'He can't do that. He doesn't own the paper.'

'No, but he's an old friend of Lord Danecliff. It was natural when they got your story that they should check with him. He denied it absolutely. Said Frank died in the crash. Said you lied just to make a story. They didn't argue: in fact, Danecliff said you'd done the same rotten thing once before. Why'd you lie, Martin? That was cruel. Awfully cruel. I don't think I can ever forgive you for that.' She said it all in a remote, sad voice and then trailed down the hill after her father. There were tears in her eyes again. 'You malicious bastard,' she said forlornly.

Kelso started to clump after them. Then he stopped and shouted, 'What are you blaming me for? I'm a good reporter. I only write the facts. You can't blame me!' But they were not listening.

He appealed to Unthank who was watching dispassionately from across the swept tarmac. 'You heard him. They didn't even believe what they saw in the photographs . . . Hey, come back. I'm not taking the blame for what's happened here.'

But now no one was listening. No one at all.

He turned and shook his head disbelievingly towards the distant, bristling peak of Stack Polly. It looked like a petrified hedgehog, jutting out incongruously from the low ground on all sides.

Somewhere out there was a wolf pack. Perhaps half a dozen packs by now. Getting bolder and a little closer every day. Christ, with the rest of the country immersed in its own problems and the Highlands cut off on the ground by miles of snow, no one else seemed to see the danger.

'For God's sake, they're out there. Can't you see them? Can't you smell them? What's it going to take for you to wake up?' His voice went hoarse and he was racked with coughing.

As he made his way laboriously back to the guest house, the sun went in. The shadow of a cloud swept across the country-side for mile after mile. From that height it would have been possible to see two hundred grey wolves in Ross-shire. And every day a few more were slipping down from the bare high ground and soulless moorlands to the north.

PART III: THE HUNTERS

TWENTY-THREE

The two Russians were very special, although you might not have guessed it to look at them. The bereft oil tycoon had sent out the word that he wanted the best, most effective wolf hunters in the world . . . and within a few days Bukhanovich and Spassky were on their way from Moscow.

One was neat and would have been handsome . . . but for his dead eyes. When he looked at you, you were immediately aware of the whiteness surrounding his milky pupils. He was a man who betrayed little emotion.

In contrast, his older and subservient companion was baggy and bearlike and wore an amiable smile.

They sat side by side, in silence. It suited them to converse only rarely. One gave instructions and the other patiently carried them out. That was the way it had always been . . . and it worked well.

A military helicopter carried them up over the familiar River Lena, where they were momentarily blinded by the reflection of the winter sun on its silver surface. They flew across the ponderous Verkhoyansk Mountain Range, astride the Arctic Circle, and then on to the city of Verkhoyansk which once recorded the world's lowest temperature: 132 degrees of frost.

Not that the weather bothered the ample Boris Spassky who carried the bags, looked after the dogs and did the cooking. He had always lived close to the Lena, and knew that the general absence of winds made the dry cold bearable and, anyway, there was always the short sweltering Siberian summer to look forward to.

The only part of his life spent away from Siberia was his five years' compulsory service in the Red Army. During this period he became the soldier-servant of Guards Lieutenant Ilya Bukhanovich in an echoing garrison barracks on the outskirts of Moscow, where he watched with some pride his expressionless officer command the elite, high-stepping guard outside Lenin's tomb.

The lieutenant sat beside him now. Apart from the fact that he had long since handed in his uniform, he was the same autocratic, fastidious man whom Spassky had looked after as batman.

As wolf hunters, they earned a bounty for every skin acquired, in addition to a basic salary paid by the Soviet Socialist Republic of Yakutia. It put Bukhanovich in the envious position of having a flat in Moscow to which he retreated twice a year, to bury himself in culture and good living and cast aside all memory of the stomach-straining work of pursuing and killing the Siberian wolf.

Spassky had not yet been privileged to see the second-floor apartment, but he had heard all about the wide marble staircase that led to a front door with the name written inside a small brass frame. *Bukhanovich I.*

He glanced at his companion, whose finely chiselled features gazed down at the slowly-moving forests and rivers: hundreds upon hundreds of miles of virgin land, encased in permafrost as far as the eye could see. But Bukhanovich's cold eyes saw none of it: his mind was far away in Moscow.

As soon as he had received Regional Commissioner Valenko's instructions that they were to report to the Deputy Minister's offices in the Kremlin, he began packing. At least, Spassky began packing while the former lieutenant paced back and forth considering the reason for the summons.

Perhaps their outstanding record of wolf kills was at last going to be officially recognized. And not before time. Possibly an award was contemplated. He relished the thought: Hero of the Soviet Union Ilya Bukhanovich. And with it, an annuity, even at the age of twenty-eight. Not much, but sufficient, when lumped together with his indecently large savings of the past few years, to allow him to return permanently to Moscow.

It still rankled with him that fellow ex-Guards officers slipped nonchalantly into jobs that had been kept waiting for their polished behinds in government departments and overseas embassies. Family connections. Whereas he was obliged to struggle, by his own efforts, into the privileged enclosure which separated him from the elegant echelon of Muscovites.

His father had been a fool; a Belgian architect with revolutionary zeal who turned his back on Brussels and settled in a brand-new steel town in the Urals. He soon found that all the authorities required of his ability was concrete conformity. However, before his ardour burned out it reached a brief, flickering zenith: his courtship and marriage to a ballet dancer, whose good looks and vanity she passed on to their son, Ilya. The highlight of her life was a minor role in an historical spectacle produced at the Moscow Film Academy and, later, as the years aged her, she refused to go out into the street under the illusion that countless cinema-goers would recognize and mob her. Ilya had worshipped his mother and had a contemptuous disregard for his father.

The two fur-clad hunters landed in a corner of the city airfield only to be immediately ushered across to a silver jetliner, bearing a prominent red star, which carried them to Moscow in a rigid discomfort but in a minimum of time.

Nevertheless, as the sun peeped out on the spartan streets of the capital, he strode out ahead of his companion who laboured along with their suitcases, packs and equipment.

He breathed in the smoky atmosphere of Moscow as if sniffing an expensive brandy. Appreciatively. In it, he fancied he could detect the lightly scented fragrance of discerning women and the grand decadence of the opera.

Bukhanovich's pale eyes glinted with pleasure and his zest showed in his walk. He had the neat, disciplined movements of a ballet dancer, which is what his mother had always intended him to be. He also had the physical attributes of a Bolshoi graduate: muscular arms, whipcord calves and a protruding bottom. Shopgirls caught his eye, but he would have none of them. His manservant respected him for that. Ilya – as he described his lieutenant to companions, but never to his face – was a cultivated man. He listened to chamber music even when there was nobody else there.

At an office in the Kremlin, their letter of introduction was examined through gold-rimmed glasses by a chief clerk to the Deputy Minister. The bureaucrat then contemplated the wolf hunter over the top of his spectacles as if to draw some conclusion. But he met with a disconcerting stare.

Bukhanovich was kept waiting in an enormous room with an elaborately decorated ceiling for nearly an hour, before being shown in to see the man who had summoned him so many thousands of miles.

He bowed slightly from the waist, and crossed half an acre of floor with his chin up. 'Comrade Minister.'

'Aah.' A squat, bald man busied forward from behind an enormous desk which rested on a carpet from Tashkent. 'Comrade. Please . . . ' He extended his pudgy hand towards an ornate chair. 'Will you smoke a cigar? No? Good. It's an excellent habit not to get into.'

They small-talked for a while about the journey out from the Lena, which the Deputy Minister professed to have swum one summer when a field commander of pioneer troops. He unbuttoned his jacket and patted a bulging stomach. 'I was as fit in those days as you are. But look at me now. I have trouble just getting out of my bath. Every day, apart from my normal work, I am expected to attend several official receptions, eating and drinking when often I do not feel like it. I tell you, no soldier ever faced an ordeal like that. Believe me, I'd rather be working in the open air thousands of miles from here. I envy you your work.'

Bukhanovich raised his eyebrows. Little did the man know how quickly he too would change places, given the chance.

The stocky administrator looked down at him in the chair. 'You know why you are here?' The wolf hunter shook his head.

'You are here because, in my opinion, you can perform a

most useful service for Russia. You and your man, Spassky. By the way, where is he?'

'He is waiting in the corridor, comrade Deputy Minister. He is used to waiting.'

'Quite so. Umm, you are an educated man. I don't need to explain to you that our country has vast untapped reserves of natural resources. You also know we have experts: scientists, minerologists, engineers who are second to none in the world.' He clenched a fist in mid-air. 'Second to none! And yet, naturally, there are some areas where Western expertise is ahead of ours. As our First Deputy Premier confided in me only last month: if others toil for years on complicated research, untangling equations and carrying out numerous experiments, we will be the first to acknowledge their heroic work as we step across their backs to share in the fruits of their endeavours. And why not? Eh?'

Bukhanovich nodded, although he had little idea where the conversation was leading.

The older man paced to one of the big windows which looked out over the domes and spires of Kremlin architecture. 'For that reason we are anxious . . . no, let us say we are *willing*, to allow certain Western participation in the exploitation of resources. You understand?'

Bukhanovich had no understanding at all. Not an inkling as to why he had been flown thousands of miles simply to listen to a lecture. The Deputy Minister revolved a globe on his desk and stopped it on Russia's eastern seaboard. He pointed at the Sea of Okhotsk, one thousand miles north of Japan. 'See here?'

'Yes, comrade Deputy Minister.'

'We have confirmed substantial oil deposits. Here, here and here, between three and four hundred feet below the surface. Millions of barrels of rich high-quality oil. But . . . and there is always a but . . . the weather there is infuriatingly unpredictable. So we need experts accustomed to the problems we will undoubtedly encounter. Wouldn't you say, in those circumstances, that it is important to get the right people to advise us?'

'Undoubtedly, comrade Deputy Minister. But I don't see...' His voice wavered uncertainly.

The squat figure turned and picked a thin folder off his desk. 'I have here your military record.' He flicked through several typewritten sheets. 'And you know what I see here? Eh? I see myself when young.' He gave a burst of laughter. 'I see a Russian who is loyal and politically reliable. I also see a reputation for discipline. It tells me that one of your men was shot at your request...'

Bukhanovich quickly got to his feet and stared ahead at a stern picture of the Premier on the opposite wall. So that was it! After all these years, they were getting back at him for that snivelling pervert who had constantly provoked his men. The circumstances flooded vividly back to mind. The man was too dainty ever to have been conscripted. He was fully aware of his disturbing influence on the whole company. His mincing little walk brought wolf whistles from an entire regimental parade and, when a lusty corporal grabbed a handful of his pert arse, there was pandemonium. After two weeks' field discipline, the same man became grotesquely drunk on his first night of freedom. When he was brought back to barracks with traces of rouge on his cheeks, he was sick over the lieutenant's calf-length boots. Enraged, Bukhanovich petitioned for a court-martial. The young soldier was shot three days later, after Bukhanovich gave evidence of his 'perpetual disorder and insubordination'.

The details flashed through his mind, as sharp and clear as on the day it happened. He saw the frail soldier slump forward, blindfolded with his arms tied behind a post. And he felt no remorse, no pity. Just a sense of satisfaction.

'I feel I must say, comrade Deputy Minister, that I was in no way...'

'Tcch, tcch, tcch.' A restraining hand cut off the need for an explanation. 'I admire a man who makes up his mind decisively, and sticks to it.' He read quickly through the remaining pages. 'You are, of course, still on the Army reserve.'

'Yes.'

'Good.' A beam accompanied the closing of the file. 'Comrade, I want you to prepare to go abroad. You and your man will leave for Great Britain as swiftly as can be arranged.'

Bukhanovich nodded, but could barely disguise his surprise.

'And now you want to know why, eh?' A beefy arm wrapped around Bukhanovich's shoulders and squeezed him almost off the ground. 'See?' The older man grunted amusedly. 'I haven't lost all my vigour. I was a young bull once. Just like you. So . . . Why are we sending you abroad? you ask. Because you are a wolf hunter. And in the northern part of Great Britain there is an American oil producer who says he has urgent need of a wolf hunter. We, in turn, could make excellent use in the Sea of Okhotsk of two analysis engineers from his North Sea oil fields. So, naturally, we will be happy to oblige.'

'Aah.' Bukhanovich, understanding at last, breathed with relief. It could have been a lot worse. He did not particularly relish working in a land where they probably could not distinguish a wolf from a large fox, but it was a great weight off his mind.

'Good,' said the Deputy Minister rubbing his hands. 'It is a simple enough arrangement, provided of course that they see it from our point of view. Heh?'

The simple enough arragement was delayed for three davs while the two Russians sat restlessly on their suitcases in the lobby of a state hotel waiting for the word to move. Bukhanovich was even refused permission to stay at his own flat.

The fault rested, far away in Scotland, with the severed communications to Elphin. And when J C Bakersman finally learned why Moscow had not responded he almost went berserk.

'Get Derek Westly off O-Oscar,' he ordered. 'I want him and that Frank Dubois, from Piper, on the first available plane to Moscow. I don't give a toss what they're doing. I don't give a damn if you have to bundle them on board in their underwear. Just get them on a plane!'

Two hours after the bewildered engineers landed in Moscow, Bukhanovich and Spassky were on their way in the opposite direction.

The Deputy Minister was so delighted with the arrangement that he went to the airport in his official black limousine, an enormous seven-litre Zil, to see them off. The farewells were interrupted by a breathless messenger from the Kremlin communications room. He handed a note to the Minister's assistant who whispered in his superior's ear.

'This man Spassky. His wife is dying in the sanatorium at Verkhoyansk. She has been ill for some months with pneumonia. But now the doctor says she is much worse. She cannot last more than a few days. Perhaps the man should be told?'

'How old is she?'

'Twenty-four, comrade Deputy Minister.'

'Tcch, tcch.' The Kremlin official shook his head in sympathy and whispered the gist of the message to Bukhanovich.

It was left to the impassive hunter to tell his companion . . . or not. But he simply finished shaking hands and both men climbed the gangway and took their seats. After the doors snapped shut, Bukhanovich passed on the news matter-of-factly. His only concession was, for once, to call Spassky *comrade.*

'Comrade.' The term was so unfamiliar coming from him that Spassky assumed for a moment that he was addressing somebody else. Then he leaned forward attentively.

'I have just heard that, today, your wife died in hospital. It is official. The Deputy Minister expressed his regrets. That itself is a great honour.'

'Umm?' The numbed words did not sink in for a while. 'Valentina?'

'Yes, her.'

Spassky tried to stand up but was restrained by his seat belt. He slumped back and stared out at the grass that flattened itself at the edge of the runway as they gathered speed.

'It can't be so.'

'I'm afraid it is.'

Tears welled into his eyes. 'Are you sure?'

'It's not the sort of thing they make mistakes about.'

Spassky said remotely, 'It was her birthday yesterday. I sent some spring flowers from the airport. Blue and yellow, her favourite colours. I hope she got them.'

Bukhanovich, who had never met his companion's wife and had never particularly wanted to, allowed himself a rare gesture of sympathy. He patted the man's limp hand, then closed his eyes restfully as the big airliner nosed up into the brittle blue sky and headed due west.

He could have managed without Spassky. But to do so would have meant abandoning a measure of comfort and cooked food, and that alone justified his decision. He had no misgivings. He was only concerned with getting on with the job.

Together they were astute and pitiless hunters. There was no breed of wolf that could match their ability as a team. At least, none they had come across. So far.

TWENTY-FOUR

Richard Unthank could not get her out of his mind. He went to sleep thinking about her, and probably dreamed about her too; he could not be sure after a muddled constantly turning night. But first thing in the morning, she immediately filled his consciousness again.

The love became an ache which only eased when they were together.

Consequently he was reluctant that evening, when he trudged along to her cottage for supper, to tell her that she would have to leave Elphin.

175

There was a rumour at the guest house that wolves had been seen roaming through Elphin at night. He told Mrs Galbraith hotly that it was rubbish. Just the same, the danger was growing and he somehow had to get Emma out.

The front door creaked open on reluctant, snow-stiffened hinges. She kissed him hungrily on the mouth, and tasted so fresh and wholesome that he came close to changing his mind. How would he exist without her until the spring?

Later, stretched out together on the sofa and touching the length of their bodies as they half-roasted in front of the fire, he said quietly and without preparing her: 'I want you to move out of here. Tomorrow.'

Her classical face was half in the shadows, but he could see the silhouette of her angled cheek bones as she turned, amused at the idea. Her long slim fingers undid another shirt button and slid down and around to the small of his back. He arched forward into her jersey, nestling against her soft, loose breasts.

'That's the nicest proposition I've ever had,' she whispered.

He began to move rhythmically, pressing her backwards into the upholstery, while his tongue explored her ear. 'It's not a proposition.'

Her eyebrows rose in good humour. 'Isn't it? You mean, you're ordering me to move in with you? I'm not sure that's practical. Shouldn't it be the other way round: you moving in with me?'

He stopped moving. 'Emma, I want you to leave Elphin and go back to Inverness. Or, better still, London.'

She sat up abruptly. 'What now? Just when things are getting interesting?'

'This is a dangerous place to be. I mean it. Mrs Galbraith claims that wolf tracks have been seen in the early morning along the main road, past your house. That means they're not far away during the daytime either. Might be watching us now.'

'Are the other women and children leaving?'

'What other women and children?'

'From the crofts and cottages. And what about the old people?'

'I don't know. It's not my responsibility. I imagine not. Nobody ever listens until it's almost too late. But there will be little help from outside. The country's already got its hands full dealing with the epidemic of pneumonia. London must be coughing and spitting all over the place.'

'There! And that's the place you want me to go? No thanks. I might as well open all the windows and catch my death of cold right here. At least I'd die in familiar surroundings.'

He moved away from her to avoid being influenced by her seductive fingers. 'Look, I know these animals. They're not hampered by this weather. It simply makes them stronger in relation to us. It wasn't so many years ago that their kind ruled this entire hemisphere. They've killed somebody already, and they'll do it again. They're almost impossible to catch in these conditions and you don't see them coming until it's too late. I've a terrible feeling that a lot of people here are going to get hurt. I can't be sure. But I do know that I don't want you to be among them.'

She softened at his reasoning. 'Why?'

He was lost in her neverending eyes. 'Because . . . Because I love you,' he said so shyly that she could hardly hear.

She held him around the neck, staring into his eyes wonderingly. On and on.

There was a crash on the door. A rat-tat-tat on the iron knocker which echoed through the house and jarred them back to reality.

Kelso stood on the front step, with two days' growth of stubble on his chin. A besotted smile died on his face as he saw Unthank also standing in the doorway.

Emma's face lit up. 'Hello, Martin. Come in and get warm by the fire. How lovely to see you.'

'Thankyouverymuch,' he slurred, raising his foot several inches too high in order to clear the doorstep and jarring it down inside. 'I came to see how you are, Emma darling.'

'How nice of you. Come and have a drink.'

She slipped a hand under his arm and helped him into the snuggery. Unthank followed sourly and the journalist looked over his shoulder in mock concern. 'Not interrupting you, am I, old man? I mean, nothing going on, was there?'

'Nothing of interest to you.'

Kelso flopped back into the sofa and slipped off his boots and socks. Unthank wrinkled his nose and fanned the air. 'Oh my God. Do you have to?'

The journalist hiccupped. 'Very necessary,' he said gravely. 'Have to massage them vigorous . . . vigorous . . . have to massage them to prevent frostbite.'

'Really,' said the scientist flatly.

'Yesh. I read it somewhere.'

Emma reappeared carrying a tray with cups of coffee and biscuits. Kelso looked glum. 'I don't like coffee,' he said dejectedly.

'Well, what *do* you like?' Unthank asked aggressively. Then a breath of alcohol made him withdraw the question. 'On second thoughts, don't tell me. I can guess.'

'Don't think I'm ungrateful.' Kelso addressed himself to Emma. 'But I didn't come here to socialize. I just want to say that I've made up my mind not to give in. Not to leave. I've got a feeling that there could be an enormous story right here in Elphin, and all I've got to do is sit tight. Nobody can sack me from here.' He directed a finger at his chest and succeeded in missing by several inches. 'I'm . . . I'm the only experienced journalist here, and I wanted you to know that, because you're the only two people who are even speaking to me at the moment.'

'Wrong,' Unthank interrupted. 'I'm not speaking to you either.'

The journalist drank his coffee noisily and dribbled some down his shirt which, as it happened, was also coffee-coloured. He sighed and set down the cup. 'Sorry I burst in. I just needed somebody to talk to.'

Emma smiled encouragingly. 'You come along whenever you like.'

'But not after tomorrow,' interjected Unthank. 'She won't be here.'

'Oh?'

178

'She's leaving for Inverness as soon as we get four wheels out of here.'

Emma shook her head. 'Oh no I'm not.'

They forgot Kelso, who was sitting between them with his head turning from one to the other like a tennis spectator. 'I told you: it's not going to be safe here. Christ, it's not safe now, only nobody else has realized it yet.'

'I'm not going.'

Unthank fixed her with his grey eyes. 'I love you,' he said adamantly.

She stared back, equally resolute. 'And I love you.'

Kelso glanced from one to the other and shrugged.

She gritted her teeth. 'But I'm not going. That's an end to it.'

Kelso sighed, as if that was that. 'We're staying,' he said to himself. 'That's final.'

Unthank had never met such an obstinate woman, and yet he had a disturbing feeling that he had barely scratched the surface of her resolve. 'If a wolf comes for you there's practically nothing I can do. If he goes for your throat – and they do, you know – you're dead. I'm not saying that to frighten. That's the way it is.'

Kelso pulled a face at the thought and gulped. 'Well, *she's* staying. But I'm still open to persuasion.'

Emma closed the curtains. In doing so, she glanced at the darkening hillside and wondered if there really was anything out there. Watching her. She shuddered, but it did nothing to alter her resolve. She drew the curtains irrevocably.

If you want to find a wolf pack, look for ravens. The Russians knew it and, no doubt, there is an old Soviet proverb on the subject. But the Russians had not yet arrived, and Emma Dancer had put aside her misgivings as she locked the house next day and scrunched into the village. She paid no heed to a low-winged raven which flapped heavily across the crest of a hill a quarter of a mile away.

Darkmind stood motionless between the trees, watching

179

until she vanished among the houses. Behind him the rest of the pack lolled, unconcerned at man's proximity because of their leader's calm.

He blinked. The sun glistened on his damp fur and pleased him, but he still felt a dull ache for Whitepatch which would not go away.

Times were better for the pack now. They knew where to get meat. It was there, on the edges of the village, for the killing. He glanced around. Even at rest, the pack looked majestic. Four other lean, intent animals in the prime of life.

There was Bent-Ear, the next strongest to himself in the hierarchy, who followed and obeyed unquestioningly. Long-runner, who had the stamina to outlast any quarry which might initially outstrip their pursuit. Hollowbelly, who was wily and snappy, and now their only remaining she-wolf. And Rabbit, the least aggressive of the pack who was always at the centre of their play.

It had been a month since another female, Brokenfang, died on an icy day when the sea wind was at its most bitter. Half-starved, she ventured too close to a cliff edge in search of gulls' eggs near Stoer, after a night on the stark Assynt Hills had left her joints stiff with rheumatism. She slithered beyond recall and somersaulted out of sight.

Darkmind stirred uncomfortably and turned back to face the weak sunshine. Life was bearable again.

There were a dozen big black ravens, some of which flapped to within twenty yards of the pack and, soon, Rabbit bounded delightedly among them in a time-honoured game.

The unwieldy birds have an age-old affinity to wolves. They regularly picked over any remains of the pack's meals, and prised open droppings as a matter of course.

One pecked at Rabbit's paws, while the wolf lay with his ears pricked forward. The predator jerked away and ran in an excited arc, before lowering itself again and moving stealthily back up to the waiting bird.

As soon as Rabbit was within striking distance, the raven fluttered into the air and landed with a great palaver a short

180

distance away. And from there they started the game all over again.

The other wolves watched with sleepy good humour, particularly as the cumbersome ravens squawked whenever they felt Rabbit was flagging.

Darkmind sniffed the breeze and stretched his back legs out, preparing for action after several hours in the same spot. He yowled discordantly, trying out his voice and bringing the others to their feet without haste.

He moved off, skirting the village, and the other predators ambled loosely after him. They appeared to be both undisciplined and uncoordinated. But appearances can be deceptive.

TWENTY-FIVE

The memorial hall was packed. It might have been freezing outside but men stood up and stripped off their jackets in the humid atmosphere and cigarette smoke drifted in layers under the exposed rafters.

Sir Marcus had never seen so many people in the little hall before. They were crammed on to every available seat and bench, standing down both sides and at the back.

He knew practically everybody by name, and was aware of their pride and the hardship they endured as a matter of course. It was their Highlands. Theirs and his, and nobody was going to separate them from it.

He glanced at his notes, putting on his glasses for a minute or two. He would have to tell them that London could not help at this stage, and probably not Edinburgh either. Almost every part of the country was fighting off a health and weather crisis of its own. But he also knew that the news would not dismay the Highlanders. If they had a problem, they would solve it themselves.

As MP and a senior church elder, Sir Marcus occupied the central chair behind a trestle table on the stage. Tacked up behind him was a sight that stirred all who saw it. A white diagonal cross on a blue field: the flag of the Cross of St Andrew.

Sitting either side of him, looking down across their restless, expectant audience were three other elders: a woman magistrate who had once been a steely-eyed force to be reckoned with but now, with a weak heart, was reduced to a waxen smile; the Rev. Pilbeam who was blowing thoughtfully on his steepled fingers and a ruddy-faced fish merchant from Kylestrome, who flushed with embarrassment whenever called upon to speak in public.

They left the running to Sir Marcus.

He banged the gavel and the hubbub subdued. Ninety pair of eyes focussed on him. He, in turn, regarded them grave-faced. His eyes travelled slowly along the front row, then the second and third rows, nodding as if satisfied with what he saw. He loved an audience; he knew how to stir and to sway a mass meeting. He knew how to use silence to its best effect and he could rise to the big occasion with commanding Churchillian eloquence. But it was not something that came naturally. He practised the resonance of his words, as well as his posture, in front of a bedroom mirror several times a week. And was all the more effective for it.

Some said he was blatantly two-faced. Pretending to be a Highlander when he was among them, but spending most of his time in Kensington where he lived when the House was in session. But none could doubt, seeing him now, that he was the man of the moment and that he fully intended to grasp it.

'Ladies and gentlemen,' he began. 'Friends. We are met here today because a shadow has been cast over our community. I know, understand and share your fears. Several of you have been to see me privately, disturbed at recent occurrences. And, indeed, you were right to do so. What I hope we can decide upon today is a course of action. Action that will speedily bring about a return to normality for us all.

'You all know of the abrupt and harsh arrival of winter

182

which caused the red deer to move down from the high ground. Tens of thousands of them have now moved on again, southwards. But, out there!' He extended a dramatic arm at the high side-windows, causing dozens of faces to turn in that direction. 'Out there . . . are lurking an undetermined number of other, more sinister, intruders. Creatures who, unless they are stopped, won't hesitate to cut down your sheep and cattle. Indeed, we fear they may have been responsible for the deaths of at least two men and a little girl. And, unless we act swiftly and ruthlessly, others of us could be in the utmost danger.'

Donald Bane, the father of nine children who divided his time between farming and fishing at Lochinver, raised his brawny arm. 'What are the police doing about it?'

Sergeant Dunceford leaned forward from his seat on the edge of the stage, for Sheerwater's permission to respond. He got it. 'We're doing all we can, which is mainly to keep a close eye on the situation and give fair warning if anything seems likely to happen. But what can two men do? We don't even know precisely what we're up against.'

Bane rose and flicked the straggly hair away from his eyes. 'Get help, that's what you can do. Get a message to Edinburgh and let's have a company of sharpshooters from the Black Watch up here at the double.'

'Aye, aye!' The cry was taken up enthusiastically, and somebody called: 'Make it the Gordons.'

Sir Marcus got quickly to his feet. 'All right, all right. But I must tell you I've already sent messages to the War Office, to the Prime Minister's Office and to the Officer Commanding the 5th Highland Division. But nothing can move in this weather. You know, as well as I do, that we're virtually cut off. And even if we weren't, I suspect nobody would arrive to lend a hand. The emergency services are at full stretch in every major town throughout Britain. We've got an influenza epidemic, old people dying in their hundreds of frostbite and exposure and goodness knows what else. Donald . . . whatever we decide to do, we're going to have to do it ourselves.'

A woman with a flushed face and a shawl around her plump shoulders rose. 'Please, sir. What the devil are we talking about? Is it right what some people are saying: that there are wolves hereabouts? And what sort of wolves are they? Big ones, wee ones? What?'

Somebody else called out: 'They're no friends of the Campbells, I'll tell you that, Maggie!'

'They're not alone in that!' retorted the woman.

There was a roar of laughter, and Sir Marcus returned to his feet. 'Mrs Campbell. I want you to see for yourself.'

A deep silence descended on the hall as the MP beckoned to one side of the stage flanked by worn green velvet curtains. Richard Unthank stepped into view.

'Mr Unthank is an animal expert employed by the Government and he's here to advise and help us.'

Unthank gave a little bow of acknowledgement. He noticed Kelso and Emma sitting together in the front row, the journalist scribbling in a notebook on his knee. Behind them was a sea of expectant faces. He gripped the heavy curtains and drew them completely back.

There was a concerted gasp from the audience and more than one woman screamed.

Standing on a broad plinth was the snarling, crouching figure of a wolf. Two rows of savage teeth were bared at whoever met his gaze.

More than one man had brought his shotgun into the hall, and the creature was so realistic that several hands tightened on barrels and stocks. But none was raised, for the animal had been transfixed in its final act of defiance for at least fifty years: unmoving since the day its snarl was set in position by a taxidermist.

Unthanks sensed their terror and rapped its black nose firmly with his knuckles. There was an immediate sigh of relief and tensed shoulders relaxed.

James Alistair MacDonald, who many years before had emigrated to Canada for a time, got halfway to his feet. He was wizened but as alert as he'd ever been.

'God almighty! That's a timber wolf. I've seen his like before. Are you saying some of those creatures are prowling about here? If that's what carried off the McDee girl, you'd better tell us straight, Marcus. They don't come any worse.'

Others jumped to their feet and Sheerwater had to quell an uproar. 'Just a moment, gentlemen! Let Mr Unthank explain. Give him a chance, please.'

When Unthank spoke there was a tremor in his voice, but he overcame his nervousness as he became immersed in the subject.

'This . . . ' He crossed in front of the crouching wolf ' . . . is *Canis Lupus*. He's been in the cellar of this hall, I'm told, since before most of us were born. Gathering dust. Even in his day, this particular specimen never walked free. Not in Scotland, he didn't. *Canis Lupus* is a much older adversary than that. But he is a creature you should be well aware of, if you're intent on staying here.'

There was a murmur from the hall, and Bane called to Sir Marcus Sheerwater: 'What's the Englishman mean by that? If we stay here? Course, we're bloody well staying here.'

Sheerwater glanced over his spectacles. 'Mr Unthank, kindly confine yourself to a description of the wolf. We'll consider what action to take later.'

Unthank nodded wryly. He exchanged a glance with Emma who looked unusually pale and tense. 'The grey wolf, or call him what you like, has not roamed the Highlands for two or three centuries. But when he did, he reigned supreme. For thousands of years he was a fearsome killer, and no other animal of these climates could match him either in ferocity or intelligence. He slaughtered at will.'

There was an uneasy stir in the hall and more than one woman held her child closer and wished they had stayed at home.

Sheerwater forced a smile. 'There's no need to be melodramatic, Mr Unthank. There are some minors in the hall.'

'There's nothing theatrical, sir, either about what I'm saying or the animal itself. I'd rather everyone heard the worst now, than find out to their cost later.'

Sir Marcus was beginning to perspire. 'All right, if you must.'

'He's a dangerous and vicious adversary. But he's not

185

invincible, as man found out when he wanted this land for himself two-and-a-half centuries ago. There seemed to be no way that man and wolf could live in harmony. So, the wolf packs were surrounded. They were smoked from their dens. They were destroyed with cudgels, claymores and rocks. Pits were dug to impale them, and Parliament put a bounty on their heads. And they died out, our ancestors believed, for all time.'

Sir Marcus quickly took over while he had the chance.

'My friends, we have marshalled together a great many facts and drawn some conclusions. Frankly the prospect is grim. Yet I don't intend to hold back anything from you. You have a right to know. But anybody who feels nervous and who wants to leave the hall, should do so now.'

Nobody stirred, although more than one person glanced apprehensively at his neighbour.

A dour, thickset man named Angus McNab, who had spent his life splitting and hauling blocks of granite, called bluntly: 'Get on with it, man. We're not squeamish.'

Sir Marcus cleared his throat and turned to a marked page in his notes. 'Lucy McDee. Vanished two weeks ago after her father swears he was surrounded and cut off by wolves. One of them got into their house and dragged her out, screaming, in his jaws. Sergeant!'

Dunceford got up heavily, also consulting a notebook. 'The girl, or her body, have not yet been found. We have no independent verification of her parents' story, but blood smears were found in the bedroom and down the stairs.'

Sir Marcus resumed, after the sergeant took a step backwards and lowered himself judiciously to his chair.

'A week later, a motor cycle was found in the hills just a mile or two from here with signs of human remains nearby. Sergeant.'

Dunceford returned to his feet, licking a finger and turning a page. 'Clothing identified as belonging to one Franklin Bakersman, an American visitor, was discovered by me and Acting Constable Shaftoe next to a motorcycle. Also some bone fragments and . . . ' he cleared his throat and glanced at

186

the rows of white faces without seeing them ' . . . small severed portions of human anatomy.'

Sir Marcus continued in a restrained voice and without apparent emotion, apart from a movement of his tongue around dry lips. 'Yesterday the body of James McDee was found at his home . . . ' He glanced at the police sergeant who responded by getting up once again.

'Sir. I examined the body at seventeen-hundred hours and found it to be decapitated.' A cold seemed to trouble Dunceford, and he extracted a large white handkerchief and coughed into it several times. 'The severed head was later found several hundred yards from the farm, bearing teeth marks but sufficiently preserved to be identified as that of Mr McDee. Thank you.' He closed his notebook and sat down with an air of finality.

Sir Marcus dabbed his forehead and spoke to his fellow elders about how warm it was getting in the limited space of the hall. Someone hurried off to open the windows.

'Mr Unthank. May we hear what you have to say, please?'

Richard Unthank stood up, relieved to see that although most people looked pale they were accepting the situation sensibly enough.

'Mr Chairman, I've been out surveying high ground to the north and west of the village for the past three days and believe I have identified the pack which has established a hunting run in this vicinity. There are five wolves, one of them an obvious leader. They seem to be in prime condition, fast-moving, alert and extremely dangerous. We will have trouble running them down.'

The woman magistrate raised a perpendicular finger. 'Mr Unthank. How big are these creatures?'

Unthank turned to the snarling petrified model. 'About the size of this specimen. He's an average fully-grown male, weighing about a hundred pounds. None of this pack is smaller, but the leader himself is considerably larger.'

'How much bigger?'

He moistened his lips and glanced at Sir Marcus. 'I'd say

187

nearly two hundred pounds . . . about *twice* the size of this one.'

The hall erupted. 'Jesus wept! What was that he said? Bugger me!' Gasps of astonishment quickly turned to anger.

'Why didn't the police do something about this sooner?'

'What the dickens have you been doing for the past two weeks?'

'What about our children? Are they in danger? Are there any plans to evacuate them?'

Sir Marcus was on his feet, ringing a brass handbell borrowed from the schoolhouse. 'Please, please. Don't let the meeting get out of hand. We need unity, not recriminations.' He had to shout to make himself heard. He had a favourite pledge which he was determined to get out. 'I can assure you all that a full and painstaking inquiry will be held into the circumstances. But, for the moment, the overriding question is how do we rid ourselves of this scourge?'

'Shoot the buggers!' A young man with a woollen hat on the back of his head waved a shotgun. He was from a fish-packing factory on the coast, to the west, and his hands were white and wrinkled from continually pickling herrings.

'Aye. There's enough of us to blast them to furry shreds.'

Sheerwater nodded with satisfaction. As a former staff officer, he approved of the idea of a voluntary hunting party. 'Could we have a show of hands from all able-bodied men willing to take part in an organized hunt?'

Some forty hands shot up.

'Would you take their names please, Sergeant?' The MP bent to consult his fellow elders, who shook their heads in turn. 'I don't propose to hold you here any longer than is necessary, ladies and gentlemen. It seems to me that the time for talking is over and the moment for action has dawned. Sergeant Dunceford will lead the hunt and be answerable directly to me. They will start operating tomorrow morning. Any of you who have specialized knowledge – such as Mr Unthank – or any of you with weapons which you wish to contribute should report to Station House. It remains only for me, on behalf of you all, to express our deepest sympathy to Mrs McDee and to Mr J C Bakersman for the personal loss they have suffered. Beyond that I remind you all that, come what may, this is the Highlands. In the coming days you will need to summon all your courage and fortitude. But Highlanders have been bloodied before, and they always come through unbowed!'

There was a burst of applause and people began getting to their feet ready to disperse.

'It . . . it just remains for me to say,' said the MP, draining the last drop of emotion from the meeting, 'good luck and God be with you all.'

TWENTY-SIX

Sir Marcus was right. The Highlanders struck back with a vengeance and three wolves were dead within twenty-four hours. Yet his hopes were unrealized. The wolves were from a quite different pack to Darkmind's and newly arrived from the debilitating north coast.

They reacted tiredly and without much cohesion. The hunting party's first enthusiastic barrage, which would have won a small battle in any part of the world, bowled over the startled pack. The lead wolf was reduced to bloody tatters and only one of the three managed to zig-zag away.

Sergeant Dunceford could hardly believe his luck. He left Shaftoe to guard the remains while he led a pell-mell pursuit. His mistake was in reacting too quickly, instead of first awaiting the return of Richard Unthank who was out reconnoitering.

The wounded wolf headed back towards the land he knew best, the bare moorland of the Reay Forest twenty-five miles to the north, dying as he limped, blood dribbling from his sagging black muzzle.

He made good time at first, loping through the dusk and leaving the pursuing Scotsmen well behind. But after first light the gap narrowed by the hour, and at midday Dunceford himself was the first to reach the exhausted, almost-lifeless body.

He finished it with a shot behind the ear, posed for photographs and then had a leisurely meal. They returned without haste and had to spend the night under canvas before rejoining Shaftoe and Unthank.

It was a day lost. A vital day for Elphin.

Unthank was restless. When the main party had not returned to the camp, he tried talking to Acting Constable Shaftoe, who was in theoretical command. But all the big policeman could do was shrug helplessly and rearrange the pelts which he had deprived of their carcasses.

'Better wait till the Sergeant gets back,' he repeated several times, scanning the horizon. His was not to reason why.

Unthank knew the dead wolves were not even remotely connected with the pack threatening Elphin. But the kill was none the less commendable, since half a dozen wolf families could be hunting that stretch of the west coast and all were potentially dangerous. Even so, he felt gnawing misgivings that the hunting party was turning its back on the village for too long.

There were too many men involved in the hunt for it to be really effective. Thirty individuals merely slowed one another down. But for all that, they were Scots and there are few better men to have alongside you in adversity.

The Sots are a dour, masculine, bloody-minded race. And Donald Bane, who went with Unthank ahead of the main party, was as abrasive as you would expect of a man who was conceived on a windswept hillside in a downpour of rain. Yet, in a tight spot, you could wish for nobody better to guard your back.

'Where in tarnation is that policeman?' asked Unthank, as darkness crept down across the moorland.

190

Bane caught his mood of restlessness. 'The man's a Sassenach . . . a typical wet, bloody Englishman. What do you expect?'

The scientist grunted. 'I'm the Englishman, Donald. He was born and bred here.'

'I know that, but he's still more of a Southerner than you are. Prancing about like a wee girl, licking everybody's boots. It turns a man's stomach.'

'At least he's out here with us. And not sitting on his arse like one or two others I could name.'

Bane, who was so short and broad that he seemed almost square at times, produced a flat half-bottle of whisky and gulped a mouthful. Then he wiped it on his sleeve and pushed it gruffly towards the younger man.

'Not for me.'

'Go on!'

The admonition in his voice made Unthank reconsider. He tipped the bottle and the spirit reached his stomach with all the paralyzing force of boiling water on frozen stones. He turned away, coughing excruciatingly, and only Bane's sharp reflex action prevented the bottle from dropping to the ground.

Unthank wiped the tears from his eyes. 'I'm sorry. It went down the wrong way.'

'That's all right.' Bane was pleased that this man from the South was seen to be fallible. It helped to reinforce his conviction that Caledonians were the only really durable men in Britain.

The next morning he went with Bane on another series of diagonal sweeps, trying to pick up the tracks of the wolf. But newly fallen snow buried any signs that might have helped them.

Eventually Dunceford and his elated group appeared over the rise and dumped the last of the pelts on a sheepishly grinning Shaftoe. 'Add that to the pile, Bobby. You'll soon have enough for a coat down to your ankles.'

Sergeant Dunceford thumped down his pack, accepted a

cup of steaming cocoa and glanced at Unthank. 'Well, what do you think of that, mister?'

Unthank turned over the remaining blood-darkened pelt and nodded. 'Quite a lad, this one. Weighed over a hundred pounds.'

'Aye.' Dunceford drank a rewarding draught of hot chocolate. 'Led us quite a chase, too.'

'You shouldn't have followed him.'

'Uuh?'

'He would have died anyway.'

'How can you say that? I thought you were supposed to be an animal expert. Isn't there a rule about finishing off what you start?'

'We haven't got time for rules. The fact is, this isn't the pack we were looking for. The big one we want could be anywhere by now. Even back at the village.'

Dunceford was not particularly put out. 'Look, I don't know what you're griping about. A wolf is a wolf is a wolf. One dead today is another one less to hunt tomorrow. Isn't that so?'

'Sure. But the Elphin pack is already blooded. They've tasted humans. So, we ought to be moving on pretty soon.'

Dunceford yawned and rubbed the small of his back. 'I've just finished chasing across half the mountains in Scotland. I've been up to my neck in drenching snow. I'm bruised all over and I've done the four-minute mile every half hour for the last two days. I'd have thought that entitled me to put my poor old feet up for a minute or two, wouldn't you?'

Unthank glanced at his wristwatch. 'All right, you have your breather. But I'll start back to Elphin and take Bobby Shaftoe and Donald Bane with me. All right? I'll feel a lot easier when I know what's happening.'

'Or isn't happening,' said the police sergeant sarcastically. 'Okay, off you go. The rest of us will be back in our own time with the skins.' He wagged a cautionary finger. 'Mind you, don't let this thing get out of proportion. If the people want to make heroes out of us for shooting a few wolves, tell them to put off any celebrations until the whole job's done.'

Unthank could not stop himself smiling. 'Don't worry, I'll tell them.'

Dunceford stared at him for a while then said exasperatedly: 'Well, get on with it. What are you grinning at?'

'Nothing. It's just that I've never been this close to a hero before.'

By nine o'clock in the morning Unthank was on his way back. But it was already too late.

The wolves came down from the high ground, through the thin trees and across a road which lay flat on its back paralysed by the cold. They followed Darkmind at a lope, spread over a front of nearly forty yards.

As they quickened their pace, their feet splayed out and left tracks which were unmistakably wolf. No longer could they be confused with stray pets, even though most unaccompanied dogs had been eaten days before.

The headmistress at the village school, Miss Amanda Haggerston, was sixty and had deferred her retirement for several years. Some said she was too old to cope with lively children, but she loved the job and there was no obvious successor.

She spent a few minutes looking for the handbell before recalling that it had been borrowed for an evening meeting in the memorial hall. She glanced at her watch and tut-tutted. Two minutes past nine. It was unlike her to be late calling assembly.

Standing out in the playground, awaiting the clanging summons, were a scattering of children. It was Amy McDee's first day back at school since losing her sister. Her mother was still in shock and she was staying with an aunt. She had arrived a few minutes earlier, pale-faced and more timid than usual, but she knew the headmistress would look after her.

Miss Haggerston was a kind woman with that additional toughness of character which most teachers acquire in the company of irrepressible children. The school building was Victorian and ought to have been replaced years before, and

13   193

the same applied to its caretaker, Bernard McQueen. He shuffled along the corridor with his arms folded across his chest and his hands tucked under his armpits. Bernard enjoyed grumbling about the everlasting cold.

'Isn't it bitter again, Miss Haggerston?'

'No worse than usual, Bernard,' she said briskly, determined not to give in to his remorseless pessimism.

'Do you know what the temperature is? Twenty below.'

'Well, that's not bad, Bernard. It's not even freezing point.'

The caretaker lifted his thick, almost impenetrable glasses to peer at the wall thermometer and blew on the mercury. 'There must be something wrong with this thing. It's been stuck on that mark for days. I'd swear it's a lot colder.'

She laid a hand quietly on his shoulder. 'If you look into my room after assembly, you'll find a pot of tea. You're welcome to a cup.'

There was a small, high scream from outside, but neither paid any attention to it. The playground was a breeding place for over-excitement.

Outside, the lead wolf slowed to a walk and prowled around the three-foot railings. Most of the children were the width of a wide stretch of tarmacadam from it, waiting their turn to run at a frozen patch under the classroom windows.

Amy did not feel like enjoying herself in the jostle. Instead she meandered alone to the far side of the playground where the dwarf wall was topped with black railings.

The wolf was excited by the sweaty pleasure of the children, despite the clamour they made. By the time he thrust his grey muzzle through the wrought iron perimeter, he had singled out his victim for the kill.

Shock took Amy by the throat. She saw the wedge-shaped face staring at her and for a moment or two she was literally struck dumb with terror. Here were her nightmares of the past week coming true. Then her thin, piercing scream was heard. It wavered on longer and was pitched higher than a normal playground sound.

Miss Haggerston paused outside her room and stiffened.

When she stepped outside she found the other children quietening into an uncanny silence.

The wolf tried to force himself forward through the ironwork. It snorted at the approach of another human, jerked up its head and displayed its teeth. Miss Haggerston tried not to run. She heard her voice issuing firm but low-pitched instructions. 'Go inside, children. Right away. Don't run, but don't dawdle. Shut the doors after you.'

She dared not take her eyes off the monstrous creature that was staring balefully through the low railings. She could hear a low rumbling coming from deep in its throat. Grizzled hair and merciless yellow eyes. Wolf. But it couldn't be! She walked quietly and determinedly towards it.

She stared rigidly at the creature, not daring to glance aside at Amy McDee for fear the animal would somehow be released to do its worst.

'Amy, take hold of my hand, please.' She stretched out a taut arm to where the girl was transfixed. 'Take it, Amy! There's a good girl!' The strain was apparent in her voice.

Darkmind drew back on his haunches and snarled. This unexpectedly direct approach puzzled him. There was no danger in it to him, and yet apparently the perpetrator saw no risk to herself either.

The angle was too steep for him to clear the railings. He wriggled back a few feet.

'Amy dear, we're going to walk back to the school now. Not run . . . walk. Are you ready?'

They were obliged to turn their backs on the wolf. The frail headmistress and the terrified leaf of a girl. But together they covered ten yards resolutely. Fifteen yards. They could see a line of white anxious faces peering out at them from behind the thick classroom windows.

Darkmind only just cleared the blunt ornamental speartips which scraped his underbelly and sensitive genitals in passing. The pain shocked all other thoughts from his mind and he landed badly.

The faces at the window showed Miss Haggerston, from their sudden change of expression, that the bluff was over, and she dragged Amy into her protective arms as she turned. But the wolf was shaking himself hugely and licking his private parts.

They had no more than a moment or two of respite, and she took it. Her old-fashioned shoes hurried frantically across the tarmac, propelling Amy before her. The only person in the building who could possibly help now came rushing out in the opposite direction.

Emma Dancer had been in the hall, arranging simple typed notes on a small archaeological display she had set up for the children. She heard the commotion, went to the main doors and took in the horrifying situation.

There was a half-bucket of sand and a stirrup pump beside the doors, waiting patiently for a fire. The red bucket had never before been lifted in an emergency, and it was desperately heavy. She tipped out half of the sand, and swung the rest through the doors.

Amy's matchstick legs took her into the safety of the corridor. Miss Haggerston sprawled over her and slid into the wall with a reassuring thud. Only Emma was outside now and the remaining sand sprayed out in an arc through the air.

Darkmind flicked his head away as the stinging grit caught his eyes. It was just enough to make him veer away while his intended victim vanished from sight.

He glanced back at the pack, scrabbling over the railings. Emma's mouth opened in disbelief at the new onrush of ferocious creatures from thirty yards away. She half-fell, half-flung herself back at the doors and crashed inside.

Small hands slammed them shut and the bewildered caretaker, who could still not see more than a blurred outline of predators, dragged a heavy desk behind the doors to prevent them being opened unexpectedly.

Someone was screaming, Emma was sobbing for breath . . . and Miss Haggerston who had dislocated her elbow in falling against the wall somehow managed to smile. 'All children,' she said in a wavering but reassuring voice, 'go back into the hall and shut the doors tight. We'll have this little upset sorted out in no time.'

When Unthank and the two other men arrived they found Elphin unusually quiet and deserted. They moved along the main street, glancing anxiously from house to house. Occasionally a curtain twitched but no one appeared outside.

'What's going on?' growled Donald Bane. It was his idea, as the father of nine, that they first check at the school.

Unthank banged on locked doors. There was no response for a while and then a quavering voice called: 'Who is it?'

'Richard Unthank.' He glanced at Shaftoe who had finally caught up. ' . . . and the police.'

They could hear furniture being dragged away from behind the doors which cautiously opened. Then Emma waded through some excited children, fell against him in relief and hugged him around the chest. 'We thought you'd never get back.'

Unthank was being observed by more than two dozen relieved faces, but that did not stop him kissing her.

'They were here. The wolves. They tried to break in. It was terrible.'

'Anybody hurt?'

'Miss Haggerston has broken her arm, I think.' She shuddered and peered around his protective arm. 'Have they gone?'

Shaftoe returned from a quick survey around the edge of the building. 'Nothing there now, miss.'

'Thank God for that. We'll have to get the children escorted home.'

'Don't worry, we'll take care of it. Don't worry about anything. It's over now.'

But as Unthank glanced at the distant hills, blurred by mist, he knew all too well that it was not over. It was only just beginning.

TWENTY-SEVEN

All MPs were urged by the party Whips to return to London. The Government had a crisis on its hands. In the Commons the Prime Minister, the Rt Hon James Beaconsfield, was holding off yet another Opposition attack. Alone and faintly aloof, he gave the impression of a dignified stag at bay.

Three million tons of coal were paralyzed in transit. Tens of thousands of men and women were put on short time at work. And still the snow continued to fall.

'I have given coal absolute priority on our frozen railways,' the Premier boomed, 'and the Trades Union Council has promised to do whatever is needed to get railway wagons rolling again.'

But Opposition MPs, and a growing number of government rebels who themselves had spent hours in garage queues for little more than a dribble of petrol, joined in the chant. 'Too little, too late. Too little, too late. Resign, resign!'

The Speaker banged for order but could not be heard at first. In his determination to restore calm, he moved so vigorously that a hot-water bottle, secreted behind his back, slid out and hit the floor with a flop which temporarily restored good-humour.

But it could not last, and the Prime Minister knew well enough that action was required. He called another emergency Cabinet meeting.

When the news reached Sir Marcus Sheerwater over the radio at Elphin, he asked to use Bakersman's helicopter. He was intent both on getting to London to support the Premier, and asking for troops to be released into the Highlands.

The elderly, sharp-eyed American was extremely accommodating. 'Sure, Marcus. You take whatever you want, and keep it on stand-by for when you come back.'

Sheerwater poured a whisky down his throat and smiled through permanently scarlet cheeks. 'Good of you. But I expected no less. Knew I could count on you in the circumstances.'

The American poured the MP another drink. 'This will help keep the chill out until you reach Westminster. There you are.'

'Thank you indeed.'

'And what will you tell them, Marcus, about our spot of bother up here?'

'Well, for a start I'll make it damned clear that we need immediate help from a sizeable contingent of troops. At least one battalion. My God, I was aghast . . . absolutely aghast when I heard about the school incident.'

The little American walked slowly around the elegantly furnished library, nodding. 'Of course you were. And I know just how you felt.' He tapped his chest. 'Gets you here, doesn't it? Right here where it hurts. After all, I had a son myself, didn't I? There's nothing anyone can do to change what's happened. But at least, on this occasion, no one was hurt.'

The statesman regarded the American millionaire sympathetically. 'Anything I can do for you in London?'

Bakersman looked out at the drifting white snowflakes. They were a lot less remorseless now and seemed to be falling only casually. He swung around, as if the thought had only just occurred to him. 'Sure. There are a couple of things you can do.'

'Well?'

'First, in all sincerity, I know you'll do your honest best for this country. I have a soft spot for Britain. A lot of us have, you know, deep down. I guess you just lost your way a little as a nation in the last ten or twenty years. But Britain has a habit of producing men like you, Marcus, just when it needs them – in times of stress. Men who aren't afraid to grasp a handful of nettles. Men you can rely on. You may not rate my opinion very highly, but I'd like you to know that I've always held you in high esteem. I make no secret of the fact. Britain could do a lot worse than make you her next Oil Minister.'

Sheerwater was quite taken aback. Here was one of the leading independent oil producers in the world, apparently taking a personal interest in his future. An interest which could weigh heavily with a Prime Minister anxious to wrest as much oil from under the North Sea as possible during the remainder of his term of office.

'I'm delighted to hear it. If it ever crossed the PM's mind to offer me the chance, I'd think about it very seriously.'

Bakersman raised his glass, which he had barely touched up to now. But this was an occasion worth breaking his abstinence. 'Here's to your future, Marcus. May it be a bright, high-octane one. I think it will, and I'm not often wrong.'

Sheerwater's haughty face beamed with pleasure as he glanced at his watch and then collected his briefcase and documents. 'We'll meet again soon.' He extended a hand. 'My dear friend.'

Bakersman took it in his own determined grasp and did not let go until he got home his real point.

'My other suggestion, Marcus, is that you put off that request for troops.'

'No soldiers? Why?'

'I simply want you to think about it for a few days without doing anything precipitate.'

'But you know the urgency of the matter. I couldn't think of delaying it.'

'Yes. I know your reasons, but now hear mine. I've got some Russians coming. Just two men. But they're very special. They hunt wolves. And I want you . . . my old and dear friend, to let me have this chance to avenge my only son. I want the wolves that killed my boy. I want to know, absolutely, that they're dead. I want . . . ' He wiped his eyes. 'I want their goddamned balls.'

The oil man still did not let go of the MP's reluctant hand.

'Sorry,' he said, blinking away a tear, 'I get overwrought at times. What I want to say is that the Russian Government has allowed me the use of its finest wolf hunters, and I don't want any flat-footed soldiers trampling tracks and scaring that pack off. They're not going to get away with it that easily.'

Sheerwater finally extracted his hand, and patted the air appeasingly. 'I know how you must feel, especially after losing your son. But surely you see that the more guns we have at our disposal, the quicker this thing will be over?'

'That's not the way it would turn out, Marcus. You've got an odd way of treating animals in this country. If this matter becomes public, some of your Southern biscuit-dipping pet-lovers are going to insist that these wolves are captured alive. Then the next thing you'll know, they'll be in zoos and living the life of Riley. I can't allow that, Marcus. I can't allow anyone to contemplate it.'

'I wouldn't let that happen.'

'You wouldn't be asked.'

Sheerwater stared into the American's unwavering eyes for several seconds. 'All right. You've got three days. I'll concentrate on other things. But if your people haven't been successful by then, the troops come in. A whole regiment if necessary.'

'It's a deal. My two guests will be here by tonight.'

The MP discovered it was not that easy to keep his promise

When he reached London, with Big Ben in darkness and the frozen stars shining over the city with a harsh brilliance, he found the population wrapped up in its own problems. They did not want to know how Scotland was, or wasn't, faring. But Sir Marcus faced a predicament.

It came in the petite shape of Sue McKenna, a television programme presenter, who arrived by arrangement at the St Stephen's entrance of the elegantly-spired Parliament buildings. She walked past a security check and into the circular Central Lobby, which is between the House of Commons and

201

the House of Lords. After enquiring at a reception desk, she sat on one of the green leather benches until Sir Marcus appeared.

She stood up. 'Hello, Sir Marcus. Sue McKenna, Independent Television World Tonight programme. Nice of you to see me.'

'Always pleased to talk to the press and television. Especially someone as attractive as you.'

He escorted her attentively downstairs to the small oak-panelled Strangers' Bar, whose long narrow windows looked out on to a snow-covered terrace, beyond which flowed the Thames.

It wasn't difficult to be flattering. She was in her mid-twenties, short, dark-haired and with a brisk manner. No fool, this one. Her figure drew attention in the mainly male preserve and Sir Marcus found himself on the surreptitious end of one or two sly winks.

They had a couple of gins and eventually she stayed to lunch, apparently charmed into it by his persistent requests. But, in fact, that was what she had intended all along. That and much more.

They went into the Members' Dining Room, the lofty walls of which were hung with historic pictures of parliamentarians. Sir Marcus, who had a normal sexual appetite but little to feed it, found himself aroused by her. She did things in a subtly physical way. Touched his hand lightly when she spoke, showed the tip of her tongue when she told a double entendre. She even had a provocative way of eating a steak, and he found himself fidgeting and clearing his throat loudly on more than one occasion when she caught him observing her.

She sipped the claret, moistened her lips and smiled at him warmly. 'I'm here for two reasons, Sir Marcus.'

He waved in mock offence. 'Marcus ... please.' He patted her hand and noticed that the fingernails were painted the same absorbing shade of pink as her lips.

'All right ... Marcus.'

She moved her legs for comfort and brushed his calf. 'First, to ask you to appear on the programme tonight. Ten minutes live on North Sea oil reserves and the contribution Scotland can make towards getting Britain back on her feet. And then perhaps a word on the growing opinion that you could be in line for the Oil Ministry.'

'All right. I'd be happy to oblige. And the other matter you wanted to raise, Miss McKenna?'

'Sue.'

He devoured her with his eyes. 'Sue.'

'I believe a former colleague of mine has been working in your part of the country. Martin Kelso? And it's raised a question in my mind.'

'Kelso? Err, I do believe there is a person . . . a journalist staying at Elphin for a day or two. In fact we had a chat the other day.'

She soothed him with another smile. 'How is the limping wonder?'

'Fine, fine.'

She slipped out of her little suede jacket, without getting up, and Sheerwater found himself confronted by two well-formed breasts which moved, and caught the edge of his attention, as she talked animatedly. She was not pushing herself particularly; she just happened to be the sort of woman who excited him.

'How are people up there managing in the circumstances?'

Sheerwater's eyes narrowed. Attractive or not, she was a journalist. 'What circumstances?'

'Well, the present crisis.'

The wine waiter reappeared and Sheerwater put a hand over his glass, something he rarely did in more relaxed moments. 'What present crisis?' he asked blandly.

She pointed out at the grey sky and the fuzzy snow floating endlessly down. 'That,' she said, faintly puzzled.

'Oh, that!' Sheerwater relaxed. 'Sorry, the bad weather's become almost a way of life. I don't think about it specifically any more. Now, what was it you wanted me to do for you?'

She grew serious. 'It's about Martin Kelso. He's landed in awful trouble with his paper. They've threatened to sack him over a couple of stories he filed. At least, that's the rumour I heard.'

Sheerwater nodded. 'I know. His proprietor, Danecliff . . .' He nodded towards the House of Lords. ' . . . seems convinced he was making up news. People will put up with a lot, but there is a limit.'

She nodded him along and gazed into his eyes. Sheerwater loved it and topped up her wine glass. 'And did he make up that story?'

He spilled some claret on to the white tablecloth and stained it a weak mauve colour. 'What?'

'The story about the wolves threatening villages like yours in Scotland.'

'Wolves?' He made the word sound preposterous.

She suddenly took off the pressure, relaxed and dabbed the damp tablecloth with her napkin. 'I thought it was far-fetched.'

'Yes, I err . . . ' He coughed into his hand, and then waved to a familiar figure passing between the crowded tables of the dining room. 'Choose your dessert, m'dear. I'll be back in just a moment. Must have a word with Hugh Leckenby. He's just been given the Foreign Office.'

When Sheerwater returned a few minutes later she talked about anything but the Highlands and their troubles. And it was he who raised the matter again while they were sipping coffee.

'Know Kelso well, d'you?'

'Quite well. We shared a flat near St Paul's for the best part of a year.'

'Oh?'

'He's the reason I left my husband. He's an ambitious bastard, but don't be fooled by his suave manner. He could charm a nightingale into his hand, then feed it to his cat if the whim took him. Of course, when my husband got a decree, Kelso decided he'd had enough. He's too dedicated to himself, and to getting on, ever to settle down.'

Sheerwater smiled sympathetically. 'I know the sort.'

'But he does have one or two attributes. He's good company

and he's an excellent journalist. Doesn't usually make mistakes.'

Suddenly they were right back to the point. The MP could avoid her steady gaze only by looking at his watch. 'I have to go soon, my dear. I hate to leave, but there's some important business coming up in the House.'

She considered his haughty looks, which the years had etched into a permanently disdainful expression, and a body which had given up the battle against over-eating. Not the most appetizing of men, but she had known worse.

'I'd like to talk to you again later, Marcus.' It was not the earnest way she looked at him, but rather the shoeless foot which purred up and down his leg which made him agree.

He swallowed awkwardly. 'I'm busy most of this afternoon.'

'Do you have a flat?'

'Yes, a few rooms I use while I'm in London. Nothing elaborate.'

'I'd like to call on you after the programme tonight.' She spoke quietly and allowed the words to soak in like an expensive liqueur.

He was circumspect. 'May I ask why?'

'I think we can help each other. You've got something I want . . . and I've got something you want. Haven't I? I'm sure we could come to a rather pleasant arrangement. No harm in talking it over, anyway.'

His hand slid under the crisp tablecloth and closed over her firm knee. They understood one another. For the moment.

The young ginger-haired nurse, who doubled as cook and part-time receptionist at the infirmary, was surprised to see Kelso appear through the double doors. There were still hours to go before official visiting time, and even then they rarely saw complete strangers.

She was not part of the general ward, but looked after two

205

or three smaller and more secluded rooms. 'You're not allowed in here,' she blushed.

The journalist hooked a thumb at the doors. 'I was told it would be all right.' He had few scruples where a story was concerned. 'I've come to see Mr Inkerman.'

'I'm sorry, that's not possible.'

'Why not?'

'He's in isolation.'

'I know.' He fumbled in his pockets. 'Do you smoke, dear?'

'No.'

'Sensible.' He sighed and gave up the search. 'Tell me, how is he?'

She glanced along the empty corridor, uncertain how to answer. 'I couldn't say.'

'I expect he's feverish, but I'm sure you made him comfortable.' He leaned casually on the reception counter and smiled reassuringly. 'Has he had the tests yet?'

She was very young with freckles high up on her cheeks. 'I believe so.'

'Don't you know?'

'Well, yes he has.'

'Good. What were they for?'

She looked around nervously, reminding him of a small cornered animal. 'To find out whatever's wrong with him, I suppose.'

She pressed the flat of her hand on an electric bell and kept it there. A distant door opened and closed, and brisk feminine steps approached. When Penny Bakersman appeared round the corner, Kelso was as surprised as she was.

'Good Lord. What are you doing here?'

The influential American's daughter plucked at her hospital-white overjacket. 'As you see, I'm helping out.'

'You? What do you know about hospitals?'

'I'm a Registered Nurse and when I heard they needed help here, I volunteered. I trained at the Northwest Texas, in Potter County, Amarillo.'

'But you didn't need a career.'

'So what? I was serious enough at the time.

206

'All right, don't get shirty.' He drew her aside, out of hearing of the ginger nurse. 'Look, Penny, you can help me. I have to see Cecil Inkerman.'

'It's not possible. He's a patient in isolation. You shouldn't have got even this far.'

'Listen, I wouldn't ask a favour if it wasn't important. Only we're old friends. Cecil and I grew up together.'

'No you didn't,' she said flatly.

'What do you mean?'

'You didn't grow up together. I've seen his admission card. He was raised abroad. You probably never got beyond the Elephant and Castle.'

He drew her even farther away from the inquisitive eyes of the other girl. 'Look, let's be honest with each other. He's got rabies, hasn't he?'

She tugged her arm free of his grip. She was open-mouthed with astonishment. 'No, he hasn't. Let go of me. What are you trying to do?'

'All right, so he hasn't got rabies. But he was attacked by a wolf, wasn't he? Otherwise, why check for rabies?'

'Martin,' she sighed. 'I'm in a privileged position here. If I told you everything that went on, I'd be betraying a confidence.'

His eyes narrowed and he held her at arm's length. 'Everybody knows what's going on but nobody wants me to publish it. Your father, the MP, the police, Dick Unthank . . . and now you.'

She shook her head sadly. 'There's nothing I can do.'

'But I simply want to talk to Cecil Inkerman for five minutes.'

'He's in isolation. It's a precautionary measure. Why not wait a day or two until he comes out?'

'I can't wait,' he said with increasing anger. 'I've got a deadline.'

'And I can't let you through,' she said pale-faced.

His eyes glinted. 'All right. I'll get what I want some other way.'

207

TWENTY-EIGHT

'Be quiet please.'

That same evening, in a brightly-lit London television studio, a sensitive young man in a canary yellow roll-necked jumper and green velvet jacket fanned his hands for silence. The ceiling was festooned with spotlights and most of them seemed to be focussed upon the member of Parliament's face, which was sweating again despite diligent powdering by the makeup girl.

It was so hot.

He forced a flattering smile in anticipation of the interview to come. Five million viewers, they had assured him. That must include several members of the Cabinet and a scattering of peers at the very least. It was not far off peak-viewing time either; undoubtedly his chance to make an impression with people who mattered.

He could see his face now, on a monitor screen, as well as a single-line caption *Sir Marcus Sheerwater, MP, Secretary of State for Scotland*. This was it. He gave his all to the camera with a small red light winking on top; the look that showed him to be a man of resolve and compassion.

For the next few moments the face of the interviewer Sue McKenna occupied the screen, giving him the opportunity to observe her from his seat diagonally opposite. A jet black trouser suit flattered her already prominent figure. It was tight enough for him to wonder if it left room for her to wear anything underneath.

The thought did nothing to cool him down.

She turned to address him. 'Sir Marcus, you had talks with the Prime Minister earlier today on the prospects of a bold expansion of Britain's North Sea oilfields. Is that not so?'

The MP touched his spotted bow tie and gave a tolerant

208

smile. He was a master of timing and presentation and was not to be hurried. He also had a superbly modulated voice.

'It would be wrong for me to betray a confidence by disclosing the precise nature of our conversations at Number Ten,' he said, giving the incorrect impression that he had visited Downing Street on more than one occasion. He leaned forward addressing the viewers directly. 'But they are of the utmost relevance to Britain's economic recovery from this disastrous winter and indeed, ultimately, could affect the standard of living of us all.'

A green velvet arm signalled to the control box, and the picture on the monitor changed to an aerial view of a North Sea rig with a pre-recorded commentary about the increasing annual flow of oil and gas into Britain.

Sue McKenna leaned across, out of camera, and touched him lightly on the forearm. 'You're doing fine. Anything you need?'

'Not at the moment,' he whispered. 'Although that may change later.'

'I hope so.' Her eyes lit up, as if she was looking forward to the night. But then mild deceit came naturally to her; she buttered up celebrities every day as a matter of course. How else would she get them to co-operate in all sorts of improbable situations? Of course, many were egotists and needed little encouragement. But some were honest and nervous and needed reassurance, and if it wasn't for them she would have given up long ago.

The producer began fanning his fingers at them. Ten, reducing to nine, eight, seven, six ...

'Tell me, Sir Marcus, is it not a fact that you have already held detailed discussions with a leading American oil company, which is showing interest in investing millions of dollars in developing new fields off the coast of Scotland?'

Sir Marcus raised his eyebrows in surprise, so that nobody would suspect that he himself was the interviewer's only source of information. 'It is indeed. As a matter of fact, a leading oil magnate is staying at my home on the Highlands this very weekend. And what I hope we can do, is to open up fresh layers of oil wealth for Britain. In some cases these layers are lying right underneath apparently spent-out wells. British technology and American resources could well unlock a whole new treasure chest for this country.'

'You make it sound attractive. But have we got the right key to open it?'

'I think so. Finance is the key. And I'm telling no secrets when I say to you that several oil finance groups have already approached me privately to express interest in investing substantially in British waters – providing they get two absolute assurances. One is that Scotland and the Scottish people agree wholeheartedly to co-operate. And the other is that we retain a stable government. In other words, they are willing to make available huge sums of money if we show ourselves to be one hundred per cent dependable. And that means having the sort of leaders on whom they, and the British people, can rely.'

'What sort of men have they in mind?'

Sir Marcus let them wait, until the studio was hanging on every word, for fear he had dried up. He leaned forward. 'Men of integrity and old-fashioned honesty. Men who keep their word and won't renege on agreements.'

'People like yourself, Sir Marcus?'

The MP pretended not to have heard. 'I beg your pardon?'

'Someone like yourself, Sir Marcus, for the vacancy of Oil Minister?'

Sheerwater laughed modestly. 'Dear me, no. My concern is for Britain; that we develop our natural resources to the best possible advantage. But I also think it's high time that this country got back to the old traditions of integrity and ability in high places. And, as a first step, appointing Ministers of State who know what they are talking about. Quite simply it means having an Oil Minister who understands the needs of the nation in terms of fuel requirements, as well as maintaining the environment, and who can keep a proper balance between the two. A man who is not afraid to get crude on his hands and can talk to the oilmen and riggers in their own language. Whether or not I'll be involved, is not for me to say.

That's a decision for people to make in another place.'

He caught Sue McKenna's eye for a split-second. No fool that one, he thought. *You'll have to watch her.* Then he quickly directed his mind back to the subject of oil.

'But I will say this: that our future prosperity undoubtedly rests on the vast reservoirs of oil and gas which are still lying untapped under our northern waters. Not Scottish, Irish or Welsh, but *British* waters. And what we need now, and indeed what we must insist upon as a complete nation, is a determination to forge ahead and make the enormous benefits available to us all.'

Sheerwater sat back and there was a spontaneous burst of applause from the studio staff. The camera even caught the interviewer nodding her agreement.

The green velvet arm twirled and Miss McKenna said: 'Thank you, Sir Marcus Sheerwater, MP.'

Later he returned to his flat opposite the sprawling Department of the Environment buildings in Marsham Street and found two messages awaiting him.

He tucked his pigskin gloves under his chin and slit open the envelopes. 'Go in, dear. Pour yourself a drink.'

Miss McKenna stretched her arms above her head and it was all he could do to prevent himself reaching for her.

One was a note from his wife, asking when he intended to return to Elphin and suggesting he pick up two tins of caviare from Fortnums. The other was terse: from Sergeant Dunceford asking him respectfully to make contact. The sergeant, who had sweat trickling down the bridge of his nose when he sent the message, had not clearly reflected his anxiety. An obscenity would have helped. Sheerwater crumpled up both notes.

Miss McKenna, conscious of his greedy eyes, rubbed her leg. 'I bruised myself getting out of the car.'

'Oh dear. Let me have a look.'

'All right.' She didn't need a great deal of encouragement. She unzipped the bell-bottom trousers and stepped out of them. She had gorgeous legs and his eyes followed them up to the hem of her short jacket. She wore flimsy pants, cut between the curve of her splendid buttocks. There wasn't much he could not see or make out.

He laid a trembling hand on her thigh. 'Is that better?'

'Much.' She murmured in his ear and let her body rest against his. 'I wanted to ask for your co-operation. I read Kelso's story about the wolves running amok.'

'I thought Danecliff tore it up.'

'He did. But Kelso's a suspicious bugger and he made sure I got a copy. He knows I wouldn't cross the road to help him if he fell under a bus. But he also knows *that I know* how good he is.'

He stroked the curve of her thigh and almost choked with excitement as she shifted her frontal weight against him. 'But it's not true,' he protested.

'I'm sure it isn't . . . in every respect.' She undid some buttons and tickled him lightly. He had never felt so reckless. 'But the main facts are correct, aren't they? Why deny it? You're only putting off the inevitable.'

'Darling,' he moaned. He widened his stance to savour the urgent little movements of her body. 'Dearest . . . Suppose some of what he wrote is true, you must understand that this isn't necessarily the right moment to disclose it. There is the public's safety to consider. I can't have thousands of people thrown into a panic because of the hasty actions of one irresponsible journalist.'

She kissed his nose. 'Right, Marcus. What you need is to stage-manage the whole thing. A news story like this is too volatile to let slip out haphazardly. First get it under control, then tell the people.'

He was surprised at her reasoning. 'Exactly!'

'Then why not work closely with me, Marcus? I can have a TV crew standing by for whenever you give the word. We can get up to the Highlands in ten hours and film you as well as the climax of the hunt.'

He explored the small of her back and pushed her panties down over the curve of her buttocks with both hands. 'Sounds very possible,' he laboured.

212

She held him off slightly. 'But only on the understanding that I handle the story exclusively.'

'Exclusively?'

'That's it. All you have to do is keep me closely in touch with the situation, and I'll film as and when the opportunity arises. It will show you as a man of action. You *are* a man of action, aren't you?'

He nodded eagerly.

She quickly took off her jacket and brassiere. The size of her naked breasts took him by surprise. 'Let's get on with it then,' she said coolly.

The barrel-chested Russian, Boris Spassky, stood up to his knees in snow and felt sorry for his hunting companion. Not that one normally felt sorry for former Red Army officers; they were well able to look after themselves.

He was in the grounds of the big house, encouraging their two wolfhounds to plunge about and find their land legs again.

He glanced through the full-length windows as often as he could without appearing conspicuous, and for the first time in his life did not envy Bukhanovich.

The fiery American, JC Bakersman, was gesticulating furiously as he paced back and forth. His words were lost behind the double-glazing, but he occasionally waved his arms to emphasize a point. The milky-eyed Russian stood white-faced and took it; he had little choice.

Spassky could only guess what it was all about. They had arrived in the little village overnight and had hardly had time to sort out their jumble of luggage before the oil man imperiously summoned them.

Perhaps it was because of the interminable delays at Moscow and London airports. Or perhaps he was making clear to Bukhanovich why he wanted so badly to avenge himself on the wolves. Either way he need not have bothered, thought Spassky. They didn't care. They had been ordered to clear away the wolves, and that they would do with clinical objectivity. Or as clinical as you can be against a cunning and aggressive foe.

He had no love for his companion, but he resented anyone who humiliated Bukhanovich. It was a slight to them both.

The Russian support man knelt in the snow and gently rubbed the forelegs of his two lovely ladies: for that was how he thought of the hirsute bitches who were so affectionate to their handler but so deadly in the chase. They were Irish wolfhounds, bigger than any other breed he had seen and twice as scruffy, but he would not change them for a hatful of roubles.

They took his mind off his wife . . . who was dead. He drew a great shuddering breath and shut his mind to the thought.

As the dogs wandered off, Spassky observed their movements through diagonal eyes which revealed his own mixed Mongolian ancestry.

Yacka and Elena had long doleful faces and were chest-high to an average man. Their big lean bodies were covered in grey wiry hair which gave them an endearing elderly appearance.

Occasionally one of them stumbled and Spassky watched anxiously, like a father observing his offspring's attempts to totter. It was obvious to him that they had not yet recovered from the journey. Another night's sleep should see them back to normal.

Why the dogs had not been incarcerated under Britain's strict quarantine regulations, he did not know. Perhaps it indicated the depth of influence that the abrasive little American possessed.

When the former lieutenant emerged from the house, his face pale with anger, Spassky knew it would be wise not to get too close. But he had to talk about the dogs' condition.

'The ladies haven't found their feet yet,' he said in Russian. 'But I think by tomorrow they will be back to normal.'

'We haven't got until tomorrow,' snapped Bukhanovich.

'Huh?'

'Call them in.'

Spassky stopped, bewildered, but put two fingers in his mouth and let out a piercing whistle. The big dogs plunged back into view, falling drunkenly and scrambling up again in their enthusiasm.

The man with the curious eyes examined them. Opened their yawning mouths, peered at their tongues and into their pupils; felt under their heaving bellies. Finally he swore and turned away. 'See that they are rested. We start without them.'

Boris Spassky puffed out his cheeks. In such unfamiliar territory they needed the dogs badly. Without them, the search would be twice as arduous and there would be no ground-covering sweeps which ranged far ahead and back along either flank.

'Can't we wait another twenty-four hours?'

Bukhanovich jerked his head contemptuously towards the house. 'That little madman wants us to kill a pack that have been breathing down his neck. He thinks he is back in Chicago, ordering hamburgers. Five, he said.' The Russian thrust out his glove and extended the stubby fingers. ' "Bring them back here to me, straight away!" he said. His thoughts are twisted like poison-ivy around a tree and it affects his judgement. I think the wolves must have done terrible things to his son.'

Spassky sighed. 'Tomorrow would have been better. How often have you said: preparation is the half-sister of success.'

The leader turned his dead eyes on the house. 'I am beginning to regret that we ever came.'

The second Russian trudged away with the dogs, to bed them down and get the guns. As he passed close to the tall white house, the little American came out on to the porch, glaring as if to indicate that they should get on with it.

Spassky waved in passing and called out in Russian. 'Hello there. A fine day.'

Bakersman grunted, but it was his only concession. 'Just get on with it, fella.'

'Old men,' said Spassky with a smile that belied his words.

215

'Old men are the same the world over. With all your experience of life you're supposed to be wise and kind. But every one of you turns out to be crusty.'

He went off singing a sad little song, but a glance back at the morose figure of Bukhanovich disturbed him. It could be dangerous for the Russian marksman to go off at half-cock. People could get hurt that way.

TWENTY-NINE

Unthank tried to remain calm. He had never seen Emma so edgy before and it disturbed him. The incident at the school, when she escaped from the snarling predator only by a matter of inches, had left her badly shaken.

He heated up some beef soup and submerged several chunks of toast into it, but she barely ate any. 'I don't feel like it,' she whispered. 'Think I've got a chill.'

He offered to walk to the infirmary, less than a mile away, and get a sedative but she would not hear of it. She clutched his arm and he realized that the fear of the wolf attack still filled her mind.

She clung to him, would not let go even long enough for him to boil a kettle. He wedged some logs on the fire with one hand and settled down with her on a sofa, tucking a soft Shetland blue rug across their legs.

It was snug and the flames threw flickering shadows along the walls of her cottage. Before long her eyelids drooped and the hands of the grandfather clock in the corner moved steadily towards midnight.

Unthank lolled back uncomfortably as the woman's head rested against his slowly moving chest. And so they slept through the dark hours that preceded the grey dawn.

The Highland mountains are deceptive: so broad and morose that their height seems diminished, but still they touch the clouds.

In the bleak half-light of the new day, Darkmind and his pack crossed the flank of Cul Mor two miles from the small community and gazed down on the humans they knew to be there, resting in silence.

They had trouble getting down from the hills. The snow was deceptively deep and they moved in single-file, travelling in a series of continual leaps like dolphins plunging through a frozen sea.

Eventually they encircled the house with windows which reflected the embers of a dying wood fire. Darkmind even cautiously nudged the back door with his moist black nose, but it was firmly secured top and bottom by horizontal bolts and he turned away.

The others circled restlessly, or sat on the road.

Darkmind knew he had to draw out his prey. Until the victim was aware of him, it had no cause either to move or panic. He sat back on his haunches thirty yards from the house and tipped back his head.

A wolf's howl is eerie at the best of times, and four in the morning is not the best of times. His lonely call wavered across the icy sheep-flats, over the meandering burn and the rigid heaps of cut peat by the side of the deserted road, and touched each of a dozen homes with fingers of fear.

Those who heard but were half-asleep, later presumed it to have been part of a shadowy nightmare. But Unthank, whose head rolled slightly at the noise, making him even more uncomfortable, came to with a start.

The melancholy notes overlapped one another as he moved Emma's limp weight aside and quickly crossed in his socks to the nearest window.

He could not see anything clearly. The shadow of the night and wisps of freezing mist blurred an impression, even though he used the curtains to rub away condensation from the window panes.

A low dark shadow moved away. Wolf! Followed by

another two unhurried shapes. They seemed to be looking intently in his direction.

A ripple of fear ran through his body and for a while he was paralyzed. His eyes strained for some sort of confirmation, but now there was nothing in sight other than deceptive rocks, and shrouded gorse bushes which moved slowly in the restless wind that blew down from Cul Mor and across the treeless slopes of the Drumrunie Forest.

Unthank quickly looked around at Emma who was sleeping as deeply as ever. He had to do something. They were here! He was almost certain of it! But what were they up to?

Jesus Christ. He carried his fleece-lined boots out to the little hall and closed the lounge door gently behind him. Sitting on the narrow wooden stairs, he tugged them on and broke a fingernail in the process.

He shook the sleep from his head and quickly dressed. Then took up his shotgun, checked that he had a pocketful of cartridges and creaked out on to the porch.

A narrow beam from his rubber-sheathed torch stretched for thirty yards. It stabbed across the road and dissected the grey half-light. Almost immediately, he picked up a reflection from green eyes. They blinked, and he had the impression of bared teeth before an indistinct form moved away with slow deliberation.

He counted the shapes that followed. One, two, three, four. *Jesus, Jesus,* he repeated to himself as he nibbled at the finger with the snagged nail. They wouldn't hurt him, he kept telling himself. He knew them too well for that. *Just don't startle or provoke them.*

He cocked his gun and moved out into the middle of the smooth stretch of snow that covered the road. Nothing could get at him there without giving him at least three seconds to shoot.

He kept quite still, hardly daring to breathe, and listened to the wind sighing down from the invisible mountains. By now, no other sound disturbed the night air. The wolf that had howled was gone . . . but three sets of prints led away into the gloom. Luring him on. Unthank glanced undecidedly back at

218

the house, where Emma lay sleeping. Somebody else could be savaged before the dawn, torn agonizingly, if he didn't give the alarm. He tucked his numb chin down into the front of his overjacket and hurried after the unseen pack.

Light streaks appeared down the flanks of dark hills, gradually lifting the mask of night. Even so, a lone grèy wolf coming down from Cul Mor was difficult to distinguish from the litter of boulders shrouded with tired moss and black lichen. Particularly if it moved only occasionally and, for the most part, stood almost motionless, allowing only its spiky tail to twitch in anticipation.

Slack-Jaw was as awake as he would ever be after napping fitfully in a damp limestone cave, and now he followed the scent of the hunting pack.

Saliva dangled from his long tongue and, when one of his hind legs jerked in a spasm, his drooping head turned aggressively on the offending limb.

Emma's house lay directly in his path. He, too, saw the glowing embers of the fire and, lacking the caution of sounder minds, stood up on his hind legs and raked the window.

The slither and scratching roused Emma from under her blankets. She half-turned and fell off the edge of the settee on to the floor. The impact jarred her wide awake in a single terrified moment.

Outside, the rheumatic wolf again clawed the slippery glass, turned his great face sideways and tried to bite it. In vain. But as Emma rose up in an erupting mound of blankets and dishevelled hair, they saw one another in frightening outline.

Emma's heart stopped beating for an instant, and Slack-Jaw drew back slavering and snarling.

'Oh, my God!' There was a jagged instant of awareness. Then a thought struck her with panicky force: supposing the door was on the latch! She turned frantically to get out to the hall, terrified of what she might find. But she was hampered by an uncooperative blanket wrapped tightly around her legs. Slack-Jaw followed her movements along the outside wall and hurled himself at the front door the instant he heard the bolts snick one way, then the other, as she checked their position. His considerable weight crashed full-tilt into the woodwork, jerking her back on the other side. She screamed as she fell, but the door held.

The wolf, snarling and licking at the pain it had unwittingly inflicted on itself, became aware of a distinctive and acrid smell of fear that reached his nostrils. He again sprang at the door, wheeling tightly and posturing.

In the darkness Emma panted as she scrambled backwards, bumping into a blind wall and crashing sickeningly down two stone steps into the kitchen. Her shoulder ached and the intense cold of the flagstones burned through her clothes, searing the skin. She rolled over in anguish, sobbing for Unthank and wondering deliriously why on earth he had deserted her.

After a while she regained her sense of direction and pulled herself up on to a plain wooden chair. She dared not switch the light on for fear of revealing her exact position, but she needed help desperately. Any help would do.

Her clawing, searching fingers found her radio set on a worktop and switched on a cassette recording. She had a long-standing love for the stirring, mystical music of Sibelius and now it carried over her in waves.

Her quick shallow breathing became gradually deeper and more regular, and her frightened mind wandered. It was as if she was dreaming again. She needed a husband, a permanent presence. A long lean body to hug in the depths of the night. But somehow Unthank became muddled in her mind with an image of the lame journalist. Not that it mattered. Anybody would do. Anyone, provided she could rely on him to be there when she needed him.

A renewed noise outside, a sliding pushing noise, jerked her back to reality and she cowered up against the bare wooden stairs. One at a time, as far as the landing. As far away as she could get. The noble, muffled music followed at a respectful distance.

Emma lay down on her crumpled clothes, upstairs on the bedroom floor under a windowsill. She felt like a hypnotized rabbit about to fall prey to a more vicious creature. It was the law of nature . . . part of the violent natural cycle of life. Human instinct is closer to animal than many people imagine. And, like many comparatively defenceless creatures, a corner of her mind had already accepted the inevitable. She lay there, sobbing.

Unthank fell forward on to his knees for the umpteenth time that night and swore foully. He was close to the back of a sheep farm, and a low trough buried in the snow did nothing to help him. Several times, he detected flitting movements ahead, but none was translated into anything more tangible than a crouching sandstone rock or a withered, disfigured birch tree.

Yet ahead of him, cut into the crisp pristine snow, were fresh canine tracks. The mark of *Canis Lupus*. The splay was unmistakable. He stopped quite suddenly. The wolves were extremely close, and obviously hungry. He did not need to see them; his skin crawled, confirming the fact.

Something moved inside a rickety outbuilding. A snorting, heaving movement through reeking straw a few yards to his left. Nothing on God's earth would have induced Unthank to venture inside. Nothing save one thing. And that situation now presented itself right behind him. A hunched snarling shape loomed out of the shadows, leaving him no choice but to plunge inside: directly into the menacing shadows of the barn.

He was face to face with a startled well-fed Shetland pony. Its beer-barrel body and stout little legs quivered with fear. It had never known hunger: its affinity to man the provider had ensured that. But it knew desperation, and now it shifted continually, facing all the minute noises of the night at once.

Unthank fumbled the latch shut and stood pressed back against the dry-stone wall in case of immediate pursuit. The shotgun hung limply from his hand. After a moment or two, he allowed his other hand to venture out and stroke the pony's damp muzzle.

'Steady, boy,' he gulped. 'We'll be all right. You just see.'

There was no indication of any pursuit and Unthank moved across to calm the shivering pony. It was a movement Darkmind was waiting for. He thrust his head under the broken-bottomed door and went for the boot. Great yellow teeth ploughed along the tough leather toecap and snapped shut on the very edge of the sole, jerking Unthank completely off his feet and tearing away a strip of leather. The man's long leg twisted painfully under him and he thrust both hands out to break his fall, only to find them protruding under the door. He could not move and there was nothing he could do if the pack leader poked his head forward a second time.

As it was, the Shetland saved him. It had seen and sensed enough. Now it plunged and jerked in the confined space, lashing out its hind legs and parting Unthank's hair in passing.

Smelling sharply of sweat and urine, the desperate pony gave a double-footed kickback which shattered the flimsy door and catapulted split planks across the yard outside. Three wolves were scattered by the onslaught.

Darkmind saw the man sprawled helplessly in the opening, but the wolf's immediate attention was drawn to the terrified Shetland, which lunged over their flattened heads and bolted into the awakening day.

There was no choice. A wolf will automatically turn after prey that flees. And, however fast the victim moves, there is nothing that can ultimately outrun five famished wolves.

Darkmind gave several gruff barks – the hunting call of the pack – and the others joined in the chase, emerging from all directions and taking up their familiar loose wedge-shaped formation behind him.

The frantic pony ran past Emma's cottage, its thudding passage drawing the demented Slack-Jaw into the chase as well. He abandoned his feverish burrowing and clawing at the front door and joined the streaming pursuit.

Darkmind saw the outcast wolf streaking to join them and lunged at him, without checking his stride. But the lone wolf persisted and Darkmind chose not to turn and fight. He revelled instead in the chase, which drew out all of his age-old skills as a hunter. He was invigorated by the wind. Nothing could stop him.

Unthank raised his head slowly from the ground . . . inch by inch for fear that he would discover another wolf poised waiting for him to move. But to his intense relief all he saw was the disappearing rump of the last dark predator: Rabbit, late as usual and spurting after the others as if he had been scalded.

The surge of relief was tempered by anxiety for Emma. They were heading straight for the last house in the scattered village, where she would by now probably be awake, wondering where he was and opening the front door to find out.

In which case they might not continue to pursue the terror-stricken pony.

Unthank struggled to his knees, raised the gun deliberately high and blasted off a shot. It was nowhere near the pack, but made at least two of them dodge aside and throw quick glances over their tails. Indignant, accusing glances.

He could not bring himself to kill any of the wolves. For years they had shown themselves willing enough to keep to the high ground, and only the exceptional winter had drawn them into conflict with people. Given a mild spring, they would return with the deer into the mountains, and an acceptable balance of nature would be restored.

Others might not see it that way, but Unthank knew it to be true. Even so, he had to warn unsuspecting families. He barged into the church, bursting the doors open and stumbling to the back of the building where a curtained alcove contained a bell rope, ready to call the faithful to worship on the coming Sabbath. His gun clattered to the stone floor where a worn inscription read *Here lyeth Murdo Mackenzie, Missionary to Elphine . . . 1790–1848.*

He unwound the tethering cord and gripped the woollen sally, then pulled mightily so that his knees almost touched the ground, before the response of the heavy bell overhead tugged him up on to his toes. For a few moments the dusty silence was unbroken, and he grunted with exertion as he again pulled the rope down almost to the floor.

Suddenly the church was filled with the noise of the bell. The movement of the heavy rope and the great pulsating envelope of noise which engulfed him made him lose all awareness of what he was doing. It was as if the bell was ringing him. He scrunched up his face and tried to think only of Emma and the danger she might walk into.

But he need not have worried.

Emma Dancer crouched under the bedroom window of her home, peering across at the church and the unexpected clamour of the copper bell. She saw the pony career past and several grey shapes streak in pursuit. She also saw Slack-Jaw jerk away from the house to join the chase. She clasped a hand to her dry mouth in unbelievable relief and uttered little whimpering noises.

There had been a time when she gave up completely. Now, it seemed to be suddenly over and she was safe. Her hands were white and shaking. She made her way unsteadily down the stairs, listened carefully at the door and then unbolted it.

A crisp new day was streaming across the burn which twisted its way over the small glen. The sharp air was a tonic and she breathed it in with eyes closed.

But when she took just one small step outside, her stomach seized up in an agonizingly tight ball. There was still something waiting! With no time to turn to safety . . . she passed out in the doorway.

Ilya Bukhanovich regarded her limp body with his curiously blank eyes, as if it represented both an inconvenience and an imposition. Behind him, his large companion, Boris Spassky, scanned the hillside and shook his head.

'Out of range. But they'll pull the little horse down in a mile or two and stuff their stomachs. And then we'll have them.'

The ex-lieutenant of rifles nodded and glanced across at the church tower, which was still echoing with the urgent and ill-spaced clamour of the bell.

'They are a noisy people,' he said in Russian. 'How can they ever expect to catch the sly ones if they behave like this?'

His companion shrugged. 'I don't pretend to understand them.' He noted that Bukhanovich seemed to be in a fairly good mood, which was rare for him. 'What are you going to do with her?'

'They have rules about these things in Western countries. It's called the closed season and, at this time of year, I think we are supposed to throw back the under-nourished ones.'

Emma recovered consciousness in time to hear the two men laughing, and to find herself regarded by a pair of unusually pale eyes. She was too drained of emotion to care even though, when she was picked up, a firm hand gripped and squeezed her buttock, as if assessing a melon. He carried her back inside and laid her on the settee and, by that time, other people had come running along the road.

For a while the pony ran like the wind: terror gave her ten miles an hour on top of her previous best speed. Darkmind kept up the pace for as long as he could without bursting his lungs. Most of the other wolves were spread out a long way behind.

But as Darkmind fell back, Longrunner took up the front running. This was the way of the wolf: hunting as a pack and each, in turn, pushing their prey to the limit.

Invariably it is the victim who suicidally allows them to make the best use of their tactics, by swerving off at right-angles and giving the rest of the pack a chance to cut corners and catch up.

Bent-Ear took over the lead just before the pony faltered, missed its sweat-drenched stride and finally went down. The second biggest wolf went in like an express train and bit savagely through the rump muscles.

15

The pony screamed in pain, got up and galloped on with frantic new strength. But the sight of streaming blood drew Darkmind back to the fore. He swerved inside, slashing more live sinew with his enormous teeth.

A hind leg gave way completely, and the pony staggered along on three. But it could not last and, finally, she collapsed into a drift of snow, swivelling wild-eyed to face her tormentors and lashing out pathetically with a single front leg. The panting wolves formed a loose circle and stood triumphantly contemplating their next meal as they regained their breath.

When they eventually attacked it was not head-on, even though the plump Shetland could do little to stop them. Instead, two wolves lunged in from the back and bit deeply into the already-mangled hocks. When the pony swivelled, they retreated. But others immediately attacked from the far side: always from the undefended side. It did not take long; the heaving pony was soon submerged in gnawing wolves. Her flanks continued to pump away even after Darkmind's muzzle was saturated in a gravy of thick rich blood.

After a while Darkmind paused to sniff the air. So far as he could tell, there was no other creature in the vicinity. He stretched his neck and found time to grieve momentarily for Whitepatch. The pack looked up, one by one, alert to their leader's movements. Soon they would be able to sleep with bloated bellies, draped snugly across one another, as if they were pups again.

Darkmind raised his head and howled, a long haunting note which carried back over the hard sandstone folds of two bare and treeless forests: Inverpolly and Drumrunie.

But the rest of the pack were anything but mournful. They were the lords of the Highlands, and this was the day of the wolves.

THIRTY

Richard Unthank sank back into the bath. His knees stuck up in the air while he submerged blissfully to nose level in steaming water, absorbing the soothing heat. It was never easy for a six-foot man in a four-foot bath, but he managed. Later he shaved, dressed in fresh clothes and devoured a pot of tea, a warm French loaf in two great hunks, and nearly half a pound of Cheddar cheese. Nothing had ever tasted so good.

Acting Constable Shaftoe had been waiting outside the cottage when he returned, to say that Emma was at the infirmary. Not hurt, he said, simply shock and exhaustion. She'd been given an injection to make her sleep heavily for the next twelve hours.

Unthank had the radio switched to full volume in the kitchen, and kept half his attention on it as he journeyed about the house. It was a bright, neatly kept home with feminine touches that intrigued him. The more he thought about Emma, the easier it was to make up his mind. He ought to have married ten years ago. He would have had children by now. Suddenly he missed whatever it was: the love, the sharing, the little anxieties which invariably sort themselves out.

He decided to go to the infirmary, as soon as she was awake, and propose. The decision made him happier and, at the same time, more nervous than he had felt for years.

The weather man's voice interrupted his thoughts.

'The long-range forecast is more promising. Warmer weather is expected to move down across the North Atlantic before the end of the month, bringing a thaw to most parts of the British Isles. Isolated snowfalls are likely to continue in the Highlands and north-west England during the next

227

few days, gradually dying out towards the end of the week.'

A wash of relief rinsed Unthank's mind. He foraged for a pencil and wrote down the gist of what he'd heard on the back of an envelope. When he peered out at the sky it already seemed a lighter shade of grey, and there was even an encouraging blue gap between distant clouds.

He trudged hopefully along to Station House. With any luck, the deer would start filtering back to the high ground within a month. They could be back to normal in two.

Shaftoe was sitting in Sergeant Dunceford's worn but imposing chair with his boots on the desk and a beer glass in his hand. Unthank's sudden arrival almost gave the untidy policeman a heart attack. He swung his feet down with a crash which sent dust up from the wooden floor and slopped froth over the edge of his glass.

He seemed desperately relieved that it was only Unthank. 'I thought you were the sergeant for a moment.'

'Is he around?'

'No. We're closed.'

Unthank waved the envelope. 'Did you hear the forecast?'

The well-meaning constable fastened the silver buttons on his black jacket. 'Yes, we listened to the six a.m. bulletin.'

'How did Dunceford react?'

'Violently. He hugged me and we danced round the room. We were half-afraid this winter was going to last forever. But he didn't stay long. He went off to see that American about some wolf hunters he's brought in. The Sergeant says we don't need them. He says we can kill off every wolf in the area easily enough, without any foreigners trying to claim the credit.'

'But there's no need for anybody to go on with the hunt. In two or three weeks the packs will withdraw to the mountains after the deer. The trouble will sort itself out.'

Shaftoe looked nonplussed. 'Well, I don't know about that. I just work here. But I do know that Sir Marcus is looking to us, in the force, to keep this thing under control. The American wants the hunt intensified and I've got a feeling that the Sergeant sees himself with some silver pips on his

228

shoulder by the summer. Can't blame him. I'd like to be a full constable myself.'

Unthank clenched his fists. 'But that's ridiculous.'

The young policeman looked put out. 'No, it's not. I think we deserve it.'

'Not you. I mean the blood-lust. It's that little madman up the hill. Why does he want to slaughter our animals when they'll withdraw of their own accord soon enough?'

Shaftoe got up, noting the distraught edge in the scientist's voice. 'You'd best ask him that yourself. It's really outside my jurisdiction. And, as I said, we're closed.'

Unthank did not like being directed towards the door, and he brushed away the other man's hand.

Shaftoe said appeasingly: 'Sorry . . . nothing personal. But we are closed. And if you see the Sergeant don't mention I was sitting down. He thinks I'm cleaning his car. Ridiculous, isn't it? As soon as I get it clean, he goes out and gets it dirty again.' The door clicked shut.

When he reached High House, Unthank heard three shots being fired in rapid succession. He went round the back to see what was going on.

Spassky was standing in a bulky army snow smock and white hood, looking down at a stag, which had been shot through the neck but still had enough feeble strength to lift its noble head.

The Russian raised his rifle in one hand, almost casually, so that the barrel rested against the velvet brown skin. Another red deer carcasse lay nearby; it looked to Unthank like a half-starved hind and he could see blood still seeping from its grimacing mouth. 'What the hell are you doing?' he demanded, hurrying forward.

The Russian swung up the gun barrel until it rested with fractional precision under the tip of Unthank's chin. He went back a step, and Spassky matched it, applying pressure with the cold edge of the muzzle.

He gingerly extended a hand towards the dying stag. 'What

229

are you up to?' he slurred, barely moving his lips in case it disturbed the man's trigger finger.

'Hmm?'

'What's going on? You can't shoot animals like this, willy nilly, especially when they come to a house for scraps.'

Spassky continued frowning at him. 'Willy nilly?'

'Why? Why you shoot?'

The Russian glanced towards the house for help but none was forthcoming. He pointed to his mouth, chewing vigorously, and then towards the house.

Unthank sighed and backed away. 'You stay there,' he said, mouthing each word articulately. 'Put gun down, and wait, Okay?'

'Hmm?'

'I say, you put gun down and wait. Okay?'

The Russian's grim expression gave way to a smile of realization. 'Okay,' he responded. 'Okay.'

But no sooner had Unthank rung the doorbell than he heard another shot. The stag was dead. He swore and put his weight on the bell. He didn't take it off until a woman answered.

It was a tired-looking Penny Bakersman. She gave him a threadbare smile and invited him inside.

'Who is that maniac?' Unthank demanded.

'I'm not sure.'

'But he's slaughtering deer. Indiscriminately.'

She shook her head. 'You'd best have a word with my father. Mr Unthank, isn't it? You're a friend of Martin Kelso's.'

She led him through the hall and opened panelled doors into the dining-room, where Sergeant Dunceford and the other haughty-looking Russian were standing in front of a long table while the little oilman tucked into an impressive array of food.

Bakersman glanced across but did not interrupt his conversation for the sake of the newcomer.

'I don't see any problem, Sergeant. You simply lead your men out to the north and east of the village. And Ivan here . . . ' He jerked a derisory thumb at the intense Russian '. . . can cover the south and west.'

Sergeant Dunceford sighed heavily. 'But the south-west is exactly where my people say the wolves are running.'

The American gnawed a bone and then wiped his fingers on a napkin before fastening his ferrety eyes on the policeman. 'Precisely. But then he is the expert. And I *do* want wolfskins brought back here, Sergeant . . . not a tale of woe about how most of them got away again.'

While Dunceford turned away huffily, and muttered about strangers hunting through his hills, Unthank took in the spread of food on the polished table. It was amazing that so much was available for a single lunch: far too much for one scrawny man to pick over. There was pheasant, venison, a great spread of salmon and numerous silver dishes containing greenstuffs and appetizers. A tray of drinks was close at hand.

Bakersman poured himself a generous amount of sparkling white wine. He slurped as he drank, and a dribble dampened the napkin tucked in at his throat.

Penny Bakersman interrupted from a distance. 'Daddy. This is Mr Richard Unthank, the environmental and animal expert.'

The elderly man glanced sourly in his direction and heaved faintly, as if controlling a burp.

She persisted. 'He wants to talk to you urgently. Isn't that so?' She gave Unthank a pleasant smile, and he suddenly noticed her boyish attractiveness. She wore no make-up, faded corduroy slacks and an unbuttoned jacket, but her clear-cut features and full mouth came through and made a pleasing impression.

'It is indeed,' Unthank said firmly.

But her father brushed the matter aside, as if of little consequence. 'Won't you have a glass of this stuff, dahlin? It's pretty good. Twenty-five dollars a bottle. Come on, you look pale. You know, I really don't understand why you're wearing yourself inside-out at that ragamuffin hospital. They've got plenty of people trained to do just what you're doing.'

231

'Daddy,' she said wearily, 'there's no one else available right now. No one at all. Anyway, it's what I want to do.'

He tilted some wine into a glass, which she picked up and handed straight to Unthank. 'Mr Unthank? I'm really not in the mood for bubbles up my nose.' She turned back to the others. 'Daddy, I'm going to lay down for a while. I'm on duty again at ten tonight.'

She went out, leaving her father to prod at the remains of a venison steak and then push it away ungraciously. He waved Unthank towards an armchair, licking his fingers. 'Sit down, all of you. Well, sir, what is it you want?'

The scientist glanced at the other two visitors. Both appeared exasperated: the sergeant because he felt his position was being undermined, and the Russian who did not want to be involved with anybody else.

Bakersman made no attempt to introduce them to each other.

'Well . . . ' Unthank slapped his legs and began. 'You may know that I was sent here because of my knowledge of deer habits and movements, as well as being involved . . . ' He cleared his throat. ' . . . in the introduction of wolves to Rhum Island.'

The American crashed his fist down on the table, making the cutlery dance. It effectively cut off all conversation until Bakersman himself muttered: 'It's not to your credit.'

'The community here has been in a precarious position for some time now because of the extreme weather conditions. The deer moved unexpectedly and the wolves followed. And . . . '

The American interrupted bitterly. ' . . . and my son was dragged off his motorcycle and bitten to death.'

Unthank again cleared his throat. 'And that too. But today we have the news from London that the winter is lifting. The weather men say that, in two or three weeks, a thaw should set in. That means the deer will return north, retreat back to the high lands. It also means the wolves will pull back with them.'

'No, it goddamned doesn't,' growled Bakersman.

'Pardon?'

'It means nothing of the sort. Those creatures you talk about so casually are going to be strips of raw flesh long before they get the chance to cower back out of sight. I've got thirty men under the stalwart Sergeant that says so. Isn't that right, Sergeant Bunchford?'

'Aye, sir.' He coughed discreetly. 'Dunceford, sir.'

'And I've got two tame Bolsheviks who'll shoot whatever I tell them.' He turned to Bukhanovich. 'Right?'

There was a look of growing distrust on the Russian's face, but he also added a slow nod.

'There,' said the oilman with some satisfaction. 'It seems we don't need your help. We can kill them pretty well under our own steam.'

Unthank flared up, irritated by the man's manner. 'There's no need to kill them. Just keep out of their way for a while, and the whole thing will abate.'

The little eyes blazed and he stood up abruptly, pushing the table away from him. 'They killed my son! Killed a little girl and her father too! Don't you know that? Where yuh been?' He made his way aggressively around the table and jabbed Unthank with the rubber tip of his walking stick. 'What in the name of sweet Jesus do you think we're going to do? Pat their heads? Wink into their beady little eyes, and send them about their business? Don't come that environmental balls with me! Each one of them's going to get a bullet in the head . . . same as you, if you don't get out of here.'

When the stick next poked into Unthank's chest, he wrenched it from the old man's grasp and flung it away.

'I don't blame you for the way you feel. I've got no right to. But vengeance won't solve anything, and it could do a lot of harm.'

'What have you done with my stick? I'll see that you are reported to your superiors for threatening behaviour.'

Unthank leaned forward, keeping what he had to say private to the two of them. 'If you had an ounce of common-sense you'd listen to what was being said. And people would

233

respect you for it. As it is, you're nothing. Nothing but a moth-eaten weasel.'

The American looked as if he did not believe what he was hearing. 'Sergeant,' he said shrilly, 'get this man out of here immediately. He's insulted me.'

Dunceford coughed mightily, got up and separated the two men. 'Mr Unthank, you'd better go now, please.'

Bakersman fumed. 'I want this man arrested and charged with contempt.'

The sergeant shook his head. 'We don't usually do that sort of thing over here.'

'I don't give a damn what you usually do! Do it, or I'll have your balls.' Bakersman swung towards the Russian, wiping the smile from his face. 'You! Don't stand there, smirking. Help toss this bum out of here and, if he comes around again, put a bullet through his kneecap.'

But the Russian would have none of it. 'You seriously ask me to threaten a British citizen on British soil. Do you know what you are suggesting? I am here as a guest, representing the Union of the Soviet Socialist Republics.'

'You're here because I sent for you!' said Bakersman, close to apoplexy. 'And if I complain about your conduct here, you're destined for Siberia, my friend.'

Bukhanovich remained unruffled. 'I already live in Siberia.'

The oilman spun to face each of them in turn. 'Get out of here you, and you. And you,' he panted. 'Just give me back my stick and I'll go myself and beat the life out of every wolf I can find. I'll show you what an old-fashioned man's made of.'

His daughter heard the uproar and returned in time to see him sweep crockery and silverware alike off the table in a crescendo of despair. He seemed to be overcome by the effort, and the sergeant helped lift him on to an elegant Victorian chaise-longue.

Unthank and the Russian waited awkwardly outside, both feeling guilty about provoking the old man towards a stroke. Finally the grey-haired policeman joined them, closing the dining-room door gently.

'How is he?'

'Too old to be showing off like that.'

'Sergeant, I meant what I said about the deer. They'll fall back in just a week or two, and pull the wolves back with them. As soon as the weather breaks.'

'I'm sure you did, Mr Unthank.' Dunceford buttoned up his coat ready to leave.

'So, what do you intend to do?'

'Do? I intend to go out and hunt wolves, just as I said I would.'

'But you can't. They're no more guilty of any crime than we are. They are simply carrying out the prime requirement of their species. Survival.'

Dunceford stared him in the eye. Steadily and disconcertingly. 'So are we.'

THIRTY-ONE

The exhausted doctor looked in on the isolation section before going off duty just before midnight. Penny Bakersman heard him coming.

'Everything all right?' he asked, smiling wearily into the shutaway room.

'Yes, thank you,' she said crisply. 'He's sleeping.'

'I just thought you'd like to know. The tests are negative. There's no question of rabies. We'll be able to move him back to the general ward tomorrow.'

'I'm so glad.'

'Me too. I appreciate you volunteering to work in here. It's not something that even the hardbitten nurses look forward to.'

She shrugged. 'Had to be done.'

They said goodnight and she was left alone. She went out-

235

side into the corridor and broke the rules. She lit a cigarette with trembling fingers. She was a fraud, and not the calm self-assured nurse he imagined. Several times that evening she had washed anxiously in carbolic soap and now she felt ashamed of having done so.

Some animals have a highly developed sense of perception. Man is not among them. But occasionally an awareness is triggered even in him. This was one such moment.

Bukhanovich was tired and irritated. He and Spassky had spent the previous day tramping across endless slopes, floundering at times waist-deep in snow and seeing nothing ahead of them but bare unmarked mountainside.

They had no dogs to help them and the domineering little oilman insisted that they report back to him each evening, so that he could keep an account of the land scoured and then advance coloured pins across an Ordnance Survey map on his study wall.

So, here they were, early the next morning hanging about outside the house. Once again wasting valuable time. The muscular Russian stroked his battered hunting rifle and thought about the possibility of the American appearing in his sights at, say, a range of two hundred metres.

Three seconds were all he would need to make absolutely sure. Two, if you insist. He swung the polished stock up to his padded shoulder and curled an index finger around the trigger.

The impression he had of a 7.62 mm bullet paralyzing the old man, stopping him in hectoring mid-sentence, cheered him no end.

He squinted up to where the sun should have been but wasn't and then let his eyes drift casually over the skyline. He noticed Slack-Jaw a fraction before turning away.

The wolf was almost invisible against the uneven crest of Spotted Hill, which rises abruptly from the main road and dominates the whole of Elphin. Only the fact that the animal moved in fits and starts, snapping at its tail, drew his attention.

He kept his eyes fixed on the distant shape, for fear of losing its position, while his left hand quietly unfastened the flap of his binocular case. The lone wolf jumped into focus. Within a second or two, he saw its ears prick up on the alert. It was almost as if it realized it was being closely observed.

Big-boned and ugly. Too thin to be healthy, but still perhaps one hundred and forty pounds. And greatly troubled by parasites, to judge from the number of times he snapped irritably behind him.

Spassky came around the corner of the house. 'So. How long before we set out? Our little ladies are ready to stretch their . . .'

Bukhanovich signalled him into silence. 'Up there. See him?' he asked, without lowering the glasses. 'We have a friend.'

The second Russian also took out his binoculars and then he, too, smiled. 'Welcome, cousin,' he said in Russian. 'We've been wondering when you would pay us a visit.'

'What's the matter with him?'

Spassky, who knew a great deal about cold-weather animals and their problems, adjusted his focus. 'He seems troubled.'

'Fleas?'

'Of course, comrade. But notice he is alone.'

The senior Russian lowered his glasses. 'So?'

'He may be the one who lags behind. If the pack shuns him, it means he could be a little crazy. Certainly unpredictable.'

Bukhanovich put his binoculars away and glanced regretfully at his slim, gas-operated rifle. It had saved him a lot of exhausting climbing in the past, but this time the range was too great.

'Bring the dogs round.'

Spassky did as he was told, but he could not shake off a feeling of foreboding. A premonition that his dogs were not yet up to a confrontation with a mad wolf.

Bukhanovich, on the other hand, had no such reservations.

237

He wanted only to press on, knowing that the wolf would by now have turned away, and would be loping across the mottled rocks which led deeper into the Cromalt Hills, where mist trailed in eerie drapes under the claustrophobic clouds.

An urgent rapping drew their attention back to the house where Bakersman, temporarily confined to a wheelchair and with a blanket around his shoulders, was tapping furiously on the glass porch with his walking stick.

A servant banged open the double windows with the heel of his palm and the oilman called, 'Where the hell do you two think you are going?'

'Hello!' Spassky continued to move after his leader, who plodded steadfastly on and refused to recognize the interruption.

Bakersman's voice reached them faintly but clearly. 'Not that way!' he called hoarsely. 'You should be moving west and then sweeping around to the south, like I told you.'

'Mind you don't get a cold, sitting out there,' called Spassky agreeably in Russian as the gap widened.

'Where in the name of sweet Jesus do you think you're going? Back to the Urals?'

Spassky gave a final wave as the outraged voice faded. 'Look after yourself, old man.'

He caught up with his companion and rubbed the ears of his frisking dogs. 'He's not so bad. He's just an *old* man who hasn't realized it yet.'

THIRTY-TWO

There were so many good stories thrown up by the weather, Kelso hardly knew which to write about first.

He did not have the field completely to himself. There was a report on the BBC early morning news about hunting parties being organized across the width of a numbed Scotland, but only in the context of farmers protecting their stock and the item was squeezed to the back of people's attention by the influenza epidemic, which had the south of England on its knees.

At Brighton, the hospitals were so full of limp, coughing patients that only the most dire cases were being admitted and all accident victims found themselves being taken to a glass-domed pleasure pavilion on one of the piers.

The weather continued to produce bizarre incidents. The pilot of a light plane, forced to bail out over the middle of the Channel when his engine seized up, came down on thick ice and walked two miles to the shore.

The Energy Minister in James Beaconsfield's Cabinet was challenged to a duel by an Opposition member after denying, in a Parliamentary debate, that he was 'incompetent and bone-idle'. But he wisely failed to turn up in Hyde Park at dawn the next day, to the scorn of his bristling rival and the disappointment of three half-frozen television crews.

In outlying districts so many vehicles had broken down that otherwise manageable roads were blocked, and people moved about mostly on foot. Petrol supplies were restricted to the emergency services, and food rationing was introduced in some isolated areas.

With so many news angles of his own, Kelso sat hammering at his typewriter for two hours.

As a consequence, he was left behind by the police sergeant's hunting party. And, by the time he was ready to follow them, Emma Dancer delayed him in startling fashion.

Emma was released from the infirmary within an hour of waking from her drug-induced sleep. The only doctor on duty, who yawned more than once and shook his head apologetically, asked about her trauma with the wolves and seemed satisfied with her spare replies.

Unthank heard that she was home from Temporary Constable Shaftoe, who was hurrying along the snow-packed street to join two dozen other thickly dressed and heavily armed men. The policeman spotted him outside the guest house and called across.

The lean scientist scrounged some eating apples and an outsized bar of chocolate and made his way to the last house in the village. After a moment or two of hesitation, a curtain twitched and she came downstairs.

She barely responded to his kiss.

Unthank slid his hand around her firm buttocks. 'I've been dying to see you.'

'Have you?' She clicked a bolt on the front door and quickly moved back into the cosy lounge, leaving him to raise his eyebrows quizzically.

'I brought these for you.' He proferred the food, but she made no attempt to accept it and merely darted another glance at the door.

He unloaded the apples on to the settee and made a play of warming his hands in front of the fire. 'Look, I'm sorry about what happened, Emma. I had to get out and warn the other people. There seemed no point in waking and alarming you. I couldn't tell there was another bugger trailing behind.'

He gazed miserably into the flames. But she did not respond and, when he glanced over his shoulder, she had retreated to the kitchen and was clinking cups.

He followed her through. 'I'm sorry.'

She shrugged. 'It's over. All that matters now is what happens next.'

'What do you mean?'

'I want to leave here.'

'Don't we all. Well, at least the weather forecast is encouraging.'

'I don't give a damn for the weather!' she snapped, making him jump. 'I just want to leave.'

He reached out from behind and caught her trailing hand, but she tugged it clear to stir some swirling cocoa in a saucepan. He persisted. 'Emma, I love you. Don't pull away from me.'

She suddenly started to cry. In a moment, he swung her

around and she buried her face against his jacket. He stroked her hair soothingly.

'I'm so frightened,' she said, rubbing her face into him.

'I know, I know . . .'

He listened to the little sounds she made; clearing her throat, breathing quickly to overcome the tears and steadying herself again.

Unthank jumped in quickly without thinking. 'Emma, let's get married.'

The words carried clearly across the otherwise silent kitchen, but she did not respond and he wondered if she had even heard. 'Let's get married,' he repeated.

She pulled away, shaking her head.

'Why not?'

'Don't ask me now. Not in the middle of all this confusion. I can't think straight.'

'Oh,' he said dejectedly.

'There's only one thing I want at the moment.'

'What's that?' he asked dully, with all the zest knocked out of him.

'To get as far away from this place as I can. Take me away tomorrow . . . and I'll marry you the next day.'

He ran a desperate hand through his hair. 'How can I? It's just not possible. Emma, there's no way out of here. The road's closed both sides of Ullapool and the only helicopter is running errands for Sir Marcus Sheerwater.'

She pulled him down on to the settee, to earnestly explain. 'But there is . . . There are boats at Lochinver only fifteen miles away. The doctor told me. They've already evacuated the old people and some of the children.'

Unthank sighed. He could not leave now. There was too much to do. Nobody else could help the gradually starving animals; and certainly nobody else wanted to.

'What's the point? In a couple of weeks the thaw will unlock the roads and the railway. Then we can get a sleeper down from Inverness. We'll be in the Dorchester Hotel a few hours later, and I'll see that they treat us like visiting royalty.'

Her sharp fingers dug through his clothing, hurting and stressing the urgency of her demand.

'I want to get out now. Or at least by tomorrow.'

'Darling, it's no good going to Lochinver,' he reasoned. 'The ice will be several feet thick. Boats won't be able to budge.'

'That's not so,' she insisted. 'It's on the Gulf Stream. The doctor said sea-going boats there won't have any trouble. None at all.'

He walked around the room, anxiously searching for some way to appease her. 'It's no good. I can't do it, Emma.'

Her mouth fell open in dismay. 'Why not? The other night you couldn't wait to get rid of me.'

He spread his hands helplessly. 'The situation has changed. People have begun shooting wolves and deer indiscriminately. It's my job to bring some sanity back into the situation. I saw a man kill two deer yesterday, simply because they got in the way of his car and made it stall in the snow.'

'Animals like that will survive whatever you do.' She looked despairingly at her hands, opening and closing them ceaselessly. 'But I'm not sure that I will.'

'No harm will come to you.'

'Won't it?'

'I promise. I'll look after you.'

She suddenly looked coldly into his eyes. 'Like you did at the school when those terrible creatures broke in?' she asked accusingly. 'Or when I woke up to find you gone and something clawing at the door?'

He walked away from the house feeling completely bewildered. His world had suddenly been turned upside down. Everything had gone wrong, and it did not help to know that the wolves and the merciless weather were really to blame.

He wiped away some tears and regretted losing his temper when she asked him to pass a message to the disabled newspaper reporter.

He had asked indignantly: 'What do you want with Kelso?'

242

'None of your business. Just tell him I want to speak to him tonight. Urgently.'

'I'll do nothing of the kind. He can't help you. He's a bloody cripple.'

'Cripple or not, he's got a lot more backbone than you.'

'That's not worth much when you're up to your armpits in snow.'

She regarded him in silence, then said quietly, 'It's my life and I'll live it any way I choose.' He heard the bolts snick shut behind him.

Unthank felt empty and sad. He was going into the raw Highlands to save wolves which, in turn, would try to drive him away. It was his job. Yet in his heart he cared nothing for them: nothing at all. Humans may have a low sense of perception compared with other animals, but they do possess complex emotions. And one of them is pride. He kept on walking.

Martin Kelso was massaging the leg which daily carried the weight of his thick invalid boot. It ached, but for once he did not mind. He had a good many other things to occupy his thoughts.

He spread a Forestry Commission map across a table in front of the fire and circled areas in which the wolf hunts were already in progress. At Shin Falls, near Lairg, nearly a hundred men and boys were said to have encircled a pack of seven. The trapped animals had been seen running desperately up and down along the precipitous brink of the rock-lined waterfalls and, even though a youth fell into the gushing icy water and was pulled out half-dead only thirty seconds later, the hunters were confident of success.

In Glen More forest park, amid thousands of acres of carefully nurtured Caledonian pines and with the brooding Cairngorm Mountains in the background, weekend hunters were said to have shot ten wolves and at least two of themselves.

On the island of Skye, the crew of a Royal Navy destroyer

were reported to have joined locals in driving deer and wolves alike on to a sea-flanked promontory of the Cuillan Hills. They were keeping them hemmed in with the aid of tracer bullets, which hissed over their heads and shattered the rocky hillside, ensuring that both defiant predators and petrified ruminants remained to await their fate.

He glanced up at Unthank hurried across the far side of the lounge and went upstairs to his room. 'Hello,' he called, but there was no response.

Later, when the tall man thudded down again, carrying a rucksack and snow goggles, the journalist tried once more. 'Going out?' he called cheerfully.

There was a grunt and then the front door slammed behind the departing figure.

Kelso raised his eyebrows, and his attention was coincidentally drawn to one of the notices pinned to a felt-covered board on the wall. *Visit the Highlands and sample for yourself all the courtesy and old-world charm of its people.*

It was nearly an hour later, when the housekeeper brought him in tea and a plate of dry-as-dust oatcakes, that he learned Emma Dancer was asking to see him.

Kelso had nothing else to do before setting out to catch up with the hunting party the next day. He went upstairs to shave and dab himself liberally with after-shave lotion. He took his time; but then he did not know quite what he was missing.

THIRTY-THREE

Bukhanovich should have known better. But he was not used to hunting in collaboration with anyone else.

Bakersman had tried to humiliate both him and the servile police sergeant, and now he asked himself: how could he be expected to pay heed to the instructions of a man who knew nothing of wolves and their sly ways?

Slack-Jaw loped on through the mist, sliding down the sprawling snow-sheeted sides of mountains. Sometimes leaping from rock to rock, as if picking his way across the frozen white landscape without touching the earth itself. And yet, at other times, limping wearily with his head almost bumping the ground.

He was not consciously seeking Darkmind and the others. But he was an animal born into an hierarchical system, who was as reliant on those who made the pack's decisions, as he had been cantankerous towards the wolves under him.

He did not need to search thousands of acres of wilderness. The bite of the wind off the side of a mountain, or the sunken hospitable face of a hollow hillside, were the indicators that led him away from remote places and towards the pack.

Bukhanovich had been one of the brightest pupils at his Academy and that had led directly to his commission in the Red Army. Now, he told a friend, he was his country's only intellectual sniper. Had he been of sufficient age during the Second World War, he would almost certainly have claimed dozens of Wehrmacht victims before the inevitable return bullet found its mark.

Spassky, on the other hand, could hardly bear to fire a rifle. He invariably shut his eyes when he squeezed a trigger and often missed comparatively close targets by up to twenty yards. He was, however, an excellent tracker and dog-handler and had a deep empirical knowledge of wildlife. The two Russians made a formidable team which needed no help from hastily formed hunting groups.

But, by ignoring the direction in which Dunceford's men were sweeping, Ilya Bukhanovich was inviting disaster. And the mist that blundered gently along at a thousand feet above sea level closed his eyes to it.

The five wolves in the main pack were nervous and excited. They sensed man in the vicinity. Darkmind himself noticed

245

the distant movement of a pair of Whooper swans, even though they were too far off to distinguish their distinctive yellow bills.

His nose twitched and his handsome head turned first one way and then the other. For a moment or two his sensory system was confused, then the indications became more definite. They were coming from both directions at once. Still a long way off . . . but drawing closer every minute.

He instinctively wheeled and, after a moment's hesitation, the pack followed. Wolves possess a natural caution. Later, they would attack unflinchingly when the moment was right – but they would pick the moment.

Darkmind chose the way and then stopped to let the others overtake him. He watched them melt into the mountain mist, brushing through bedraggled heather and over rocks that protruded from the snow like the tattered remains of a faded tartan.

A few minutes later, Slack-Jaw came out of the mist, padding blindly forward with his head trailing, to be faced by the motionless figure of Darkmind on a granite outcrop. A low rumbling from the back of the pack leader's throat made the demented wolf jerk to a halt.

Slack-Jaw flattened himself and backed away, his tail swishing and his teeth bared. The way ahead was blocked, but he was equally aware of the methodical pursuit closing in behind him.

Rabbit gave him the way out he needed. The distant and least aggressive of the pack howled back anxiously for his leader, and Slack-Jaw took advantage of the distraction to bolt after the vanished pack.

Darkmind spurted to head him off, but could not chase for long and had to return to his vantage point on the rock to determine the nature of those who followed.

In a few minutes, Yacka and Elena bounded out of the mist to be confronted by the snarling figure on top of a hillock.

The Irish wolfhounds, with their gangling legs and long necks, would normally have towered over any wolf. Together,

246

they could chase and bowl over most predators. But the muddled scents of so many wolves made them uncertain and they sank down in the snow, whining, but well apart and still some distance from Darkmind.

It was an acceptable stalemate. The enormous dogs waited for their masters to catch up and make a decision, while the big wolf knew that time gained ensured the safety of his departing pack.

Both Russians were breathing hard. Spassky's chest was slippery with perspiration and his mind was far away, dreaming of a kind and simple Valentina and her fresh grave lying under the wintry flowers she had loved. There were tears in his eyes and he was totally unprepared for the wolf that was waiting for him.

Bukhanovich was no better off. He was wondering if his embassy would heed the puritanical American and whether or not the man's low opinion of them would be relayed back to Moscow.

His long-barrelled rifle was resting on his shoulder the wrong way up: the muzzle in his grasp and the butt protruding into the air. He was humming, under his breath, the catchy tune that countless Red Army men had sung to themselves to whittle away the miles. Except that now he hummed it in a grim, funereal way. *Oh, Kalinka. Kalinka. Kalinka my love . . .*

Man and wolf came upon each other through the slow-moving mist, separated by no more than thirty yards. The Russians were momentarily too startled to do anything. The men's eyes met briefly, almost furtively.

Bukhanovich was the first to act. He cartwheeled his rifle, caught it by the stock and cocked it for firing, all in one blurred movement. One of them yelled 'Wolf! Right ahead!' He didn't know if it was Spassky or himself.

Their two dogs leaped up, galvanized by the shouts, and ran diagonally towards the motionless wolf. Spassky wiped the tears from his eyes, acutely aware of the danger his ladies were running into. 'Hold! Hold!'

The dogs dropped again, but their second or two of hesitation prevented Bukhanovich from shooting and allowed Dark-mind to wheel around and slip out of sight.

The leading Russian said something obscene and waved the dogs forward. 'Get after him!'

They bayed as they cleared the rocks with great raking strides, ears pricked at the prospect of a real chase at last, and plunged into the mist on the far side.

Spassky clambered to the top of the outcrop, shielding his eyes as if it would sharpen his vision. A murmur of wind on the downslope lifted the drifting veil long enough for him to see the zig-zagging chase, down through a litter of rocks, across rivulets and plunging through suffocating drifts of snow. Down, down.

'My God! Look there!'

Bukhanovich jumped up to join him, clutching him around the waist to steady his own precarious foothold. 'What is it?'

'Down there. Beyond the trees. Men.'

The Russian leader peered at a dozen tiny figures, far below but just discernable for a moment before the mist thickened and hid them from view.

'It must be the policeman and his little army. What are they doing here?'

'The wolf's heading straight for them.'

Bukhanovich fired his rifle over his head. Once, twice, three times.

Far below in the glen, Sergeant Dunceford and the others were sprawled on ground sheets, or idling about checking their equipment; one was digging corned beef out of a tin and sandwiching it hugely between oatmeal biscuits. Another was lying on his back holding a small battery radio in the air while it played music at him.

The shots made Dunceford jerk up, ricking his neck. He pulled himself on to his knees, straining his eyes into the mist but seeing nothing.

Most of the men were on their feet now, puzzled. 'What the devil's that?'

'Somebody's in trouble.'

But Dunceford had something of the primitive about him

and was suspicious by nature. He rubbed his strained neck. 'Get your weapons and spread out in a line. It could have been a warning. Better not take any chances. First man to see anything, yell out.'

There was a great deal of speculation and some embarrassed laughter as they settled into a firing line, but none of them could see beyond a dip in the hillside thirty or forty yards ahead.

The first Scot actually to spot anything was a gentle youth called Angus Murdoch, whose ginger hair was so long and fine that he was obliged to keep a felt band around his head to control it.

Darkmind came out of the swirling grey cloud like a demon: down the steep slope at well over thirty miles an hour. Yards between each leap and unable to stop even if he wanted to.

'Christ!'

Twenty yards behind him, the other men were still unsighted. 'What is it?'

The great shape sailed over Murdoch's head, giving him no time to duck and leaving an impression of massive strength and rows of jagged and uneven teeth. The eyes were wickedly slanted and ears pressed back against the big skull.

'Wolf! Wolf! Coming straight at you!'

'Jeeesus!' Somebody stood up, horrified by the satanic shape hurtling towards them and unwittingly took the full force of the predator against his shoulder, cartwheeling him over and over until he finished up fractured and winded against a heap of rucksacks.

Darkmind himself landed in a great flurry of snow, scrambled back to his feet and snapped ferociously in Dunceford's direction. The policeman sat transfixed, staring open-mouthed at the wolf's sudden arrival and unable to make his petrified hands move towards the rifle.

Darkmind jerked his head towards the baying animals in pursuit and then continued down the hill and into the mist.

'What in the name of Jesus was that?' somebody called incredulously from the far end of the line of stunned men.

Dunceford recovered himself, and gulped: 'Kerr . . . rist. What a size. Did you see that?'

'Wolves!' They all heard a high-pitched yell from Murdoch higher up the slope. 'More on the way!'

Dunceford flung himself forward into the snow, digging frantically with his knees and elbows. He could not be sure if he was doing it from fear or simply to find a comfortable firing position. Bodies crouched behind rocks and well-oiled bolts snapped on rifles.

Two ragged, grey shapes sailed into sight, covering prodigious distances with each leap. First one, then the other. There was no time to clearly identify them.

The men blasted away with everything they had: rifles, shotguns, airguns and even a heavy old Webley handgun. The first dog, Yacka, landed with her legs spreadeagled as if she had been pole-axed, only to get up seconds later with her tail wagging pathetically and half her stomach blown away. Her intestines were visible through a long tear in her lean stomach.

Elena crashed among the men in a welter of jutting legs and scrambled miraculously to safety behind some barely adequate stones. The men recovered and went after her, whooping. Bullets crashed and whined off the black moss-covered rocks.

The dog lay whimpering and, after the men pressed forward and a silence descended, rolled on its back and also wagged its tail. It clung apologetically to life for some time.

Angus Murdoch staggered down the slope, his face the colour of porridge. 'Did we get them? God, I've never seen such beasts. I thought I was wolf-meat for sure.'

Someone sniggered among the knot of men staring down at the wolfhound, and soon they were all laughing uproariously.

'Let him through. Come and see what scared you, Angus. A dog. A bloody great scarecrow of a dog.'

The youth examined the remains and joined weakly in the laughter. 'But there were others,' he said, remembering the confusion of bodies overhead.

250

'One was a wolf, and two were dogs. Guess which two we got?'

They were almost helpless with laughter, which came all the more readily now that any danger was past.

Spassky, who had drunk his fill of death during the past few days, panted down the mountainside. Stretching out so far that he almost overbalanced in his wild and fearful dash ... tripping and stumbling.

His wife was dead, and now his lovely ladies had vanished into the sound of guns. He slowed up, sobbing for breath, only when he reached the threadbare remains of Yacka.

'Oh, no,' he groaned, falling on his knees and cradling the bloodstained remains in his arms, nuzzling the gentle face of the dead Irish wolfhound. Then stumbling on to find Elena, who was just being put out of her agonizing misery by Dunceford with a shot through the neck.

Spassky saw it happening but was just too late to prevent it. He was appalled. He flung himself on to the policeman's broad back with a despairing cry and bore him down with a thud that made men grimace thirty yards away.

It took two Highlanders to drag him off and club him into submission.

The other Russian came down the mountain a few minutes later and saw Sergeant Dunceford sitting dazedly on the ground with blood trickling from a cut lip. Bukhanovich examined the dogs without comment, pushed through the silent men and studied the wolf's lone tracks leading away across the foot of the glen. Then he returned to the policeman.

'What happened to you?'

Dunceford indicated Spassky, whose unconscious body was sprawled nearby.

Bukhanovich turned his countryman over with a push of his foot and regarded him distastefully. He inflicted his own summary punishment: a violent kick in the chest. Several of the men winced but nobody knew quite what to say.

The Russian hunter said, 'You must forgive him. He's rather emotional. But perhaps it was excusable under the circumstances.'

Dunceford coughed busily. 'Well . . . I, err.'

'I apologize. No disrespect for the law was intended.'

'He flung himself on me, like a madman. There was nothing I could do. I'd ricked my neck, you see.'

'Do you intend taking any action against him?'

'It's possible. He can't go about attacking people like that.'

'Then I, too, must consider whether or not to make an official protest to your government about the irresponsible and callous slaughter of two valuable Russian animals.'

'Steady on. There was no time to differentiate.'

'Ah. You saw the wolf then?'

'Oh yes, we saw him all right. He was like something out of a nightmare. Came charging right through the middle of us.'

'And you shot him?'

Dunceford looked at the others for support and shrugged helplessly. 'Couldn't. He was much too fast. He was through us and away before any of us had half a chance.'

Bukhanovich stared disconcertingly. A flat, derisive stare which made the policeman shift uncomfortably.

The Russian asked himself again and again: *Why did I ever come to this godforsaken country?* The shrivelled oil magnate would not forgive his lack of success. Neither would his own embassy. He had to do something quickly and spectacularly, otherwise he stood to lose so much. His pension at an early age, the gratitude of his country and perhaps even his cherished apartment in the heart of Moscow.

He shouldered his rifle and heaved Spassky's pack on top of his own.

'Where are you going?' asked the policeman.

'After our unpleasant friend.'

One of the Scotsmen shook his head as if he doubted the sanity of the venture. 'I hope for your sake that you don't catch up with him.'

'Don't worry for my sake. We Russians are not all soft-hearted.'

Dunceford stood up, still rubbing his neck disconsolately. 'You can say that again. Look, I've got to get these people back to town for a rest and a re-think. It could be that we'll have to try something else.'

'Do what you like. I only ask that you keep well clear of me.'

'No need to get huffy. We can still help each other.'

'I don't need your help.'

'All right, do it your way. But Bakersman isn't going to like it.'

'He can . . .' The hunter thought better of what he intended to say, and reconstructed the sentence. 'He can do as he wishes.'

Dunceford glanced down at the sprawled figure. 'And him?'

Bukhanovich kicked his companion lightly. 'Leave him. He'll know what to do when he wakes up.'

With that the Siberian walked away from the villagers, cleared the ridge and vanished from sight. In a few minutes, the barely moving mist shut him off completely. But the tracks he was following were still easy to discern and he set a steady, inexorable pace.

He was walking to his death. Not immediately . . . he still had time to slay several wolves. But what he did not realize was that his real enemy was no longer the wolf.

THIRTY-FOUR

Emma Dancer poured herself a drink and sat at her dressing-table, staring endlessly at her own reflection. She sipped the gin. Time had been good to her face and body, but had done nothing to improve her judgement. How could she have been so wrong about Richard Unthank? She carefully straightened the perfumes and make-up that were scattered over the surface in front of her, her mind ceaselessly churning over the events of the last few days. She had always considered him a confirmed bachelor, a man totally engrossed in his world and those wretched animals that were so much a part of it, but surely she had meant more to him than that. How could anyone be so weak and so stubborn at the same time?

Suddenly Emma was gripped by an uncomfortable fear. The memory of the wolf scraping at the pane, the thud of its body straining at her door, unleashed the same panic she had felt at her own helplessness the previous night – she would not go through that again! She would not stay in a situation that was beyond her control.

Emma turned her mind to Martin Kelso and smiled. Martin would not let her down. She had known from that first day on the bus that she could get him to eat out of her hand. He would get her out of Elphin.

Emma stared into the mirror and waited.

Martin Kelso, always the gentleman, decided that he needed flowers if he was to call on a lady. There were none showing through the crisp mound of snow under which the garden was buried, and no florist's shop within fifty miles. So he compromised.

He leaned over the banisters on his way downstairs at the guest house and lifted a bunch of dusty artificial carnations from a long-stemmed vase. He kept them under his coat knowing that Mrs Galbraith, an honest straight-laced Gael, saw things in a different way to him.

After plodding through the hindering snow to her home, he bent the crushed flowers back into shape in the shelter of her porch, and fastidiously blew any remaining dust from them.

She was a long time answering his knock.

'Hello there.' Judging by her flushed cheeks, it appeared that she had either been sleeping in front of the fire, or drinking to calm her nerves.

He produced the flowers from behind his back. 'For you.'

'Ooh.'

'Like them?' He shifted modestly. 'Marigolds, I think.'

She inhaled, as if the plastic had a scent to be cherished. 'Carnations.'

'Same thing.' He stepped inside, rubbing his hands appreciatively. 'Well, here I am.'

She helped him out of his fur topcoat. 'I'll pour you a drink, Martin.'

'Fine. Nice to see you again.'

'Nice to see you.'

'How's that big fiancé of yours?'

As she turned away to fetch his drink, he pulled the settee closer to the fire and smoothed out two places. But she settled opposite. 'Are you wondering why I asked you over?'

'No. We're friends, aren't we?'

'Richard and I have broken it off.'

It was neat gin, and he winced as the first mouthful went down. It was rather like drinking expensive perfume. 'Broken what off?'

'Our engagement.'

'Oh, I'm sorry.'

'So am I. But perhaps it's just as well we both found out what kind of people we really are.'

'I'd have said you were admirably suited. What caused it?'

'We had an argument . . . over you.'

Kelso managed to get another mouthful halfway down before coughing violently. So violently she patted his bent back. 'Sorry, sorry,' he wheezed.

'Are you surprised?'

'No, no,' he lied.

'I asked him to take me away from this awful place. I've hardly slept a wink since the incident at the school. But he wouldn't, and we had a row.'

'I'm sorry to hear that.'

'It's for the best. Apparently he thinks more of animals than people. Says it's wrong to shoot deer, even for food and when families are going hungry. Can you believe it?'

Kelso held his glass up to examine the contents and instead found himself observing the attractive line of her breasts.

They were more prominent than he'd remembered, in a salmon pink jersey. 'Doesn't seem possible,' he said, not taking in the conversation.

'I had a really bad night last night. A wolf . . . I think it was a wolf . . . tried to get at me through that door. It was terrifying. I've never experienced such naked, cold-blooded aggression before.'

'Oh, you poor girl.' He was concerned, but not sufficiently to shift his attention away from her jumper. 'I only wish I'd been here.'

'You're very understanding. I knew I could talk to you.' She seemed greatly relieved and touched his hand. 'Martin, I'm going to ask you a great favour.'

'Of course.'

'You won't be shocked, will you?'

'Me? Shocked?' he scoffed, hoping for the worst. But she remained at arm's length.

'I've always been a fairly calm person, but this wolf business got under my skin. I'm frightened. More frightened than I've ever been. I must get away from here.'

'I can understand that.'

'I thought you would . . . Will you take me?'

'Me?' He was genuinely astonished.

'Yes, I'd pay you what I could. A hundred pounds. Is that enough?'

He shook his head and puffed out his cheeks.

'I could stretch to a hundred-and-thirty,' she beseeched him, 'if you'll trust me for a week.'

She was close to tears and he slipped a comforting arm around her slim shoulders. 'Look, I want to get out myself. But there's no way. It's not a question of money. There's no transport, no roads are clear and there's no sign of any help. I'm afraid we're both stuck.'

'There's a snowplough behind the police station. It was left there just before the last big fall.'

'What!'

'And, although the road south may be blocked, the one to the north isn't.'

'My God!' Kelso got up and limped around the room, even beaming delightedly at his handicapped foot. Then he stopped. 'Wait a minute. Even a snowplough has limits. What if we got stuck a few miles north of here? It's in the middle of nowhere.'

'All we have to do is get to Lochinver,' she said urgently, 'There are boats.'

He tilted back his head, squeezed his eyes shut and made an instantaneous decision. 'I'll do it! I've got as much reason as you for getting out. But we'll need that money of yours.'

'I'll get it now. It's under the bed.'

'No, no. Let me think for a moment.'

He could see his story being wired from Ullapool or Liverpool, or somewhere similar, by tomorrow evening. The paper couldn't afford not to print it. That meant his by-line would be on the streets of London the following morning, and he would be famous by breakfast. He savoured the taste in his mouth. *Famous by breakfast!*

'Emma,' he said, his voice intentionally low.

'Yes?' she looked up with little girl eyes. Maybe her judgement was not so bad after all.

'I think I can pull it off,' he smiled wryly.

'Oh thank you, thank you,' she drew him to her, but already her mind was elsewhere.

Emma Dancer was hardly aware of him feverishly unfastening her clothes or even getting into bed. Her thoughts were locked on the journey to come.

In the middle of the night, he awoke drowsily to find Emma staring down at him. She gripped his face in her hands.

'Martin,' she said in a voice he hardly recognized. 'Promise me you won't back out of this.'

'Of course,' he said, uneasy at her tone.

'Good . . . I knew I could trust you.' She kissed him softly and fell asleep almost immediately.

In the morning, he slid out of bed and made breakfast for

himself. He was unable to wipe a silly smile from his face. A woman like that and famous by breakfast! As he limped back to the guest house that cold grey morning he whistled to himself. Life was improving. Martin Kelso was getting on top again!

Sergeant Dunceford, on the other hand, could see his ambition of achieving two silver pips on his shoulders, slipping from his grasp. Everything was turning against him, despite his strenuous efforts to comb the hills.

Once Bakersman learnt that he had let the wolf leader wriggle through his hands, the cantankerous American would complain bitterly to Sir Marcus. The policeman knew his type only too well. Generous to a fault when things were going well, but quick to anger and wickedly unfair when they weren't.

All the years of endeavour and bustling energy which he'd put in towards promotion would be wasted. He'd end up with no more than a sergeant's wafer-thin pension, worn out and with no proper home.

On the long trudge back to Elphin he dropped his equipment more than once, and swore at anyone who was close enough to be blamed. It was not like him, and it made the other men uneasy.

'Clumsy young bugger,' he snapped at someone who had inadvertently fallen against him while sharing a narrow path along the edge of a frozen burn. 'Get out of a man's way.'

When next he called a halt for ten minutes' rest, Dunceford settled some distance from the others and dug secretively into his rucksack. He kept a little waterproof bag at the very bottom; one which he occasionally opened, but never before with any intent of using its contents.

The police sergeant loosened the draw-string and tipped a dozen or so grey-green beans into his hand. They were part of a shipment confiscated from a Dutch steamer when it put into Ullapool from the East Indies two years earlier.

A crofter named John Duffy, who had an unkempt head of

hair not dissimilar to his herd of shaggy Aberdeen Angus cattle, sauntered over. 'What are you up to?'

Dunceford jumped and his hand closed tightly. 'Nothing.'

'Bit early for planting beans, isn't it?'

The hand relaxed and opened slowly. 'You don't plant these beauties. They're *nux vomica.*'

'They're what?'

'For feeding wolves.'

The crofter laughed uncertainly and moved away, his attention drawn to somebody else's conversation. He shrugged; the sergeant was under a strain. But what he did not know is that *nux vomica* beans contain a white crystalline powder which kills wolves and all who digest it. Strychnine.

Sergeant Jack Dunceford slept heavily and late the next morning, and missed all the excitement. By the time he awoke at midday, stiff and aching all over, the snowplough had left with three people on board.

Kelso had called at Station House much earlier for a routine chat with the suddenly talkative Constable Shaftoe and heard of the hunting group's brush with the wolf and of the lone Russian's determination to track it down.

Again, it was too good a story to keep for ever. He sat down at the sergeant's desk, pushed the entire contents to one side and wrote his copy in longhand.

People were being reduced to shuffling figures on the road between their homes and a few thinly-stocked shops. They were being starved by the weather, terrorized by wolves and apparently ignored by the rest of an uncaring Britain. It was good stuff. He could already see his by-line, prominently boxed in. Perhaps with a little head and shoulders of himself. *Martin Kelso, in the Highlands, Tuesday.*

The ambling young constable was intrigued that something was being written about Elphin, and kept him supplied with slopping mugs of tea.

'They tell me I might get a boat out of here if I can get to Lochinver. How far's that? Ten or fifteen miles?'

259

'Road's blocked.'

'Not to a snowplough.'

Shaftoe followed his thinking and glanced towards the rear window.

'It's not ours. Belongs to the regional authority. You can't touch it.'

'Why on earth not? I'm a ratepayer like everybody else, and that truck is public property paid for on the rates.'

'But you can't go driving it off anywhere you fancy.'

'I wouldn't be going *anywhere*. I'd be going *somewhere* to get help for this forgotten toenail of the British Empire. It seems to me that the only way Elphin will get any outside help is if someone ploughs his way out and tells the authorities what's going on.'

The temporary policeman drew back in embarrassment. 'Well, I can't go.'

'Don't want you to. I'll do it myself.'

'Not without the driver's consent. He's staying up the road with the MacTavish family.'

'All right, I'll get it. Him too, if I can.'

Martin Kelso was a persuasive man, and not given to adhering to the letter of the law when it did not suit him. He had the timorous council driver out of his lodgings within ten minutes and even sent him along to rouse Emma Dancer.

She arrived white-faced and breathless a few minutes later, a suitcase banging at her legs. 'I thought you'd gone without me.'

He blew her a kiss. 'Me? Would I do a thing like that?'

The meek young Gael pulled a knitted hat down over his ears and climbed up into the high cab of the yellow Foden truck. As he warmed up the six-cylinder engine, Emma walked aro   the outside and felt reassured by the six huge black tyres and the angled snow blade fixed to the vehicle's predominant bonnet. Fifteen miles was obviously well within its range.

She busied herself in the kitchen at Station House, making sandwiches and vacuum flasks of tea with Shaftoe's amiable help.

The pretty American girl, who was wearing a nursing hat, came down and talked earnestly to Kelso for a while. She seemed stunned that he was leaving without telling her, but she hung around and watched them leave.

Emma had never felt so relieved in her life as when the roar of the engine filled her ears and the vibration made her bracelets rattle together. In an hour or two they would be thumping massively down the hill into the little fishing port of Lochinver, where a cluster of high-prowed vessels are berthed the year around.

The Foden's cab was surprisingly warm and the driver gave her a darting smile whenever he was addressed. He understood English but preferred to restrict his monosyllabic conversation to the Gaelic.

Elphin was soon left behind. They progressed steadily but noisily along the lonely road, pushing back the snow and not seeing a soul on the majestic white hills. They passed a half-buried hotel at Inchnadamph, which was their halfway mark, and soon afterwards the ruins of Ardvreck Castle on the shores of deep-running Loch Assynt.

There seemed no reason to stop, but the driver set his handbrake and climbed laboriously down into the kneedeep snow. He stood quite still, blowing on the bent fingers of his mittened hands and listening to the abrupt silence.

'What's he up to?' asked Kelso, emerging from the soporific warmth of his upturned collar.

'Stretching his legs.'

They watched the man climb over a leaning gate and walk around the frozen water's edge to the foot of the ancient grey tower wall.

Kelso began to get irritated. 'Where the hell does he think he's going? We're wasting time.'

He even got down into the wet snow himself and cupped his hands around his mouth. 'Come on, old lad,' he bawled. 'This isn't a bloody coach outing.'

The man returned presently, without any explanation. Before he restarted the engine Emma noticed he was shivering slightly. 'Cold?' She poured him a mug of tea and stirred in some sugar. He shook his head, but took the tea.

'*Cunnart.*' He pointed towards the ruins less than two hundred yards away.

'He says there's danger. *Cunnart.* Over there.'

'I can't see anything to worry about, except a few sheep tracks. Sheep tracks?'

The driver shook his head faintly. '*Madadhallaidh. Mactire.*'

'Oh God,' she whispered.

'Well?' demanded the reporter.

'Wolf tracks.'

Kelso leaned across Emma who separated him from the driver. 'What did you see?'

The man, who seemed to have withdrawn completely into the Gaelic, avoided his eyes. '*Am fear nach can mi. An droch-chreutair.*'

She translated quietly, the long manicured nails of one hand digging into the palm of the other. 'The one I won't mention. The evil creature.'

The cab was strangely silent even though the engine turned over noisily. Kelso glanced across at the snow-draped ruins. 'Bollocks,' he scoffed eventually. 'Let's get out of here before we work ourselves into a state over nothing.'

The vehicle lurched back on line with the thin grey and red poles which marked one side of the hidden road to a depth of seven feet. They bumped reassuringly on their way at no more than ten miles an hour. It was fast enough. To go off the road would be disastrous; they could never get the Foden back on again.

Kelso took her hand. 'Soon be there.'

A short distance behind them, loping along the high ground with its curious mixture of obdurate Torridon sandstone and soft pliable peat, were five wolves.

They were invisible to the occupants of the truck.

The lead wolf occasionally glanced down across the mountainside to the labouring vehicle, as if he was only mildly interested. But he knew time was on his side. There was no turning back for the truck and no way out ahead.

PART IV: THE RECKONING

THIRTY-FIVE

There is no room in the world for more than one species of predator bent on domination.

The wolf had merely fought for a place in the balance of things as ordained by Nature and evolution. But gradually it lost its way to a more ruthless species which was not content to obey even the basic laws of mutual survival.

Unthank did not realize this as he tried to make his presence felt in the snowbound community, his mind still filled with Emma Dancer and the loneliness that stretched ahead of him now she had gone.

But Darkmind knew only too well.

The real killer was about to emerge in all his cunning and ferocity.

THIRTY-SIX

The house on the hill took on a gaunt appearance. The cook and two other servants made their excuses, gave up their claim to payment for days worked, and left. They returned somewhat fatalistically to their families to face whatever the neverending winter had in store for them.

Dust sheets were draped across rooms full of furniture and the living space was drawn in, more and more each day, until

Penny Bakersman was cooking for her father from a kitchenette while he moved a camp bed into the adjoining lounge.

Not that he appreciated her attention.

He swung out wrathfully with his stick, convinced that everybody was against him. It was little wonder that when the last of the servants left, they whispered their apologetic goodbyes and a Celtic blessing on Penny alone.

'Where are they all?' demanded JC Bakersman in the morning, after being confronted by a cold and empty grate. 'We paid them enough. Whatever happened to their sense of loyalty?'

His daughter twisted old newspapers and laid a fire to warm his veined hands. 'They've all gone, and I don't blame them. It's nothing to do with money. People have an instinctive feeling about these things. They say that, if the winter won't relent and something dreadful happens, they would rather be back in a place of their own choosing.'

Bakersman muttered as he crossed to the window and looked out at the grey, overcast sky, checking that there was no sign of the company helicopter. The three days' grace he had extracted from Sir Marcus Sheerwater had run out and, thank God, the helicopter had still not reappeared. He was relieved for the breathing space. Every extra day gave his marksmen a better chance of slaughtering another wolf.

'There.' She knelt back on her heels to watch the newborn flames devour paper and wood, and lick at sullen lumps of coal. 'Now, for heaven's sake, sit down. I want to talk to you.'

Her father ignored her and crossed to his large-scale map of the area, on which he kept track of the wolf hunt. But the lines of orange and blue pins were muddled.

'The idiots are going round in circles,' he complained.

She steered him to his purpose-built straight-backed chair. 'Never mind about other people. Just listen to me for a while.'

He grumbled, but finally settled. 'Well?'

'Where's the helicopter?'

'In London, I guess. Marcus Sheerwater needed it on urgent Government business.'

'But that was a lifetime ago . . . last week, when things were vastly different. Now we desperately need it back here. You've got to get it for me. Today.'

'Why, what's the matter with you?'

'It's not for me. It's for Mrs McDee and little Amy. The girl's having constant nightmares. She thinks that one particular wolf is intent on getting her personally.'

Her father turned his head away with an impatient noise. 'That's ridiculous.'

'That may be. But, if we don't get her far away from here, she'll frighten herself to death.'

Bakersman grunted and gnawed his fist with frustration. 'It's those goddamned wolves. They took Franklin, then the girl and her father. They're to blame . . . not me! We've got to wipe them out, you know. Every goddamned last one!' He swished his walking stick like a sabre and broke two fine tumblers in the process.

'Forget the wolves just for once. Think of the girl's sister.'

'I am thinking of her! I'm thinking that, if she dies, she won't go unavenged. I'll have every one of those evil bastards nailed to the door within a week.'

Penny Bakersman took hold of her father's lapels and stared into his eyes. 'Don't you understand? She hasn't got a week.'

'That's too bad,' trembled her father. 'But there's nothing I can do. As soon as Marcus gets back, the lid comes off the pot. The press will pour in and, pretty soon, all the do-gooders will arrive. If that happens, we can kiss goodbye any chance of retribution. And then who's going to avenge your brother? Huh? Answer me that.'

She stared at him in astonishment. 'Vengeance? Are you serious? I'm trying to save a girl's life . . . not avenge somebody who's dead and gone. Daddy, face it. He's dead. You can't bring him back.'

His face twisted with anger. 'Careful, darling! You're not so sweet and innocent that I wouldn't smack your face.'

'Daddy.' Her voice cracked with despair. 'I just want you to see things clearly.'

265

'Oh, I see better than you imagine. Like I saw what you were up to at that ski resort. Shafting! That was it, wasn't it? Shafting while your brother was dying. Any normal sister would have been filled with remorse. But not you. Oh no. You couldn't wait to fall backwards into bed with that newspaper fella, and get yourself laid!' He bent forward in his wheelchair and coughed up his heart.

'Get out of my sight,' he sobbed when he eventually straightened. 'Get outside and pray for forgiveness. I might have been guilty of a lot of misjudgements during my life, but one thing I never forgot is the sanctity of the family. No sir. Nobody can accuse me of turning my back on my kin.'

She left the house chalk-faced and wiping her eyes. She was gradually losing everyone she loved: Franklin, Martin Kelso, and now this . . . but she was more determined than ever to get her way. She made for the guest house where one of her father's bespectacled aides was staying, trapped by the last snowfall.

'I want you to get in touch with the company.'

'I'm sorry, Miss Penny, I can't even get through to the local operator. The line's dead. Been dead for days.'

She ignored his problems and repeated, 'I want you to get in touch with the company. Tell them I want the helicopter flown back here immediately. I don't give a damn what it's doing or where it is. You understand?'

'I understand right enough, miss. But what will your father say?'

She took a deep breath and her eyes hardened. 'My father's dying. I own nearly one-third of all the stock in Parallel Oil. He won't be here next year, but I will. So just do as I say.'

The man suddenly became a lot more attentive. 'Yes, madam, I understand. But I don't know how to get the message through.'

'That's your problem. Just do it . . . and do it fast.'

Sergeant Jack Dunceford trudged up to the MP's house in an attempt to retain some of the shattered pieces of his career.

No one answered his knocks and he ventured inside, calling hesitantly as he went.

'Anybody in? Are you there, sir?'

He knew the staff had left, but was still surprised at the extent to which the house had been shut up. Dust seemed to have settled thickly within only a day or two and already the place had a damp, unused smell about it.

He found remains of sandwiches and a bottle of curdled milk in the tiny kitchen. The oilman was lying shivering on a sofa, with an overcoat pulled up to his chin. His ferrety eyes were closed, but no sooner did the policeman peer down than they opened and fastened on Dunceford.

'What the hell are you creeping about for? You should be out hunting.'

Dunceford jerked back. 'I thought you were having a nap.'

'You should be out hunting.'

'Aah.' The sergeant twisted his peaked cap in his hands and smiled craftily. 'I don't need to, do I.'

Bakersman sat up, like a walrus emerging from the sea. 'What?' He waved a hand towards the kitchenette. 'Do something useful. Make me a coffee.'

Dunceford busied himself, filling a kettle and opening and shutting drawers. In the meantime, the American sat on edge of his bed and put on a jacket over his crumpled shirt and tie.

He accepted the coffee with a grunt and pulled a face as he swallowed the first mouthful. 'Errr! Goddamnit, that's awful.'

'I'm not much of a cook,' Dunceford said apologetically.

'You're not much of anything if you ask me,' muttered the oilman. 'Now, why aren't you out hunting, like you're supposed to be?'

'I'm a policeman. It's not part of my job to go wild goose-chasing across the mountains in the middle of winter. I've already been out for several days, and I've killed my share of wolves. But enough's enough. The snow keeps coming down, and nobody can go out there at the moment with any certainty of ever coming back.'

Bakersman screwed up his face in agony as he drank. 'Goddamnit, this is really atrocious. Where did you learn to make coffee?'

'I didn't. I only drink tea.'

Bakersman shuddered as he set down the cup. 'You heard anything from those Bolsheviks yet?'

'No.'

'Well, if they don't come up with some positive results soon, I shall be on to their Foreign Ministry. When you find them, I want you to tell them that, and then give them such a kick up the arse that you never get your boot back.'

'I don't know why you put so much reliance on foreigners.'

'I don't. That's one of the reasons I'm not relying on you.'

'But I don't need to shoot wolves.' Dunceford gave a devious little smile. I've already got them where I want them.'

'Help me into my chair.' The American grunted as the sergeant lifted him solidly into the big wheeled invalid chair. 'What do you mean?'

'I've got something special up my sleeve.'

'Special?'

Dunceford nodded foxily. 'A day at the most, and I'll have something for you in the way of pelts.'

The American frowned, trying to make up his mind whether or not Dunceford was fantasizing, when the drone of an approaching aero-engine cut across his thoughts.

Helicopter. Damn and blast it! He quickly hand-wheeled himself across to the broad windows and scanned the clouds as the noise grew more distinct. Tense hands gripped the chromium rims. *Go away,* he willed it. *For pity's sake, go away.* He needed just a day or two more. Two miserable days at the most and the wolves would be his. Was that too much to ask?

Penny, who had just returned from the infirmary, burst into the room and pushed open the double windows. The noise became a roar. 'Where is it? Can you see it?' She leaned out into the bitterly cold air, straining her eyes up at the impenetrable clouds. 'Oh come on. Come on,' she pleaded.

'Don't encourage them,' growled her father.

'We need that helicopter!'

'No we don't. It's no use getting flustered over a kid who's halfway into her grave anyway.'

She pulled back into the room and twisted furiously, catching him with a stinging slap across the face. Even the policeman winced.

'Don't you dare say that! I've worked for three exhausting days to save Amy McDee's life, and I'm not going to give up now. God, she's worth more than you ever were.'

Bakersman was stunned by her outburst, but he had no time to react before a change registered in the aircraft's pitch. It was fading.

The policeman pointed. 'There it is! Looks like an old Tiger Moth heading for Skye.' A frail, high-winged plane skimmed slowly into view under heavy clouds on its way towards the sea.

Penny covered her mouth in dismay, and she was aware of her father's triumphant gaze as she ran from the room.

Dunceford missed the drama as his eyes followed the receding plane. 'He's still got one or two mountains to dodge. And, if he comes a cropper, there's no way I can help. Nobody could move far in that snow. It's neck-deep in places.'

He sighed and, as his gaze descended to street level, he saw for the first time a distant figure, walking purposefully off towards the isolated peak of Suilven, pulling a sledge behind him.

Bakersman also noticed and twirled his wheelchair expertly, the better to see. 'Who the blazes is that?'

Dunceford gulped. 'Professor Pope-Watson. He's an eminent ornithologist.'

'He's a what?'

'A bird-watcher. In his eighties. He goes off to look for peewits and that sort of thing, for weeks at a time.'

'But you said the snow out there was impassable.'

'I know.' Dunceford laughed weakly. 'Would you believe it?'

THIRTY-SEVEN

The snowplough forced its way over the crest of the hill, building a wall of snow to one side, and Emma saw for the first time the beautiful fishing village of Lochinver. It stretched out before her, at the foot of tree-lined hills, around the gentle curve of a loch for nearly a mile until it reached the quay.

A road followed the edge of the water and, on its landward side, the roofs of the church and a hotel glistened in unexpected sunshine.

The driver switched off his six-cylinder engine and braked on the downslope. It was no problem. Travelling at less than ten miles an hour and hampered by a deep carpet of snow they stopped within a few feet.

Emma made an appreciative noise. 'It's breathtaking.'

But Martin Kelso was already peering anxiously ahead. 'How many boats do you see? One. I can see two!' Relieved, he kissed her soft cheek and then leaned across and pumped the Highlander's hand. 'Thanks. Thanks a lot.'

The Scot smiled wanly and glanced again into each of the long side-mirrors, checking the hillside behind him. But there was no apparent movement.

Lochinver was curiously silent as they drove across a little bridge and swung along the lochside, making for the distant turreted hotel which adjoined Culag pier. There was no movement in the modest row of houses and, by the time they reached the halfway point, a grey-stone war memorial on the lochside, Kelso had an uneasy feeling that all was not well.

Emma stared, intrigued, at the lifesized figure of a kilted Highlander in a glengarry, advancing bayonet-fixed into eternity.

'Oh, hell,' groaned the newspaperman as he got a closer look at the first vessel. 'It's a hulk. Looks as if it was beached a hundred years ago.'

They rounded a curve on to the last few hundred yards of road to the quay, where spars and stiffly-frozen nets still held the promise of a way out by sea.

'Come on. Get a move on,' he urged the driver.

They had hardly reached the broad courtyard of the hotel, before Kelso swung from the cab and jumped into the snow. Then, he limped rapidly across the quay to a second boat.

He shuffled down a gangway, cautiously dislodging virgin snow a foot deep. Once on deck, he waved back enthusiastically.

But Emma's attention was drawn the other way. The hotel doors opened and a brawny-armed young woman with red cheeks appeared. She wore a scarf, wrapped under her chin and tied on top, like a toothache bandage.

'Hello there,' called Emma Dancer. 'Are we glad to see you. We were beginning to think this was a ghost town.'

'Oooh.' The woman laughed embarrassedly and stepped out in glossy yellow Wellington boots. They shook hands.

'Where is everybody?'

'Oh, most of them have gone. They left a week ago on the last boat.'

Emma started to smile an acknowledgement, then twisted around. 'Last boat? What's the matter with that one?'

The woman smiled like a polished apple. 'No engine. She's just used for storage. Old tackle and the like.'

'Wouldn't you bloody well know it!' Kelso reappeared scuffing his boots aggressively. 'Hello, I'm with them.' As he shook hands, he noticed that their driver was gazing back down the road. 'We've got to get out of here, to the south. Do you understand? Is there anything that can take us?'

The girl smiled. It seemed she smiled at everybody and everything; she was that sort of person. 'I understand all right. Won't you all come in?'

The spacious hotel had once been a home of the Duke of Sutherland, and Kelso could still sense the brandy and cigars

271

atmosphere it had exuded. But for now it was under siege. The double lounge was temporarily converted into living quarters for about six people – all extremely elderly so far as he could see.

One or two waved feeble hands and moved slowly from camp beds to a long, central table on which there were various pots and plates, and an urn of tea.

The big girl rubbed her raw hands briskly. 'Now, won't you have a hot cup of tea? If you've come from Elphin, you must be chilled through.' She operated a silver lever and sweet, scalding tea gushed out into elegant crockery bearing an ancient coat of arms.

'There, that should warm you.'

'Are there any men here?'

'No, just me and the older ones.'

Kelso went to one of the far windows and gazed out at the white, unmoving water. 'Looks frozen stiff to me,' he muttered.

The group trailed after him. 'It can't be,' said Emma. 'There's the Gulf Stream somewhere around here.'

'Aye,' volunteered the Scotswoman. 'It's only a few inches thick. But you could walk on it for a mile or two if you were really set on the idea.'

Kelso grimaced at her plain, matter-of-fact face. 'May I inquire? Are you a spinster?'

'No. I'm a MacLeod.'

'No, I mean, do you have a husband, or a father or brother who might help us? It's imperative that we move on. We have to get down to Ullapool and then to England. And I certainly don't fancy walking on the water.'

'There'll be no boats back here until the thaw,' she said apologetically. 'Most people voted to leave after we'd been cut off from outside contact for more than a month. These few old folk, who've lived here all their lives, refused to budge. So I stayed too.'

Kelso gulped. 'That's courageous of you.'

'Not at all. I get seasick. Anyway, I've never been outside Sutherland in my life and no wish to start now.'

272

They all laughed, and Emma sat down with Kelso while their timorous driver fell, somewhat uncharacteristically, into a deep conversation with Ella MacLeod.

'We've got to get out of here,' whispered the reporter. 'This is worse than Elphin. At least there, we had the chance of that bloody elusive helicopter coming back.'

Emma's face twitched. 'I'm not going back,' she said firmly. 'You do what you like, but I'm going on.'

'Going on? Where to?'

'Anywhere,' she shivered. 'I'll walk if I have to, but I'm not going back to face those demented creatures.'

Kelso remembered seeing an Ordnance Survey map pinned to the lobby wall. He threaded his way through obstacle-course furniture, past the main reception desk, a disconnected telephone and brown trout mounted in glass cases on the wall.

Sure enough, the road back towards Ardvreck Castle branched off to the north, touching the coast several times on its lonely way to Durness and the relentless North Atlantic.

'Ella,' he called. 'Would you come over here, please.'

'What is it, sir?'

He rested his fingertip on the map, a few miles up the coast from Lochinver. 'Any boats to be found up here?'

She nodded. 'Aye. Kylesku has the ferry. A big car ferry, but there won't have been any customers for a month or two.'

'But does it go? Does it work?'

'Work? Oh, yes. It's a powerful vessel. It'll be tied up there until the spring.'

Kelso turned to Emma whose face had come alive again. 'What do you think? Fifteen miles. It's a ropy-looking road and, when we get there, we might find someone else has had the same idea and already pinched it ...'

Ella MacLeod interrupted. 'Oh no, they wouldn't do that. It belongs to the regional authority. Everybody knows that. They'd never get permission to take it.'

Kelso regarded her honest face sympathetically. He even squeezed it gently between his hands. 'Of course not. It wouldn't be proper. Look, can we rest here tonight and set out for Kylesku first thing in the morning?'

'Of course you can. We're pleased for the company.'

The newspaperman spent an uncomfortable night. A fire burned sleepily enough in a big carved-stone fireplace, but an elderly man with paper-thin lungs coughed incessantly and Kelso was unable, for appearances' sake, to creep under Emma's pile of blankets.

They huddled on the floor. No one even suggested going upstairs where countless beds remained unaired and untouched. But, as Ella said, it was not their hotel and they would not touch more than was absolutely necessary in the owner's absence.

In the early hours Kelso heard a distant howling. The mournful sound froze his marrow, and was all the more disturbing against the weird shadows thrown along the high walls by the fire.

The howls were far away. Perhaps a mile or two. It was even possible that they came from animals on the far side of the hills and moving in quite the opposite direction.

He got up to get another cup of tea from the tepid urn and noticed the snowplough driver standing out in the lobby with Ella MacLeod. They were talking in low voices, in the Gaelic. But when the woman shrugged helplessly and pointed in three quite different directions, she repeated a word which he recognized. *Madadhallaidh*. Wolf!

The road was blocked. Snow was piled in an enormous drift, twenty feet deep on an exposed bend, leaving no room either side for manoeuvre.

They tried to bulldoze their way through, but only got stuck. The driver raced the engine and grated a number of forward and reverse gears, but the Foden was hopelessly buried.

It was mid-morning and, otherwise, not an unpleasant day. They had left a subdued Lochinver two hours earlier after a tinned breakfast of black pudding, bacon and beans.

Ella MacLeod had piled them up with flasks and yet more

tinned food and seen them off: a sturdy reassuring figure in the trampled snow of the hotel courtyard.

'Sure you'll be all right here, alone?' Emma asked for the last time.

'I'm not alone. Anyway, we've got two ship-distress rockets on the roof.' She laughed merrily. 'I can always fire those and hope a nice plump bachelor will come running.'

None of the old folk ventured outside and the three of them kissed Ella MacLeod goodbye before swinging up into the high cab.

Kelso gave a final wave. 'Take care.'

'You're the ones who need to take care,' she called. She did not explain and they did not press her.

At first their progress was better than they had imagined possible. Soft snow skimmed effortlessly off their diagonal bow-blade and they followed the track they had cleared the previous day. But after turning abruptly north off the familiar road, at desolate Skiag Bridge, they began steadily to climb and the new road twisted like a scarcely-ridden horse.

The big solitary mountain of Quinag began to dominate their view on the left and they felt the push of a sullen wind off its downslopes. It was the same current which had caused the snowdrift and brought them to a halt about a mile short of the Kylesku Ferry.

Not once since leaving Lochinver had they seen any sign of human activity, and Emma began to despair that they would find anyone at the loch crossing-point ahead.

Kelso forced open a door against the crushing weight of snow, thumping it with his ugly surgical boot, and grinning maniacally, almost as if he enjoyed making his foot suffer.

'Bring the flask,' he grunted to Emma as he thrust himself out backwards and elbowed an escape corridor. She floundered after him followed by their white-faced driver, who uttered little gasps as he jerked through the chest-high snow.

Back on a cleared stretch of road, they shook themselves dry and took stock. The sun was still glinting from a patchy grey and white sky and, under any other circumstances, they would have laughed at their bedraggled appearance.

On one side the ground fell gently away, dipping down towards Quinag and a point where it began to soar again to a towering 2,500 feet. On the other they were flanked by a line of small grumpy hills. Along their crest was a power cable, which sagged between widely spaced pylons and only just made it across the hundred-yard gaps.

The lonely hillside itself was flanked in wiry snow-covered heather. Kelso shaded his eyes against the white glare and squinted up at the crest. 'I think we'd be better off up there. At least we'll get a clear view. But if we stay down here we could stray off the road without realizing it and disappear down a hole. What do you think?'

Emma glanced around at the magnificently hostile mountainside, and shrugged. 'Whatever you think's best.' Their driver acceded with a shy smile.

They plodded up the slope, helping one another where they could. Stumbling, occasionally missing their step on loose, invisible stones and breathing more heavily the farther they went.

After ten minutes, when barely out of sight of the drift which devoured their snowplough, Kelso called a halt. It was then that Emma Dancer realized she had left her bag in the Foden.

'My God, all the money's in it!'

Kelso wiped his perspiring face. 'You bloody fool.'

'Don't speak to me like that!'

Kelso looked round for support, but their driver kept well out of it. 'Women, bloody women,' the newspaperman muttered with an exasperated jerk of his head.

'Swearing won't help,' she said sharply.

'Call that swearing? You should hear me when something really goes wrong. It would make your curlers drop out.'

'Well, what are we going to do? It's all the money I had.'

'You'd better go back for it,' said Kelso.

'Me?'

'It's your money and you forgot it. Christ, you certainly don't imagine I'm going, do you?'

Their exchanges were becoming steadily more acrimonious

until their driver got up, without a word, and set off abruptly down the hillside.

Emma tried to stop him. 'Hey, I didn't mean you.'

But the Gael merely waved sheepishly and continued on his way. He made swift progress and Kelso told her to sit down.

'It's okay. He knows what he's doing. We'd better relax. We won't reach the ferry for the best part of an hour at this rate.'

The sun winked in agreement and they fashioned back-rests in the snow in order to sit and stretch out their legs: admiring the austere majesty of a landscape fashioned three hundred million years before man ever walked upon it.

They might never again have seen their driver, but for the muffled blare of the Foden's horn. It disturbed the silence for several seconds, as if somebody had his hand pressed down on the bar, before petering out.

Emma got quickly to her feet. 'What on earth's that?'

'It's him. Probably just letting us know he's found it.' Kelso smiled reassuringly as he settled back against his hump of packed snow, but he felt less certain than he appeared.

The horn started up again. Abrupt and insistent. Five, six, seven times. Then stopped for good.

Emma grabbed her blue woolly hat and tugged it determinedly down over her ears. 'I'm going to see. He may need help.'

Kelso pulled her back down. 'You're bloody well not! There might be something down there!'

She stared at him with a rigid awareness. 'What do you mean?'

Kelso zipped and buckled his jacket. 'I don't know what I mean. I'll find out though. You stay here.'

He set off, following the blurred footsteps of the Gael, and covering the steeply descending ground at a speed which surprised even him. But every step brought him closer to the realization that something was seriously wrong. Emma followed at a distance.

They stood panting for breath at the half-blocked culvert

of snow in which the Foden was buried. All was silent and curiously eerie. As Kelso leaned forward to peer inside, the snow creaked under his weight. She gasped and grabbed his hand for reassurance.

'Stay here,' he whispered. 'If he's in there, he's been caught by a collapse of soft snow. There's no point in us both . . .' His sentence trailed off as he stepped warily along the corridor.

At first he could see little difference from when he had left the Foden earlier. The high door was still half open, although now there was something substantial inside.

Kelso crouched behind the truck for nearly thirty seconds, waiting for something to happen and ready to jerk back out of the way the moment it did.

Jesus Christ, there it was! There was a faint movement inside, and he strained his eyes to see through a frosted glass panel at the back of the cab.

Whatever it was stopped moving and, after another long wait, he steeled himself. He squeezed along the side of the vehicle and climbed up on to the big front wheel, easing the door open. Immediately there was a rush of movement and something struck his arm forcibly.

'Jeeee . . . sus!' He jerked back off the giant tyre, falling blindly into the shock-absorbing snow and landing with his head several feet lower than his legs. For a moment or two he was helpless, and whatever was coming out would get at him before he could regain his feet! He rolled desperately over in the wet snow, ending up in tangle under the truck and cracking his head on the chassis as he tried to straighten up.

Nothing followed him down. And, when he inched his head back into view, he saw the Gaelic driver's arm dangling from the door. The young man's head was pressed against the instrument panel and there was a trickle of blood down the ridge of his nose.

Kelso half-lifted, half-dragged him clear and laid the limp body down behind the vehicle, still within the cavernous gloom of the towering drift.

As he turned the limp head, he saw raking claw marks,

278

which had torn open the man's face from the corner of his eye, down across his neck to the edge of his shoulder. 'Oh, my God.' One of the hands was ripped and bloody, and already turning stiff with cold.

The driver's eyes fluttered and his lips moved wordlessly, until Kelso propped him up. Blood was pumping from a severed neck artery and the back of his coat was soggy with the weight of it.

'What is it, old chap?' Kelso bent low to catch the words, but they were in Gaelic and meant nothing to him.

'I don't understand,' he said desperately. 'I can't hear you clearly. Talk in English.'

The man tried again, struggling feebly to lift his head. 'Out on . . . out on the road. Two wolves waiting . . . waiting for me.'

Kelso swung around savagely and bellowed out a warning. 'Emma get off the road. Wolves! Get in here. Right now, woman. Move!'

She came scrambling in, whimpering and falling on to her knees. But she stopped feeling sorry for herself as soon as she saw the driver's condition. 'You poor, dear man. Let me have him, Martin.' She cradled the ashen-faced youth in her arms.

Kelso shaped a rough pillow of snow, then stripped off his own topcoat and two jumpers before reaching his shirt. He wrenched it off and yanked out an unco-operative sleeve with an oath that would have shocked a naval stoker. Then tore it roughly into bandages. He wound them deftly around the man's thick neck and under one arm, twisting them as best he could to cut off the endless flow of blood.

But he was too late. The youth was barely alive and looked the colour of old putty with a bluish tinge to his lips. Yet still his face held a pathetically grateful expression.

Kelso could not bear to watch him die. He went outside into the weak sunshine and stood numbly, not much caring whether or not a wolf returned.

The meek young Gael moved his eyes after the self-indulgent Englishman and whispered to Emma: 'Siad. Siad.' Then he closed his eyes and died.

When she joined Martin Kelso her eyes glistened with tears.

'Did he say anything?'

She shook her head.

Siad is the Gaelic for *A fine fellow*. But it would not be appropriate to tell him. The real *Siad* had died.

THIRTY-EIGHT

The helicopter came fluttering down out of the sky before most people even realized that it was on its way.

But they had a second chance to welcome it five minutes later. First it unloaded Sue McKenna, a TV cameraman and a sound engineer, then took off and circled as if arriving for the first time.

By now, Dunceford had appeared outside Station House, working his way into his braces and wiping traces of a fried egg sandwich from his mouth. The vicar made his way to the school playground accompanied by several women, and a scattering of other people filtered out as if from nowhere.

The helicopter door was flung back and Sir Marcus stood there smiling and waving dramatically.

'Hold it right there,' called Miss McKenna from between cupped hands. 'Now, jump down and shake hands with the first person to greet you. That's it!'

She snapped her fingers at Sergeant Dunceford who was rapidly approaching, buttoning his uniform jacket. 'You! Over here, please. Come straight in and embrace your MP.'

'Who, me?'

'Yes. Go on, don't stare at the camera. Try to look natural. You're delighted and enormously relieved to see him. That's it. Now both turn this way and smile. Great. Great. Cut!'

Dunceford pumped the MP's hand. 'Am I glad to see you,

sir. You ought to know what's been going on. It's been a madhouse, but I've got it under control now.'

'Over here, Marcus,' called the energetic dark-haired girl. 'We want a shot of the vicar giving thanks when he sees you.'

Sheerwater brushed the policeman aside. 'Later, Sergeant. Later,' he muttered. Then louder: 'Coming, Sue. Nice to see you again, father. Everything all right?'

There was turmoil for the next hour or so. The exhausted doctor was called down from the infirmary and told he could have a box of emergency medical supplies right away.

'It's not supplies I need,' he said, 'so much as a good night's sleep.' But he was ignored while the TV crew elaborately filmed the Red Cross box being handed over by Sheerwater.

Sue McKenna, however, was still not satisfied. 'Hold it. The whole thing looks like a damned funeral. We need something to liven it up. Doctor, have you got any decent-looking nurses we can get our hands on?'

The doctor shrugged hopelessly. 'Err, I don't really ... '

Penny Bakersman arrived at an opportune moment, but she looked jaded and had to force a smile. 'Doctor, I'm delighted to tell you that the helicopter is now officially at the hospital's disposal. Use it for patients, or medical purposes, or whatever you think fit.'

'Are you sure?'

'Absolutely.'

'Thank you, nurse.' They shook hands warmly.

'Wait a minute,' called the exasperated woman TV producer. 'What are you doing?'

Penny pretended not to be aware of her hostility. 'Me? Oh, I'm making arrangements for the helicopter.' She beckoned the pilot down.

'Well sod that ... ' Sue McKenna turned her around by the elbow. 'We've just flown all the way from London, by arrangement, and at considerable inconvenience. And I'm not about to have my crew dumped in the snow by you or anybody. So just you hold your horses.'

The MP noticed the women growing increasingly resentful

of one another and broke away from his conversation with the vicar.

'Darling,' he said, bustling across full of bonhomie, 'this is . . . ' Then remembered that the Highlands are less broadminded than London. 'Miss McKenna, this is Miss Bakersman. Her father owns Parallel Oil.'

'How do you do?' The TV woman was coldly polite, then turned to the uncomfortable MP and said, almost in the same breath, 'Marcus, we've got a busy schedule. Tell her to keep out of the way, or she'll get her arse kicked.'

Penny smiled with acid sweetness. 'Marcus. Father's not well. So, if you need any help from the company, talk to me. In the meantime, we're taking the helicopter back in order to fly a sick girl south.'

'What?' exploded the hard-bitten TV journalist. 'How the hell are we going to film a pack of wolves without it?'

'Find some other transport. You could try the bus.'

'What bus?'

'You'll find it near the police station. Of course, it is under ten feet of snow, but you could dig it out.'

Marcus Sheerwater was vastly relieved to be interrupted by the arrival of Bobby Shaftoe on a Shetland pony. He seemed to be in a desperate hurry, pumping his legs against the pony's plump flanks to urge it forward.

The temporary constable was in a muck sweat. 'Sir Marcus!'

'What is it?'

'Trouble. Up there, on the Spotted Hill.' Shaftoe dismounted awkwardly and fought for breath. 'There must be a dozen or more animals in a heap, all dead. Including a wolf. Looks as if they've been hit by a whirlwind.'

Sheerwater frowned at the hill which rose steeply from the side of the road at the far end of the village. 'Are you sure? Where's the Sergeant?'

But Dunceford had scurried back to Station House to get his high helmet on which was the silver crest of the county constabulary. He knew, immediately Shaftoe panted into view, that the results of his previous day's work had been found. The strychnine had been abruptly effective, just as he knew it would be. There were probably several dead wolves, not just the one. Trust Shaftoe to get it wrong. In any event, he had been the only man in Elphin with the foresight to use a swift and deadly method of control.

Dunceford quickly wiped his face over with a flannel and examined his reflection. *You'll be on television tonight,* he promised himself, adjusting his chin strap.

Some thirty people straggled up the snow-covered slope to see for themselves what Shaftoe had discovered. The acting constable laboured on ahead, perspiring in his enthusiasm to show them.

They came upon the carnage in a dip protected from the wind-blown snow, just over the crest of the hill. Sheerwater's nose wrinkled in disgust as he surveyed the remains of a disembowelled cow with the residue of its stomach spread about. This was the animal that Dunceford had killed and stuffed with poison. Scattered beyond it was a petrified tableau which included a fox, two badgers, several squirrels and more than a dozen gulls.

Farther on was an enormous grey wolf, with a bent ear. It was stretched out dead, in the middle of a whirl of tortured tracks which indicated some of the dizzy agony of its dance of death.

Dunceford puffed up the slope, minutes behind the others and peered intently at the motionless animal. 'We got one of them! Is it dead?'

'Course it's dead,' grumbled a farmer, kicking the furry bulk, which barely shifted under the impact of his boot. 'But it's not the only one.'

He pointed down the slope to a dozen woolly mounds. 'Seven of my best ewes and a ram,' he said bitterly. 'Wasted mutton. Poisoned! Which of you mad buggers is responsible for that?'

For the first time, Dunceford felt a pang of doubt that his actions had been correct. He glanced quickly at the MP who was talking busily to Sue McKenna. A cameraman was focusing his lens on the wolf, then panning around to the stiff-legged sheep.

He edged across and heard Sir Marcus say, 'It's despicable. Whoever spread poison on the remains of that cow intended it to be eaten by wolves, without any heed to the other consequences.'

An interview was set up, with Sir Marcus facing the camera. He posed behind the dead wolf.

Sue McKenna said, 'Aren't you glad that at least one wolf is dead?'

'Glad, yes. But horrified at the irresponsible way it was done. Of course, we must rid populated areas of these savage animals. But there is a limit as to how far some people can afford to go, and this sort of indiscriminate killing is criminal. Strychnine is passed on to carrion eaters which in turn are consumed by people. In addition, there's the very real danger that sick animals will regurgitate on to land used by normal grazing cattle and sheep. This is a virulent and long-lasting poison.'

Sue McKenna asked, 'And who is responsible?'

'I've a good idea,' the MP said grimly. 'And you can be certain that the culprits will answer for their actions.'

Dunceford turned pale and tugged at each of his fingers until it cracked. But he felt a wave of intense relief when Sheerwater called him over and said, 'Find those damned Russians! I want them back here straight away!'

'Yes, sir.' Dunceford pushed his way blindly through the little knot of people and stumbled back down the hill.

When he arrived at Station House, he had resolved his dilemma. It was basically the Russians' fault anyway. After all, their arrival had aggravated the situation in the first place, and prevented his volunteer hunting party finishing off all the wolves.

Serves them right. Bloody foreigners.

THIRTY-NINE

Richard Unthank spent the day covering a great deal of ground without getting anywhere. It took several hours for him to catch up with the Russians and try to persuade them to stop hunting. But he would have found it more rewarding talking to a brick wall.

When he got back to Elphin, and learned about the poisoned animals on the hill, all other considerations were pushed from his mind. He clambered up to investigate and scooped a sample of the cow's intestine into a plastic bag to take along to the infirmary.

In his haste, he slipped outside hospital reception and bit his tongue. Consequently, blood was dribbling from the side of his mouth when he was explaining his request for an analysis of the poison.

The doctor was not unhelpful, but he had plenty of other things on his mind. 'I'll do what I can, but it may take a day or two. Why don't you go along with Miss Bakersman here? She'll clear that cut and give you a cup of tea. Think you can manage that?'

'Thank you.' Unthank turned wearily to find Penny waiting with a half-smile of acknowledgement.

'Hello.'

'Hi.'

She took him into a room no bigger than a cupboard and got him to perch on a worktop while she shook a bottle of iodine. She spread some on a lint pad and told him to open his mouth wide.

'Uh-huuh.'

'Hold still now. It won't hurt.'

'Aaah!'

285

'Don't be a baby.'

Her eyes held a measure of amusement for the first time in days, and Unthank was aware how attractive she could be, even with no make-up, tired lines under her eyes and hair which she continually blew out of her eyes.

She paused, sensing that he pitied her in some way.

'I was sorry to hear about Miss Dancer leaving,' she said, catching him at a disadvantage.

'Sorry for me?' He was about to put her straight, but she wedged a lint pad into his mouth.

'Hold that on the cut,' she said crisply. 'It will go on stinging for a minute or two, then you'll feel fine. That's all.'

He nodded and left the tiny dispensary.

She packed up the items she had used and sighed. A minute or two later, when she walked into the corridor, he was waiting by the front door, glancing at her with his grey eyes.

She pretended not to notice until almost the last moment. 'Something you want, Mr Unthank?'

He nodded thoughtfully, still holding the pad to his mouth, and plucked a sprig of mauve heather from a window vase, kissed it and handed it to her.

She smiled sadly, and walked away brushing it lightly against her cheek. It simply made her think of the limping Martin Kelso, and how much she missed him.

Professor Norman Pope-Watson had wispy hair under his thick fur hat, and watery eyes: an elderly erudite man who would have looked more at home lecturing at the Royal Academy on ornithology, or sitting placidly in his Kensington drawing room contemplating walls lined with endless cases of British birds.

Whether or not he was past his prime, he did not miss much. At that precise moment, after setting up a makeshift hide on the rocky lower slopes of Suilven, he had an air of great expectancy. His binoculars swept the three-pointed ridge at the top of the lone mountain and followed the majestic flight of a golden eagle. About two hundred feet below and to its left a pair of beautiful peregrine falcons were circling.

It was a superb sight in the cold, clear air and he felt elated.

He knew there were wolves in the vicinity, but they did not bother him. In the past he had frequently faced them over comparatively short distances but merely averted his eyes and went about his breakfast preparations. And, quite soon, they too lost interest and went on their way.

Pope-Watson's idea of excitement was not connected with danger, but in identifying fractionally different aspects of similar birds through fluctuations of their mandible or tail feathers. He would have dismissed any mention of ferocious wolves with a flutter of his hand; pointing out that because he did not interfere with them, they consequently did not encroach on his territory. He was only concerned with making copious notes about the northern birds he spotted in the solitude of the Highlands.

From his fixed vantage point – under some sheep hurdles roped together and strewn with heather – he noted three indications of human presence that day.

First, his binoculars picked out the helicopter pulling up from Elphin during the late afternoon, a red light blinking regularly under its fuselage as it headed south-east.

Shortly afterwards, he noticed two distant figures in snow smocks, who would have been almost impossible to see but for their black telescopic rifles and their tracks, moving eastwards with the practised speed of northlanders.

And finally, as dusk descended and he adjusted the double weather skin over his tent, he spotted a puff of black smoke far to the north. From Kylesku. That could be the ferry clearing its engines after months of inactivity, he thought. Curious that. He would not have expected the ferry to re-awaken from its icy moorings for at least another month.

He focussed on the spot, but the big shadow of Quinag obscured his vision and he could not detect any further movement. He stirred some more tea into his pot: there were more important things to think about.

FORTY

Emma rubbed her aching eyes and again tried to scan the glaring white landscape. 'I don't like this at all. Surely they wouldn't attack somebody, and then just disappear?'

Kelso was perspiring. He had forced the Gael's awkward body back into the cab of the snowplough and locked the door, so that some unfortunate passer-by would find him in the spring. But at least they would find a whole body, and not the grisly remains of a predator's meal.

'Perhaps the noise of the horn scared them off. It must have been deafening in an enclosed space. But, you can bet your boots, they're not far away. Probably watching us right now.'

'What are we going to do? We can't wait here for the spring.'

Kelso's eyes shifted uneasily around the hilltops without seeing anything untoward. But then human eyes have been dulled by centuries of sheltered living. And, from the opposite direction, several other pairs of eyes had no such problem. The clear, sharp vision of the wolves was firmly fixed upon them.

'We've only got about a mile to go. I don't see any point in waiting. It's just a question of putting one foot in front of the other.'

'I'm ready,' she said quietly.

He showed her a transistor radio he had retrieved from the cab of the Foden. 'Could be useful. If anything happens to me, make sure you take it. If they don't like noise, it'll come in handy.'

They started up the hillside, following their earlier tracks, until the journalist suddenly stopped. A wolf was sitting in

288

the narrow channel of footprints, about forty yards ahead of them, blinking sleepily as if almost indifferent to them.

'Oh, God help us.' She gripped his hand from behind. 'There's another one up on the ridge.'

'I know,' he muttered. 'I can see four of them. They seem to want us to know, too.'

The wolves sat idly, one or two bathing their faces in the distant sun. Another nuzzled her shoulder fur in search of a skin mite which would in time cause mange. All apparently disinterested. Yet, any sudden movement from the humans would bring their heads jerking intently round, ready to race down in pursuit.

'We're not going anywhere,' Kelso said as firmly as he could manage, without actually opening his mouth. He was afraid she might do something rash, especially as she must have been aware that his legs were trembling.

'We can't stay here.' She gripped his hand so fiercely that he could no longer feel it.

'We have to go down. Down and around the foot of Quinag . . . if they'll let us. It's twice as far, but I don't see what else we can do.'

She whimpered. 'They're moving. Oh God, they're moving.'

It was Darkmind who tried to stir them into action: walking quick-legged across to Longrunner and then swiftly back to his original position.

Kelso switched on the radio. Full volume.

A raven flapped curiously overhead, and looked down at the motionless specks on the hillside. A considerable noise echoed up, although still nobody moved.

'Here is the weather forecast for the twenty-four hours, beginning midnight tonight.' A precise English public school accent boomed across the frozen hills, informing several square miles of deserted countryside what the prospect was for any warmth tomorrow.

'In the north of Scotland and Northern Ireland . . .'

Emma covered her ears with her fur gloves and Kelso grimaced at the noise. Higher up the slope, Darkmind sniffed from side to side, turned a full circle and pawed the snow.

The other wolves shifted uncomfortably and watched their leader for guidance.

Darkmind made up his mind and set off up the hill, glancing furtively over his shoulder before disappearing over the crest. The rest of the pack followed, scrambling with indecent haste to escape the echoing ear-aching details of the forecast.

The limping man and a terrified woman hurried in the opposite direction, across the obliterated road, and on down to the foot of the snow-filled glen. Kelso dropped the radio which slithered some thirty feet ahead of them. He plunged recklessly after it, risking breaking a leg to get it back before anything could hurtle out of the sun and take advantage of them.

But nothing appeared and he cautiously switched off and tucked the portable set down inside his anorak.

They got no further glimpse of the pack for a considerable time, until they cleared a hump of land and found the narrow road again: dipping and curving down to a landing stage at Kylesku.

They hugged each other with joy. The village itself consisted of only two or three tiny houses and an hotel closed for the winter. But the sight which made Kelso's heart pump with utter relief was the big ferry boat, moored on their side of the narrow-necked loch with sheets stretched over much of the superstructure.

He took her hand and ran cumbersomely down the road. Snow had been trampled within two hundred yards of the landing stage, indicating that there were still some people in the vicinity.

Emma tugged him to a halt, gasping for breath, and pointed desperately up at the sheer rocks on one side of them. The wolves were back in sight, running in single-file some forty feet above them.

Kelso tugged out the transistor and switched it on. This time an orchestra played 'Land of Hope and Glory' with all of Elgar's original, crashing fervour. The noise was deafening and almost made them stumble.

But they kept going. Just twenty yards to the first house now, and a door opened. A man in a roll-neck jersey with a bald head and look of incredulity stared at them.

It was not altogether surprising. After two months of isolation and utter silence, he and his family were now being rapidly approached by two frantic strangers, accompanied by the might of the London Symphony Orchestra and a line of wickedly lean wolves.

He jerked back instinctively, allowing Kelso and the woman to career inside, then crashed the door shut behind them and securely bolted it top and bottom.

The man pressed his back against the door. 'What on earth is it?'

Kelso switched off and gasped with relief in the sudden silence. ' "Land of Hope and Glory",' he panted. 'Elgar. From his Pomp and Circumstance marches, Opus 39.'

Emma stared at him with a wild relief, then started giggling and found she could not stop.

When the ferry operator and his homely wide-eyed wife learned that the wolves had followed the snowplough all the way from Elphin, they were as disturbed as the new arrivals. It took little effort to convince them they should all take the ferry and sail south.

The ferry man had initial doubts about his employer's reaction, but the journalist brushed them aside. 'My newspaper will deal with the regional authority. Don't worry about them. By the time I've written this up as a news story, they'll pop their buttons with pride. All you've got to do is make the vessel work. Get up steam, or whatever you need to do.'

After several hours of preparation – food cooked, blankets rolled and valuables packed in suitcases – and no further sign of the wolves either from the front or back windows, the two men ventured outside.

They had to cross forty yards of open ground to the ferry.

They ran to it . . . but nothing streaked out in pursuit. They worked swiftly, almost desperately, to strip away any hindering tarpaulin and get the engines ready.

It was a new vessel and the motor spluttered into life at the third attempt. In a few minutes, the main engines were turning and a throb could be felt throughout the heavy flat-bottomed vessel.

Kelso left the bald helmsman on the bridge and went back for Emma, as well as the ferryman's wife and his shy, clumpy daughter. They scurried to the side and clambered in. It was a shallow-draught vessel and touched the concrete road where it met the ice-encrusted loch. Kelso refused to let down the hinged gangway flap and instead made the heavily-built wife heave herself on board.

'Let her go,' he bawled when the daughter also tumbled on to the deck, and a ship's hooter sounded a deep triumphant response.

But it was not to be that easy. The frozen loch gripped the vessel tenaciously and, although water churned and the ice cracked in twenty different directions, they could not at first break free.

The ferry man, perspiring and freezing at the same time, told Kelso to wait until he could generate enough heat to use a steam hose. Then the journalist would have to drag it around the blunt bows, dangling it over the rails, and melting ice as he went.

They started manhandling the unwieldy hose into the bows during the afternoon. It was slow, laborious work and by the time the ferry floated free it was dusk. Kelso was also drenched in perspiration.

Once again the engines turned over, and water churned back on to the road, as the vessel mounted the ice and leaned its enormous weight down on it. With an enormous crack, which sent a fissure hissing more than one hundred and fifty yards ahead, they broke through.

The engines immediately took on a deeper note and they moved visibly forward into the gathering darkness.

'Look, mummy!' The girl pressed her finger against the

bridge window, and they hurriedly rubbed away condensation to get a better look at the rim of high ground sliding off their port beam.

A line of yellow eyes watched them from the half-circle of land. Slanting eyes, unblinking in the light thrown out from the ferry.

Emma buried her head against Kelso's shoulder and shuddered. He stroked her hair. 'It's all right. It's over.'

But, when she looked back half a mile later, she was sure in the darkness that the last pair of eyes were still on her.

FORTY-ONE

The two Russians were getting steadily more frustrated. Bukhanovich pressed on, ignoring rest periods and sometimes trudging up to a quarter of a mile ahead of his hunting companion, until darkness forced him to stop.

Spassky plodded behind, rueing the loss of his two lovely wolfhounds. Apart from Valentina, he had found them more loving and less demanding than any females he had ever met. Now they were gone, and the warmth was replaced by an aching void. An empty, endless ache.

Yet, paradoxically, he chose them in the first place because of their cruel streak. Male dogs were no good for hunting. Over the years, in which he and Lieutenant Bukhanovich had acquired an enormous tally of wolfskins which eventually became Red Army officers' greatcoats, they found that dogs occasionally mated with she-wolves instead of killing them.

A she-wolf on heat can distract an attacking dog. In fact, some packs are alert to hunting dogs' vulnerability, and will purposely leave behind a female in order to delay pursuers long enough for the rest to escape.

A wolfhound bitch, on the other hand, shows no such

mercy. It makes no difference to her that a wolf is on heat, carrying pups or arthritic. In she goes, harrying and turning the predator until it comes within range of the waiting guns.

But now, both of his bitches were gone. He and the lieutenant had now to make their own chances, and they found it exhausting and unrewarding work.

That night, while Bukhanovich was sitting huddled in his sleeping bag, brooding, and his companion was lying on his back too tired even to sleep, a distress rocket arched into the sky to the north and hung in brilliant red splendour until it waned.

Spassky forced himself up on one elbow. 'What on earth was that?'

A second rocket flashed into the clouds, and re-emerged in a dazzling red glow. Then faded. Bukhanovich stared morosely at the spectacle, his cheekbones silhouetted by the artificial light.

Spassky waited for another one, but the show was over. 'Someone in trouble perhaps?'

'Probably.' The hunter squeezed his chin thoughtfully. 'Perhaps they've found what we are still looking for. How far away would you say they are?'

'Four, maybe five kilometres.'

Bukhanovich nodded and yawned. 'Good. We'll try that direction in the morning.'

'Just as you say, Comrade Lieutenant. Goodnight.'

Bukhanovich merely grunted and huddled down on the iron-hard ground. He dreamed of Moscow and a pair of sheets and the little brass door plate which contained his name.

In the morning, at a time when the rest of the country was contemplating breakfast, the two Russians had covered three kilometres due north, almost in a straight line. There was no need for subtlety.

They picked their way through frozen clumps of reed in a burn paralyzed by ice and were starting up a slope on the far side when Bukhanovich stopped and reached back to grip Spassky's arm. They both became statues.

There was a faint brushing noise overhead and, a moment later, a great raven flapped slowly over the crest of the hill and passed into the distance.

Bukhanovich raised his eyebrows optimistically and, together, they edged forward. Halfway up the incline they again stopped. Spassky gestured ahead and the other man unfastened his binocular case to focus on the point of interest.

The sharpening image revealed several wisps of steam, or condensation, curling up above the ridge. Spassky whispered jubilantly in the other man's ear. 'It's them! For sure!'

The marksman from Siberia pulled his white snow-hood down to the bridge of his nose. Then wriggled to the top of the ridge and inched his eyes over the skyline.

There were three wolves: two frisky black males and a pathetically thin grey she-wolf. They had spent most of the winter in the disciplined rows of pines of the Achfar Forest, at the northern end of Loch More, but after saturating themselves in an early bloodbath of stranded sheep, and cutting down aged red deer left behind by the fleeing herds, they found in recent weeks that their easy food supply had run out.

Now, with unaccustomed hunger pains gnawing at their stomachs, they had moved south-west for a week before coming across the defenceless community of Lochinver.

The she-wolf stretched out under the half-exposed roots of a spruce tree, not more than forty yards away. Apart from the frugal shelter of the tree, there was nowhere for her to go; beyond her was half a mile of open gently sloping snow.

Bukhanovich knew without doubt that he had them, and he concentrated on the two black wolves which were so alike in build and marking that they might have been brothers. Yet what were they tugging and scuffling over? He motioned Spassky to join him.

The bulkier Russian wriggled forward, displacing large quantities of snow with his chest. He was still thinking about Valentina and the shock of her sudden death. He relied so much on her large warm bosom and the understanding way she drew his tired body to her when he returned from a month's hunting. Soon he would be too old to struggle with the elements. And what then?

His head cautiously cleared the ridge and he saw what had puzzled his comrade.

The two black wolves were absorbed in tugging, in opposite directions, a glossy yellow object. A Wellington boot. He shrugged at Bukhanovich, who simply pulled a face and snicked the bolt softly back on his rifle.

He savoured the moment, like the enjoyment of mounting and penetrating a woman, allowing the foresight to caress one of the creatures from its generously-shaped mouth to its flanks and back. The rifle stroked its distant victim lovingly.

The former prize-winning Moscow Academy graduate and parade-ground martinet repeated his unrequited courtship on the other wolf. He even toyed with the idea of firing his first shot through the yellow boot, in order to give the pair a startled thirty yards start before killing them.

It was too large for a child's boot. Yet, surely no normal man would wear anything so hideously bright? Bukhanovich raised himself a fraction higher than was necessary. He was contemptuously confident of his ability.

His companion darted a look at him. 'Something wrong, Comrade?'

The ex-guards officer shook his head and, at that moment precisely, the black wolf facing up the slope sensed man. It let go of the plastic as its glinting eyes focussed on the ridge.

For an infinitesimal moment in time, wolf and hunter stared straight at one another, and for a fraction of a second they were on the same keen-edged level of understanding.

Recognition bought the superb wolf to his feet, fully alert. His brother snapped his wicked head around, and even the she-wolf rolled off her back and scrambled to her feet in the heavy ensuing silence.

Time was suspended for Bukhanovich. It was always like that for the best of his kills. Whereas he could still move at his normal unimpaired speed, everything else seemed reduced to slow-motion. Thus, there was no way he could miss.

He inclined his right cheek into the rifle and felt the stock fit snugly into his shoulder. He squeezed the trigger when he was ready, without haste.

The first bullet took the wolf facing him, through the front of its neck, severing the windpipe and paralyzing it. The second animal slewed away and leapt more than twenty balletic feet on its way towards oblivion. The bullet anticipated its arrival back on earth and sent it ploughing a trench through the snow, still moving towards the horizon, but coming to a halt before much more distance was covered.

The she-wolf was no more than a pathetic bag of bones. She had been useful to her brothers, but shared little of their food. There was nowhere she could go without running into a bullet and yet she made it extraordinarily difficult for the hunter. She backed, snarling, into the shadows of the half-exposed tree roots. Bukhanovich sent a bullet in after her, but it ricocheted off the gnarled and twisted roots and whined into the distance.

The marksman pulled another face. 'Trust a woman to make things awkward.'

Spassky felt a curious emotional sensation. Wolves had never meant any more to him than wages at the end of a hunt. The fact that they had feelings had never occurred to him before. The only females he ever previously considered were Valentina and his two lovely wolfhounds. Yet now, for a moment or two, his heart went out to the trapped and terrified female under the tilting tree.

Spassky was nothing of a shot; in fact he had as little to do with rifles as possible, apart from cleaning and priming them. Yet now he wanted the animal finished off quickly and humanely . . . and he knew he could not rely on Ilya Bukhanovich to do that.

'Leave it to me, please, Comrade.' He stood up and walked over the crest before his surprised companion could stop him.

'Where do you think you're going?'

Spassky knew his place in the order of things; it was always subservient to Bukhanovich, but on this occasion he was convinced he knew better. He turned, blocking the other man's view. 'Please. I know what I am doing.'

She-wolves, like their human counterparts, prefer to let their males display all the aggression that is normally called for. But they can be unbelievably courageous when the occasion arises.

This was one such occasion.

The she-wolf took her chance and came out of the shadows like an avenging wind. She was halfway up the slope and baring her irregular teeth before Spassky spun to face her.

It was too late for him to shoot. He raised his arm simply to defend his face, as he did so, a bullet cracked through the gap under his forearm.

It stopped the wolf as abruptly as if she had run into a wall and knocked her sideways. But she was up in an instant and limping away down the slope. A second bullet nicked Spassky's ear and broke the wolf's tail.

'Sit still!' snapped Bukhanovich, leaning sideways for his third successive shot. The Russian helper scrunched up his face and closed his eyes.

The wounded wolf was not an easy target, mainly because she was zig-zagging back and forth illogically. In the end she simply ran out of steam, near the slumped carcasses of her brothers, and stood whimpering and nuzzling their uncommunicative bodies.

Bukhanovich got up, swore at Spassky and pushed him aside with his boot. Then he strolled down the hillside with his rifle dangling casually in one hand.

He walked right up to the wolf, who wagged her tail in submission, laid the barrel against the grey undernourished neck and executed her.

Bukhanovich returned to a protruding rock and lit a thinly-rolled cigarette. Spassky simply lay where he was and stared at the sky, thinking about Valentina and the flowers on her grave.

Without her there was nothing to go home to, and for a while he envied the she-wolf.

Britain is less than six hundred miles from tip to toe: a mere eight or nine degrees of latitude. Yet the variety of weather it encompasses is sometimes extraordinary.

Two muggy days of ochre mist slowed London to a walking pace and preceded a thaw which quickly transformed hard-packed snow into a sea of slush.

Rivers, pinched with cold and imprisoned by unrelenting ice, were now suddenly released. Swollen water gushed and bullied its way into the Thames. The river, where it passes Westminster and the Isle of Dogs, is several feet above the level of surrounding land and, when the sea tide came into the capital from the Estuary that evening, cracks appeared in the retaining walls.

It was nothing like a national disaster, but sufficiently dangerous to occupy the south's complete attention. Troops with sandbags and women's voluntary organizations with unlimited cups of scalding tea arrived on the scene and worked through the night under floodlights.

A double-decker bus was swept away by a sudden deluge and, miraculously, when it swirled to a halt fifteen minutes and one mile later, the driver was still clutching the wheel white-knuckled and with a sickly smile on his face.

There was sufficient warning for most people to go home, or at least climb to first-floor level. But the Underground system was flooded and communications came almost to a halt.

The Prime Minister was not altogether surprised by the sudden turn in the weather. He had been promised by the Meteorological Office for two weeks past that a thaw was on the way, and when at first nothing happened he regarded the forecasters with the disapproval that schoolmasters have of exaggerating boys.

But he became convinced one morning when pausing on his way to breakfast and tapping the wall barometer, as was his custom. It was definitely falling. He cleared his throat and frowned over his glasses at the mounds of snow covering Horse Guards Parade behind Number Ten.

A few miles away in Hampstead, John Ogleby, the head of

the Meteorological Office, awoke with a start and was conscious of a remarkable clarity in the air. The fog had cleared and he could hear train whistles from the other side of the Heath for the first time since he was a boy.

The weather was definitely on the change. Cats began sneezing, and horses in the anachronistic stables of a national dairy in south London sweated and moved restlessly about their stalls.

By the end of the day, trampled snow on the pavements no longer felt like concrete, and an evening newspaper carried the front-page headline *Siberian Winter Over!*

People danced in the street and the Rt Hon James Beaconsfield and leading members of his Cabinet promised to attend a service of thanksgiving at St Paul's.

But within two days the Premier was exasperated. He summoned an anxious Ogleby to discuss the flood problem, and demanded to know: 'Where's all the damned water coming from? There wasn't *that* much snow.'

'It's not the depth of snow that's important, Prime Minister, but the water equivalent of the snowpack.'

'Don't muddle me with scientific explanations, man. I have to face a good many disgruntled members of Parliament, and what they want are straightforward, honest-to-goodness facts. Well, sir?'

Ogleby shrugged in painful anticipation. 'I'm afraid the situation is bound to get worse before it gets better. Water is heavy and, therefore, destructive. I understand that some power and telephone lines have already been severed. And, in my opinion, we are in for a good deal worse . . . roads subsiding, drinking water cut off and all that sort of thing.'

'Good God, man. I thought the snow was bad enough.' He shuddered slightly and turned to his personal assistant. 'What's your opinion, Marchant?'

'Well, there aren't many votes in this situation. So I would get the first blow in, if I were you. Warn the House tomorrow that there is a new emergency ahead, and the country needs one last effort to pull us through to the spring. You could call for some of the Dunkirk spirit.'

Beaconsfield groaned. 'Not again, Marchant. That line's wearing a bit thin even for you. Still, I take the point. I've got to be seen doing something. Look, I think I should visit some schools in low-lying areas of London. Find me a few basements where elderly people are living. Then I can inspect one or two emergency centres. You know the sort of thing. Get the Press Secretary on to it. Then in the afternoon I'll announce that, as a result of all the personal hardship and suffering I have seen inflicted by the thaw, I am putting an immediate £10 million into a government emergency flood relief fund.'

His assistant scribbled in a notebook. 'Sounds about right, sir.'

Beaconsfield grunted. 'You'd better tell the Chancellor.'

'Will do, sir.'

The assistant retired smoothly, leaving the meteorological man standing uncertainly behind the Prime Minister, while the latter sorted through a despatch box. 'Where are my blasted spectacles,' mumbled Beaconsfield, patting his pockets and feeling under documents on his desk.

Ogleby retrieved them from a windowsill and handed them over. The great man seemed startled to find anybody still in the room. 'What do you want?'

'I'm Ogleby, sir,' he reminded the Prime Minister obsequiously. 'Controller, Meteorological Office.'

'Yes, yes. Well make sure you bring better news next time. I don't like these gloomy forecasts of yours. It's all too easy to get into that sort of habit. Right?'

'Yes, Prime Minister. Absolutely.' Ogleby bowed his way out, bumping into the door post on his way.

The Prime Minister stared after him for some time. Then gave another little grunt and returned to his official papers.

FORTY-TWO

Spassky raised his white-caped head over the ridge, invisible to all but the sharpest eyes. 'We've got company,' he said quietly.

Bukhanovich lifted a rifle and rolled on to his chest in one fluid movement. His eyes followed the direction of his companion's nod and saw the shape of Sergeant Dunceford moving wearily down a parallel slope, away from them.

Spassky neatly ejected some saliva. 'Shall I shoot him and peg out the skin?'

Bukhanovich contemplated the policeman, who had paused to drink from a pocket flask before examining the hillside through his binoculars.

The Russian hunter-helper smiled cynically. 'He stares hard enough, but sees nothing.'

'Better call him over.'

'If you say so, comrade. But I think he is more trouble than he is worth.'

'Do it.'

Spassky stood up and put a thumb and forefinger in his mouth. A piercing whistle halted Dunceford and made him turn, whereupon the Russian waved hugely.

'Join us, Sergeant,' he shouted in Russian. 'It is better that you come up here and make our lives a misery, than blunder on and disturb all the wildlife within five miles.' A broad smile belied his words and Dunceford made towards them with the impression that he was welcome.

He puffed and heaved, and eventually settled on a rolled sleeping bag and accepted a cup of Russian tea. He pulled an excruciating face.

Spassky played the indulgent host and again proffered the flask.

Dunceford smiled painfully, as if loath to allow duty to interrupt such a gastric delicacy. He dug into an inside pocket and extracted two long white envelopes. 'There. It's my duty to hand you these.'

Bukhanovich noted the official edge to the policeman's voice and glanced questioningly at his companion. But when he stretched across to accept the letters, Dunceford withdrew them out of reach.

'Sorry. Only one of them is for you.'

Bukhanovich frowned. He disliked unexpected situations, and his general dislike for everything in this strange and awkward country grew more intense each day. He carried his official-looking envelope off to a distant rock to read it in private.

Spassky, on the other hand, was intrigued by the fact that someone had typed his name in full across such an immaculate envelope. He settled down, wriggling himself into a comfortable position. But within a few minutes both men were stunned at what they read in two quite different contexts.

Bukhanovich's sensitive fingers felt the embossed hammer and sickle emblem on the thick, expensive paper even before he saw any words, and knew it was from the Russian Embassy. He read under his breath:

The Ambassador, representing the Union of Soviet Socialist Republics in London, instructs me to inform you that he is gravely disturbed at your capricious attitude towards the vital task entrusted to you. You are to complete the work without further delay, and return to London for instructions. No additional deterioration in your relationship with J Bakersman must occur and you are to apologize fully for any misunderstandings. Consideration of disciplinary action will take place in your absence. Signed J Gregorvich, Second Secretary.

The hunter stared blankly at Dunceford without seeing him. Capricious? A feeling of bottomless desolation overtook him. My God ... the malicious American could say whatever he wanted and it would be held against him, however vehemently he denied it.

Dunceford got up guardedly as the Russian approached him, his flat white eyes curiously glazed.

'Not bad news, I hope?'

Bukhanovich heard the words but they did not register. 'It will soon be getting dark. You had better go.'

'I thought you might ask me to stay for a bit of dinner.'

'Go home!' snapped the Russian in a voice that brooked no alternative.

Dunceford looked around for his fur gloves and spotted them under the hunched shape of Spassky, who was poring ponderously over his own letter. 'Excuse me, will you?'

He had to shake Spassky's meaty shoulder for the words to mean anything. And, even then, the policeman was obliged to tug his gloves out from beneath the Russian's great posterior.

The second letter simply contained a telegram from Verkhoyansk, which had been automatically forwarded by the embassy in Kensington Palace Gardens.

To: B Spassky. Regret to inform you your wife, V Spassky, died today. Please accept sanatorium director's condolences.

What puzzled the Russian was the date. Yesterday's date ... *your wife died today* ... He rubbed his face bewilderedly. How could that be? He himself knew days ago.

Dunceford was about to leave when he noticed the three wolfskins bundled together. 'Hey, you got a few, then. That's good. That's very good.' But Bukhanovich walked slowly away from him, the embassy letter trailing in his hand.

The policeman turned to the other, normally amicable hunter. 'I must admit, I didn't think you stood much of a chance. Not against animals like ... '

But the second Russian also brushed past, ignoring his words. 'Comrade Bukhanovich,' he called. 'I wish to talk with you.'

The gap was some forty yards. 'Comrade,' Spassky called urgently, thrusting his own letter into the air. 'I want to hear your opinion on something!'

Dunceford backed away, stumbling up to his thighs in deep snow, and clearing his throat noisily. 'I think I'll be going then. I'm sure you two have plenty to talk about, without me getting in the way. Yes, well . . . '

He turned and made for Elphin at a much faster pace than he had arrived.

FORTY-THREE

Days passed and the winter in the far north showed no real sign of abating. Bitter winds conceived in the Arctic wastes, blew unchecked across the ominously-heaving seas and cut cruelly into the Highlands.

An elderly wolf was found near Wick, frozen to death at the side of the main road, apparently caught in a blizzard. A police patrol discovered the animal petrified in mid-stride.

In Elphin, JC Bakersman grew more prickly by the day and his daughter bore the brunt of his complaints. One afternoon he yelled at her.

'You did what?'

'I told the helicopter pilot to bring Martin Kelso back here on the next flight.'

'Well, you had no right to. I don't want journalists poking about here.'

'I want to see him for my own reasons . . . not because he's a journalist.'

'But that doesn't make sense. He ran out on you!'

Tears welled into her eyes. 'That's an awful thing to say.'

'It's a pretty awful thing to do. But he still ran out on you. He's nothing but a self-opinionated second-rate journalist who can't walk straight.'

Penny bit her lip and tasted blood. Her father was probably right. Martin Kelso might indeed be self-centred and an

305

indifferent reporter. But it did not alter the fact that she was irresistibly drawn to him, and the more she thought about him the worse it got. Anyway, there were qualities she admired: frankness and humour. And, on top of that, he had a funny way of trying to get his own back on his disfigured foot.

'He's not like that at all. He set out in a snowplough, unarmed, to get help for the rest of us.'

Bakersman laughed scornfully, but she continued to defend him. 'It's not his fault that the helicopter got through first.'

'I know his sort only too well. He did what he did, for his own reasons, not for yours. I also know what he wants.'

She ignored the innuendo and walked past him to gaze out of the window. 'I know what I want, too: I want to marry him.'

'What!'

'If he asked me, I'd marry him tomorrow . . .'

'Over my dead body!'

' . . . but he hasn't asked me, and I don't think he intends to.'

Bakersman groaned. 'Honey, don't tie yourself in a knot over this guy. He's nothing special. Believe me, there are much better men around. Important and healthy . . . and properly educated.'

She looked out at the deceptively placid snow. 'He'll do fine.'

Bakersman tilted his head back at the ceiling. 'Give me strength. Of all the gilt-edged chances you've had, you have to go and fall for a lame smart-arse.'

He sat with his head in his hands for most of the afternoon, but at supper time he took her hand and patted it. 'Promise me you won't do anything rash, honey.' And she knew that he had something up his sleeve.

But during the night he had a dream: a vigorous, argumentative dream which brought on a heart attack. He died the next day in the small general ward of the infirmary, scarcely mourned.

A crofter in threadbare pyjamas, who occupied the adjoining bed, was attended by a continual coming-and-going of acquaintances while Bakersman had hardly any. One of the villagers glanced sympathetically across at the man who had been a millionaire five times over and noticed he had no flowers or fruit, let alone visitors.

He slipped some winter jasmine into Bakersman's bedside vase.

She was now a millionairess. Strange . . . she didn't feel any different. Two days after her father died, Penny Bakersman faced herself in the mirror again: hesitantly at first, as if not quite sure what the reflection would reveal. Certainly nothing that gave the impression she had access to almost limitless money . . .

She stroked her dry skin and decided it was high time she improved her appearance. She had been a drudge for long enough.

A long soak in the bath, followed by a face massage and fingertip creaming, made her feel a lot better. She sighed with relief and brushed out her damp hair.

Her cheeks were still flushed from the heat of the water when the helicopter came stuttering across the Cromalt Hills. She did not know for certain that Martin Kelso was on board but, just in case, she wrenched the curlers painfully from her hair and scrambled into a new spring suit.

She kept telling herself, excitedly, to calm down: that he would not be on board. But she was wrong. When she jumped up from her dressing-table for the umpteenth time, she recognized the familiar jerky stride as he made directly for the house on the hill.

'Oh . . . Oh my . . . Where's my lipstick? Damn, it's rolled under the bed.'

The doorbell rang and she was out on the landing and calling downstairs like a teenager. 'Answer it. Answer it, please!' Except that there was no one else in, and she flew down herself and slid back the noisy double bolts.

Kelso's eyes twinkled. 'Hello.'

'Hi.' She felt like a piece of limp pastry and they stared at one another inanely for a long time, until finally she moved back to allow him inside.

'I heard about your father. I'm very sorry.'

She nodded.

'Come inside. You've had a long journey. I'm really glad you came.'

He grinned sideways at her. 'Thank my news editor. He insisted.'

'Oh.' She flapped her hands inarticulately, trying to explain the cluttered state of the house. 'Things changed a lot after you left. All the servants went, and we didn't see any point in keeping the entire house open. So . . . '

She shrugged and wondered desperately why he had not kissed her. Something was wrong. She guessed she still looked a mess. Probably it was something to do with all that damned money she had inherited.

'How long are you back for?' she asked brightly.

'Not long.'

She felt a stab of disappointment. 'Why's that?'

'I got my old job back on the paper. Temporarily, at least. If I make it through the next week or two, I can keep it. They want me to wrap up a few things here, then scoot back to London. That's why I have to ask you something important.'

'Oh?'

He shifted awkwardly, moving the weight off his distended foot.

She stopped breathing. If he proposed . . . She blanked out her mind, not even allowing the thought oxygen in case it prospered only to be snuffed out.

'I wondered if I could use the helicopter to take me back, after breakfast.'

'Umm?' She fought not to gulp, or show her emotion in any way, although the room suddenly took on disproportionate and faraway dimensions. 'No, no. You do that.'

'Thanks.' He leaned forward, and she smelt his familiar masculine and slightly smoky aroma. 'I haven't even kissed you yet,' he laughed and put his lips against her cheek.

She glanced at the main staircase, as if someone was expecting her back upstairs. 'Well, I've got things to do.'

'Will I see you later on?'

'Of course,' she said perkily. 'Of course you will.'

'Fine. Right. I've got a couple of people to talk to, just to tie up the wolf story. I'll see you before I go back.' He wiggled his fingers at her and backed out.

And she walked blindly back upstairs. Feeling desolate.

The next morning she determined to stay in the house until after the helicopter had left, but at the last moment she dragged out her suede, fur-edged coat and rushed to the school playground.

He turned just as she arrived. 'Hello. I was beginning to wonder if you'd bother to see me off at all.'

'Of course.'

She stood on tiptoe and kissed him softly somewhere between the chin and cheek, just catching the sensitive edge of his mouth. But not a lover's kiss.

'*Why* are you going back, Martin?'

'Why?'

She took her courage in both hands. 'You could stay here with me, if you really wanted to.'

He tried to be honest, and he even faced her for a moment before his eyes slid away. 'It's what I do best.' He shrugged hopelessly. 'I haven't got much else to be proud of.'

'But it's only a job.'

'I know . . . that's the thing. You don't realize how valuable something is until you lose it.' He held on to her hand, shouting over the roar of the engine. 'What are *you* going to do?'

Penny Bakersman cupped a hand to her mouth. 'Stay here until it's all finally over. Then go home, I guess.'

'But it is over.'

She shrugged. 'Not quite. Give it a day or two, then I'll pack my bags.'

The pilot tapped Kelso on the shoulder and he waved an acknowledgement. 'I've got to go.' This time he kissed her squarely on the mouth, and she started to respond. But it was already too late, and he clambered on board.

Before the little door slammed shut, he met her eyes and shrugged. 'Have a good life.'

'And you,' she whispered.

She turned away with tears streaming down her face, and walked back to the house, deafened by the engine and without looking where she was going. She fell over once, but got up without caring. She locked the great door behind her and sobbing filled the otherwise empty house.

But, even as she grieved, she could still not believe she had seen the last of him.

FORTY-FOUR

Darkmind and his pack moved south from Kylesku, their hollow stomachs rumbling as they contracted with hunger. After hesitating, he swung back towards the coast and the fishing village of Lochinver. But when the pack ranged along the curving road to the hotel and pier there was nothing edible to be found.

They poured in through a flapping door of the hotel, across the beleagured lounge and upstairs. All was deserted. The people had gone, or fallen victim to whatever had come before.

The big pack leader sniffed about and remembered Elphin and, with it, memories of Whitepatch. Late that afternoon he swung south-east again, barely pausing to rest.

They reached the village soon after daybreak, when the sun had risen and broken clear of the ground mist. They were grateful for the thin warmth on their backs, but the overriding consideration now was food.

Any prey they spotted from now on, or any tracks they crossed, would receive their avid attention.

Jack Dunceford was up at six o'clock. He never required an early call, nor did he rely on alarm clocks. Years of practice had built in his own infallible system, even after late-night duty.

It was a curious morning. And, like the weather man hundreds of miles to the south a few days earlier, he immediately sensed a change. There was absolute stillness outside as he drew back the dull, heavy curtains.

As he blinked in the face of unaccustomed sunshine, he smiled with relief. He turned back to the humped shape of his wife under a pile of blankets but then, on second thoughts, refrained from shaking her. Plenty of time later for her to enjoy the first day of the thaw.

Downstairs, after dragging on heavy wool-lined boots, he stepped out on to the snow-packed road to savour the long-awaited change in the weather. No particular reason to be cautious.

Yesterday had left him at a low ebb. But today, with the sun on his face, he felt new hope. Spring would bring a return of the deer to the high ground and a pulling-back of the wolves.

He walked down the middle of the silent road. It was incredible, unbelievable. He bathed his face and neck in the sun and was happily blinded by it.

When he regained his focus, Darkmind was in the road ahead.

Dunceford tried to blink the image away. But another look simply confirmed it. *Wolf*.

The policeman retraced his deep tracks without turning or deviating from them. The smile was frozen to his face and it only altered when another wolf slipped out from the shadow of the church slightly behind him.

Then a third and a fourth.

Dunceford had about fifty yards to cover if he was to reach the safety of Station House. He made the mistake of trying it.

He ran ponderously, flailing his arms, while Darkmind cleared the intervening distance in great leaps: twenty or thirty feet at a time, until he landed squarely on Dunceford's back, crushing him face-down in the suffocating snow.

Rabbit ran excitedly around the threshing pair, snapping and harrying. He drew blood, and swallowed a glove containing one-and-a-half fingers in an unconsidered gulp.

Darkmind would normally have pulled back after the initial onslaught and allowed the others to dart in from all sides. But his paws got entangled in the jacket hood, and he bit deeply and angrily at the man to make him let go.

Dunceford's jugular vein was severed and blood welled out in great quantities. He gurgled and struggled like a stranded leviathan, but never regained his feet or even managed to face the long-awaited sun again.

At least two other people were awoken by the noise. One was the thin-faced widow of postman Albert Henry Tudor, who slid up her squeaky bedroom window opposite the scene of the attack.

She was not particularly brave, but a shocked and affronted woman makes a formidable adversary. She vanished from sight, to quickly reappear at the front door wielding a long-handled broom.

Longrunner and Hollowbelly spun around, but she scurried at them dealing out blows at head height and they gave ground, snarling. Rabbit also scrambled clear.

Only Darkmind remained hunched over the still-breathing body, eyeing the new arrival malevolently and not releasing his mouthful of jacket and loose back flesh.

'Let go . . . you big brute!' she admonished, sweeping snow frantically into the huge wolf's face.

Darkmind let go. And, at that moment, a man yelled from the top window of another house and drew Mrs Tudor's attention away. Darkmind launched himself forward: crushing her backwards and severing the thin broom arm with a single upward sweep of his terrible carnassial teeth.

The arm was all but wrenched off as, moments later, she tried to drag herself back to the house. The man's head re-emerged at the distant window, and a blast from his wobbling shotgun blew out the top half of a lead-strip window in the austere Free Church building opposite.

The second uncontrolled shot boomed obliquely across the road towards Station House, peppering the polished bonnet of Sergeant Dunceford's immaculate Cortina where it was parked, under a lean-to.

Acting Constable Shaftoe heard the noise, lumbered to a side window and regarded the rip marks across the bonnet with horror. It was the sergeant's private car: the pride of his life. And, when he wasn't about, it was entrusted to the care of Bobby Shaftoe . . . on the strict understanding that he never drove it without explicit permission.

Shaftoe pulled on his trousers and thudded downstairs, unsuccessfully trying to button up the neck of his long-sleeved vest.

'Oh my God . . . my God,' he kept saying to himself. 'He'll kill me if anybody's buggered up his car.'

Outside, he gave a moan of anguish after running his hands gingerly over the wings and rippled windscreen. There were now five people on the road: two of them being pursued back into their homes and the others calling frantically to one another.

Shaftoe looked over his shoulder, puzzled. The car was bad enough, but it did not rate the whole town getting into a frenzy.

He saw Darkmind at the very moment he himself was seen by the wolf. Shaftoe was stunned, but he had the sense to reach for a shovel as he advanced bewilderedly on to the exposed road. What helped him was the fact that he had no time to consider how one-sided was the contest. Then he spotted Dunceford's shape up ahead.

'Sergeant?' he called around the fearsome, snarling predator. 'That you?'

Darkmind rocked back slightly before exploding forward, his teeth bared in undisguised ferocity. But the policeman, like many heavy men, was nimble on his feet and neatly side-stepped.

As he moved, he shut his eyes and flailed the shovel. It landed with a thud which sent shock waves up his big arms. The point of contact was at the back of the wolf's skull, around the ear. The pack leader landed heavily in the snow, stunned and temporarily out of the fray.

When Shaftoe pulled the sergeant's bleeding shape towards him, something came away stickily in his hand. 'Oh my Christ,' he sobbed, resting his glistening forehead against the one untouched patch of uniform he could see. 'You'll be all right. You'll see. I'll take care of it.'

But he knew there was no hope for his superior and the sight of Rabbit scrambling through an injudiciously opened window, had him back on his feet. 'Come out of there!' he shouted dazedly. 'That's private property!'

Somehow he got back to Station House. How, he could not recall later. He knew only that he stumbled across the wolf leader's stirring body and used it as a pushing-off point to gain a few more yards.

Longrunner went for him, but the policeman staggered to safety in the nick of time. The rapidly closing door shuddered under the weight of the predator's impact and held fast.

Shaftoe fumbled the bolt across and made his way confusedly through the two adjoining rooms: falling over a chair on the way and eventually squeezing out through a tiny back window. He edged around the building and into the rear of the lean-to.

Standing there was Dunceford's Cortina saloon: the only object of consequence the sergeant had ever owned. The police force paid him a modest additional sum each month for it to be used on official duties, but he still pampered the car like an only child, frequently waxing and polishing, and religiously checking the oil level and tyre pressure each Sunday, even if it had not been used.

Shaftoe knew he only had to lean an elbow on the roof during conversation for Dunceford to bristle. You'd have thought it belonged to the Royal Family. The sergeant would push him away and polish the tainted spot assiduously.

As always, the key was in the glove compartment. There was no need to lock the vehicle. Nobody in the county would have dared take it.

For once, Shaftoe had considerations other than the sergeant's wrath. The engine roared into life. He crashed the gears and jerked into motion, driving the car around the edge of Station House and into the middle of the road.

There it stalled. He gave it too much choke and accelerator, and only succeeded in flooding the carburettor. *Shit!* He jerked his head away as Longrunner appeared at the window, snapping furiously and stretching up on his back legs.

Shaftoe managed to restart the engine, by gentling the accelerator down to the floor and keeping it there while he turned the ignition key, but in the meantime the wolf scrambled on to the bonnet, blocking out most of the light. Shaftoe pressed himself back into the upholstery and switched on the windscreen wipers: only to see one bitten off.

He was past caring about the car now that the wolf was making frenzied efforts to break through the windscreen. Despite the freezing temperature, sweat soaked through Shaftoe's vest as if he'd just run a mile.

'Sweet-Jesus,' he croaked, forcing the car into second gear. All four wheels spun for a grip before hurling the Ford forward. He wrenched the wheel and saw the great animal crash off against the wall of a house.

Shaftoe kept driving: two hundred yards to the far end of the village where his desperate eyes spotted Penny Bakersman and the ginger-haired receptionist hurrying down from the infirmary to give whatever help they could. He blared his horn at them, and rapidly wound down a window.

'Get off the road!' he wheezed. 'Off the road! Get into that house and stay there!'

He did not wait for a response but spun the Cortina around and started back at speed, snow flying out from his snow-chains like a bow wave.

The first wolf to come into view, Hollowbelly, was in a predicament. She had forced her lean body into a box-framed window only for it to drop like a guillotine. Her rump and back legs were pumping for leverage when Shaftoe saw her.

He bumped up the kerb on to the pavement and scraped the side of the car discordantly along the row of buildings as he lined up his target. At nearly forty miles an hour, the

315

wing-mirror was plucked off along with most of the paint-work. Then the boot cover vanished as he gouged out a long channel of brick and cement dust, before catching Hollow-belly's exposed flank a thud, throwing her high into the air.

The injured wolf picked herself up and scudded on ahead with her tail between her legs. The Cortina followed like an avenging angel, swerving to the far side of the road. It caught up outside Station House, and jolted over the despairing grey shape.

The car skidded to a halt. Then reversed and thumped over the shape once more. Back and forth until Shaftoe could stop gritting his teeth and turn the Cortina.

Longrunner saw how the she-wolf had fared and came at the car bent on revenge. He again made for the bonnet and bit the glass, splaying his forelegs wide and laying flat to hold his balance.

Shaftoe could not rely on the thickness of the windscreen to protect him and jerked back in the driving seat whenever the wolf lunged. He picked up speed, hardly able to see around the ferocious face and wind-flattened fur which blocked the windscreen. He went into a series of wild snaking curves, trying to throw off the predator, but Longrunner stuck like glue.

He braked so hard that his own head hit the windscreen. The wolf slid back a foot or two, but his feet were wedged securely in the ventilation grills and he scrambled into a more secure position.

Shaftoe was perspiring so freely it almost blinded him. It stung his eyes and made his hands slip on the wheel. He twisted the car and gunned the engine, aware that something was making its back wheels labour.

He accelerated back through the village for the last time, with a resolution born of desperation. It was now or never, and he held his foot down on the pedal as if nailed.

A blurred line of frozen milk churns came into view along the side of the road. He flattened them one after the other like skittles. Each was nearly three-foot high and heavy with milk. It was like driving at speed along the sleepers of a railway line. The wheel juddered out of his hands and the wolf banged helplessly up and down on the bonnet.

Back in the clear, he swerved sharply across the road, up on to the pavement, snapping a six-inch-square post supporting a balcony and ploughed straight through a shop front.

The Cortina disappeared up to its rear wheels in bricks, shattered glass and a disintegrating display of tinned food. Longrunner was flung back between the car and the wall: the life crushed out of him in a moment of blinding pressure.

Seconds later, the first-floor balcony collapsed on to the Cortina's roof and more plaster dust showered down. Silence ensued and, after what seemed like an extremely long time, Shaftoe forced open the jammed door and surveyed the wreckage.

He saw Rabbit nuzzling a bruised and unsteady Darkmind in the distance, as both wolves limped away to the north. The big pack leader did not look back until he had crossed the frozen waterfall beyond Cnoc Breac and, by that time, he could no longer see the village.

Shaftoe could not stop trembling. He leaned across the dislocated radiator and inspected the bonnet, which was so buckled it was a work of art. The front wheels had been jolted off their axle and the exhaust pipe poked several feet from the rear of the car.

He polished dust off the roof with his sleeve, but it looked only marginally better. Sergeant Dunceford would go berserk, if he lived . . . And, if he lived, there was now no chance of Shaftoe being made a substantive policeman.

Even so, he would rather have Jack Dunceford back. He wiped his eyes. The blinding sun made it appear that he was crying.

FORTY-FIVE

Martin Kelso walked into the desk-cluttered, neon-lit newsroom.

'Hello there, Mr Kelso,' said a copy boy.

'Hi, Jack.'

Familiar faces glanced up from typewriters as he threaded his way towards the day news editor's phone-choked desk.

'Martin, you've come back for me!' someone called. 'And to think they said you'd done a bunk.'

He grinned and kissed a wrinkled blonde, who wore several ornate and chunky rings. 'Hello, Marlene. I'd never leave you ... or your husband. I'll see you later over the road.'

Even the day news editor said *welcome back* and sounded as if he meant it. 'Ready to start, Martin? There's plenty to do.'

'Ready as I'll ever be.'

'Right. Give your attention to this. I've got the address of a curate in Hove who's building an Ark in his back garden. Wants to get two of everything on board before the tidal wave arrives. He's predicting noon tomorrow. In the meantime, the local council has had complaints from his neighbours. They say they can hear roars and screams coming from his room. Look into it, will you?'

'Okay.' Kelso took the proffered slip of paper and then paused. 'Oh, Harry, just one thing. Why the change of heart? I mean, what made Danecliff decide to forgive me?'

The big news editor shrugged. 'You know the way he is. First he gets a complaint from somebody whose wife plays bridge with his wife, or who knew his son at Eton, and suddenly he's breathing hellfire. Then somebody with a little more influence puts in a good word for you ... and all is

318

forgiven. I don't know. These things are beyond me.'

Kelso looked thoughtful. 'I think I'll do a little checking, just for my own peace of mind.'

A big hand deterred him. 'Now, Martin. You've been given another chance. Take it, gratefully and on the basis that it's simple justice . . . and leave it at that. What's the point in risking upsetting his lordship if you don't have to? Just concentrate on the future and let the past take care of itself.'

Kelso shrugged, as if he accepted the advice. 'Okay. Just as you say.' But he sauntered off, far from satisfied.

He manipulated his club-foot up the main staircase, step by thick-soled step up three floors: past advertizing administration to the rarely visited top floor where the boardroom was situated and where the proprietor was said to have a penthouse, although Kelso had never seen it.

He crossed a discreet walnut-coloured carpet and into an elegant reception room, where a well-groomed woman with ash-blonde hair streaked with grey was adjusting a sheet of paper in an electric typewriter. She looked up in mild surprise.

'Why hello, Martin.'

'Hello, Martha.' He lowered his voice. 'Is the Only Begotten in?'

She regarded him benevolently, without answering the question. 'Haven't seen *you* up here before.'

He smiled. 'Well, you know how it is. Hallowed ground. It makes barbarians like me feel uncomfortable.'

'You wanted to see Lord Danecliff?'

He backed off slightly. 'I'm not sure.'

She was not surprised. Nothing seemed to surprise Martha. 'It's just as well,' she said. 'He left for Deauville this morning. He's spending a week at his villa: sitting in the sun mostly and dictating the odd telegram back here, just to keep me on my toes.'

'Well, that's the way it is in a capitalist society. But come the revolution, Martha, you and me are going to change all that, aren't we?'

She smiled endearingly. 'We certainly are.'

319

A gentle buzz indicated that somebody wanted her on the telephone. She directed him to a long low settee which looked as if it had never before encountered the seat of anybody's pants. He flicked through a glossy mazagine until she set down the receiver.

'Now. How can I help you, Martin?'

'I need some information.'

'What about?'

He said quietly, 'About me.'

'I see.'

He looked intently at his hands and then rubbed them together as Penny came into his mind again. 'Danecliff,' he began, 'wanted me out of the way a week or two ago. You remember?'

'Of course I remember. He went a most unusual shade of enraged scarlet when your name was mentioned.'

'Why was he so anxious to see the back of me?'

'Because you went too far with a story . . .'

'But that's the editor's prerogative, Why should Danecliff get involved?'

She wetted her lips and looked over her discreet shoulder at the proprietorial inner sanctum. 'Because the Minister of Health rang him personally in a great lather and demanded retribution after you caught him bending.'

Kelso raised a hand to stop her going further. 'Fine. That's what I thought. Now, later on, I went to Scotland and I filed another, quite different story. And, all of a sudden, the world fell in. When I next spoke to the office downstairs, I could hear the thunder rolling. His lordship wanted my balls. But why? I mean, again, why would he be interested?'

'Because somebody else rang up and complained about you. An American who he'd met a year or two ago at a White House reception, and who has a lot of influence on both sides of the water. Baker, something.'

'J C Bakersman.'

'That's him.'

'Right. Now, here's the question . . .

320

She pulled a wry face. 'You mean, they haven't been questions up to now?'

He laughed to cover his anxiety. 'All of a sudden, I'm back in favour. I'm the Prodigal returned. But why? That's what puzzles me. Why the change of attitude?'

'Oh, is that all?' Lord Danecliff's confidential secretary seemed relieved. 'I thought you were going to ask if he's got a love-nest, or what he wears in bed! It's simple. Bakersman's daughter sent a message. I took the call. Apparently she's inherited half the North Sea and has an awful lot of pull. Said she wanted to untangle an unfortunate error of judgement made by her father. Said they had absolutely no quarrel with anything you wrote, and hoped we would see you were reinstated forthwith.'

'Did she indeed? And what did his lordship say?'

'What could he say? He almost grovelled with charm. That girl's got a way with her. He claimed that he never really lost faith in you. The liar.'

'Well, I never.'

'She just said "fine" and rang off. Of course I wasn't really listening to any of this, you understand.'

Kelso nodded, but his mind was far away and there was an idiotic smile on his face. So Penny was behind it. What a beautiful thing to do. He suddenly had an irresistible urge to see her again . . . to face her and hold her hands.

He bounced to his feet, leaned across the typewriter and kissed Martha on her startled mouth. Within a minute or two he was back at street level and stepping into the incessant traffic noise of Fleet Street. Another reporter was making his way in through the glass doors, muttering and shaking the damp off his trousers.

'Bloody water gets in everywhere. There are certain parts of me that could easily go rusty.'

'Hello, Percy. Tell the desk, will you? I've got to go to Scotland. It's personal.'

'You're kidding. You've only just got back, and I heard them say you've got to knuckle down this time.'

Kelso flagged down a taxi which veered in towards the

kerb. 'How long will you be gone?' called the other reporter.

'About thirty years with any luck.'

The cabbie slid open a separating window. 'Where to, guv?'

'Elphin.'

'Where.'

'Oh . . . Euston Station, quick as you can, please.'

The driver knocked down his For Hire sign and swung back into the traffic.

The two Russians had been arguing on and off for an hour. Such a thing would have been unthinkable between them in Siberia, but Spassky was desperately disturbed and he ran through the soft unhelpful snow to keep up.

'But, comrade, it says the sanatorium regrets to inform that Valentina died two days ago, our time. Yet you told me over a week ago.'

Bukhanovich's face was a mask. 'Don't push that absurd piece of paper in my face again. You are harassing me. We have been admonished for capriciousness already . . . and we have a lot of time to make up.'

The bigger Russian, who had rims of snow on his eyebrows, spread his arms helplessly. 'I don't understand. There is something drastically wrong somewhere.'

Bukhanovich took out his binoculars and swept the folds of hills ahead. 'Perhaps the sanatorium made a mistake.'

His companion leapt at the possibility. 'A mistake? You think Valentina may still be alive?'

'No, no. I mean a mistake in the date.'

Spassky thrust the sheet of paper in front of the long black field-glasses. 'But it says March 1st. See? *Today, March 1st.* So, it cannot be a mistake.'

The leading hunter swept the other man's arm aside. 'Evidently,' he said testily.

'Then how could you have told me on board the plane,' persisted Spassky, 'that she was already dead?'

Bukhanovich gave up trying to focus the binoculars and swung savagely on him. 'All right, all right. So, she was not quite dead when we left.'

Spassky stepped back into the deep snow, his mouth opening in disbelief.

'She was on the very brink,' continued his former officer. 'What difference does it make? The Kremlin wanted us here without delay, to kill wolves. It suited their purpose, and I took it upon myself to spare you the agony of returning home and watching your wife die there.'

Spassky stuttered, 'I don't understand.'

'It was inevitable that she would die,' his companion insisted. 'I thought *It's better for him this way.* I did it for your own good.'

Spassky regarded him dumbly and, when no more explanation was forthcoming, turned into the sun and buried his face in his hands. 'Valentina. I should never have left you.'

Bukhanovich let him make anguished noises for a while, then put his binoculars away and snapped the case shut. 'Come,' he said impatiently. 'We have work to do.'

He trudged down the slope towards straggling fingers of farmland which reached up the hillside. But it was a long time before Spassky moved, or even uncovered his agonized face.

From then on there was never less than sixty yards between them. Spassky plodded far behind, as if only half-awake. And Bukhanovich did not appreciate the danger he was now in.

McDee's gin trap had waited – unaffected by freezing temperatures or time – for sufficient pressure to bring it back to life. The yawning jaws remained transfixed. Waiting for today.

Now, with a rusty screech, two hidden rows of metal teeth arced together.

It was Ilya Bukhanovich's foot which pressed down on the circular metal plate and released the spring, just at the moment he glanced back at his sullen, lagging companion.

The triangular metal edges bit through unprepared flesh and soft calf muscles. Raw, pyramidical teeth grated against the frontal bone, ready for their serrated counterparts to snap

323

forward and make contact from the other side.

The Russian's odd, white eyes widened in astonishment. At first there was no gasping pain: simply the impression that he had been brutally clubbed across the knees. He pitched forward into the ironhard ground, stunned.

Spassky was so far back that, at first, he could not make out what had happened. He shaded his eyes and came on cautiously, not prepared to risk a similar misfortune. When he did draw level, Bukhanovich made an agonizing effort to roll on to his back.

They looked at one another in silence: one, whose mind was still thousands of miles away on a vision of his wife's cornflower blue eyes, and the other grimacing in agony, with his palms slipping on the ice-smooth bank behind him.

Spassky crouched down and ran a fingertip along the jagged edges of the barely separated iron jaws, then shook the long tethering chain free of snow. But that was all he did.

When he stood up, the trapped hunter could see no pity in his eyes. He reached for his dropped rifle, but Spassky was quicker and slid it out of reach.

The bulky Russian glanced around at the frozen landscape and rubbed his forearms briskly against the cold. Then picked up his rucksack, ready to leave.

Bukhanovich grunted with pain as he sat up and regarded his blood-soaked leg. His white eyes looked beseechingly at his servant-companion before he tried to force the rusty jaws open with his own hands.

His companion watched, indifferent to the outcome.

It seemed he might succeed for a while: the gap widened as the hunter's face concertina'd with effort. But the time-stiffened springs were obdurate and snapped back, trapping not only the bloody leg but pinning his forearm in with it.

'Aaaaaaah!' It was more a resigned groan than a cry of agony.

Spassky thought about his wife's grave and his lovely dogs and his home, far away beyond the Verkhoyansk Mountains, and set off.

The ex-Guards lieutenant sat hunched up against the pain.

'If you leave me here, I could die. You realize what you are doing?'

Spassky trudged on: twenty or thirty yards away now, while the other Russian grew steadily more desperate. 'You'll be shot. You know that, don't you?'

'Who will ever know, Comrade Lieutenant?'

'I'll know, won't I? I'll know.'

Spassky was nearly half a mile away, and the wind was whipping powdered snow into an occasional dance, when he last heard the other man's voice calling plaintively.

'I did it for your own good. Believe me, Boris.'

He had never called Spassky by his first name before. But it made no difference.

FORTY-SIX

When the helicopter's skeletal fuselage next descended on Elphin, Kelso did not expect anyone to be waiting. After all, he had arrived unannounced. But before the rotor blade had stopped whirling, the slide door jerked open and a hand reached in to grab his suitcase and dump it, unceremoniously, outside.

'Out, man. Out!'

He responded to Shaftoe's order, and was half-pulled through the gap and bundled aside. 'Stand over there out of the way!'

'Why? What's all the excitement?'

He recognized Richard Unthank trussed up in a fur flying coat and gauntlets, when the scientist lifted a pair of snow goggles up to his forehead. 'Oh, it's you. Look, we're commandeering your helicopter for a long-distance reconnaissance flight.'

'It's not mine.'

'Well, whoever it belongs to, we're taking it over.'

Kelso shivered with apprehension that something had gone badly wrong; perhaps involving Penny. 'What's happened?'

'Happened? Since when?'

'In the past two days.'

Unthank clambered on board and strapped himself in, while the temporary policeman did the same from the other side and gave the pilot some instructions. They carried maps, field glasses and provisions.

'Are you kidding? Wolves swept through the village yesterday. Killed several people before the last pair disappeared north. We're going after them.'

He slammed the little door shut and the engine took on a higher, faster pitch. Kelso ducked under the slipstream, pulling the door open again. 'Who was killed?' he yelled.

'Let go of that bloody handle.'

'Who?' he insisted.

'Dunceford for one.'

'And the girl?'

They were engaged in a ridiculous and dangerous tug of war. 'Get your hand off the door, you madman! What girl?'

'Penny Bakersman.'

'She's all right.'

'Are you sure?'

The helicopter pulled away and upwards, the door shutting with a bang. Kelso's streaming hair calmed down and he limped back to his suitcase.

A crofter had watched the entire incident from the edge of the school playground and shook his head as he shuffled away to his home.

Kelso picked up his case, closed his eyes tight with relief, and hurried down towards the infirmary.

The professor was in heaven. He was comfortably perched in his reserve hide on the edge of the treeless Glencanisp Forest between the peaks of Suilven and Canisp, which stood two miles apart like brothers who hardly deigned to talk to one another.

He had a clear view of both from his vantage point in an abandoned stone-strewn croft on the shores of Loch na Gainimh. For ten minutes he had been watching the antics of distant ptarmigan, which would have been invisible against the snow had it not been for a few black markings on their otherwise white wings and tails.

Careful observation had revealed their nest, a hollow in the ground, and now they were scurrying back and forth across the bare mountain slope: their heavily-feathered legs giving the impression of fluffy trousers.

Professor Pope-Watson hummed contentedly to himself as he made field notes on a pad strapped above his left knee. He could hear the grating croak of the ptarmigan, calling to one another, and was fascinated by the ease with which the two plump birds tunnelled into the snow in search of shoots and buds.

Suddenly they stopped and listened and, before any sound was audible to the human ear, took off in alarm.

'Oh, really!' The professor swung his binoculars until he picked up the distant, emerging speck of a helicopter. 'This is too bad!'

The pilot treated Suilven with great respect and swung north-east before skittering in across the surface of the bottle-shaped loch, causing little grey ripples to disturb its partly-frozen surface.

The professor glanced anxiously up at Canisp where he knew *Aquila chrysaetus*, a particularly fine female golden eagle, to be nesting on a ledge. She had three young. 'For heaven's sake, go away,' he tutted, as the helicopter hovered.

But it would not go away and he was obliged to slither down a stairway of tumbled stones, which once formed the dividing wall in a nineteenth century crofter's home, and hurried into the open.

Unthank saw him immediately and tapped Shaftoe's arm, indicating the direction. The policeman cupped his hand to the other man's ear. 'Who's that?'

'An ornithologist. He's a strange old bugger, but he knows what he's doing.'

'Well, he seems to want to talk to us. May have had trouble with the wolves.'

'I doubt it, he's too scraggy. You'd have to boil all his bones for a cupful of soup.'

They landed carefully on the flat edge of the loch and allowed the professor to make his way indignantly across to them. The blade eventually stopped revolving and the noise spluttered away to nothing.

'Who the devil are you?'

'Constable Shaftoe, sir,' responded the younger man, promoting himself for the additional impression he imagined it would give.

'What on earth are you up to, clattering about making all that infernal noise? Don't you realize, you are disturbing valuable bird life. There are rare and protected species in this area.'

Shaftoe flushed with embarrassment, but Unthank stretched out his long legs and walked around the aircraft with his hand outstretched.

'Professor Norman Pope-Watson, isn't it? Hello, sir. I'm Richard Unthank, environmental research with the government.' He ignored a resigned grunt of disapproval. 'Sorry to disturb your studies, but this is vitally important. A matter of public safety. There's been a wolf attack in the village of Elphin, and elsewhere for all we know. Constable Shaftoe and I have the task of finding out where the survivors of the pack have got to.'

Pope-Watson quickly calmed down. 'Anybody hurt?'

'Two dead.'

'Good God. How can I help you?'

Shaftoe felt sufficiently sure of himself to rejoin the conversation. 'Two wolves got away. One of them, a big grey bastard, was probably hurt. They set out due north toward Inchnadamph, but there are no tracks that we can detect. We think there's a chance they swung off westwards, in this direction, during the night.'

'You're right, Constable . . . Sorry, old chap, I didn't get your name.'

'Me? Oh, Shaftoe, sir.'

'At dusk yesterday, two grey wolves, one very much bigger than the other and in the lead, came through on the far side of the loch there. I had my glasses on them for the best part of thirty minutes.'

'Did they see you, sir?'

'Hard to say. The big one gave the croft a long going-over. He was the best part of a mile off but I'm sure he sensed me. Then they went on . . . towards whatever's out there.'

Unthank shaded his eyes to the north-west. Miles of sandstone highlands deeply scored by streams. Moorland and bog. A beautiful desolation . . . that's how Emma described it.

A distant screech took Shaftoe's attention. 'Sounds like an eagle.'

The elderly bird-watcher glanced anxiously towards Canisp. 'She's got three young ones up there.'

The rangy scientist jerked his head at Shaftoe. 'Ready? I think she's telling us we're trespassing.'

Within five minutes the helicopter was pulling vertically up over the naked forest with a magnificent view to the coast and the Outer Hebrides beyond.

Shaftoe stared until his eyes ached. They saw occasional tracks in the snow but whether or not they were wolf could not be confirmed unless they set down, which they did on four separate occasions. Unthank scrambled out, once disappearing up to his neck in a frightening bottomless drift, but all the tracks turned out to be red deer.

He struggled back into the helicopter, panting as he shook wet snow out of his hair.

'You all right?'

'Fine,' he grinned.

'I'm glad you're taking it so well. I know a lot of people who'd have given up by now.'

'Not me. And I've got what I really came for. See those tracks? They mean that the strongest deer have sniffed out the changing weather and are on the move again. A lot more will be back in the Highlands within a month.'

The tubby policeman nodded as he continued to sweep the

barren expanse of snow-covered hills. Then he stiffened. 'Hey, what's that? See? Down there.'

Unthank tapped the pilot's shoulder and adjusted his own binoculars. Two grey elongated shapes were crossing a hilltop at a steady lope. Moving north-west towards the bleak coast and solitude.

They came in low, overtaking the animals and giving Unthank a glimpse of Darkmind's lifted head and the uneven line of his teeth before both wolves angled off into the shelter of some rocks.

Shaftoe slid out his rifle, butt first, although the scientist restrained him. 'No need for that.'

'But it's them, surely?'

Unthank scratched his head undecidedly. In his mind he had no doubt at all. His clear view of the hilltop, if only for a moment, confirmed that it was Darkmind and the last of his pack.

'Can't be certain.'

'Well, what do we do now?'

'Put me down. I'll have a closer look.'

Shaftoe was horrified. 'After what they did to the sergeant? Not on your life!'

'Look, I know what I'm doing. Don't fuss.'

'So did I at Elphin. I was in a car, protected on all sides by metal and glass and doing fifty miles an hour, but they still made me feel like a winkle about to be prised out of its shell and eaten.'

'I'll take the rifle if it makes you feel any better.'

The pilot made a face at his instrument panel. 'Make up your minds, you two. We haven't got much fuel left, and I'm not walking back.'

'Put her down,' ordered Unthank. He planted his hand firmly against the policeman's chest to prevent him following, as the helicopter settled on a table of rock some distance from where the two animals had taken refuge.

'Be careful,' Shaftoe called hoarsely.

'I will, mother.'

Unthank knew precisely what he wanted ... but Darkmind

might well not want the same thing. And, if he didn't, one of them would be killed. Perhaps all three of them.

It was not just fear that slowed him down. The unpredictable snow, which was at first knee-deep, let him down without warning and he floundered up to his waist. He found solid ground again and moved on.

Nothing untoward was visible as he cautiously circled the mound of rocks. Out of sight of the helicopter he simply stood still and shivered, turning his back to a gust of Arctic wind which swept in over the gnarled coastline and lifted some of the top snow into drifting shrouds before lapsing.

He meant to remain there, out of the policeman's sight, without doing anything. Pretend he had searched, and leave it at that. If Darkmind was there, he could have the benefit of the doubt. And why not? He had a right to it. His forebears had possessed these numb heights long before man ever set his dissatisfied eyes upon them.

But it was not to be. Rabbit's head jerked up high and to the right of the jumbled rocks, exposing the wolves' position.

With no further need for stealth, Darkmind's handsome head also lifted into view. A huge alert face. With slanting eyes that devoured him. The bristling countenance turned sideways, displaying incisor teeth which closed with the abrupt snap of a piece of wood breaking in two.

Green eyes that recognized the observer. Unthank gulped and fought back the need to clear his throat noisily. He was hypnotized, like a hare, and the only creature to move was Rabbit who glanced inquiringly at his leader to discover what to do.

Eventually it was Unthank who moved. At first just a tentative moistening of his dry lips. But it was a start and, thereafter, he edged back one foot and then the other.

He climbed into the helicopter, stuttering with cold and immensely relieved at being safe back on board.

'Well?' asked Shaftoe.

'Just some deer, scared out of their wits. Red deer. It's a good sign.'

The pilot looked bored and glanced at his watch. 'Right,'

said the policeman. 'We'd better try farther west.'

'No need,' said Unthank. 'We've done enough. I know wolves and they'll be past the point of no return now. Once they abandon their usual hunting grounds, they'll keep going until they reach new food or get a feeling of complete safety.'

'Think so?'

'I'm certain of it. They won't come back now. Look it's Sunday. Isn't it time we went home and put our feet up?'

Shaftoe gnawed his lip undecidedly. 'I'm not so sure about that.'

'Well, I am. I'm sure enough for both of us.' Unthank shook the pilot's shoulder and indicated that they should return south.

On the flight back he wondered if he had done the right thing. But, with Darkmind out of sight, in time the wolves would slip from people's minds. He had little doubt that the predators would continue heading north-north-west to an area where few humans wandered and where they had as much right as anybody else to whatever territory they discovered.

They had a place in the natural order of things and Nature would provide for them.

FORTY-SEVEN

It was a pious grey Sunday, and the single bell in the church of St Andrew the Martyr summoned the faithful to worship.

The villagers who had remained in Elphin despite the wolf peril arrived in their dozens sombrely dressed in Sunday best, one or two of the men running fingers around their necks to ease the unaccustomed starchiness of their detachable collars; the women nodding to one another with a graciousness reserved for the Sabbath.

They came, to some extent, to give thanks for their salvation from the wolves, but mainly out of habit. Most would attend two services that day; others all three.

In the lofty porch hung a time-dulled 'Notice to Worshippers', which instructed them:

> *Be on Time,*
> *Go Straight into Church,*
> *Kneel,*
> *Don't Whisper to Your Neighbour,*
> *Don't Look Round Everytime the Door Opens,*
> *Fix Your Thoughts.*

The most prestigious of the reserved spaces on the front pew, to the right of the aisle, was empty. Sir Marcus Sheerwater was in London. He had handed a graphic description of the wolf-killing to the Home Secretary with a considerable flourish; giving the impression that, but for his intervention, things would have been considerably worse.

Penny Bakersman arrived at the church in a contingent of five patients and nurses: settling towards the front and turning discreetly, despite the porch instructions, to scrutinize the congregation.

Eventually her eyes found Martin Kelso, who limped in late as usual and breathing hard. He grimaced faintly from the back pew as he knelt on a threadbare hassock.

The longing in her eyes and his steady reciprocal gaze reflected the fact that they had spent the whole night locked together. One body, enwrapped in love and warmth until well after breakfast time.

The only reason they reluctantly separated was because she felt it her duty to be seen as part of the hospital.

Whenever she glanced around his eyes were on her; she blushed, glowing in the knowledge that he needed her as much as she did him.

Kelso fumbled the pages of *Hymns Ancient and Modern* and joined lustily in the first verse, but all that his eyes saw in the book was an image of her beautiful Dresden face.

The Rev Stanford Pilbeam processed from the vestry,

preceded by three choristers and his vicar's warden. He steepled his hands and pressed the fingertips to his mouth in satisfaction. It was a better turnout even than Harvest Festival.

As he proceeded around the church and down the centre aisle, he thought about the collection and the impetus it would give to his new fund for heating the vestry.

The organ played 'Onward Christian Soldiers' and voices sang with a zeal that echoed around the rafters. Penny Bakersman's eyes glanced to the side and quietly back at the reporter, and he sang as never before. 'With the Cross of Jesus going on before!'

Communion began. The congregation filed forward, front pews first, ready to kneel at the altar rail. Kelso watched her move forward and accept a wafer from the vicar in cupped hands. Then a sip of red wine from a solid silver chalice. *The body and the blood of Christ.* The vicar's benevolent but firm grip ensured that none had more than a taste of wine.

The vicar moved to the next communicant in line and, as Penny stood to return to her pew, she uttered what those nearby took to be an expression of adulation.

'Jesus Christ . . . Almighty.'

A shadow crossed Kelso's mind and he frowned slightly. There was a tension in her face that had not been there before. Almost alarm.

Slack-Jaw had stood up on his hind legs, paws outstretched to force open the double doors. Now he was hunched and snarling: framed in the doorway at the back of the church like a malevolent demon.

Kelso, sensitive to draughts on the back of his neck, turned slowly and stared with utter incredulity.

Others turned and a girl gave an astonishingly high-pitch shriek. A grey-haired man with a rather scrawny neck called out his grandson's name and wrapped his arms protectively around the boy. The vicar stared down the aisle with a paralyzed smile.

334

The organ played on for a while but no one sang and it finally trailed away into silence. Quite suddenly there was pandemonium.

People scrambled away from the doors, some clambering over the top of heavy-backed pews until one toppled massively forward, collapsing the half-dozen rows in front, one after the other.

Everybody seemed to be shouting and screaming at once; calling to members of their family or struggling to get by. Curiously, a man with a perspiring bald head, who was trapped at the waist by the crushing weight of the pews, made no noise at all. Simply opened his mouth like a stranded fish and panted.

The cruel narrow-eyed wolf eyed the congregation dementedly.

This was his moment of triumph. For too long he had chased only shadows and lived in a state of perpetual shivering. No longer would he be shunned by the pack and forced to live on what the others discarded as unpalatable or indigestible.

White spittle around his jaws gave him a fearsome appearance.

The vicar tried in vain to calm the swirling flood of congregation. This was his church: his and God's. But he was like a swimmer in a white surplice battling against the current.

Martin Kelso swung over the pews with the rest of them, encumbered by his crippled foot which needed both hands to raise it to waist height. He reached Penny and encircled her slim shoulders. The din was intense, and his own shouting made it worse.

'There must be a back way out of here!'

In the midst of the chaos, Slack-Jaw fixed his eyes on the vicar who seemed determined neither to flee from the aisle nor to advance any closer. Stanford Pilbeam was ashamed of himself; he was fervent in his outrage at this manifestation of evil entering his church, but his flesh was weak and his hand trembled as he stretched out an arm.

'Get out! Out of here, immediately!'

By thrusting out his arm he unintentionally dislodged his spectacles, and with them went his hearing aid and much of his field of vision. He stumbled over a pile of fallen psalm books and lost his sense of direction.

The wolf moved forward snapping and snarling, until a suddenly fleeing figure at the side of the church drew his attention. It was a gangling figure of a boy with fine, straight hair, running for the steps which led up to a long thin gallery.

In a moment's reflex action, Slack-Jaw's previous intentions were forgotten and he leapt in pursuit. The youth went up the winding stone steps three at a time and reappeared fleeing along the gallery, above the distraught congregation.

But when a stone wall blocked his unconsidered progress, the youth turned and backed up on to a precariously narrow balcony ledge and made tight little animal noises in his throat. 'Maaam!' he called desperately, as he eyed the distance he needed to lunge away from the balcony towards a flag pole embedded high in the wall. 'Where are you? Help me, Maam.'

Slack-Jaw came at him fast, snapping for his legs a moment before the boy plunged out into mid-air. His fingers reached for the pole, bearing the faded colours of a former Highland Regiment-of-Foot, and made it: tightening desperately around the varnished wood.

But the link with history was older than it seemed and the pole snapped, tipping the boy over backwards as he fell. He landed on his spine with a thud which made Kelso pull his head away.

Slack-Jaw stood on the ledge and peered down at the congregation. The journalist was among those who remained. He had seen Penny swept outside to comparative safety in a crush of struggling worshippers. But he himself was winded by an elbow in the stomach and now he had a sickening premonition that he would be the wolf's next victim.

Slack-Jaw scrambled back down the twisting staircase, although his wild eyes were glazing over again and he was overtaken by a fit of shivering.

Kelso recognized that the wolf was in trouble and, in a

336

moment of penetrating but inconsequential clarity, saw both himself and the deranged wolf for what they really were: two cripples isolated by their shortcomings.

His fleeting sympathy was not reciprocated. Slack-Jaw's upper lip pulled back to reveal snarling teeth before, illogically, he plunged off after another victim.

Somebody blundered heavily into Kelso. It was the vicar, whose desperate fingers felt the journalist's face, seeking to identify the features.

'My God, what's happening?' sobbed the older man. 'Oh dear Saviour, send help and guidance to thy flock!' Kelso took him by the shoulders and bundled him towards the safety of the vestry.

The church was almost empty now, but frantic cries drew Kelso back. The wolf was jerking in and out of a pew, biting the bald, trapped man's legs and barely distracted by a barrage of hymn books that were being heaved at him.

Kelso groaned. He had hardly any idea of what he could do and the fact that all the lights had gone out, leaving the church in gloom, did nothing to help.

He clumped towards the bristling grey shape and swung his clubfoot into the boney rump with all his force. So hard that he almost swung himself off his feet.

The stiff-haired wolf yelped and spun around, sinking its yellow teeth into his mis-shaped boot. There was no pain because there was no penetration. But Kelso bellowed at the top of his voice and continued to do so. It was his last deterrent.

The wolf wheeled away, biting objects real and imaginary as if in a brainstorm. He attacked the oak lectern and succeeded in toppling its enormous Bible, which crunched to the floor only inches from his maniacal face.

Slack-Jaw bit everything in sight with demented fervour. He sank his teeth into woodwork and prayer books, tore tapestry from the wall and tried to bring down a wooden frame containing numbers of the next hymns.

The Rev Pilbeam, who had vanished from sight for a minute or two, re-emerged from the vestry, to one side of the altar. The door remained open behind him and Slack-Jaw ran into the shadowy room, his attention taken by a faintly-moving line of cassocks and surplices dangling from wire hangers.

Kelso saw his chance and crashed the heavy vestry door shut, turning a big metal key in the lock with shaking hands. He was barely in time. A moment later the wolf disentangled himself from the empty clothing and threw himself frenziedly at the oak panels.

Emma Dancer spent several days at a friend's flat in North London trying to forget about the experiences she had been through. She almost succeeded.

But the evening's television news brought back reality, by referring to Scotland and, 'extraordinary reports of savage wolves running free in parts of the Highlands: posing a threat to isolated communities . . . '

According to the bulletin, the trouble was already over and pictures were shown of Sir Marcus Sheerwater emerging triumphantly from the helicopter at Elphin.

A cup of tea trembled in her hand, but the thought that perhaps she owed a debt to the people who shared the ordeal at Elphin made her telephone the MP the following morning: Sunday.

A cultured voice informed her that Sir Marcus Sheerwater was not at home; he was on his way to a press conference in a hall off Victoria Street, Westminster. She dashed out on impulse and got a taxi to take her there through slush-strewn streets.

An elegant little hall was crowded with journalists, TV crews and various hangers-on. She might have been turned away, had she not insisted she was there at Sir Marcus's express invitation.

Four great wolfskins were pegged out across a wall and the MP spent some time posing for pictures in front of them.

'I didn't shoot them,' he said with assumed modesty. 'Other people did that . . . people with a lot more courage than me.

338

My part was to swiftly recognize the very real danger that these predatory beasts posed, and I was determined that the lives of women and children should not be endangered by any misguided deference towards ecology or animal protection. Those things have their place in any ordered community; I'd never deny that. But here was a situation in which fear-some killers were on our very doorsteps.'

Somebody called: 'Are you sure there's no chance of any more wolves turning up?'

'There's always that chance while we allow wild animals to roam unchecked.'

'But will they kill again?'

'What can I say? I can only tell you that the experts tell me it is most unlikely.'

Emma heard herself call out stridently, without previously intending to. The pompous air of self-satisfaction exuded by Sir Marcus drove her to it. 'Did they also tell you that your own action amounted to too little, too late?'

The MP frowned in her direction and got back to his feet. 'Madam,' he snapped, 'the action for which I was responsible was both measured and considered. And I am not here to face criticism on that account.'

He sat down looking considerably ruffled. Sue McKenna, who seemed to be acting as chairman of the press conference, patted the air for calm. 'Are there any further questions before Sir Marcus leaves? He has an appointment with the Home Secretary in half an hour.'

Emma glowered at the back while journalists put one or two further detailed questions. They were letting him get away with it, she thought bitterly. The man who did nothing was being allowed to become the hero of the episode.

'Well, if that's all,' said Sue McKenna.

'I'm still not satisfied!' called Emma. 'I'm not at all happy about the complete lack of warning after the first few deaths had occurred. The situation was allowed to go unchecked while VIPs pretended it was all too trifling for words. And why was an American business friend of yours then allowed to order the police to delay the hunt further?'

339

Sir Marcus sprang back to his feet. 'There was no delay,' he said indignantly, and pointed to the spreadeagled wolf-skins. 'And there is all the evidence you should need. Once we were aware that people were in physical danger, there was immediate and bloody retribution. I see no further point either in making recriminations or holding witch-hunts.'

He had overdone it, and an uneasy silence settled on the hall. One of the TV men shifted uncomfortably. 'She may have a point, Sir Marcus. Who was the American?'

'American? I don't think I recall . . . ' For once the grey-haired MP was flustered. 'Oh, just a minute . . . perhaps she means Mr J C Bakersman, who happened to be in the area at the time.'

'Staying at your home!' shouted Emma.

'Err . . . That may be so,' stammered the MP, 'but it was all perfectly proper. We are simply casual acquaintances.'

'And he lent you his helicopter for several days so that you could fly to London!'

'Well, yes. I . . . I did take advantage of an unexpected and generous offer to return here for a cabinet meeting about the influenza epidemic. But I resent this young lady's tone, and I refuse to be hectored in this manner.'

He sat down abruptly, but Emma was not to be put off.

'How many people had already been savaged to death when you flew back here for three days of talks about another matter entirely, and elegant dinners and fat cigars,' she persisted. 'Three days while others you had left behind died?'

The meeting quickly got out of hand. Voices were raised in anger and several photographers fought their way to get pictures of Emma Dancer brandishing her white fists.

'I refuse,' said Sir Marcus into the microphone, and holding it so close to his mouth that it gave off a metallic whine. 'I refuse to be insulted.' But he got no further. A television news editor pulled it from him. 'Harry, get the crew outside. I want you on your way back to Scotland as soon as we can arrange some transport. You get the boys to Heathrow and check with me from there. I'll be at Euston Road. Okay? Go.'

'Excuse me . . . Do you mind?' There was some distracted

grappling for the microphone before it went dead.

Marcus Sheerwater drove straight back to his flat. It was a reckless speed considering the conditions of the road, and he almost skidded into a bollard before panting upstairs to his rooms.

He poured himself a stiff glass of port and drank it without savouring the bouquet. If that ridiculous woman marred his chances of a ministerial switch, he would gladly strangle her. He was breathing hard and it was some considerable time before his heart stopped palpitating.

Emma, on the other hand, went home feeling satisfied in her own quiet way. And slept better than she had for weeks.

FORTY-EIGHT

The approach to the church was like a battlefield. Ashen-faced villagers bent over bandaged victims and others sat hugging themselves with despair as they waited for assistance.

Penny had rushed to the infirmary to organize emergency dressings and to help the hurriedly-awoken half-dressed doctor gather whatever sedatives and pain-killers he needed.

Kelso made sure that the double doors of the church were securely latched and sent a boy galloping off to the vicarage for a key. Stanford Pilbeam was too dazed to help, and nobody seemed to want to take charge.

He scanned the far end of the high street angrily and wondered where the hell the overweight policeman and the tall, taciturn scientist had got to. Surely not sweeping barren mountain slopes to the north-west? Not still searching for predators where there were none?

Dull thuds and an occasional muffled snarl reminded him only too sharply of the menace inside the church. He clenched and unclenched his hands. Somebody ought to do something!

The grandfather who had earlier wrapped protective arms around his ward approached the reporter, holding out a rifle uncertainly. 'I've got this,' he blinked. 'Don't you think we should do something about that . . . that thing in there?'

'We?' Kelso was startled by the thought.

'Well, somebody's got to.'

'The constable should be back soon. I think we ought to leave it to him.'

'But that might not be until tonight, or even tomorrow morning. And the wolf could break out by then. You saw how strong he is.'

Kelso ran a hand through his hair. He was beginning to shout again. 'All right, all right. I know. But what can *we* do?'

The man seemed hurt by his attitude. 'Shoot it, of course. If you hold the door, I'll go inside there and finish it.'

Nobody else seemed interested, or even aware, of their dilemma, and Kelso groaned at the unfairness of it all. 'For Christ's sake. How old are you?'

'Eighty-nine.'

Kelso pulled the rifle out of the man's hand, rudely. 'You hold the door. I'll do it.'

It was some time before he was ready, and by then a half-circle of people had formed. He asked for, and got, a coil of rope and was about to go back into the now quiet church when Penny arrived breathless.

'Where do you think you're going?' she demanded.

'In there.' He hoped fervently that he would be dissuaded.

'Oh no, Martin.' She covered her mouth.

'It's all right.'

'Please don't, darling.'

He wiped some perspiration from his face. 'No, it's all right. I want to.'

Kelso turned the big black ring-handle and opened the

creaking doors, nodded to the old man and stepped inside. They had almost closed on him when he thought of another question.

'Wait,' he hissed. 'Don't be in such a godalmighty hurry! How do I fire this bloody thing?'

The grandfather slipped into the eerie shadows beside him, and explained the reloading mechanism. Then left him alone. The long key turned and stillness closed in.

Kelso stood, peering down the aisle, trying to discern the vestry door beyond two dust-filled pillars of daylight which leaned up to narrow Gothic windows. When he moved there was an accompanying creak and he heard a distant snuffling as the wolf's interest was aroused. Then came a growling and snap of teeth as if Slack-Jaw was irritated with his own tail.

He moved infinitely slowly around the fallen pews, avoiding patches of light on the floor in case they in some way identified him to a wolf who was still the thickness of a door away.

The wolf sneezed and Kelso listened to it – just as it, no doubt, was also listening to him – in the silence. Finally he picked the spot he needed to position himself: high up in the pulpit. He was able to block off the little twisting wooden steps and perch out over the body of the church with an uninterrupted view.

It was not perfect, but he could not think of anything better. So, he uncoiled the rope, looped one end around the pulpit rail and then walked gingerly to the vestry door and looped the other through the latch ring.

Finally and ever-so-gently, he unlocked the intervening door and backed away. Slack-Jaw sneezed again to clear his head, but did not move.

Bathed in sweat, Kelso settled himself in the pulpit and waited. When his hands stopped shaking he tugged the rope. The door opened inch by creaking inch.

He stared until his eyes hurt but nothing emerged. He even began to harbour the desperately welcome thought that the wolf might by now have squeezed out through some half-open window.

343

Eventually he sensed, rather than saw, a dark muzzle protruding into the church. A shadow bellied quickly forward under the debris of shadowy pews: too indistinct to make a clear target.

Kelso gulped hugely and wound the rifle strap firmly around his shoulder, so that it gripped like a tourniquet and pressed the cold barrel to his cheek.

The old man picked that moment to drum on the double doors at the far end of the church and call thinly: 'You all right in there? What's happening? Do you need any help?'

The reporter winced and took his eyes off the vestry entrance.

Slack-Jaw chose that moment to go berserk. He burst down the aisle towards the sound of the shaky voice and leapt at the double doors as if they did not exist. Nearly one hundred and fifty pounds of bone, muscle and demented jaws crashed snarling into the woodwork, level with the old man's head who, although he was on the other side, staggered back.

The wolf spun around biting, snapping and raking his great paws along the wall. Hymn books and collection boxes went flying and the speechless reporter was forced into action.

He squeezed the trigger and felt a soft recoil. Not surprisingly, he missed in a confusion of shadows. The bullet hit a brass plate and whined off into the rafters where it ricocheted among forgotten prayers.

Slack-Jaw turned his malevolent eyes on the pulpit and came back along the aisle with a savage rush, uttering a series of staccato barks. Kelso was aware of its supple grace as well as streaks of spittle around its mouth.

Wolves are superbly equipped for hunting. They have strength, speed and ferocity interwoven with innate cunning. They are also intelligent enough quickly to recognize another predator and know when not to attack.

Slack-Jaw turned away at the last moment and disappeared into the gloom. But the second bullet was already on its way and took him high up on the shoulder, glancing off bone. His howl reverberated around the roof.

The speed of the continually twisting, weaving shadow told

Kelso that the wolf was not badly hurt, but he could not see clearly and he leaned so far out of his perch that he almost fell.

At last Slack-Jaw saw his tormentor and came out into the open. The wolf was desperately fast. The third bullet gouged out a chunk of pillar behind his head as he launched himself up in a supreme effort to get at his enemy.

The impact stunned Kelso. The snarling head, with ears flattened against its skull, burst through the pulpit rail. A paw raked open the sleeve of his jacket and enormous teeth crunched into the varnished woodwork an inch or two from his hand.

Kelso was flung back against a stone pillar, and the rifle went off. The fourth bullet went through Slack-Jaw's mouth, creasing his face into a demonic smile, before the weight of his body slid back and crashed to the church floor.

Kelso remained in the pulpit for some time, trembling as he stared down at the motionless shape. 'Poor bugger,' he said quietly.

AFTERMATH

The summer that followed was a particularly good one. Memories of the winter were pushed to the back of people's minds and, as the days lengthened, the few wolves which remained retreated.

When the snowploughs got through to Elphin, the ravens also left. They flew off heavy-winged to the north where the hazy sun made less of an impression upon the frozen land; perhaps to renew their affinity with the surviving predators.

From then on, *Canis Lupus* kept clear of man.

He limped northwards until he found solitary areas which had been abandoned during the great population shift to the East Coast at the height of the North Sea oil boom. There, at least, he could gradually regain his belligerent pride. He had learned his lesson, but any attempt to dislodge him from this last barren territory would be prodigiously defended.

The government decreed that part of the Lake District and certain of these inhospitable stretches of the North West Highlands should be set aside for wildlife. *No-go areas* where people who wanted to fish or climb were warned they did so at their peril.

So it was that in parts of the British Isles, which remained as cold as iron, wolves again prowled unseen. Icy winds ruffled their fur as they watched for ungulates through narrowed eyes.

Man also had to accept limitations. For, as the world's dominant hunter, he too had reached a significant stage in his evolution.

There is a natural law that all species are interdependent.

And man came to realize that, unless he showed tolerance, he himself might not survive. None can survive alone, and no predator can continue to kill indiscriminately without ultimately destroying himself.

Thus man and wolf became territorial neighbours.

There were anxious moments, of course. Occasions when visitors wandered farther than they intended, only to panic at the sudden, silent appearance of a wolf. But inevitably, when the patrolmen arrived, the tracks of the predator were found to have touched the edge of civilization only to turn away as if confronted with an invisible barrier.

It seemed as if a balance had been achieved.

But deep in the frozen wastes, an uneasy intelligence was torn by conflicting interests. Shifting softly through the desolate shadows, followed by a new and stronger pack, Darkmind considered the heritage that had been systematically torn from his grasp. As the humans drifted into their summer slumbers, he realized that time was on his side.

ABOUT THE AUTHOR

Ivor Watkins spent two years in Berlin in Army Intelligence before returning to England to become a newspaper reporter. He worked on regional papers for several years and then joined the staff of a national paper in Fleet Street. He now does public relations for local government. Blood Snarl is his first novel.

Great Reading from SIGNET

Recommended Reading from SIGNET